WAVES OF RAPTURE

Sun Eagle strode pantherish toward her. When he reached out his arms to her, then placed his hands to her shoulders, it was as though the whole world stood still.

"*Lau*," Sun Eagle murmured in a slight greeting.

His lips moving downward toward Kiriki's, his hands pulling her closer to him, did not cause any alarm, but only passion to sweep through her, causing her to respond in kind.

Crushed now against his powerful, bare chest, his arms holding her tightly, Kiriki closed her eyes as waves of rapture flooded her when Sun Eagle's mouth bore down upon her lips. His tongue sought entrance into her mouth. His hands had slipped down to her buttocks, clasping his fingers onto her, forcing her to yield.

Kiriki's face became hot with a blush as he slowly began . . .

SAVAGE DANCE

CASSIE EDWARDS

JOVE BOOKS, NEW YORK

SAVAGE DANCE

A Jove Book / published by arrangement with
the author

PRINTING HISTORY
Jove edition / May 1991

ISBN: 0-515-10579-1

Jove Books are published by The Berkley Publishing Group,
200 Madison Avenue, New York, New York 10016.
The name ''JOVE'' and the ''J'' logo
are trademarks belonging to Jove Publications, Inc.

PRINTED IN THE UNITED STATES OF AMERICA

10 9 8 7 6 5 4 3 2 1

For Alverda and Charlie Klucavich, childhood friends of mine, and longtime, dear friends of my parents, Virgil and Mary Kathryn Cline,

and

For Nancy Demuth, a reader of Indian romances whose admiration of the Pawnee Indian matches my own.

Author's Note

▼ ▼ ▼

The Pawnee, *Pi-ta-da,* have been known to the white men
since perhaps 1541, and certainly since 1673. They were
the most numerous and powerful of the tribes constituting
the Caddoan linguistic stock, and one of the most important of the entire Plains area. Since the earliest definite
historic mention of them, they have been residents in
Nebraska and in the extreme northern portion of Kansas,
particularly on the Loop, Platte, and Republican rivers.

As a tribe, the Pawnee were friendly. They never fought
against the United States. They decided that their day was
done and the only course was to keep the peace and try
to learn from their conquerors. They were also motivated
in good part by a fondness for the white way of life.

The Pawnee were one of the few North American Indian
tribes who practiced human sacrifice. They believed that
long ago the Morning Star, celebrating his conquest over
the Evening Star, brought light and fertility to the world
of the Pawnee. They further believed that the mating of
these two great stars produced the first human being—a
young girl. At times, the Morning Star would demand the
return of the first human being. To propitiate the Morning
Star and ensure a bountiful harvest, the Pawnee would
capture and sacrifice a young girl.

The name, Pawnee (Pa'ni) is conceded to mean Wolf,
and was given to the Pawnee because of their method of
warfare, their skill as scouts, their custom of simulating
wolves while on the war path, and their tireless endurance.

The Pawnee were also great fighters and raiders against
their neighbor, the Comanche.

One

Nebraska, 1821

THE hush of evening lay over everything. The rays of the setting sun streamed between the trunks of lofty trees, casting alternate lines of golden light and deep shade across a land that was unique in its raw beauty. It was a startling combination of hearty vegetation, rivers and lakes, and abundant wildlife. . . .

Upon a bluff, a lone Indian warrior was silhouetted against the blazing sunset as he sat stiffly on his beautiful black gelding. The warrior's eyes grew dark with hungry passion as he watched a barefoot, lithe, and shapely Pawnee maiden carrying wood from the darkening forest toward her village. Her hair was worn in two braids, the part in the middle daubed with red paint. She was dressed in a deerhide blouse and wrap-around skirt that fell to below her knees.

Sun Eagle looped his horse's reins more tightly around his fingers, his gaze absorbing the seductive sway of the maiden's hips, driving him almost to madness with wanting her. One day not long ago he had accidentally come upon her bathing in the river, and had only observed her up closely for a brief time.

But that had been enough for him to have memorized her slender, golden body now blossomed into a woman of perhaps seventeen or eighteen winters. Beneath the golden color of her skin a glow of red just barely showed through, but her blue eyes and the lighter texture of her brown hair puzzled him.

This, and her intense loveliness, had intrigued Sun Eagle so much that he felt driven to learn all of the secrets about her. She did not know it, but she was going to be his wife!

Having lost sight of her as she now walked among the earth lodges of her village, Sun Eagle wheeled his horse around and pressed his moccasined heels into its flanks. Riding toward the sunset, his breechcloth flapped in the wind and his muscled, bronzed body shone in the dimming light. His long, unbraided raven-black hair floated around his shoulders, spreading out on the wings of the breeze, a beaded headband holding his hair back from his brow.

Nahosah, tomorrow, perhaps even tonight, she will know me," Sun Eagle whispered. "Soon she will *widosususuri*, lie down, with me. She will not say no, for she will know that one day Sun Eagle will be a powerful chief!"

Sun Eagle frowned, wondering about the maiden's true parentage. She was of the Chaui, Grand band of the Pawnee. Sun Eagle was of the Skidi, Wolf Pawnee, so he did not know that much about her. Except that her eyes were different than any other Pawnee maiden's that he had ever seen!

"But it does not matter," he said, shrugging. "Blue eyes the color of the sky are beautiful, even if they are the color of a white man's."

Sun Eagle's eyebrows rose in wonder. "Eyes of a white man," he said. "Yes! It *has* to be!"

The load of wood heavy in her arms, Kiriki glowered at the warriors sitting around the outside communal fire talking and smoking their Killikanick, a mixture of bark, leaves, and a slight bit of tobacco. Though it was accepted among all Pawnee that the women were the backbone of the village, doing much of the camp and village work, Kiriki did not like having these menial chores forced upon her.

Though she had been taught from childhood that a girl

learned all of the tasks done by her mother, as the lodge and household possessions were handed down from mother to daughter, she could not believe that that was all life had in store for her. Her mother's back was already bent and ugly, and it was all because her mother did nothing but hard labor from morning to night.

Kiriki wanted to better herself. She had no intentions of slaving away her youth in a few years of hard labor herding sheep, hoeing corn, and packing firewood. These things would cause her to grow square across the hips, flat in the face, and heavy in the legs!

No! She had seen the white women. They were not ugly and wasted away. Kiriki was part white! She desired to live the life of a white woman. Perhaps she could leave with a white pony soldier. They came from time to time to parley with her father.

"My father, *Skur-ar-a-le-shar,* Lone Chief," she whispered. "If only he were my true father. If Pawnee blood alone ran through my veins perhaps I would not be so restless!"

Though she saw the pony soldiers as a way out of her dreary life, she knew deep down that she must be wary of them. They were not all kind and trustworthy. One had raped her mother eighteen winters ago. Only out of kindness had her husband allowed her to keep the child borne of this rape—a child with her true father's blue eyes and brown hair! A child who was branded half-breed, forever!

"This child is Kiriki!" she whispered, a sob catching in her throat. She would never meet her true father. He had been hunted down and slain by the Pawnee soon after the brutal rape.

Rushed footsteps behind her made Kiriki stop and turn, to see who was moving in haste toward her. She smiled warmly when she saw that it was Durah, her best friend. While waiting for Durah to catch up with her, she shuffled her feet nervously, the bundle in her arms growing heavier by the minute. She looked over her shoulder at her lodge that was only a mere footstep away, wishing that either

her mother or father would come and relieve her of her burden.

She glanced over at the men who still sat around the outside fire, smoking and talking. Her chieftain father was among them, the biggest storyteller of them all. He did not even notice her, his dark eyes filled with mirth as he talked to those who looked at him with admiration.

As for her mother, *Baa-ubirid*, Moonstar, Kiriki did not have to see her to know what she was doing. This was the time of evening that she busied herself making bread for the next day.

"Kiriki!" Durah said, waving a hand. She ran faster, then stopped breathlessly before her friend.

"Durah, you look as though you have been up to trouble again," Kiriki said, laughing softly. "When your parents named you Durah, little did they know how mischievous you would be when you became sixteen winters old instead of being 'very good.' What have you done, Durah? Tell me."

Durah saw Kiriki's load of wood, and having already gotten her own wood supply for her family earlier in the day, took pity on her friend's patiently held burden. She began eagerly picking pieces of the wood from Kiriki's arms and tossing them at the door of her friend's lodge.

"Kiriki, wait until you hear what I have done and what I have *seen*," Durah said, her dark eyes dancing.

"Tell me," Kiriki said, sighing with relief as the last log was lifted from her arms. She began rubbing her flesh where it had been pinched by rough bark. "Must I wait forever for you to tell me?"

Grabbing Kiriki by the hand, Durah drew her into the shadows of the lodge. "Kiriki, did you see him?" she asked excitedly.

Kiriki looked at Durah with puzzlement. "Did I see who?" she asked, wishing that her friend would learn not to speak in circles. Kiriki was always blunt and to the point.

Durah released Kiriki's hand and turned to point at a

butte that overlooked the Pawnee village of many earth lodges protected by means of an earth and sod wall surrounding it. "A lone warrior sat on the hill observing our village," she said. "He was not of our village. I did not recognize him."

"And from such a distance how *could* you have recognized him?" Kiriki scoffed. "Durah, again you see just what you want to see to try and bring excitement into your life. Surely it was one of our warriors who enjoyed viewing our village from afar."

Durah leaned into Kiriki's face. "But you are wrong," she whispered, looking from side to side, making sure that she was not being observed, and most definitely not *heard*. "When I saw the warrior I became curious. I left the village and climbed the rocks until I was close enough to see him."

Kiriki gasped, yet not surprised at all at her friend's daring. Each day she grew bolder, it seemed. One day it could be fatal. "Durah, you did that?" she said. "Did he not see you?"

Durah shook her head, then smiled devilishly at Kiriki. "No, he did not see me," she giggled. "For his eyes were too full of *you*."

Kiriki blanched. "What do you mean?" she asked, her voice guarded.

"Kiriki, while you were leaving the forest with your arms filled with wood, that very handsome warrior was watching you," Durah said. "My friend, he did not miss one sway of your hips. Is that not exciting? To have a warrior from another village watching you, probably even wanting you? Oh, if but it were me! Surely he sees you as ravishingly beautiful, Kiriki. Or perhaps his attraction to you is because he is intrigued by your difference . . . by how you do not have all features that are Pawnee."

Kiriki looked up at the hill. She saw nothing as the sun was slowly setting, casting long purple shadows. A tremble coursed through her at the thought of being observed by a stranger, yet her fright was slowly turning into a strange sort of thrill. That she had been singled out by a warrior, to be watched, was nothing less than exciting!

Yet she did not wish to be pursued by a warrior. Her dreams did not include marrying into the same sort of life that was turning her mother into an old woman too soon. When she dreamed, she let herself dream big! She let herself dream of a white husband—a husband who would cater to her whims and give her luxuries that white women had.

"I do not care to hear any more about this warrior who wasted his time viewing my activities," Kiriki said, lifting her chin haughtily. "He is just a mere Indian. Nothing more, Durah. Now I must be on my way. Mother awaits the wood that I have gathered and brought for her evening fire."

She started walking away, but Durah grabbed her by the wrist and stopped her. "You are foolish!" Durah scolded. "You speak of dreams too often. My friend, dreams are for the foolish! And how disrespectful you are! A mere Indian, indeed! Kiriki, you are part Indian. Never forget that! You are more Indian than white! You were raised by the Pawnee!"

"I mean no disrespect," Kiriki said, sighing. She eased her wrist from Durah's grasp. "You know how I feel about things. Only you! And you know why."

Durah could hardly bear the soft pleading in her friend's voice. Guilt washed through her for having just shamed her. Durah *did* understand Kiriki's torn feelings about how she had been conceived, and by whom. And that she was torn between two cultures because of it.

Durah hugged Kiriki affectionately. "Durah knows that you are haunted by much that you have no control over," she murmured. "You cannot help it if your father was white. It is his blood flowing through your veins that makes you restless. Durah is sorry, Kiriki. So very sorry."

Kiriki slipped from her friend's embrace. "Meet me tonight by the waterfall?" she encouraged softly. "Let us talk? Let us even sleep beneath the stars again, Durah?"

"My parents are suspicious of me now that they caught

my bed empty the other night," Durah said sullenly. "But I shall come for awhile and talk. It is even warm enough to swim." She threw her arms around Kiriki and hugged her again. "Tonight, Kiriki. I shall see you tonight!"

Kiriki smiled, then her eyes rose slowly upward. She stared at the butte. She could not help but wonder about the warrior. Durah had said that he was handsome.

Just *how* handsome was he? Who could he have been? Would . . . he . . . return . . . ?

Sun Eagle's thoughts were distracted from watching the beautiful maiden, when on a slight rise in the land, silhouetted against the backdrop of sky, he saw his warrior friends awaiting his return on horseback so that they could continue with their journey homeward. They had humored Sun Eagle, by stopping long enough for him to take another look at the woman who intrigued him.

Proud, his gaze shifted to the many horses that were grazing alongside his Pawnee raiding companions. It had been a fruitful day. They had taken thirty head of horses. The raid against their neighbor, the Comanche, had been as easy as a falcon sweeping from the sky to capture a snake within its talons. The Pawnee had been as cunning. Not even one life had been lost during the raid.

His shoulders squared, his back straight, Sun Eagle sent his gelding into a faster gallop across the land toward his companions. He was eager to take the stolen horses on to his people. Captured horses were the legitimate spoils of war. The wealth of the Pawnee was in their horses. Horses were the only property that could be carried easily away.

A smile flickered across Sun Eagle's handsome face, again thinking of Kiriki. If a Pawnee bought a wife, he paid for her with horses!

Sun Eagle was willing to pay dearly for Kiriki because he had never seen anyone as beautiful and intriguing!

A lone horseman broke away from the waiting warriors and began riding toward Sun Eagle. He did not have to wait for long to see that the approaching warrior was his brother, Brown Bear.

Sun Eagle set his jaw firmly. His eyes narrowed. Of late, he had become annoyed more often than not with his brother, who was younger than he by two winters. Brown Bear had recently begun to show jealousies over everything that Sun Eagle accomplished in life. Though Brown Bear understood Sun Eagle's position in the village, that he was next in line to be chief, Brown Bear seemed to want to challenge this right. More than once he had tried to outdo Sun Eagle, to belittle him in their chieftain father's eyes.

But their father, Chief Antelope Buck, had only scoffed at Sun Eagle's worries, truly believing that Brown Bear's actions were guided by jealousy and ignored it as something foolish, something that would be outgrown in time. Though he did not speak it aloud to his father, whose word was everything to his people, Sun Eagle could not be swayed to believe that his brother's jealousies could be outgrown.

Sun Eagle nodded a silent hello to his brother, then rode onward as Brown Bear wheeled his horse around and began riding alongside him. Sun Eagle looked over at his brother then looked away, again reminded that Brown Bear was an almost exact replica of himself except for the coldness in Brown Bear's eyes and the drawn expression that jealousy paints onto one's face.

"My brother, did you see her again?" Brown Bear taunted, smiling devilishly at Sun Eagle. "Is she beautiful? Is she as intriguing as the other time you saw her?"

Sun Eagle cast his brother a questioning, nontrusting glance. If Brown Bear was jealous of everything else that Sun Eagle possessed, would he not become obsessed with wanting the woman of Sun Eagle's desire? Perhaps even after Sun Eagle had taken her as a wife? This could cause brothers to become the bitterest of enemies, for no man should covet his brother's wife.

Afraid of this possibility, causing Sun Eagle to perhaps be forced one day to challenge his brother to the death with knives, Sun Eagle frowned and shook his head. The lie that he was about to tell was very necessary.

"No, she is not beautiful," he said, his fingers circling his reins so tightly that he could feel the leather cutting into his flesh. "Nor is she as intriguing. It is her father's horses that I became intrigued with this time."

"But she is Pawnee," Brown Bear said, raising an eyebrow. "The horses of her people are Pawnee. We take only from the Comanche!"

"It does not matter if they are Pawnee or Comanche horses," Sun Eagle said in an annoyed grumble. "One horse is as beautiful as the next, are they not? One does not have to have intentions of taking when one looks to admire."

Brown Bear looked over at Sun Eagle. He chuckled. "Are you truly speaking of horses or women?" he teased. "She *is* beautiful, isn't she? You just do not want to share such knowledge with *me,* your brother, who also admires soft beauty in a woman."

Brown Bear's words were like knives piercing Sun Eagle's heart. Sun Eagle now knew that if he was going to pursue the lovely maiden's affections, it must be done in haste. His brother would be seeking her out also. It was in Brown Bear's eyes—in his words—that he would.

Sun Eagle glowered at Brown Bear for a moment, then thrust his heels into the flanks of his black gelding and thundered away from him. After delivering the captured horses to his village, he would return to see the maiden. Perhaps if things worked out, he could be beside the river before daylight broke on the horizon. He would watch for her arrival at the river for her morning bath and then he would approach her!

Flames of desire scorched his insides. Never had he wanted a woman as badly as now! She *would* be his. Nothing could stand in the way. Nothing.

Especially not his brother.

A waterfall accented the pine canyon. Moonlight tipped the trees white and cast silver designs across the land. Muted laughter rang through the night.

Kiriki filled her hands with water and splashed Durah

once again, only their shoulders and heads exposed above the moonlit water.

"Please, Kiriki, no more!" Durah pleaded as she wiped the wetness from her face. "I have had enough! My skin is wrinkled like an old lady's."

Kiriki swept her wet hair back from her eyes. "I have had enough also," she said, following Durah from the water onto a grassy knoll of land. She shivered as she drew a loose buckskin dress over her head. "But it was fun, was it not?"

"The true fun was in sneaking from my lodge where my parents slept so soundly," Durah said, giggling mischievously. She pulled her dress over her head and smoothed it down over her slender body, then combed her fingers through her midnight black hair, arranging it sleekly over her shoulders.

"If you enjoyed that so much, why not make it more daring by sleeping with me here beneath the stars?" Kiriki encouraged, spreading a blanket on the ground, close beside the river. "*Suk spid*. Sit down. We could talk the whole night long, Durah." She sat down on the blanket and pulled another snugly around her shoulders, enjoying its warmth after the chill of the water.

Durah sat down beside her and enveloped herself with her own blanket, clutching it around her shoulders. "What would you talk about?" she said, giving Kiriki a teasing smile. "The handsome warrior?"

"I do not know a handsome warrior," Kiriki said stubbornly, setting her jaw.

"Kiriki," Durah said exasperatingly. "You know who I am talking about. The warrior who watched you from afar today. Would you not like to know about him? Exactly what he looked like?"

Kiriki gave Durah an annoyed look. "Durah, in your eyes handsome is handsome," she sighed. "There is no need for explanations. Please forget that you saw him, will you?"

Durah scooted closer. "Kiriki, what if he watches you because he wishes to abduct you?" she whispered, looking over her shoulder into the darkness of the trees. The noise of the splashing waterfall close beside them suddenly sounded ominous. "What if he is of the Skidi band of Pawnee? They are not closely bound to other bands of Pawnee. They even practice some sort of human sacrifice! What if he watches you, thinking *you* are perfect for the sacrifice?"

A chill soared across Kiriki's flesh. She reached for a *nezik,* knife, that she had brought with her for protection and scooted it closer to her side. "You are saying these things to frighten me into returning to my lodge tonight because you are unable to spend the night with me out here beneath the stars as free as the forest animals," she scolded. "Durah, how can you be so spiteful?"

"Spiteful?" Durah said, her eyes wide. "Is it spiteful that I speak of truths? That I warn you that perhaps this man looks at you for all the wrong reasons? What if he does look at you because he is thinking of the sacrifice the Skidi offer to the Morning Star?"

"I know not of what you speak because my parents have forbidden me to ask about it," Kiriki said, her gaze moving to the sky, searching for the Morning Star, the god of their corn crop. "You should not be speaking of it, either. It is evil, Durah. Forbidden!"

"Do you not wish to know what I know?" Durah prodded. "Though forbidden, Durah knows much about it."

Kiriki looked slowly over at Durah, curiosity itching at her brain. "What do you know?" she blurted. "Tell me."

"You know that it is a Pawnee belief that long ago the Morning Star, celebrating his conquest over the Evening Star, brought light and fertility to the world of the Pawnee," Durah began.

"Do not all Pawnee know this?" Kiriki snapped. "You tell me no more than I already know. Why do you not go on home, Durah?"

"I know more!" Durah said, scooting closer to Kiriki. "Because the mating of these two great stars produced the first human being, a young girl, at times the Morning Star demands the return of this first human being. To please the Morning Star and ensure a bountiful harvest, the Skidi Pawnee sacrifice a young girl.''

Kiriki paled and gasped. ''They kill a young girl for the sacrifice?'' she asked in a frightened whisper.

''From what I have heard among the whispering women of our village, they say that only the most beautiful of girls are used as the sacrifice,'' Durah said, becoming breathless in her haste to tell the complete story. ''It is believed that the soul of the girl leaves her body at the moment she is struck with a club, and goes straight to Tirawa, the creator of the universe, who sends the girl's soul on to the Morning Star. Things are then born from it, and the earth is fertilized by it.''

Durah reached for Kiriki's hand and clasped it. ''The most beautiful of young girls are chosen for the sacrifice,'' she repeated. ''Kiriki, there is none more beautiful than you!''

Kiriki swallowed hard, then stared in surprise as Durah started laughing hysterically. ''Durah, why do you laugh? First you tell such a morbid tale and then call me beautiful? Which of these things do you find so amusing?'' she asked, jerking her hand from Durah's.

Durah rose from the blanket and looked down at Kiriki, mischief flashing in her dark eyes. ''I failed to say that the ones who are used for the sacrifice are taken from the women who are already in their village as captives, who for the most part are Comanche.'' She flipped her hair back from her eyes. ''Kiriki, do not be afraid. You are safe. You are not Comanche, and you are not anyone's captive.''

Durah's gaze moved to the butte high above the river. ''Do not fear that handsome warrior, either,'' she said. ''What I saw in his eyes was not a look of someone wanting to steal a woman only to have her slain. It was a look of wanting to possess, to love.''

Kiriki stormed to her feet, angry. ''You are my friend, yet you enjoy teasing me so!'' she said, placing her hands on her hips. ''I am glad you are not staying the night with me. *Wissgutts!* Go home! *Looah*—Go! Durah, leave me to the nightmares I now will most surely have, thanks to you!''

Durah's eyes softened with regret, her teasing smile faded. She lunged into Kiriki's arms and clung to her. "Durah is sorry," she said softly. "Durah teases no more.''

Kiriki sighed heavily and hugged her friend tightly. "Kiriki is sorry for getting so angry," she whispered. "But speaking of sacrifices and handsome men in one breath is unnerving. Let us speak of neither again. Promise?''

"Durah promises," she said.

"You had best return home before you are missed," Kiriki encouraged, waving Durah away.

Durah turned and walked away, downcast.

Kiriki settled down on the blanket and stretched out on her back. She worked hard at making herself conjure up more pleasant thoughts. Alone, it was going to be a long night.

Ah, but was this not a beautiful, mystical land? The air was filled with such sweet scents of cedar and pine. At this moment she felt as though she could reach up and touch the stars.

Her gaze settled on the morning star. A foreboding swept through her, recalling Durah's mystical tale of sacrifice—and of death.

Flipping over, she stretched out on her stomach. Her heart was beating so hard that she felt as though it was going to leap from inside her chest. She closed her eyes and tried to sleep. Yet she could not. But it was not because of thoughts of any morbid ritual. Instead, images of a handsome warrior kept forming in her mind's eye. She clenched her hands into tight fists, wondering again just why he *had* been watching her!

TWO

THE splash of the waterfall near, Sun Eagle swung himself out of his saddle and looped his horse's reins over a low limb of a cottonwood tree. The ride from his village should have been peaceful, with the stars and moon so brilliant overhead. But all the while he had been riding he had been thinking of how he might approach the beautiful maiden without frightening her. She would recognize right away that he was not a warrior from her village and would become suspicious of him.

Was it not nearing the time of the Morning Star rites? Could the maiden think that he had come to steal her away from her tribe to be the sacrifice?

Was she even aware of such a ritual? The Skidi had tried to keep it a secret throughout the years.

"But something as vicious as the sacrifice has surely not been kept unknown to other tribes of Pawnee," he whispered to himself, now moving stealthily along the banks of the moonlit river. "When I become chief, such a practice will be banished from the tribe as though it is an evil person. My people will be taught to see the wickedness of the ritual."

Sun Eagle's moccasins made scarcely a sound on the spongy moss as he broke into a soft trot. He squinted his eyes as he looked for just the right hiding place to watch the maiden as she came to the river for her morning bath. He would not have long to wait. The world would soon become christened with another sunrise. Shortly after that, Sun Eagle could expect to see the maiden with the seductively swaying hips and blue eyes as luminous as the sky.

14

Once again he would feast his eyes upon her golden, wondrous curves. Surely no other maiden had such a small waist, or such long and slender legs.

Heat rose in his loins as he recalled her high, rounded breasts. Ah, how he ached to touch them. They were surely as soft as a butterfly's wings!

Sun Eagle stopped beside the river for a moment to enjoy watching the miracle of the waterfall as its waters tumbled over the edge of the land and down the smooth rocks to the river below. The sound of the water tumbling downward, then fusing with the river in fiery crashes, was almost deafening yet, in a sense, peaceful. It brought back memories of Sun Eagle and Brown Bear enjoying the waterfall close to their village. As small children they had splashed beneath the water. They had even not only found a cave behind it, but also another cave they had found while exploring that was not at all close to their village.

All of this . . . this in the days of innocent fun and camaraderie between brothers.

But now it was all changed by jealousies. Even tonight, before Sun Eagle had left his village, he had checked to see if Brown Bear was asleep so that his brother would not follow him.

"And it will never be any different," Sun Eagle whispered again. "My brother's obsession divides us. Our hearts, our minds, are no longer as though one!"

Disgruntled at himself for letting thoughts of their torn brotherhood ruin this time set aside for thoughts of a lovely woman, Sun Eagle continued his journey alongside the river.

But his footsteps faltered. His body stiffened suddenly. He could not believe his good fortune!

He stopped and gazed disbelievingly at the beautiful sleeping form of the maiden of his midnight dreams, who now lay only a few more footsteps away from him. The blanket under which she had meant to sleep had fallen aside, allowing the moonlight to play along her buckskin-clad body, and to illuminate her beguiling facial features that were so delicate and innocent.

Sun Eagle's breath was almost stolen away.

Then his eyebrows forked. Why was she sleeping away from her village? Was she this daring? This adventurous? Was this not a reason to be even more intrigued by her? Surely no other woman would be as brave.

His handsome face creased into a frown. *She is not as brave as she is foolish!* he thought to himself. *Look at her now. Any animal could creep up on her and devour her!* His pulse began to race.

Suddenly Kiriki sprang to her feet like a tigress, poised for an attack with her knife held high, ready for the death plunge should Sun Eagle move any closer. Having learned all the sounds of man and animals, she had heard his approach. She had only pretended to be asleep.

Sun Eagle took a quick step backward, startled. Never had he seen a woman move as quickly! He was the foolish one to have thought *her* foolish. It was apparent that she had prepared herself for anything or anyone that might be a threat to her in the night.

He looked slowly up at the knife and how its sharp blade shone threateningly beneath the moonlight. Then he looked down into the maiden's eyes. "Do not be alarmed. I mean you no harm," he said, making a fist with one of his hands and placing it above his heart. "I come in friendship."

"Friends do not come sneaking around in the night," Kiriki said, hoping that he had not heard the frightened tremor of her voice. "Nor is it the best time to make acquaintance with *new* friends."

"I did not come searching for friendship in the night," Sun Eagle said, disturbed by the knife still poised in the air. "Sun Eagle did not know that you were here. It is not a usual thing for a woman to sleep alone beneath the moon and stars."

"Why are you here?" Kiriki asked guardedly, her insides trembling. His nearness did have an unsettling affect on her, but it was now not so much from fear as it was from fascination. Could this be the handsome warrior whom Durah had seen? If so, Durah had been right to sing his praises to the sky. This warrior's face was so handsomely sculpted it made Kiriki's heart beat recklessly. Never had a man stirred her in such a strange way.

"You are not familiar to me," she blurted. "You are not of my village."

Sun Eagle was at a loss for words. With the knife still a threat, and with a woman whose eyes were filled with fire holding the knife, how could he tell her that it was because of her that he had come? If he told her that he had become intrigued with her from afar, would she not become even angrier to know that she had been spied upon?

No. He did not know what to say. Either way, he could be condemned in her eyes. It seemed that his dream of having her for his woman seemed to be fading with the approaching dawn.

"Though it is not usual for a woman to be sleeping alone away from her people, it *is* usual for a man to be wandering in the night, communing with the land," he defended, lowering his doubled fist from his heart, to hold his arm stiffly at his side.

"Do you always commune close to a village that is not your own?" Kiriki snapped angrily. "Where *is* your village?" Her gaze raked over him, seeing his buckskin attire, and more. She saw a muscled body beneath the tight buckskin. She saw a long, lean torso that displayed narrow hips and a wide chest.

She drew a ragged breath, again looking up at his face. It was strong and determined, with hard cheekbones. There was a sensual fullness of his lower lip . . .

Forcing herself to emerge from her moment of reverie, Kiriki challenged him again with her eyes. "You could even be Comanche!" she said in a hiss, not wanting to let down her guard—not wanting him to see that he had disturbed her in any way other than to instill anger in her heart for having been there, an intruder in the night. "Tell

me that you are! I will enjoy plunging the knife into your
enemy heart!''

Sun Eagle smiled to himself. He had seen her look at
him like a woman looks at a man who is intriguing to her,
instead of frightening. He recognized much in the way she
now looked up at him with her luminous blue eyes. The
fire had left their depths, replaced by something beautifully
warm. Though she still spoke threats to him, he knew that
she now felt that her real threat was how he had truly
affected her. He was used to this. Though sometimes an
annoyance, he had accepted that women enjoyed looking
at, and being with him.

''Comanche?'' Sun Eagle said, chuckling. ''If I were,
even *I* would plunge your knife into my heart. My hate
of them equals yours.'' His eyes touched her everywhere,
branding her. ''I am Pawnee, just as you are Pawnee.''

Her arm having grown tired, the knife heavy in her
hand, Kiriki slowly lowered it. A hot blush rose to her
cheeks as she felt Sun Eagle's eyes traveling over her,
warming her flesh.

''You truly mean me no harm?'' she asked softly, blinking her lashes nervously as his eyes locked with hers.

''None,'' Sun Eagle said firmly. He looked down at the
knife. ''You wish not to harm me?''

Something made Kiriki unclasp her fingers around the
knife and drop it. ''None,'' she said, laughing nervously.

''Why do you sleep alone, away from the safety of your
family?'' Sun Eagle asked, moving to sit on his haunches,
staring out at the moon-splashed river. ''Are you restless?''

Now feeling safe enough with the stranger, Kiriki sat
down on her blanket and followed his gaze to the water.
''Are you?'' she asked, now wanting to know everything
about him. ''Are you restless?''

Was he the warrior who had spied upon her?

If so, why?

Was she the true reason for him being there now?

If so, she should send him away! She wanted to be

intrigued by a white man, not Pawnee. A white man could
take her away and introduce her into a world of wonder.

Did she want too much out of life just because some
white man's blood ran through her veins? Was she shamed
for wanting too much? . . .

"Sun Eagle is restless because of something he has
seen and now wants," he said, his heart thundering wildly
against his ribs.

His eyes moved slowly to Kiriki, mesmerized anew by
her haunting loveliness. She was a most beautiful maiden.
Her features were perfect. Her delicate cheekbones were
blooming with color. Her ripe and curving breasts, defined
so clearly beneath the buckskin fabric of her dress, were
heaving with what he hoped was excitement brought on
by his nearness.

"You have seen? You have wanted?" Kiriki said, her
voice soft and lilting. "What have you seen? What have
you wanted?"

Her pulse began to race, reading so much into what he
had said. If he was the warrior who had watched from the
hill, he had seen her! Did he now want her? Should she
flee?

But no, she could not. A strange sort of ache was troubling her at the juncture of her thighs. Never had she felt
this before. Was she awakening to feelings of a woman?
Could a total stranger cause this painful sort of pleasure
to blossom within her? Should she not run because of this?
No, she could not. She was enjoying these moments
shared with a stranger, whose fathomless eyes were now
almost hypnotizing her with their dark, hidden fires.

Sun Eagle moved to his knees and turned to Kiriki. He
framed her face gently between his hands. "Do not be
frightened by what I have to tell you," he said, looking
at her with tenderness. "Just listen. Measure my words
very carefully. They will be spoken from the heart. . . ."

Brown Bear stirred in his sleep inside his great earthen
lodge, the moon casting its beams down through the
smoke hole above him, to fall upon his face. The light

reflected farther inside the lodge, revealing guns, metal tools, and pots, beads and cloth that the white man had introduced to his people.

It also revealed that the Pawnee were extremely religious. They viewed their home as a miniature of the universe itself. The domed roof represented the sky, cottonwood trunks supporting the roof stood for different directions, and through the smoke hole in the center the star gods were thought to pour down their strength.

The lodge's doorway faced east to the Morning Star and god of light, fire, and war. The western end faced the goddess of night and germination.

Between the central fire pit and a buffalo skull altar to the west was the sacred spot where no one was to step. . . .

Brown Bear tossed and turned on his pallet of furs, sweat beading his brow as his dreams became filled with a strange, glaring light and the shape of a godly figure emerged, as though floating toward him.

"Who are you?" Brown Bear whispered in his sleep. "What do you want? Leave me in peace!"

Suddenly the godly figure turned into a great, brilliant star, fully engulfing Brown Bear within its powerful gleaming light.

"Brown Bear, it is I, Morning Star, who commands you to go across the land and find the most beautiful of all the young maidens," a voice said, emanating from all points of the universe. "You will be blessed, Brown Bear. Blessed. . . ."

The light began to dim and the voice began to fade. Brown Bear awakened with a start, his heart pounding so hard that he felt faint. He looked wildly around him, seeing that everything was as it had been when he had retired for the night.

Yet, deeply within himself he knew there was a difference.

He was recalling the command. Something drew him to his feet and from his lodge. His gaze, as though drawn by a puppeteer's strings, moved slowly upward, looking eastward into the heavens. He was startled by the intensity of one star that stood out from the others with such brilliance it almost blinded him.

It was the morning star, as though it was beckoning to him . . . commanding him. . . .

"The dream!" he gasped. "Morning Star came to me in the vision! It beckons to me even now! I have been chosen to find the maiden for the Morning Star ritual! I, only, am the one to search and find the maiden that is the most beautiful of all maidens for the sacrifice!"

Humbled by this honor, tears began to roll down Brown Bear's cheeks. He knew that he must go and share this news with the Morning Star Priest, but first, he must tell his brother, Sun Eagle. Ah, how wonderful it would be to see his brother's expression. This time Brown Bear had something to be envied by Sun Eagle!

Wiping tears from his eyes, he watched the star's brilliance fade. It now only sparkled, mingling with the other thousand points of light in the sky. . . .

Swallowing hard, Brown Bear spun around and ran through the village until he reached Sun Eagle's private earthen lodge. Without hesitation he rushed on inside, then stopped, numb. His brother's pallet of furs was empty. His brother was gone. In the middle of the night? Where could he be? If he was with a woman, he would have invited her into his dwelling; he would have gone not to hers.

And as far as Brown Bear knew, there *was* no special woman in Sun Eagle's life.

Brown Bear's heart skipped a beat and his eyes widened with remembrance. "Ah, but there is," he whispered, curling the fingers of one hand into a tight fist at his side. "Did he not gaze upon her today? Is he with her now?"

Jealousy and disappointment soared through him. Jealousy for a woman he had never seen, and disappointment over not being able to tell Sun Eagle that the Morning Star had appeared to him in a special vision!

Spinning around on a heel, he left Sun Eagle's lodge, downcast. Then he again began to remember the honor

that had been bestowed upon him. He must go to the
Morning Star Priest and share the good news with him!

Hurrying to the priest's lodge, Brown Bear was stunned
to find him awaiting his arrival at the door. Without words
spoken between them, Brown Bear followed the priest
inside his dwelling. He sat down close to the firespace.
Brown Bear watched the priest fill his pipe and light it,
then accepted it when it was offered to him.

He took a draw from the long and narrow stem, then
offered the pipe back to the priest and began telling him
of his vision, yet at the back of his mind he was anxious
to leave. Brown Bear must ride from the village and find
Sun Eagle.

He must also take a look at the woman of Sun Eagle's
desire. Perhaps *she* was the loveliest of them all! Perhaps
she would be the one sacrificed for the Skidi band of
Pawnee this year.

When Sun Eagle placed his fingers so possessively to
her shoulders, Kiriki flinched with alarm. Yet she did not
try to move away. There was something in the way he
spoke to her that made her know that he had no intentions
of harming her. There was too much in his eyes that led
her into wanting to hear what he had to say.

As the moments passed, he seemed less and less a
stranger to her, as though she had known him forever.

Oh, how could it be?

How?

"Moments ago you called yourself by the name Sun
Eagle. Where do you come from?" she asked, searching
his face for answers. "Why do you single me out? Why?"

She would not let herself think of Durah's tale of sacrifices. Of murder!

No! She would not. Not at a time like this, when she
was discovering so much about herself that was strange to
her.

Ah, the feelings that were swimming through her. Were
they not delicious? Yet, almost frightening?

"Yes, Sun Eagle is my name," he said, loosening his

grip on her shoulders. "I have already told you I am Pawnee. My village is a half day's ride from yours. I only recently saw you for the first time, or I would have pursued your affections earlier. Do you not know how lovely you are? You are not married or you would not be sleeping alone. Why are you not married?"

His gaze swept over her, stopping at the great swell of her breasts. "Your age has surpassed that which is normal for the Pawnee women to marry," he said huskily. "Most become wives at fourteen winters, when they are just maturing into womanhood. You are how many? Surely seventeen or eighteen."

Kiriki's head was spinning, trying to comprehend all that he was saying. "I am eighteen winters in age," she said. "You have observed me how many times?" she quickly added, her eyes innocently wide. "It was *you* who was observing me today?"

"You saw me?" Sun Eagle said, smiling down at her. "That is good. You expected me to come again."

"No, I did not see you," Kiriki said, easing away from his fingers. She toyed with the fringes of her dress, looking away from Sun Eagle. "My best friend, Durah, saw you."

Slowly she looked up at him. "She also surpasses the age of what is normal for Pawnee women to marry," she murmured. "Neither of us wish to become old before our time. I, Kiriki, as well as Durah, look in the other direction when anyone talks of marriage!"

Sun Eagle settled down on the ground beside Kiriki's blanket. He drew his knees up to his chest and circled them with his arms. "Kiriki," he said, nodding. "Now I know your name, and I find it as beautiful as you."

"You did not answer me," Kiriki said, staring over at him. "How many times have you watched me that I do not know about? If you had come later this morning you would have even seen me ba—"

She stopped short and her face blushed hotly again. "Oh, please tell me that you have not watched me bathe," she said, her voice fading away when she saw him look slowly over at her with a soft glimmer in his eyes.

Embarrassed, she turned her eyes away quickly. "You *have* seen me bathe," she gasped. "You are here this time of morning to see me bathe again! Is nothing sacred to you? Do you not know the meaning of privacy?"

She rose quickly to her feet, grabbing her blankets. "Kiriki has nothing else to say to you," she said curtly. "You go and find yourself another innocent Pawnee maiden to spy on. Kiriki shall be more careful in the future. Kiriki will check all the bushes beside the river before shedding her clothes!"

Sun Eagle rustled to his feet. He grabbed Kiriki by the wrists, causing her to drop the blankets. He drew her to him, holding her immobile against his powerful body. "Sun Eagle does not want to sneak around watching Kiriki," he said gruffly. "I wish for Kiriki to be with me *willingly*. I have come to court you." He feathered kisses across her brow. "Sun Eagle will pay many horses for you. Your father will not be able to say no."

His kisses were causing Kiriki to become mindless. Her pulse was racing. Her throat was becoming dry. The pit of her stomach felt strangely queasy, and she knew that it must be passion that she was experiencing. It felt deliciously sweet, as though she was ready to take flight!

But what he was saying caused her to keep some of her senses. He wanted to marry her! He was ready to deliver many horses to her father to pay a bride price for her!

This was not the way it was supposed to be. A white man was supposed to come and rescue her from a future of a crooked back and wide hips. If she married this intriguing, handsome warrior, her future could be filled with many intimate moments with him at night, but she dreaded and feared the days the most.

Oh, but she just could not bear to think of the days! From morning to sunset she would be forced to do hard and grueling work. . . .

Wriggling free from his grasp, Kiriki grabbed her blankets from the ground and began to run. Sobs of despair

leapt from her throat. She had never felt so beautifully
wonderful inside as when in this man's embrace, yet she
must turn her back on it. She must!

Not to be denied what he hungered most for in the
world at this moment, Sun Eagle ran after Kiriki. When
he reached her, he grabbed her around the waist and pulled
her to the ground beneath him. With a knee he eased her
legs apart and placed his hand at the juncture of her thighs
and began softly caressing her. His mouth crushed hers
with a fiery kiss.

Breathing hard, trying to catch her breath, her eyes
wild, Kiriki pushed at his chest and jerked her lips free.

Yet she could not deny the exquisite sensations that
were blossoming where his hand so daringly caressed.

"Please, let me go," she cried, melting inside from the
flames burning and spreading within her. "Please. Do not
take me like this. Do not rape . . ."

The word "rape" was like a jolt to Sun Eagle's mind.
He had not even been aware of where his desires had
taken him. He jerked his hand away from her and let her
slip from beneath him. He held his head in his hands, his
loins burning with need. "*Looah!* Go!" he said thickly.
"Now!"

Half stumbling, Kiriki moved away from him. She was
torn with feelings. She now understood what the word
desire meant. She was filled with desire at this moment,
and knew that surely no other man could cause such wondrous feelings inside her again.

Yet, it was not what she wanted. She *must* flee. Not
only him, but also that which he had awakened within
her.

Forgetting her blankets and knife, Kiriki broke into a
mad, blinding run. But so much told her that she was
running in the wrong direction. It was toward him that her
heart told her to go!

Not . . . home . . .

She continued running away from the river.

Sun Eagle rose slowly to his feet. He picked up one of
Kiriki's blankets and placed it to his nose. Inhaling, he

smelled her sweetness which still clung to the fabric. His
eyes became filled with pain, his heart ached. He could
not give her up all that easily. He would return to sit
beside the river again. She would, also. He had seen desire
in her eyes. *He* was the one to feed that desire.

Only he.

Three

WITHIN the safe confines of her village, Kiriki stopped to catch her breath, having run so hard that her side ached. She looked over her shoulder at the butte just barely outlined against the lightening sky of morning, wondering if Sun Eagle had gone there after her flight from him. Would he stay and observe her some more today? Or would he leave, thinking that she would confide in her parents about the near-rape?

Not seeing the outline of an Indian brave on a horse, Kiriki turned her eyes away and held her head in her hands. Rape. Had history almost repeated itself? If she had been assaulted sexually would she not, forever, suffer the same humiliation that her mother had carried around with her these past eighteen winters?

"Yes, except that the rape would not have been done by a white man," she whispered to herself.

Raising her eyes from her hands, a sensual tremor coursed through Kiriki. The remembrances of Sun Eagle's lips and hands awakening her into wondrous feelings would never leave her. And he had felt the same about her, or he would have not gotten so carried away with the need of her.

Would it have truly been classified as rape if he had continued with his gentle caresses? Had she not wanted him surely as much as he wanted her? Had her body not responded to him in ways that she had never known existed? . . .

Shaking her head, Kiriki wanted to place her confused feelings behind her, but that was impossible. They were so vivid, it was as though he was still with her—touching her, kissing her . . .

"I must talk with someone," she whispered harshly.

Her gaze moved to Durah's earthen lodge. Smoke did not yet rise from the smoke hole this early in the morning, which meant that everyone was still asleep. Perhaps she could slip into the lodge and fetch Durah without awakening the rest of the family.

She set her jaw firmly, knowing that she must take that chance, for she needed Durah's camaraderie now more than ever before. Durah would not break a confidence. She would listen. She would give advice . . .

Moving barefoot across the dirt-packed earth, so quiet that her footsteps were as those of a panther stealing upon its prey, Kiriki stopped at the entrance of Durah's lodge. She inhaled a shaky, nervous breath, then lifted the buckskin entrance flap and tiptoed inside.

From having been in their lodge so often, she knew exactly where Durah slept. She inched her way around several sleeping mounds of bodies, then knelt down beside her friend.

Bending close to Durah's ear, Kiriki whispered her name, glad that Durah was not one to become alarmed easily. Durah's eyes opened quickly. She turned silently to Kiriki.

Kiriki placed a finger to her friend's lips, encouraging silence between them, and nodded toward the door. Durah understood. She slipped free from her blankets, pulled on a dress, then tiptoed with Kiriki from the lodge.

Once outside, Kiriki grabbed Durah's hand and led her hurriedly away from the dwelling into the dim pewter light of morning, then turned to her friend, her face warm with excitement.

"Durah, he came to me," she said in a rush of words. "The warrior came to me!"

Annoyed, Durah rubbed sleep from her eyes. "Kiriki, did you awaken me just to tell me about a silly dream?" she said scornfully. She turned to walk away, but Kiriki grabbed her hand again, stopping her.

"I am not talking about a dream," Kiriki said, her voice anxious. "I speak of reality! The handsome warrior that you saw watching me came to me only moments ago as I lay beneath the stars."

Kiriki's eyes began to dance as she smiled. "Durah, do you not see something different about me?" she said in a silken purr. "If so, it is because this man has awakened strange stirrings within me that I have never felt before. I even believe that he loves me. He says he will pay a bride price of many horses to my father for my hand in marriage!"

Durah was speechless, even numb. She eyed Kiriki with disbelief, yet she knew that she had been told the truth, because Kiriki was not the sort to lie. The warrior *had* come to her and *had* spoken of marriage to her. If Kiriki said it was so, then it was so!

"Kiriki, please tell me everything," Durah said, unable to quell the envy that was building up inside her. Durah had not wanted to get married at the age of fourteen winters, but now, at sixteen winters, she was becoming enchanted with the idea of having a man to keep her warm during the long, cold nights of winter.

Oh, if only the handsome warrior had come to her. Had offered to pay a high bride price for her. She would have said yes, many times yes!

Kiriki looked cautiously around her. "Here?" she asked in a hushed whisper. "What if someone should hear?"

Durah looked over her shoulder at her lodge, then back at Kiriki. "Mother and Father were sleeping soundly, so we have time to go and sit by the river to talk before they rise," she said. "Let us hurry. I want to hear everything!"

Giggling like small mischievous children, they ran hand-in-hand through the village, on past the protective walls, and then toward the river. The sunrise was bringing the drab clay bluffs to life with reddish light. A soft breeze made the leaves rustle and whisper.

Her heart almost stilled with a sudden thought, Kiriki jerked herself and Durah to a stop. She looked wildly ahead, then at Kiriki. "What if he is still there?" she whispered. "Perhaps we had best return to our village!"

"No, we must not return home," Durah argued, her heart pounding with the thought of possibly seeing the handsome warrior up close, perhaps even eye-to-eye. "Is this not all just too exciting?" She tugged at Kiriki's hand. "Come. Let us see if he *is* still there. What harm can come of it if he is?"

"What harm?" Kiriki said, her voice shallow. "His nearness confuses me. *That* is the harm."

"You are intrigued by him," Durah said, her eyes wide. "Why is that so confusing?"

"Because I wish to be intrigued only by a white man who can take me away from backbreaking duties," Kiriki argued.

"Kiriki, you are impossible!" Durah said, sighing. "I wish to keep my slender figure as much as you, but I abhor the thought of sharing a bed with a white man just to ensure it. Do you not remember how evil the white man can be? You are on this earth because of one such evil man."

Kiriki hung her head. She dug her toe into a thick layer of dried leaves. "As I said, I am confused," she said, then Durah yanked her hand and pulled her along as they began running again.

The closer Kiriki drew to the spot where she had shared a brief moment of ecstasy with the handsome warrior, the more the pit of her stomach fluttered. When she saw one of her blankets that she had left behind, she looked quickly around for the other one.

"He must have taken one of my blankets," she said, glad that Durah had finally released her hand when she also saw the blanket, and then the shine of the knife lying within its folds. "How can I explain its absence to my mother?"

Durah plopped down on the blanket and smoothed it out for Kiriki to sit beside her. "Come, Kiriki," she encouraged. "No one is here, we can speak in private. I have waited long enough. Tell me all that happened between you and the handsome warrior.''

Arranging her dress neatly beneath her, Kiriki sat down beside Durah. She gazed into the river, the flush of the sunrise streaking it a muted pinkish-red. When the moon had been silvering the water with its mystical beams, she had been in the arms of Sun Eagle. . . .

''He calls himself Sun Eagle,'' Kiriki said dreamily, thrilling inside at the mere mention of his name. ''Is that not a beautiful name, Durah?''

Durah gazed in longing at Kiriki, knowing that her dearest friend was experiencing true pangs of love for the first time in her life. It was in Kiriki's voice. It was in her eyes. . . .

Brown Bear crouched behind a thick stand of cotton-wood trees deep in the forest, his horse tethered far away from him. He had ridden hard through the night and had been sidetracked only once, when he had heard a rider approaching. Brown Bear had found a hiding place just in time, for another moment longer and Sun Eagle would have discovered him riding in the direction of the village where Sun Eagle's heart had been captured by a lovely maiden.

After Sun Eagle had passed on by, Brown Bear had arrived at the river just before the two lovely maidens he was now viewing. He had heard Sun Eagle's name spoken by the loveliest of the two women. She was still talking while the other one was raptly listening. Brown Bear had to get closer; he had to hear what she was saying. Perhaps with the very first try he had found Sun Eagle's woman!

Moving stealthily from tree to tree, Brown Bear was careful not to step on a twig that could snap and alert the maidens of his presence. When he got within hearing range, he crouched behind a thickly leafed lilac bush and listened. A slow smile began to crease his face, for what he was hearing was a confession of everything that had transpired between this beautiful maiden and Sun Eagle.

She was telling her friend every intimate detail and how her insides thrilled even now to recall Sun Eagle's kisses!

Brown Bear leaned closer when Kiriki's name was spoken by Durah.

"Kiriki," Brown Bear whispered to himself. "She is called Kiriki—'bright eyes.' " His gaze traveled over her, now understanding why his brother hungered for her. Except for the strange blue color of her eyes and the pale brown of her hair, everything about her was perfect, as though born into this world for a purpose other than being a wife. . . .

Now Brown Bear wanted more than ever to do what was necessary to deny his brother this woman whose loveliness inflamed even Brown Bear's heart. Sun Eagle always managed to get everything his way. This time he would not! Brown Bear would make himself the most admired warrior of his village by stealing Kiriki for the sacrifice. *That* was Kiriki's destiny! From the moment she had stirred that first time in her mother's womb, her destiny was to please the Morning Star.

His eyes narrowed as he became lost in thought. Kiriki's abduction must be planned carefully, and he would have to keep her hidden until the time was right to present her to his people for the sacrifice. It must be perfectly timed, when Sun Eagle could not stop him.

Finally, Brown Bear's cunning ways would win over Sun Eagle's!

Brown Bear smiled devilishly as he envisioned the moment Kiriki would take her last breath on this earth. It would be as it had been for centuries, when the most beautiful captive's heart had been torn out and her body filled with arrows, as thick as the quills of a porcupine. . . .

Sun Eagle rode across the land, his village now in sight. He enjoyed this time of morning when everything was fresh and new, a new beginning always within reach. The sunshine brushed the tops of the trees, and the waist-high grass was still being caressed by sparkling dew. The breeze was too soft to feel. Soon the sun would be warm and comfortable upon him.

Riding into the village, Sun Eagle gazed at his parents' lodge. He smiled. Smoke was spiraling from the smoke hole. His mother was awake and preparing breakfast. His father would be taking a walk, having his early morning commune with nature. Sun Eagle would be free to share feelings alone with his mother. She could help him decide on a special gift to take to Kiriki, to show her just how much he cared for her.

Quickly dismounting his horse, Sun Eagle tied it near the door of his parents' lodge along with two other fast horses that were tethered there. It was the custom of the Pawnee to tie up the best of their horses close to the lodge door where they would be under the eye of their master as much as possible.

Sun Eagle walked on toward the entrance flap, feathers hanging and swaying on the lodge and rows of animal hoofs hanging down the sides. His footsteps firm as he entered the lodge, he felt all warm inside when he saw his mother bending over before the fire, patting and rolling out dough for bread. The lodge already smelled enticingly of cooked rabbit and boiled turtle eggs.

Kidibattsk looked up from her chores at Sun Eagle. "Welcome, my son, and sit down," she said.

Going to his mother, Sun Eagle kissed her fleshy, copper cheek, then settled onto his haunches before the fire. He stared into the flames coiling themselves over a log cut from an elm tree, feeling his mother's eyes on him, studying him.

"You come so early in the morning to visit your mother?" Kidibattsk asked, accidentally smudging corn meal on her face as she brushed a wiry, gray hair back from her puffy eyes. She went and placed a thick arm around Sun Eagle's shoulders, so short and squat herself that when she stood next to him while he sat on his haunches, she was almost his exact height. Her name, Kidibattsk, meaning "very little" had been rightfully given to her at birth.

"You are troubled, my son?" Kidibattsk asked softly. "You want to talk to your mother about it?"

Sun Eagle placed a hand on her arm, relishing her closeness. She had always been there for him, as his confidante. "Mother, there is suddenly a special woman in my life," he said thickly. "But she does not return my affections. Tell me what I must do to win her heart."

"Who is this woman?" Kidibattsk asked as she sat down beside Sun Eagle. She looked into his eyes and saw the pain that loving this woman was causing him. "Is she of a neighboring village?"

"Yes, she is of the Grand band of Pawnee," Sun Eagle said, picking up a stick, stirring the coals of the fire with it. "Mother, she is most beautiful!"

"She has seen you?" Kidibattsk asked softly. "You have approached her? She has seen your handsomeness?"

"Yes, I have approached her," he said dryly. "Yes, she has seen me. But she must not see me as handsome, for she turned from me and fled."

Kidibattsk gasped. She squared her shoulders angrily. "A woman does that to my son?" she asked heatedly. "She is not the woman for you! You must look elsewhere."

Sun Eagle rose to his feet and began pacing nervously back and forth. "That is impossible, Mother. For you see, I already know how she feels in my arms." He doubled his hands into tight fists at his sides. "She is meant to be there. She must be."

Kidibattsk rose to her feet and placed a firm hand on Sun Eagle's arm, stopping his pacing. "You say she turned away from you, yet you say that you have held her," she said, her puffy eyes squinting up at Sun Eagle. "Did she turn away from you after you held her?"

"Yes," Sun Eagle said, tormented by remembrances.

"She is not for you!" Kidibattsk reaffirmed. "No woman who turns away from my handsome son deserves to be pursued by him! Do not make a fool of yourself. Let her go."

Feeling a strange sort of pain squeezing his heart, know-

ing that for the first time in his life he must ignore his
mother's advice, Sun Eagle looked solemnly down at her.
"I cannot turn my back on her, nor can I let her go," he
said hoarsely. "If that is your advice, I am sorry but I
must ignore it."

Stunned, Kidibattsk stared at Sun Eagle. "My son, you
are in love if you cannot listen to what your mother tells
you," she said, her voice breaking. "I must say to you,
then, that you must find a way to make her love you in
return."

"You understand?" Sun Eagle asked, placing his hands
on his mother's thick, stooped shoulders. "You give me
your blessing?"

"Always, my son," Kidibattsk said, sniffing back a
tear.

"Then help me to find the perfect special gift to take
to Kiriki," Sun Eagle said, knowing that he would be
returning to Kiriki this very day. He had purposely brought
one of her blankets with him to his village. It was a perfect
excuse to return to her. At the same time, he hoped to
have a special gift for her so that her feelings toward him
would, perhaps, soften.

"Kiriki?" Kidibattsk murmured, arching a gray eyebrow. "That is her name?"

"Yes," Sun Eagle said, again gazing down into the
flames. "A perfect name for such a lovely maiden."

Kidibattsk stared at Sun Eagle again, then went to the
back of the lodge and picked up a small cedar box. She
took it and handed it to Sun Eagle. "Choose from my
necklaces that one which you think your Kiriki would
admire the most," she said, her hand trembling.

This son, her first born, would one day be chief. How
could she tell him that his wife must be strong and very
caring, for the ordeals of being a chief's wife were sometimes quite trying. The chief's wife had to carry all the
burdens of the tribe the same as he, as well as be a wife
and mother.

Kidibattsk grew tired of it at times.

But other times, *most* of the time, she would not trade

places with anyone on earth. Oh, but how she loved her husband! That special love—that bond—made everything in her life worthwhile. Surely any woman married to Sun Eagle would feel the same.

Sun Eagle held the small chest in one hand, while with the other he opened it. He looked down upon an assortment of necklaces, most of which had been made with colorful beads. They were all beautiful, yet one stood out from all the rest in its rare loveliness. His mother had plucked several pink-tinted sea shells from the river and had cut and shaped them to look like pink flowers, then had strung them. Sun Eagle ran his fingers over the smoothness of the shells, then smiled.

"This is the one I choose for Kiriki," he said, handing the cedar box back to his mother. "She is like the shell flowers—exquisite and dainty."

"You have chosen wisely, my son," Kidibattsk said, closing the lid on the box. "You will give it to her today?"

"Yes," Sun Eagle said, nodding. "Today."

Heavy footsteps entering the lodge drew Sun Eagle around. He gazed with pride at his father, *Alligatus,* Chief Antelope Buck, who, attired in only a brief loincloth, displayed that he was still well-muscled at his age of fifty-five winters.

Sun Eagle went to his father and embraced him, the necklace held tightly within his hand.

"*Lau,*" Chief Antelope Buck said in fond greeting. "At least my eldest son is in the village to greet his father this morning." He chuckled as he fondly patted Sun Eagle on the back.

"What do you mean? Is Brown Bear not in his lodge?" Sun Eagle asked, alarmed at the thought of where his brother might be. If Brown Bear had discovered Sun Eagle had been absent throughout the night, he surely would have guessed where to find him. Brown Bear could have decided to go to Kiriki's village himself, to take his *own* look at the lovely maiden. When Brown Bear discovered that Sun Eagle was no longer there, he might even try and win her affections before Sun Eagle. Sun Eagle must return to Kiriki. Now!

"Brown Bear's lodge showed signs of his having slept there, yet he is gone," Chief Antelope Buck said, shrugging. He sat down before the fire and reached for his pipe. "I checked his horse. It is also gone. Where? I do not know."

"I must also leave," Sun Eagle said, rushing toward the door.

"My son, where do you go in such haste?" Chief Antelope Buck asked, gesturing with a hand for Sun Eagle to come back and sit beside him.

"Let him go in peace, without questions," Kidibattsk encouraged, placing a gentle hand on her husband's bare, muscled shoulder. "He has other things besides a wandering brother on his mind."

"Oh?" Chief Antelope Buck said, raising an eyebrow.

Kidibattsk leaned down and kissed her husband on the brow. "A woman," she whispered. "Our son, Sun Eagle, has found a special woman. He goes to her now."

Four

UNABLE to get Sun Eagle off her mind, Kiriki had hurried through her morning chores, knowing what she must do. Determination in her steps, she left the village behind, not even telling Durah where she was going this time. She had to be alone, to think, but already she knew it was imperative that she see and be with Sun Eagle again to prove to herself that she could live without him. Her feelings for him were too strong to deny. Never had she felt this way before. Perhaps, she never would again.

Flipping her long brown hair back from her shoulders in frustration, Kiriki continued barefoot beneath towering elms toward the shine of the river. "Oh, what must I do?" she fussed to herself. "My dream has always been to feel something special about a white man. I want to live as though white, myself."

Lifting her buckskin skirt she stepped over a gnarled tree root that had worked its way up through the earth and lay twisted across the moss-covered land. Her mind was catapulted back into time, to the moment she had first been held in Sun Eagle's arms. She had experienced something wonderfully sweet; a strange sort of melting that went from the top of her head to the tip of her toes. It had been as though she had become a part of the sunshine, all warm and mellow.

The river reached, the waterfall splashing over rocks nearby, Kiriki plopped down on the ground beside it and stared into the clear water where minnows darted and played. She ran her fingers through her long hair, her frustration no less than only moments ago.

"I cannot imagine ever feeling as strongly for a white man as I do Sun Eagle," she whispered, feeling foolish for talking to herself as though she were two persons.

She drew her knees to her chest and hugged them, her skirt hiking up, way above her knees, revealing the silken, golden flesh of her thighs. Slowly she rocked back and forth, her concentration momentarily distracted as she watched a water spider skip across the water's surface.

Dismounting, Sun Eagle tethered his gelding far enough away from the river so that its hoofbeats would not be heard, just in case Brown Bear was there spying on Kiriki. If Brown Bear *was* there, Sun Eagle would have to challenge him, whether or not he wanted to. Things were getting out of hand with his brother. His jealousy was placing a barrier between brothers.

The lovely necklace that his mother had given him for Kiriki lay hidden in a buckskin pouch attached to the waist of his loincloth. Sun Eagle began to move stealthily through the dense forest, the smell of the river sweet and refreshing in the air. The sun spiraled its rays through the roof of heavy vegetation overhead, like golden satin streamers waving in the wind. Squirrels snapped acorns from the trees; bluejays squawked, breaking the silence.

The splash of the waterfall up just ahead made Sun Eagle grow tense. His brow was furrowed into a deep scowl, his eyes were two points of fire as he searched for his brother's reined horse.

His shoulder muscles relaxed somewhat as Sun Eagle slowed his pace. Hope was swelling inside him that his brother had not come to spy upon Kiriki after all. There were no signs of Brown Bear anywhere. This time, had Sun Eagle's suspicions wrongly accused a brother? Was Brown Bear on a different sort of mission this morning; perhaps a mission of his heart?

At this moment, Brown Bear could even be with a woman, loving her! He surely did not need Kiriki at all, for it was well known that Sun Eagle's brother was most virile, with a number of women willing and ready to marry him. . . .

Sun Eagle's frown changed slowly into a smile when through a break in the trees ahead he saw what surely was a vision! Although he had hoped to see Kiriki, he had not ventured to guess that he would be in luck a second time; that she would actually be there!

Stopping to gaze at Kiriki before actually going to meet her face to face again, Sun Eagle could not control the beating of his heart. Never had he wanted a woman as badly as Kiriki. How perfectly natural she had fit into his arms when he had embraced her.

And, ah, her lips! They had tasted of wild flowers, of the sweetness of raindrops, and of the wonders of the breeze on a spring day!

Suddenly she was everything to him.

Everything!

Sun Eagle had to have Kiriki to awaken to each morning. He wanted her beside him when he went to bed each night. He wanted to hold her as he slept. He wanted her there to hear him when he breathed her name in his sleep.

He wanted her with him, always!

"And so shall I have her," he whispered to himself. "I have come today with not only my offered love, but a very special gift. How can she deny me?"

Not wanting to waste anymore time worrying and wondering about how Kiriki might receive him, Sun Eagle stepped into full view and walked hastily toward the river. When Kiriki turned with a start and their eyes met and held, he saw much in her expression that revealed that he may have also been on *her* mind. . . .

Kiriki rose quickly to her feet, almost falling into the river as she lost her balance from being so startled by Sun Eagle's sudden presence. It was as though she had silently bid him there, and he had come.

Oh, but if she could only stop the crazy beating of her heart! If she could just turn and run away from him and never think of him again, she would be so much better off for it.

But she knew that all of these things were impossible. Now that she had seen Sun Eagle again, and saw so much in his eyes in the way he looked back at her, she realized that she had truly not come to the river to try and purge herself of this handsome man at all. She had come to see and be with him, because she longed for him. Deep within herself, where her desires were formed, she knew that he was the only man who could ever kindle such desires.

His dark, fathomless eyes were rendering Kiriki mindless as he kept gazing at her, drawing closer to her as he now strolled pantherish toward her. When he reached out his arms to her, then placed his hands to her shoulders, it was as though the whole world stood still as Kiriki's breathing was momentarily halted.

"*Lau*," Sun Eagle murmured in a slight greeting.

His lips moving downward toward Kiriki's, his hands pulling her closer to him, did not cause any alarm, but only passion to sweep through her, causing her to respond in kind.

Crushed now against his powerful, bare chest, his arms holding her tightly, Kiriki closed her eyes as waves of rapture flooded her when Sun Eagle's mouth bore down upon her lips. His tongue sought entrance into her mouth. His hands had slipped down to her buttocks, clasping his fingers onto her, forcing her to yield her pliant body into the shape of his.

Kiriki's face became hot with a blush as he began slowly gyrating himself against her, the buckskin of both their garments not enough shield to keep Kiriki from feeling the largeness of his manhood that probed where her thighs seemed to open at his silent will. Her mind spinning, wanting something from this sort of body play that she did not quite understand, she was drawn to place her hands to the fringed hem of her skirt, to slowly begin lifting it so that she could feel his strength more pronounced where she suddenly felt inflamed with a need of something she had no control over.

"Kiriki," Sun Eagle whispered, drawing his lips away. He combed his fingers through her hair and feathered gentle kisses along the delicate slope of her cheek, then lower, to smother her with kisses along the column of her throat. "My sweet Kiriki. I need you. I need you so much. *Sicks-tah*. Give me. *Dacki!* I give you!"

Kiriki swallowed hard as his hands lifted her blouse and cupped his fingers around the throbbing, swollen nipples of her breasts, while his body arched closer against her as she offered her lifted skirt to his beckoning manhood.

Then when she felt just how large and hard he was as he moved himself more intently against her, Kiriki blinked her eyes nervously and suddenly realized just where her wanton behavior had almost taken her. She placed her hands at his bare chest and shoved him away from her. She dropped her skirt and turned to run, but his hand was on her wrist, turning her around to face him.

"Please let me go," Kiriki cried, tears streaming from her eyes.

She lowered her face, embarrassed. "I do not know why you affect me in such a way," she said in a strained whisper. "You are the first! The first!"

Her eyes shot upward to meet his. "It is not right," she said, her voice breaking. "I must return home. Now! You are not what I want!"

She placed a cupped fist to her mouth and bit down onto her knuckle. "I can't want you," she said softly. "I can't."

Sun Eagle was taken aback by her sudden denial; by her attitude toward him. He had felt it in her kiss and embrace that she *did* want him. It was only natural that they should share in lovemaking if they wanted each other in the same way. She was already beyond that age in which most Pawnee girls were married. Why did she keep denying herself that which was natural and beautiful?

But he had to be careful not to voice these questions aloud to her. She was different from other girls. She was already a woman, and surely not yet even touched intimately by a man! If she *had* been with a man before, being with Sun Eagle would come easy for her. She would have lain down with him willingly!

"Kiriki, do not go," Sun Eagle said, his voice drawn. He reached a hand out to her, yet did not touch her. "*Suits*. Come here. I meant you no harm. I should have not approached you in such a way." He saw that a small lie was necessary. "I have come today only to return your blanket." He gestured toward the forest, where his horse was tethered. "If you will come with me to my horse, I will give the blanket to you. I did not bring it with me to the river because I was not sure you would be here."

"I do not need the blanket," Kiriki said, curving her lip into a pout as she peered up at him through tear-hazed lashes. "You keep it."

"If you do not wish to go with me to get your blanket, then perhaps you will at least consider sharing a moment longer with me here by the river?" Sun Eagle asked, seeing her reserve softening in the way her eyes cleared and her lips were no longer curved into a pout. "Let us share in small talk. Nothing more, Kiriki. I have traveled far. I am too weary to return to my village just yet."

"That is not my concern," Kiriki said, lifting her chin stubbornly.

"I know that it is not," Sun Eagle said, resting a hand on his buckskin pouch, so badly wanting to offer her the gift. But the time was not right. "But all I ask is that you just sit down by the river with me while I rest. Then I shall leave you in peace."

Kiriki cast a look over her shoulder in the direction of her village. As far as she knew, she had completed her chores way before the rest of the young women. None would be coming to bathe for awhile yet. And she did so badly want to talk with Sun Eagle. She wanted to try to discover the source of her fascination for him. If so, perhaps she could place it all behind her and get on with her life as it had been before setting her eyes upon him that first time.

She must.

"All right," Kiriki said, sitting down at the river's edge, dangling her legs so that the soles of her bare feet skimmed the surface of the water. She glanced over at

Sun Eagle. "But for only a moment. No longer. I have
more things to do than just sit and talk with you."

Sun Eagle nodded. "I am sure that you do," he said,
sitting down beside her. His hand went to the buckskin
pouch at his waist, anxious to give the gift to Kiriki.

But it still was not the right time to offer a gift to her.
Would it ever be? She was fighting her feelings too much.
He had to wonder why—he was not an ugly Pawnee!

And he had much to offer her. If only she would allow
it!

"Why did you come to the river today?" Sun Eagle
asked, frowning down at her as she peered up into his
dark eyes.

Kiriki shrugged casually. "I come to the river every
day," she said matter-of-factly. Then she frowned at Sun
Eagle. "I come here because it is usually quiet and peaceful. Only recently have I had interferences in my time of
solitude."

She pointed a toe down into the water, watching as a
minnow came and nibbled painlessly on it. "Need I ask
why you came to the river today?" she said, looking
guardedly at Sun Eagle. "It is because of me, is it not?"

Sun Eagle wanted to save face by not telling her of his
deepest feelings for her while she seemed less interested
in him. He plucked a blade of grass and thrust it into his
mouth. He ignored her steady gaze and looked out across
the river, where wild flowers grew in myriad colors on
the opposite shore.

"Why did I come today?" he said deeply, idly chewing
on the blade of grass. "My brother. I came searching for
my brother."

Kiriki's eyebrows rose inquisitively. She peered studiously at Sun Eagle, suspecting that he was lying. "Oh?"
she asked, amused. "A brother?" She laughed liltingly.
"And does your brother come to my river often?"

Sun Eagle's face flooded with color. His jaw tightened.
He challenged her with a set stare. "You own this river?"
he said with an edge to his voice. "Neither my brother
nor I should come and sit beside it? Ever?"

His words and sarcasm stung Kiriki. She lowered her eyes. "I did not mean to imply—" she began, but was stopped when Sun Eagle placed a finger to her chin and lifted her gaze back to his.

"Never humbly lower your eyes in my presence," Sun Eagle said flatly. "Nor anyone else's. You are a woman of substance! Never let anyone make you feel less than that."

Kiriki was awash with confusion, not understanding this man who seemed to reach clean into her soul and grasp onto her feelings. Nor could she understand how he could feel so protective of her feelings. She wanted to be glad that he cared so much, yet there was still that part of her that rebelled against loving him.

Again, she had the strong urge to flee. Intimacy between them was inevitable if she stayed. There was a strange sort of bond flowing between them, something that she had no control over. His eyes were setting her afire inside. They said what she knew he did not feel free to say aloud to her. She had caused him to refrain from being as open with her as he seemed to want to be, that she wanted to be with *him*. If only her heart—her dreams—would allow it!

"You said that you were searching for your brother," Kiriki said, wanting to break this tension that seemed to be building again between them. "Do you have more than one brother? Do you have sisters?"

Sun Eagle drew his hand away from her, calming when he realized that she was finally willing to relax with him and share in small talk. He now knew that he had to be patient where any other sorts of sharing were concerned. She was not the sort to force intimacies upon. She would not be unmarried at her age if she took such intimacies lightly! She was carefully waiting to choose the right moment, it seemed. He hoped that the right moment of her choosing would be with him.

"I have but one brother and no sisters," Sun Eagle said. "And you? Do you have brothers and sisters?"

Kiriki got a strange sort of forlorn look in her eyes as

she looked away from Sun Eagle. Her mother had been unable to bear any more children after Kiriki's birth. How was she to know if she had sisters or brothers who had white skin? Her father had raped her mother, and then he was killed. Perhaps he had children from a wife before his death. Perhaps many. She had not pondered over these questions often, because she had always known that she would never know the answers. Her father was dead. So was his past.

"No," she said blandly. "I have no brothers or sisters."

"I wish that I could say that I am sad because you have no brothers or sisters, but I am not sure that I would be telling the truth," Sun Eagle said, thinking of the problems he now faced with his brother. Life would be much simpler without a brother's interferences.

Kiriki knelt and turned to face Sun Eagle. "Oh?" she said, quirking an eyebrow. "And why do you say that? Are you not happy with your brother? What is his name? Is he older or younger? What does he do to irritate you?" She smiled up at him. "He *does* irritate you, doesn't he? So often brothers do aggravate one another."

Sun Eagle peered down at her, mystified by the color of her eyes. He so badly wanted to question her about them; whose they mirrored. But he could not. Perhaps later, when she would feel free to tell him all of her hopes and desires, and torments.

His gaze swept slowly over her face—a face of innocence, untouched by age, for there was not one line that ruined the beautiful copper flesh.

It took all of his willpower not to reach out for her and draw her lips to his. To be lost in her kiss again would be magnificent.

Yet he felt as though he were less a man for such strong feelings. Did not women sometimes destroy the virtues of men? Their strength? Their courage? Their destiny?

Was it meant for Kiriki to cause all of these downfalls for Sun Eagle?

Even if it was so, and he knew beyond a shadow of a

doubt that it was, Sun Eagle could not step away from what he had found in this beautiful Pawnee woman.

He wanted her.

Regardless of the consequences, he *would* have her!

"My brother and I do seem to have a running feud these days," Sun Eagle finally responded. "But I find it hard to understand why. For the most part, he is the cause." He swallowed hard. "It seems that my brother has decided to become jealous of all that I achieve or own. There is nothing I can do about it. He is a stubborn man, with no ideals of his own. Seems he wants to be a mirroring of me in every way!"

"Why, I think that you should feel honored that a brother cares so much," Kiriki said, her eyes wide. "I don't see his actions as jealous behavior. I think that he only does these things because he apparently idolizes you! You are the older brother, are you not?"

"Yes, I am the oldest."

"Well, then see? Younger brothers always fantasize about being like their older brothers! I have seen it often in my village—brothers behaving in the same way."

Sun Eagle wanted to believe her, yet *he* knew the truth. Not she. "There were times when my brother and I were very close and happy," he said thickly, looking at the waterfall. He pointed at it. "My happiest memories with my brother are the times we played in a cave behind a waterfall close to our home, and even more so in one that was discovered quite a distance from our village when we were out riding and hunting one day. We went back often and explored the cave, and caught rabbit and cooked it over a fire there. It was as though we were the only two people on the earth, my brother and I. But now it is different. The cave behind the waterfall has been forgotten by my brother. It is best that I forget, also."

Hearing his melancholia, his sadness, made Kiriki's heart go out to him. She suddenly reached for his hand and yanked at it as she rose to her feet. "Come," she said with a flip of her skirt as she turned and looked at the waterfall. "Let us go and explore. Let us see if there is a cave behind this waterfall. If so, you and I will share the secret—forever.''

Sun Eagle was momentarily taken aback by her sudden change of heart, but he was more than willing to take full advantage of it. He did not want to pass up any opportunity to stay longer with her. The longer he stayed, the more chances were that she would eventually give in to her feelings about him. He desired her more than anything else in the world at this moment.

"You have not explored the cave before with your friend?" Sun Eagle asked, moving anxiously to his feet.

"By friend you mean Durah," Kiriki said, prodding him onward as she yanked at his hand, walking away from him.

"Yes, Durah," Sun Eagle said, catching up with her. He matched her, step by step, in awe of her energies. She was walking as boldly and quickly as any man. Her eyes were suddenly sparkling and vivacious. Her cheeks were rosy.

"Durah and I usually do not take the time to explore," Kiriki said, shrugging. "When we are together, we mainly talk of things we share with no one else." She cast him a quick smile. "We are the closest of friends, you see. The best any could ever be. I do not know how I could get along without her."

"When you marry, your husband will become your confidante, and you will no longer need a woman friend to tell your secrets to," Sun Eagle said matter-of-factly. "Husbands and wives are best friends—the best in the world."

Kiriki tossed her head haughtily. "Hah!" she exclaimed. "No man could ever take Durah's place when it comes to sharing my secrets! I cannot fathom telling a man my deepest desires."

Her face flooded with a blush when she felt Sun Eagle looking at her. She looked slowly over at him, seeing a quiet amusement in his eyes.

"Well? It is *true*," she reiterated. "How could a woman tell a man secrets of her heart? How?"

Sun Eagle stopped suddenly and placed his fingers to her shoulders, swinging her around to face him. "How can a woman tell a man the secrets of her heart?" he asked huskily. "She doesn't need to. He can read it in her eyes. He can hear it in her voice. He can feel it in her touch. That is enough for a man, Kiriki. No words could ever compare with such silent emotions."

Kiriki was experiencing the same flames igniting within her that she had felt before, while again beneath the brand of his eyes and caught up in the huskiness of his voice. She had been wrong to feel sorry for him. He had most surely told her his woeful tale of brothers to draw out her sympathy. And it had worked! She was again being caught in that trap of passion, of ecstasy, of rapture. . . .

She squirmed uneasily when Sun Eagle's lips began lowering to hers. She pleaded up at him with her eyes. "Please don't," she murmured, her voice quavering. "Oh, Sun Eagle, if you kiss me again, I don't think I—"

Her words were stolen along with her breath as he yanked her against him and kissed her hard on the mouth. Her knees grew weak as a languorous sweetness overcame her. She could not help but twine her arms around his neck and respond in kind, her lips parting, accepting his demanding kiss. She clung to him, throwing all caution aside, her dreams now as though lost in a fog somewhere back in the farthest recesses of her mind.

When he swept her up into his arms and began running with her toward the waterfall, she let him. Even when they reached the waterfall and discovered there was no cave behind it and he lay her on the ground beside a thick flowering forsythia bush, she let him.

She even let Sun Eagle's fingers awaken her to more desire as he drew her blouse over her head and tossed it away, to then cup her breasts into the warmth of his palms. Her insides became as though molten lava as he slipped her skirt off and placed a hand at the triangle of dark hair at the juncture of her thighs, slowly inserting a finger inside her.

Kiriki forgot all shame, enjoying this man that she now

knew she most surely had been destined to meet. She closed her eyes and nibbled on her lower lip nervously as he broke that thin layer of skin within her that proved that she was still a virgin.

The pain was short.

The bliss that followed was wonderful as he caressed her with his fingers while he kissed her, his lips and fingers transporting her into a world that seemed to have no boundaries of time.

She was being awakened to something wonderfully joyous.

And there was no longer any turning back. . . .

Five

Sun Eagle twined his fingers through Kiriki's lustrous brown hair and drew her lips partially away from his. "I want you to be my woman," he whispered, his breath hot against her cheek. "I will pay your father many horses for you. We will be wed soon." He looked down into her eyes, seeing a sudden resistance in their depths. "Say yes, Kiriki. I want you forever. Forever!"

Kiriki's heart screamed the answer yes to him, yet her lips would not follow her heart's lead. She was still not prepared to give up all of her dreams. She had had them for so long.

She lowered her eyes and swallowed hard, knowing that Sun Eagle expected her to say yes, for had she not already given him the answer with her body?

She clenched a fist at her side, knowing that her body had betrayed her this day. It had been the willing participant of what had happened here, not herself—not totally.

Her body had even screamed out for completion of the act that had just barely begun between her and Sun Eagle. She had been introduced into the beginnings of how it felt to be with a man intimately. She could not deny that she wantonly wanted to experience it fully. She was shameful. Shameful!

Sun Eagle knew her answer without her even speaking it, for she had turned her eyes away from him. Why was she fighting what they had so magically found together in such a short time? His loins ached to feel himself inside her; to feel the tight warmth of her love canal enwrap his

51

throbbing hardness! But he did not only want it for *now*. He wanted it for all tomorrows.

Why was she rejecting him? Rejecting this passion that could be hers every day for the rest of her life? Why was she torn with wants and desires she refused to express? Why did she not see him as sincere in every way?

"I could give you the world!" Sun Eagle exclaimed, giving her hair a slight jerk so that she would be persuaded to look into his eyes again. "I one day will be Chief of the Skidi! You will reign at my side! You will be the princess of my people! Tell me that you deny yourself even this? You will never want for anything. Do you hear?"

He did not wait for an answer that he feared she was not ready to give, for whatever reason. He knew that there was only one certain way of persuasion. He would make love to her so completely—so beautifully—that she would not be able to say no to a lifetime of such lovemaking.

With one hand still twined in her hair, he drew her lips up to his mouth. While kissing her heatedly—passionately—with his other hand, he slipped his loincloth off, baring his manhood.

He then moved his hands to her wrists and raised her arms above her head and held them gently to the ground while he nudged her legs apart with a knee. Slowly, his heart beating profoundly, he began inserting his manhood within her. The tightness that he found was as he had expected, causing him to moan with pleasure against Kiriki's lips.

When she arched her hips and returned the same sort of moan against his lips, he knew that she was entering the same plateau of pleasure as he.

He made one last plunge and was finally all of the way inside her. Slowly, he began his thrusts, his mind floating as the pleasure mounted. It was as he had expected, something wonderfully unique, which was proof that destiny had brought them together.

It was only right that they should marry! And they *would*.

He would not take no for an answer!

He removed his hands from her wrists and began caressing her breasts, eliciting another soft moan from her. He moved his lips to a nipple and sucked it between his teeth and softly nibbled on it.

Her eyes closed, Kiriki thrashed her head back and forth as tremors cascaded down her back, her breathing ragged. His lips were no longer on her breasts. Without even looking she could feel his eyes on her as his fingers began teasing circles around her belly, then up to her breasts again, just missing the nipples each time, causing her to strain them toward him with added anticipation.

Opening her eyes, Kiriki looked up at Sun Eagle, disbelieving that she was so willing to share with him. It was as though his dark fathomless eyes had cast a spell over her.

Or was it his hands? His body?

No matter, the wondrous feelings soaring through her were too beautiful to be denied. They were giving her a strange sort of inner peace never experienced before.

When her mother's face flashed before her eyes, a reminder of who Kiriki was and what was expected of her, she willed the vision away. She did not want to experience shame. She wanted to absorb the moment and remember it as beautiful, always. Her mother had been viciously raped. She now most surely looked to all lovemaking as ugly. The many times that Kiriki had heard her mother and father's lovemaking at night after the fire in the firepit had burned down to dying embers, she had never heard her mother cry out with pleasure. Only her mother's husband emitted noises of passion.

Kiriki did not want to live a passionless life. She wanted to feel alive—needed—adored!

While within Sun Eagle's arms, she felt all of these things.

Sun Eagle stroked more maddeningly within her. His hand crept down her body. With a forefinger he began kneading her throbbing center. His mouth bore down upon her lips in a heated kiss, nearing that point where he was almost ready to go over the edge, into ecstasy. His hips bucked against her open, willing thighs. His finger moved in a quick circular motion over her womanhood. He could feel it growing tighter as it enlarged against his flesh. He flicked it with the tip of his finger, then squeezed it. Her more rapid breathing was proof that he was doing everything right.

He continued kissing and caressing her, his own heartbeat seemingly ready to swallow him whole. . . .

A spinning sensation was rising up and flooding Kiriki's whole body, filling her with currents of warmth. It seemed that her whole universe was spinning around, pushing at the boundaries of who she was or who she was with. All that she could feel were these wondrous sensations spiraling through her in surges of tingling heat. Each of his strokes within her promised fulfillment.

She knew that she was . . . almost . . . there. . . .

Suddenly ecstasy was reached. It traveled through her like white lightning lighting up the universe. She drew her lips from Sun Eagle's mouth and gently sank her teeth into his sinewed shoulder, to stifle her cry of bliss.

When his body stiffened suddenly, then vibrated in static tremors against her, she knew that he had most surely just experienced the same wonders of the flesh, as she. . . .

Her heart beating soundly, perspiration pearling her brow, dampening the loose tendrils around her face, Kiriki did not want to let go of Sun Eagle. She clung to him, their bodies pressed tightly together. She kissed his shoulder, the powerful tendons of his neck, and then looked up at him, her eyes seemingly hazed over with the aftermath of rapture.

Sun Eagle gazed raptly down at her, a smile on his lips. He stroked her silken buttocks, then cupped her furry mound with a hand, inserting a finger within her. He watched her expression as he began moving his finger slowly inside her. When she sucked in a breath and her body vibrated again, he knew that he had brought her to another climax.

This pleased him. He wanted a wife who had the same passions as he! Kiriki seemed to have, and perhaps even more. Her whole body had become aflame during their lovemaking!

Kiriki blinked her eyes up at Sun Eagle, unsure of what had just happened, the wondrous feelings overwhelming her again so quickly. She had again felt the same blissful release.

But again, so soon? And from him having only achieved this goal with his finger?

It frightened her, this ability of hers to experience passion so freely!

Suddenly she felt the urge to flee, to put this all behind her and never think about it again. She did not want her life to be ruled by her body. She wanted, oh, so much more in life than what the body offered her! She wanted to live a life where she would not turn old before her time from hard work. No matter if she married Sun Eagle and became his princess, she would still have to carry on the duties of a Pawnee wife. She would have to carry wood. She would have to labor hard in the fields planting and harvesting food products. All of this she did not want.

Yet, oh, how she wanted Sun Eagle! If only she could have him without the hard life of a Pawnee wife, but she knew that could never be.

In an act of desperation, Kiriki placed her hands to Sun Eagle's chest and tried to shove him from atop her. "I must return home," she said, her voice foreign to her, startling her in its deep huskiness. Had making love changed her voice? Would her mother know by this that she had been with a man? What else about her would be noticeably different?

She was suddenly filled with dread. So much about her was changed. She was no longer an innocent girl of eighteen. She was a woman, with womanly desires. And she knew that she would always desire Sun Eagle, even if she refused his marriage proposal over and over again.

Sun Eagle saw the desperation in Kiriki's eyes and understood. She was coming down from her cloud of pleasure and realized what she had willingly shared with him. It was up to him to make her know that it was all done out of love and that it was not wrong to share such a love.

She *was* going to be his wife. He would make it so.

"Do not want to leave me just yet," Sun Eagle said, enwrapping her with his arms. He drew her breasts against his bare chest, causing him to tremble with passion. "There is much to be said between us. Our hearts have spoken, now let us speak with our mouths."

"Our bodies have spoken!" Kiriki softly cried. She turned her eyes away, tears silvering their corners. "I should have never let you! What was I thinking?"

Sun Eagle placed a finger to her chin and forced her head back around to meet his steady gaze. "I have told you before not to turn your eyes humbly away from mine," he said thickly. "What we shared was beautiful, not shameful! You know that I want you to be my wife. Never would I have approached you in such an intimate way had I not already asked you to be my wife."

He kissed her lips softly. "Kiriki," he murmured. "We can have a lifetime of embraces like we have shared today. How can you say no? Tell me that you will go to your father and prepare him for my visit. I am prepared to pay a great bride price for you. I will come tomorrow with many horses for your father. Tell him, Kiriki. Be ready to leave with me."

A sob stole from deeply within Kiriki's throat. Sun Eagle had never been a part of her dreams of the future. Nor had *any* Indian brave.

"I can't," she blurted, giving him a great shove, causing him to finally roll away from her. She grabbed her skirt and blouse, and ran away from Sun Eagle to dress behind the forsythia bush.

Sun Eagle's heart was troubled, feeling that something was quite amiss in her reaction to his proposal and their lovemaking. There was so much she was hiding from him. Did it have to do with the color of her eyes? Was it because she had most surely been fathered by a white man?

It tore at his gut to think that she might want a white man for a husband because she was part white, but what else could it be that was drawing her away from him? He was offering her everything a Pawnee brave could offer, and it wasn't enough.

Slipping his loincloth on, his gaze settled on the buckskin pouch that had been tied to its waistband. The gift. He had forgotten about the special gift. Perhaps it could persuade her just a little.

He opened the pouch and took out the necklace with its tiny pink shells shaped into blossoms. He was not a woman and was still quite taken by the necklace. Surely she would adore it, as well.

Kiriki hurried into her clothes, breathless. When Sun Eagle stepped up to her and held out his hand, within it a lovely, pink necklace, she gave him a wondering stare.

"It is a gift I have brought for you," Sun Eagle said thickly. "Of my mother's necklaces, she gave me this to give to you because it is her favorite. It is also mine."

Kiriki was taken aback by his generous offering, and as she looked at it, seeing its dainty loveliness, she so badly wanted to accept it.

Yet to accept anything from this man could possibly be taken as a commitment to him, which she did not wish to give.

"No, I do not wish to have it," Kiriki said, flipping her skirt as she started to walk past him.

Growing angry, not understanding her behavior at all, especially after they had shared such beautiful lovemaking, Sun Eagle grabbed her wrist and stopped her. He swung her around to face him.

"It would matter not that you refuse my gift if it were mine alone to give," he growled. "But it is my mother you humiliate by your refusal. She chose this gift especially for you. I will not return it to her and say that it was not favorable in your eyes! It took her many hours to shape those shells into the beautiful flowers for this necklace. Her efforts will not be mocked just because you are too stubborn to accept it."

"I did not ask that you go to your mother and ask for anything for me," Kiriki said bitterly, jerking from his grip. "Nor will I ever!"

Again she tried to walk past him, only to be stopped by him once more. She glared up at him as he turned her to face him and took it upon himself to fasten the necklace around her neck. Her wrist paining her as he began forcing her toward the river, Kiriki winced.

"Let me go!" she cried. "What are you doing now?"

Taking her to the very edge of the riverbank, Sun Eagle pointed down at the water. "Look!" he commanded briskly. "Look down into the water and if you think the necklace looks ugly on you, then take it off and throw it away. If you see how beautiful it is, wear it proudly! Forget that it was I who placed it there. But remember whose fingers formed the flowers of the necklace. My mother!"

Loving the feel of the necklace around her neck, Kiriki could not help but look into the river to see how the necklace *did* look around her neck.

When she leaned over and peered at her reflection and saw how the pink flowers hugged her neck as though kissing her, she sighed and touched them thoughtfully.

"So you see that your beauty is enhanced by the necklace?" Sun Eagle said, angrily folding his arms across his bare, copper chest.

Kiriki smiled shyly as she looked over at him, her fingers running over the smoothness of the shaped seashells. "The necklace is beautiful, not I," she murmured, momentarily forgetting her reasons for wanting to flee and forget him. "Thank you for giving it to me. Tell your mother that I accept it and will wear it proudly."

A slow smile touched Sun Eagle's lips. "She will be happy," he said, squaring his shoulders. "I am happy."

Kiriki looked past him, in the direction of her village, then up into his eyes. "I really must go," she said softly. "I have already been gone too long."

Sun Eagle placed a hand to her shoulder. "I will always remember the moments with you today," he said huskily.

"No other woman but you has touched my heart in such a way. I would be the proudest brave in our Skidi band of Pawnee if you would be my wife. I will bring horses tomorrow for your father."

Kiriki's face grew pale and her breathing became shallow. She took a shaky step back from Sun Eagle, causing his hand to drop clumsily away from her. His having just admitted which band of Pawnee he was a part of was enough to send her heart into a tailspin of fear. Had not Durah revealed to her the horrors practiced by the Skidi? And he was to one day be a chief of that band of Pawnee? Surely he believed in the sacrificial ritual practiced by them.

Could he even be showing her all of this attention because he had plans for her other than marrying her? Was he actually planning to use her as this year's sacrifice to the Morning Star?

Panic rose within her. She gathered her skirt up into her arms and ran away from him, her heart pounding.

Sun Eagle raised a brow inquisitively, and was jolted with alarm at her decision to flee so suddenly from him. What had he said? Was it because he had again told her that he was going to bring horses to her father? Was she going to refuse to leave her village to be with him as his wife, even after all that they had shared this day?

Their lovemaking had been perfect! How could she not see that?

"I *will* bring horses to your father tomorrow!" he shouted, not letting anything stand in the way of having her.

Not even her strange bouts of stubbornness.

This repeated promise echoing behind sent a rush of dread through Kiriki, then despair, for she did love him so much! Oh, what *was* she to do? How could she ever trust him now that she knew which band of Pawnee he was born into?

As she continued to run away from him, her hand went to the necklace at her throat. Although she was afraid of committing herself fully to him, she *would* wear the necklace, for it would forever represent the moments of wonder shared with him.

But she must keep the necklace hidden beneath her blouse, for she was not ready to reveal it or her feelings for Sun Eagle to anyone, except, perhaps, Durah. . . .

Six

SUN Eagle rode square-shouldered toward Kiriki's village, several valuable horses trailing behind him. When not so far in the distance he saw several women working in cultivated gardens, he cupped a hand over his eyes to shield them from the sun and looked more intensely at the women. It did not take long for him to single out Kiriki in her own private garden. Her braided hair was lighter than the others; her skin was not as dark.

As his gelding moved along the meadow in an easy canter, he continued to watch Kiriki. She was busy making furrows in the ground with a hoe made from a bison shoulder blade. As she lifted the hoe, her buckskin blouse was drawn taut across the mounds of her breasts, causing Sun Eagle's loins to react with a gnawing ache of remembering how it had felt to caress her breasts with the palms of his hands and to taste their sweetness with his tongue and lips.

But he was also recalling how she had fled from him after their shared lovemaking. Something he had said had frightened her, and he knew that it had not been the mere mention of marriage.

It had been something else. But what?

Continuing to ride closer to Kiriki, Sun Eagle's shoulders tensed when she turned and caught sight of him and the horses that followed along after him. He did not read her expression wrong when he saw that his presence was not a welcome one, but instead something to again cause her a strange sort of fearful pain.

But he would not stop and question her about it.

Whether she liked it or not, he would go on and see her father, pay the bride price, then take her home with him.

Let her then look at him as though he were a terrible vision. There would be nothing she could do about it!

She would be his. His!

Drawing rein at the edge of Kiriki's garden, Sun Eagle gestured with a hand toward her. *"Lau!"* he said in greeting.

When she ignored him, he edged his horse closer. *"Suits!* Come here," he said, in more a tone of command than he had intended. He tried to lessen the strength of his voice. "Take me to your father, Kiriki. As promised, I have brought a great bride price."

He looked over his shoulder at his prized horses, then back at Kiriki. "I have brought the best of my horses for your father," he said, gazing back at her. "He will not be able to say no to what I ask of him."

His lips lifted into a slow smile as he continued to stare down at Kiriki; she no longer eluded him. "Tonight you will lie with me in my dwelling, Kiriki," he said firmly. "We will have the celebration of marriage tomorrow."

Kiriki was numb, seeing his determination, so desperately wanting to feel joyous about it herself. Had she not shared the most blissful moments of her life with him only yesterday?

Oh, why had he told her that he was of the Skidi band of Pawnee? Even the thought of what he had surely witnessed through the years at the time of the Morning Star ritual made her heart sick. If he agreed to such a practice of sacrifice, he most surely was not the sort of man she wanted at her side every night for the rest of her life.

Could he want *her* as the sacrifice? Once he got her away from her village and her parents, would she in truth become his captive instead of a wife? Was it all a ploy to get her away from the protection of those she loved, so that her body could be pierced with hundreds of arrows at the time of sacrifice?

The thought made her insides ripple with cold.

Yet, in his eyes she saw so much love. In the way he

had held her, she had felt so loved. Surely he loved her for herself, only!

"Kiriki, will you take me to your father, or must I enter your village and go from dwelling to dwelling until I find him?" Sun Eagle asked, impatience thick in his voice. "You will be mine! You want it as much as I. Why are you behaving so strangely? Did you not give yourself to me yesterday? Only the blessing of your father and the wedding ceremony is now needed to complete our union."

Blushing, Kiriki gazed at the women who were in the gardens adjoining hers and watching her knowingly, Sun Eagle's declarations having reached all of their anxious ears. Now they all knew that she was no longer a mere girl but, instead, a woman.

Oh, how embarrassing it was for her!

Throwing her hoe down angrily, giving Sun Eagle an exasperated look, Kiriki turned and began stomping through the freshly overturned dirt, the earth warm against the bare flesh of her feet. She held her chin haughtily high as she heard Sun Eagle's handsome black gelding and the other dutiful horses following behind her as she stepped from her garden into knee-high grass.

Kiriki refused to look over her shoulder at Sun Eagle as she went on through the opened gate into the village. She set her sights on her lodge, then sighed cheerlessly when she saw her father sitting outside around the communal fire, chatting and smoking with the elders of the village.

Would Sun Eagle make his presentation in front of all of the elders? Or would he choose to do it in private?

Chewing on her lower lip, Kiriki looked up at the heavens and silently prayed to Tirawa, the Supreme Power who was in and of everything, asking that she would be spared anymore embarrassment. "Oh, let Sun Eagle go inside my father's house to speak with him in private," she prayed. "Oh, please!"

Kiriki became suddenly aware of an utter silence around her, and looked slowly down at her father and his friends. Their questioning eyes were on Kiriki, then Sun Eagle.

Kiriki's pulse began to race as her father rose to his feet and began walking toward her in his dignified stance, bronzed and naked but for a loincloth, which flapped against his muscular thighs with each of his bold steps. His expression was bland, his jaw tight. His hands were clenched into soft fists at his sides.

Stopping just before her father reached her, Kiriki bowed her head humbly, staring blankly at her feet. When her father's shadow fell over her, she winced as though shot. Never had a man offered a bride price for her before! All of the men of the surrounding villages knew that her father frowned upon such a gesture, saying that she was special, and that if a man should come forward, he must be prepared to pay dearly for her.

She had no idea what he considered "dearly."

If Sun Eagle's horses were enough, would her father so easily bid her farewell? Did she want him to?

Or was her fear of Sun Eagle's Skidi heritage more overpowering inside her heart than her love for him?

It seemed at this point in time that it did not matter how *she* felt about anything. It was now all up to her father and Sun Eagle. . . .

"Daughter, who is this man who follows you on horseback and who leads horses behind him?" Lone Chief asked in a deep and resonant voice. "Why do you not look your father in the eye? What does all of this mean, Kiriki?"

Sun Eagle dismounted and went quickly to her rescue, speaking on her behalf. He stepped between her and her father. "It was not of Kiriki's bidding that I come," he said thickly. "Nor is it of her bidding that I offer you many horses for her." He gestured with a hand toward the horses. "I come on my own. I have watched your daughter from afar. I would like to make her my bride. Please accept my gift of horses as bride price for her."

Kiriki looked up slowly. Scarcely breathing, almost afraid to, she leaned somewhat sideways so that she could look past Sun Eagle at her father. She swallowed hard when she saw the anger flashing in his dark eyes and the way his shoulder muscles were corded tightly in his anger.

But she knew to not expect an explosion from him just yet. He was for the most part gentle, with a temper that was slowly roused to a raging point. First he would measure his words carefully while observing Sun Eagle, deciding the worth of this young man who had come forth for his daughter's hand in marriage.

Oh, surely Lone Chief would not give her away all that easily! Did she not mean more to him than mere horse flesh?

Yet she knew the love the Pawnee had for horses. Most were captured from the Comanche in raids. To have them given to her father without so much as a challenge, surely they would not be as valuable.

Lone Chief looked Sun Eagle square in the eye and stared at him for awhile without saying a word, testing him for courage. When Sun Eagle's eyes did not waver at all, Lone Chief nodded and finally looked past him and down at his daughter, who was looking up at him with a look he did not recognize in her.

It was then that Lone Chief gathered that Sun Eagle had not only seen Kiriki from afar, but also that he had been with her. They were already acquainted. Kiriki's face was flushed and her eyes were anxious. She would not be acting this way if she did not know this man who had stepped forth on her behalf. She would have not even accompanied the man to meet with her father!

"Kiriki, return to your garden," Lone Chief suddenly said, pointing at the open gate that led out to the massive fields of gardens. "You have chores that are not yet completed. While the sun is still high, do not waste time!"

Kiriki was taken aback by her father's command. Her lips parted in surprise, her heart sank, for she did not want to leave Sun Eagle and her father alone. She wanted to see what transpired between them. If she were to be bargained over, she deserved to be there to see the end result!

But her obedience to this man who had raised her as a daughter all of these years, when, in truth, he could have banished her from his life as though worthless, made Kiriki swallow hard and nod in agreement. She stared up at Sun Eagle's back, seeing how stiffly he stood. Surely he had not batted an eye while awaiting her father's attention. He was like an unwavering tree in a storm, not to be ruffled by wind or rain.

"I go, Father," Kiriki murmured, turning quickly on a heel. Her heart pounding, she walked briskly away. She did not glance back because she knew that she would be scolded by her father's eyes. He was surely waiting for her to get back to her duties before continuing the discussion with Sun Eagle. He was determined that she would not know how Sun Eagle and his horses were going to be received.

Not until later.

Going back to her garden, Kiriki picked up her hoe and began to pound the earth with it again. She looked up, seeing the other women watching her with amused smiles, realizing that her father had ordered her back to work.

"It is not funny!" Kiriki said to them all, stopping to place a hand on her hip. "Not Sun Eagle coming to demand that I am his wife, nor that my father made me leave so that they could discuss me as though I am an object. A thing!"

Durah rushed to Kiriki's side. She slipped an arm around her waist. "Kiriki, no one is making fun of you," she whispered. "They smile because they expect you to be wed one day soon. You know that everyone thinks that you and I have waited too long. They are happy for you that you have found a man that you have feelings for."

Kiriki jerked away from Durah. She shook her head. "Oh, Durah, I do not know how I feel about *anything*," she whispered back. She leaned closer to her friend's face. "Durah, Sun Eagle is of the Skidi band of Pawnee! The Skidi!"

Durah paled. She looked to the ground. "The Skidi?" she whispered. She looked back up at Kiriki, her eyes narrowing. "He is not as handsome in my eyes as before," she hissed.

Kiriki followed as Durah walked toward her own acre of ground designated as her private garden, all Pawnee women's gardens being of that exact size for which to plant large crops of corn, sunflowers, squash and other foods that would one day be stored in bell-shaped pits, called *cache pits,* located beneath the floors of each of their lodges.

She grabbed Durah's hand as she reached for her hoe, stopping her. Kiriki urged Durah around to face her. "Surely we are wrong to have such feelings about the Skidi," she murmured. "They cannot *all* believe in that horrid ritual. I cannot even imagine Sun Eagle participating. He seems a man of heart—of morals! Surely he does not agree with such a practice!"

Durah's face twisted into a studious frown, then she smiled at Kiriki. "Of course you are right," she said, laughing softly. "He would not have come to pay such a high bride price for you only to take you to his village to slay you."

A coldness surged through Kiriki, doubts assailing her in great waves. "Of course not," she said, her voice breaking.

Her pulse racing, she went back to her own garden and picked up a digger made from a fire-hardened stick. She dropped to her knees to the fine, dark dirt and began making grooves in which she would drop seeds that had been saved from the previous year's crops. She tried to concentrate on her planting instead of what was transpiring at her village. She let her thoughts wander to the tales of her mother—about her mother telling her about long ago, when myriads of wild pigeons roosted in the trees, their excretions fertilizing the soil to an amazing degree of richness. Birds had been known to gather in flocks so dense that they would eclipse the rays of the sun, and by the sheer weight of their roosting bodies broke large limbs from the trees.

Shaking her head, a sob escaping from the depths of her throat, Kiriki threw the digger aside and sat down on the ground. She drew her knees up to her chest and circled her legs with her arms, hugging them as she looked toward the village. Her entire future was at stake. How could she be expected to just do her usual chores while awaiting the verdict of her father? She was so torn with how she wanted the verdict to be decided! She wanted Sun Eagle so badly that her insides ached with the need, yet he could not fulfill her childhood dreams. If she married him, she could no longer watch for that white soldier who would take her away from the wretchedness of a Pawnee squaw's life.

Warm arms around her shoulders made Kiriki look over at Durah, who had come to sit beside her in her time of anxious waiting.

"However your father chooses, it will be best for you," Durah encouraged. "You know that he has always chosen what was only best for you. He loves you more than he could have ever loved his own flesh and blood, Kiriki. Do you not see how fortunate you are?"

Tears streamed down Kiriki's face, so aware of the truth in Durah's words.

She was aware of something else. The necklace that Sun Eagle had given her now lay hidden beneath her blouse. After today, she could wear it, always. Whether or not her father approved of the marriage, she would no longer have to keep hidden the necklace that Sun Eagle had given her. Even if her father did not approve of the marriage, he could surely not disapprove of a mere necklace—a necklace that meant the world to Kiriki.

"Come into my dwelling," Lone Chief said, turning to walk away from Sun Eagle. "We will talk there, in private."

A young brave came and took charge of Sun Eagle's gelding and other horses. Sun Eagle followed Lone Chief into the earth lodge. The sun poured through the smoke hole overhead, fusing with the golden flames of the fire where a scintillating pot of stew cooked and simmered in the warm ashes at the edge, a close-by bent-shouldered Moonstar laboring, kneading dough for bread.

"*Sukspid,* sit," Lone Chief said, gesturing toward a pile of furs beside the firepit. He ignored his staring wife and sat down opposite Sun Eagle, folding his arms across his chest. "We shall talk."

Sun Eagle sat square-shouldered, his chin held high. "Your daughter is as beautiful as this mystical land in which we live," Sun Eagle said dryly. "Our children— your grandchildren—will be as beautiful. Say that you will accept the bride price, and I will promise you grandchildren soon."

"When you speak of Kiriki do you not know that you speak of someone special?" Lone Chief asked, ignoring any reference to grandchildren, though his heart ached to have many sit on his lap before he died. "Most Pawnee girls marry at fourteen winters. Kiriki is eighteen. Though this is of her choice, it is also mine, because Lone Chief has been waiting for the right man for Kiriki—the right bride price."

"I do understand that she is special," Sun Eagle said, nodding stiffly. "She will be treated special also as my wife." He leaned his head forward and stared determinedly over at Lone Chief. "As for waiting for the right man and the right bride price, I, Sun Eagle, am the right man! I have brought a great bride price. If it is not enough, I will even double the amount of horses brought to you today. I will do this in order to have Kiriki."

Lone Chief sighed heavily. "As you know, the Pawnee women are the backbone of all Pawnee villages," he said, taking a deep breath. "My daughter labors hard for her mother and father. When she is gone, her loss and her labors must be compensated. It will require many horses to make up this difference."

Hope swelled within Sun Eagle, feeling as though he was making some sort of headway with this stubborn father. Sun Eagle smiled cunningly. He had many horses! If need be, he would give them all to this father, then go and just take more from the Comanche to make up for his losses.

"Sun Eagle will bring more horses tomorrow," he said, smiling cleverly at Lone Chief.

Lone Chief nodded. "Tell me a little about yourself, young man," he said, picking up a long-stemmed pipe, lighting it.

"Sun Eagle is of the Bear Society," he said proudly. "I am a Bear Warrior, of the great spirit Bear, receiving power from the sun. This is why we Bear Warriors are always successful. Your daughter will be proud to call me Bear Warrior husband."

"You are of the Skidi band, are you not?" Lone Chief asked guardedly, his pipe resting on his lap.

Sun Eagle heard the caution in Lone Chief's voice, understanding why. There weren't many Pawnee outside of the circle of the Skidi who approved of the Morning Star ritual. Sun Eagle agreed himself, the practice was barbaric—something that should be done away with.

It was obvious that Lone Chief felt no less adamantly opposed to such a practice, and perhaps would not want his daughter to be a part of it, even if only in the role of observer.

"Yes, I am of the Skidi," Sun Eagle said, never wanting to show anything less than pride for his people, no matter how badly their practices were looked upon.

Lone Chief lay his pipe aside, having waited to offer it to Sun Eagle if his answers had been acceptable. They had not. He rose to his feet. "No bride price is acceptable from you for my daughter," he said thickly. He pointed toward the door. "*Wissgutts*. You will now leave."

Sun Eagle's face flooded with a heated, angry blush. He rose to his feet and took a step toward Lone Chief. "I will leave the horses already paid for Kiriki," he said flatly. "Tomorrow I will come with more. There will be too many for you to say no! Kiriki *will* be my wife, Lone Chief. I will one day be a great chief of my people. Your daughter will be well provided for. You cannot let bitter feelings against a sacrificial practice of my people keep your daughter from a future of much happiness and Pawnee wealth.''

Sun Eagle stomped to the door and turned to face Lone Chief again. ''Tomorrow,'' he said solemnly. ''I shall return tomorrow.''

He started to leave the dwelling, but stopped to peer down at the middle-aged woman sitting in the shadows, molding and shaping bread with her hands. When their eyes met and held, something strange happened within Sun Eagle, for it was almost the same as looking at Kiriki many years into the future.

It was Kiriki's mother.

His insides rebelled, for this woman's back was bent out of shape from hard labor and her face was wrinkled from having spent many long hours in the sun.

He tightened a hand into a fist, swearing to himself that this would not be allowed to happen to Kiriki. As his wife, she would still be beautiful even in middle age.

Sun Eagle rushed outside and accepted the reins of his horse as it was brought to him. He swung himself into the saddle and rode quickly away from the village. When he looked across the land and caught sight of Kiriki laboring hard in her garden, an ache troubled his gut. He peered up at the scorching sun, and then at Kiriki's tender flesh being turned into leather by it.

His jaw set, he sank his heels deeply into the flanks of his horse and rode across the furrowed land of the garden. When he reached Kiriki, he leaned an arm down and swept her up onto his lap.

Kiriki's eyes were wild, her breath stolen away by Sun Eagle's sudden actions. She clung to him as he rode away with her toward the butte in the distance. She had to believe that her father had paid the bride price, or why else would Sun Eagle have stolen her away from her duties in such a manner?

She looked over her shoulder at her village, trying to understand a father who would give her away so easily without even first asking her what *she* wanted to do.

Was he truly this anxious to be rid of her? Had she not been a dutiful enough daughter?

Numb, not knowing how she should feel about anything, she leaned her cheek against Sun Eagle's warm, bare chest. . . .

Seven

AFTER reaching the river close to her village, Kiriki was surprised when Sun Eagle drew his reins taut, stopping his horse, letting her down from his lap near a gathering of golden-centered, bluestemmed, pricklepoppy flowers. Confused, wondering why he had not taken her to his village where she would expect a wedding ceremony on the morrow, she watched as he swung himself out of the saddle and came to stand over her, his eyes dark as he peered intensely down at her.

"What is it?" she asked, studying his troubled features. "Why have you brought me here?" She had decided not to fight this decision agreed upon by the man she loved and her father. She had decided to accept what fate had handed her. If her father had accepted the horses, so be it.

Durah had been right. Dreams *were* foolish!

Deeply within her heart, she now could not wait to become Sun Eagle's wife. Oh, how she loved him! No matter that he was of the dreaded Skidi band of Pawnee. She loved him. He loved her. He would protect her from all ugliness.

Sun Eagle reached a hand to her hair and wove his fingers through it, recalling her strange attitude toward him the previous night. He was recalling her attitude when he had arrived to prove his love by the many horses he brought to her father for the bride price. What had made her change into this sweet, agreeable person that she was now? Where had all her fight gone?

This was not the Kiriki that he had seen only a short

while ago while she was standing in the garden, peering angrily up at him as though he were a devil.

"Why have I brought you here?" he asked, weary of searching his soul for answers. "Because I do not yet have the right to take you to my dwelling."

He placed his hand gently at the nape of her neck and drew her close to him, so close that when he leaned down to her face he could smell her sweetness. He could feel her warm breath upon his lips.

"Your father did not accept my bride price, Kiriki," he said thickly. "He said that he would not accept any bride price at all from me, a Skidi warrior! But I left the horses for him anyhow. I told him that I would bring many more tomorrow, for I will not take no for an answer. You *will* be mine, even if I have to fight every warrior in your father's village for you."

He engulfed her within his arms and brushed his mouth across her lips, eliciting a soft moan from deep within her. "You will be mine, Kiriki," he whispered. "Tell me that you go willingly with me!"

Kiriki was confused by her father's rejection of Sun Eagle's proposal, having thought from the moment that Sun Eagle had swept her up into his arms she was his, forever!

But her father had refused. And because Sun Eagle was of the Skidi.

Oh, how wonderful to know that her father was this cautious. That her father, who was not her true father at all, cared this much. She should have known. How could she have ever doubted his true love for her?

How?

Yet here she was, more than willing to become Sun Eagle's bride, and it was impossible. How she was torn! She had even accepted the fact that she was going to have to cast all dreams aside to be with him.

Now everything was changed. Everything was muddled.

Sun Eagle sensed Kiriki's confusion and hesitation. He kissed the hollow of her throat, then brushed another kiss across her lips. "You do not answer me, Kiriki," he whispered. "I will ask you again. Will you go with me? Will you be my wife?"

Kiriki closed her eyes as a sensual shudder encased her, his lips hot on her ear now, nibbling at its lobe. "How am I to be expected to think when you continue to distract me with your lips?" she fussed softly, her pulse racing as his hands cupped her breasts through the buckskin fabric of her blouse. "Sun Eagle, oh, Sun Eagle. . . ."

Sun Eagle no longer required any answers from her. He heard the passion in her voice. He could feel it, even, by the vibrations of her body.

She wanted him. Oh, how badly she wanted him!

Lifting her into his arms, he began to carry her away, but was stopped when a voice filled with alarm came to him from behind.

"Kiriki, your father is filled with rage!" Durah said, rushing toward Sun Eagle and Kiriki. Trying to catch her breath, she stopped and looked wide-eyed up at Sun Eagle, completely in awe of his handsomeness now that she was up so close.

Then, when Durah realized the way in which she had found her best friend and this handsome Pawnee, she lowered her eyes bashfully. "I am sorry," she murmured. "But I had to come."

She raised her eyes back up at Kiriki. "Kiriki, I have never seen your father so quickly angered as now! He is rounding up many braves. I think they are either going after Sun Eagle, or surrounding the village to protect you from him!" Durah swallowed hard. "You had best return to the village quickly, Kiriki, for if not, your father will come and find you and drag you from Sun Eagle's arms," she said, swallowing hard again. "I do not wish to even think of what would happen to Sun Eagle if he was discovered here, with you in his arms."

Sun Eagle placed Kiriki on the ground. His eyes had narrowed, the anger inside his heart grew fierce! He clasped his fingers to Kiriki's shoulders. "I will leave now," he said sternly. "But I will come tomorrow, Kiriki. I see now that I will not come alone—I will bring many warriors with me." He lowered his hands from her shoulders and spoke down close to her, his mouth only a kiss away from her lips. "Tell your father that never shall I take no for an answer. Never!"

He swept his arms around her waist and drew her briskly against him, kissing her long and hard, then let her go and swung himself up into his saddle. He gave her a lingering, determined stare, then rode away.

Kiriki watched him until he merged into the thickening forest. Then she turned to Durah and smiled awkwardly. "Is he not the most . . . ?"

A stirring in the brush close beside them made Kiriki's words fade. Tensing, she turned around just in time to see a warrior rush from hiding, his face painted in red zigzags, a knife poised in the air. A scream froze in her throat when the warrior went to Durah and sank his knife deeply within her chest, then turned to her—his dark eyes wild, his breathing harsh. . . .

Kiriki was lightheaded with anguish, so wanting to go to her friend who now lay prone on the ground, lifeless, blood gushing from her knife wound.

But even fear for herself could not give her the energy needed to move. Just as her throat had frozen, her legs would not move. She was at the mercy of this madman who had taken her best friend's last breath from her, and who was most surely now ready to take hers!

"It is not my intention to take your life," Brown Bear said, lowering his bloody knife to his side. "It is unfortunate that I was forced to kill your friend. But she was an interference in my plans." He took a step closer to Kiriki. "You will come with me now. Do not scream, or I will be forced to add more blood to my knife."

Kiriki still could not move or speak. She could not even cry to show outward remorse for her dead friend. All of her emotions except fear now seemed to have been robbed from her.

It was apparent that this man had been spying on her. Even while Sun Eagle had been there!

Oh, but if only Sun Eagle had not been forced to leave!

He would have been here to stop the evil man's attack on Durah. Sun Eagle would have slain the man!

And now? Kiriki doubted if she would ever see Sun Eagle again.

Brown Bear recognized utter fear when he saw it. This, too, would work to his advantage! Sneering, watching Kiriki all the while, he bent and wiped the blood from his knife on the tall grass, then stood up slowly and moved stealthily toward Kiriki. "You will go with me to my horse," he said in a snarl. "I plan to take you far away. As long as you cooperate with me, you will not be harmed. My plans for you are to treat you grandly."

With him now so close to her that he could reach out and touch her, or even thrust his knife into her body, should he decide to, Kiriki's strength returned. She looked past the evil man and gave Durah a sorrowful glance, then she spun around and began running. Her hair blew in wisps around her face. Her breath came in short rasps, her eyes searched for signs of her village in the distance, or for her beloved father who was supposed to be coming for her to take her inside the protective walls of the village.

Suddenly a painful grip at her wrist stopped her escape. She was yanked to a quick halt and forced around to look up into the narrowed, angry eyes of her assailant.

"Please let me go," she cried, breathing hard. "I promise not to identify you as the man who killed Durah! I will tell my father it was an unknown assailant, who escaped without harming me!"

She looked anxiously past him, then back up into his eyes. "My father is due to arrive at any moment," she said guardedly. "He is! Durah had just told me!"

"I know that perhaps he may come," Brown Bear said, tightening his grip on her wrist, now forcing her to walk hurriedly beside him. "I heard your friend explain about your father's anger, and why. I also heard her say that he *may* come for you. Not that she was certain of it. But I will waste no more time here. My horse will take us swiftly away. No one will find us. I have many skills at eluding the most skillful tracker. You see, I am a mighty hunter!''

Tired and weak from her ordeal, Kiriki sobbed. "You are a mighty *nothing!*" she cried. "When you choose to murder innocent sweet women, your title of warrior is stripped from you! You . . . you . . . are nothing! Nothing!''

"Soon I will be known as the greatest of warriors; the greatest of the Pawnee!" Brown Bear bragged, his tethered horse now in sight. "So what you say now is worthless. It means nothing to me.''

When Kiriki was only a footstep away from his powerful black stallion, she knew that if she did not escape now, she never would. She glanced over at his knife held solidly within his left hand. She knew that if she grabbed for it and missed, she could not only get cut badly but possibly murdered if he grew angry at her attempt to save herself.

But as she saw it, she had no other choice but to at least take one last chance at doing . . . just . . . that . . .

In one mighty jerk, Kiriki was free from Brown Bear's grip. She lunged for the knife, but he was too quick. He jerked it farther back, her awkwardness causing her to fall with a painful thud to the ground.

Crying out with pain when one of her wrists twisted beneath her as she fell, she rolled onto her other side, only to be put in the position of looking square at his beaded moccasins, inches away from her eyes.

"You cannot escape," Brown Bear said, squatting down before her. "You are mine, not Sun Eagle's." His dark eyes softened as his gaze raked over her. "My brother was right in wanting you. You are the loveliest of the women in all Pawnee camps.''

Kiriki's breath was stolen from her by his confession as to who he was. "You are Sun Eagle's brother?" she gasped, rising slowly to a sitting position. She rubbed her sore wrist, thankful that it was not broken. "You would do this to your brother? You know that I am to be his wife!''

A triumphant look appeared in Brown Bear's eyes. He

squared his shoulders proudly as he helped Kiriki back to her feet. "My brother and I, we challenge each other over many things," he said thickly. "Now even a special woman."

He thrust his knife into its sheath at his side, then lifted Kiriki upon his horse. "Too often my brother wins," he said sourly. "But this time he didn't. You are mine, Kiriki. Mine!"

Kiriki squirmed uneasily on the saddle of blankets, yet knew not to try to escape again. But she would try later.

Never would she give up trying!

She looked past Brown Bear. Oh, where *was* her father? Was he too busy rounding up his warriors and giving them instructions to worry about what could already be happening to her beyond the walls of the village? Just when *would* he leave the village to go and search for her?

When it was discovered that both she *and* Durah were missing . . . it would then be too late.

It already was for Durah.

She silently watched as Brown Bear swung himself up into the saddle behind her. She winced and turned her eyes away when he slipped an arm possessively around her waist and gathered his horse's reins in his free hand. Her body lurched and bumped hard against Brown Bear's hard chest and thighs as he wheeled his horse around and urged it into a thundering gallop away from this place of murder and kidnapping.

"Your brother will kill you for this!" Kiriki shouted, glancing over her shoulder at him. "You will never be able to arrive into your village with me, for Sun Eagle will be there to cut your heart out!"

Just the thought of how he *was* to arrive into the village with her filled Brown Bear's mind. To offer her to his people for the special favor of being the Morning Star sacrifice, saying that she was his captive Comanche maiden instead of Pawnee, it would be a time of great victory for him.

Somehow he must find a way to enter the village when

Sun Eagle was not present. Sun Eagle would ruin everything. Everything!

"When Brown Bear arrives with you at our people's village it will be with much celebration," he bragged. "Sun Eagle will have nothing to say about it. You see, I have won you just by my cunning ways of abducting you. He will not argue that!"

"Cunning?" Kiriki shrieked. "You call murdering an innocent young woman—my best friend—cunning? Sun Eagle will not agree. I still say that he will kill you. Your heart will be offered to his dogs!"

"We shall see," Brown Bear said, chuckling. He strengthened his hold on her around her waist. "For now, you may as well accept me as the man in your life. For, Kiriki, you have no other choice."

"Soon you will see just how wrong you are!" she shouted, the wind stinging her flesh, the horse thundering across the land. "As soon as you enter your village you will understand the wrath of a brother whose woman has been stolen from him!"

"Do not fret so, blue-eyed woman," Brown Bear said, glaring down at her as she challenged him with a set stare. "Brown Bear will not take you immediately to the village. It will be necessary to wait a few days before doing so. Because of Sun Eagle, this is necessary."

Kiriki's eyes began to gleam. "You are nothing but a coward," she hissed. "You are afraid of Sun Eagle!"

Then she tensed, realizing the danger she was in, now more than ever, because he had admitted to her that he was not going to take her anywhere near Sun Eagle. He was going to take her into hiding! Anything could happen to her while alone with him. He could even plan to rape her over and over again.

The thought repelled her. . . .

She turned her eyes away, feeling as though a dark cloud was closing in on her. . . .

Accompanied by several warriors, Lone Chief rode tall in his Indian saddle as he went to Kiriki's garden, then startled when he noted her absence there. Quickly dismounting, he went to the neighboring garden and looked down into the wavering eyes of a young woman. "Kiriki," he said, his voice resonant. "Where is she?"

The woman pointed toward the butte in the distance. "She went with handsome warrior on a horse," she said, her voice slight. "Durah followed later on foot."

Anger was swelling inside Lone Chief. His stomach muscles tightened and his chest swelled as his breathing became harsh. "It was Sun Eagle," he said beneath his breath. His brow furrowed. "You say Durah followed?"

"Yes, Durah followed," the woman humbly confessed. "She seemed anxious to tell Kiriki something. She ran. Not walked."

Lone Chief shook his head as he looked up at the butte in the distance. "Yes, I am sure Durah was anxious to warn Kiriki of my intentions," he said, suspecting what Durah's news to Kiriki and Sun Eagle could have caused. She could have fled with the young man once Sun Eagle knew the plans of surrounding the village with many fierce warriors to protect Kiriki from him tomorrow.

Yet, would she flee with Sun Eagle all that easily without much thought and deliberation about the rights and wrongs of her decision? She had much respect for her family. Surely she would not turn her back on them. Why, she did not even seem anxious to be his wife. She had not come all that happily to her father with Sun Eagle.

He frowned down at the waiting, silent young woman. "I must ask you," he said guardedly, "how did Kiriki leave? Willingly? Or by force?"

"It is hard to say," the woman said, shrugging. "The warrior swept his arm around her and carried her away on his horse with him. But I did not see Kiriki struggle, so who is to say whether she went willingly or by force? I cannot say, Lone Chief."

Lone Chief kneaded his brow feverishly, again shaking his head. He grumbled something unintelligible to the woman beneath his breath, then went and mounted his steed. Motioning with a raised fist, then dropping it to his side, he gave notice to his warriors to follow him.

Like a great, angry bear, Lone Chief rode across the land, up the butte, then moved with caution toward the river. When he got close enough to the death scene, his heart seemed to plummet to his feet. All that he could see was a dead Pawnee maiden lying in a great pool of blood. But he could not yet tell which maiden.

Durah?

Or, Kiriki?

For what seemed hours, Brown Bear carried Kiriki on his horse across vast stretches of land, through rivers cutting across rugged, pine-studded canyons, then across terrain that was most spectacular to the eye, where the North Platte River yielded its water for green and fertile fields that contrasted sharply to the buttes—where the plains ended and a rugged landscape began.

The land rivaled the sky in an uncluttered expanse. Delicate wildflowers softened the rugged dunes. Meandering streams danced through the hills and splashed their music into the air. A land that at once was harsh and serene.

Nebraska, to the Pawnee, meant "land of flowing rivers."

Kiriki watched everything around her, trying to memorize it in case she managed to escape and had to find her way back to civilization as she had always known it.

Suddenly ahead, there was a conical mound rising out of the naked plain. From the summit shot up a shaft, or column, about one hundred twenty feet in height. She had heard of this awe-inspiring sight that had been named "Chimney Rock." It was a spire of solitary grandeur, visible for miles across the onstretching prairie.

But even this was left behind, and Brown Bear continued his journey until the sun lowered in the sky and there came upon them an eerie quality to the twilight. In this twilight, the thickness of the pines and the scent of cedar and the sound of water was again the most pronounced. Up just ahead the splash of a waterfall was heard.

Hope sprang forth within Kiriki. A waterfall! She had heard Sun Eagle's tale of the waterfall and the cave he and his brother had discovered and had shared as youths. If Brown Bear took her there, perhaps Sun Eagle would eventually find her.

But would it be too late?

Would his brother have already ravaged her, time and time again, until she would not even be fit to be Sun Eagle's woman?

Remorse and fear battled within her aching heart.

Eight

THE sun was low. The shadows of evening were deep pools of violet seeping across the land. A solemn procession of warriors, led by Lone Chief holding the lifeless form of Durah within his arms, entered the village. Wailing among the Pawnee began as Lone Chief surrendered Durah to her father. After the exposure of her body on a scaffold in a tree, the bones would be gathered and placed in an *ossuary*, a place of mass bone burials.

Lone Chief raised a fist in the air. "We must now go and reclaim Kiriki!" he shouted. "She was last seen with Sun Eagle. So shall we find her with him *now!*"

"Death to Sun Eagle!" venomous voices rang out in unison. "We must avenge Durah's death! We must avenge Kiriki's abduction!"

"Yes, we *shall* avenge Durah's death and my daughter's abduction!" Lone Chief shouted. "But not with immediate death. That comes too swiftly. The pain lasts for only a moment. We must see that Sun Eagle lingers long with his discomfort."

"Yes! Let us make him suffer for the pain that he has caused us all by his actions today!" a warrior shouted, followed by several more enraged voices.

"We must find Kiriki before Sun Eagle takes her as his bride," Lone Chief said, his eyes taking on a painfully haunted look. "My grandchildren must not be fathered by Sun Eagle!"

He wheeled his horse around and rode from the village, his warriors following him, lances grasped angrily within their hands. The world was a place of contrasts, for the wailing continued behind him, and the sun was strikingly beautiful before him as it crowned the world with its disc of orange.

There was beauty and ugliness all at once, everywhere!

Lone Chief raised his eyes to the heavens, and when he saw the first twinkling of a star on the darkening sky, something seemed to stab him at the pit of his stomach. Since Kirkiki's abduction, he had been too troubled and filled with remorse to even think about the true reason why Sun Eagle could have taken her. Could it be that he did not want her as a wife at all, but instead for the Skidi's sacrifice to the Morning Star?

Was not Kiriki the loveliest of all maidens in all surrounding camps, Pawnee and Comanche alike? Did not everyone always speak of her uniqueness? Would not she make the most favorable of sacrifices?

The thought burned deeply into his soul.

Tied and gagged, shivering from the night chill as it crept around her inside the cave, Kiriki watched Brown Bear add more wood to the fire. Thus far he had not made any sort of sexual advances toward her. He had just looked at her from time to time, smiling, as though she were the recipient of some great joke not yet revealed to her.

She glared at him. With the war paint removed from his face, she could see his likeness to Sun Eagle. But that was all that was alike about them. Their hearts spoke, oh, so differently!

One man was wonderful. The other deranged. . . .

Yes, surely Brown Bear *was* deranged, or why would he have gone to such lengths to steal her away from Sun Eagle? Did he not realize that the end result would surely be his death? Neither Sun Eagle nor her father would let Brown Bear get away with this! Her father was probably already hot on Brown Bear's trail, and when he discovered Kiriki bound and gagged and at this crazed Pawnee's mercy, her father's wrath would be merciless.

"Soon we will eat," Brown Bear said, kneeling down close to Kiriki. His gaze swept appraisingly over her, then stopped at her eyes. "My brother never told me how it is that you have blue eyes."

He slipped the gag away from Kiriki's mouth. She licked her parched lips and coughed. "Your brother never questioned me about my eyes," she hissed. "He is a gentleman who does not pry into the most private parts of my life." She spat at Brown Bear's feet. "Nor shall I tell you!"

Brown Bear rose quickly to his full height. "It matters not to me who fathered you," he said, laughing dryly. "Of course that *is* the answer, is it not? Your father was white! You are a bastard child, are you not?"

"But of course knowing that I have white blood running through my veins does not change your mind about wanting me as your woman, does it?" Kiriki spat, trying not to let his abusive tone shame her in any way. "You want me only to keep Sun Eagle from having me."

Again she spat at his feet. "If this is the sort of loyalty found in brothers," she hissed, "I am glad that I do not have a brother!"

She began wrestling with her bonds, wincing with pain as the leather ropes began to cut into the flesh of her wrists. "Release me!" she cried. "I will never marry you, much less allow you to touch me! Somehow I will manage to kill you first!"

Brown Bear was becoming unsettled from Kiriki's attitude toward him, and he had to make sure that she never suspected the *true* reasons she had been abducted. He had heard some of the elderly Skidi brag of having captured maidens for the Morning Star sacrifice long ago, and how the captured maidens had been treated with the utmost courtesy and kindness. Not a whisper of the approaching ordeal had the captives heard, for it was then, as it was now, the sole aim of her captors to keep her in ignorance of it and to lull any fears or suspicions she might have.

If she asked questions, she was told that she was being reserved as the bride of a great hero—which was, of course, half true. She was not told that the hero was a god in the skies, and that the path to the marriage bed was through the grave.

The idea was to have the sacrifice go to her Divine Lover joyously, without fear or sorrow.

That meant that Brown Bear must find a way to get Kiriki to trust, even admire, him. If he was to ever get her into the village for the sacrifice, she must have cause to enter it in peace, with tranquility in her heart.

He picked up his lance and began walking toward the entrance of the cave. The moonlight silhouetted him against the darkness as he turned and faced Kiriki. "I will go and spear some fish for our evening meal," he said, his voice soft, with forced apology. "When I return, I shall untie you long enough for you to eat. In time, if Brown Bear can learn to trust you, the bonds will be cast completely away."

He stopped and cleared his throat. "You see, Kiriki, it is not in Brown Bear's plans to cause you distress," he said. "It is my wish that you learn to love Brown Bear. Left in my hands, your life will be filled with great rewards!"

"You will never have my love," Kiriki cried, straining her back up against the wall of the cave. "Only Sun Eagle will have my love." She gulped back a deep sob. "No matter what you do, even if you kill me, I will die with Sun Eagle's name on my lips!"

Understanding that he had quite a battle ahead of him, if he was ever to have Kiriki's trust, Brown Bear sighed resolutely, turned, and left. Kiriki saw this as perhaps the only chance that she would have at trying to escape. She eyed the fire, then the leather bonds at her wrists and ankles. Nervous perspiration broke out on her brow with the thought of what she had to try. She must burn herself free! That seemed the only way, though painful it would be. She could even accidentally set herself afire while doing it.

"But I have no other choice," she whispered to herself. She scooted over to the fire and slowly reached her tied hands toward the dancing flames. . . .

*   *   *

The sky was sprinkled with stars and the land was still, as a lone horseman was silhouetted by moonlight against the ground. Troubled by today's outcome of his bride price offered and denied, Sun Eagle rode with only half the eagerness generally found in him while atop his valiant steed.

But he did not see an easy time ahead for him and Kiriki!

It was obvious that no matter how large a bride price he offered, her father was determined not to let her marry him. Because of the sacrificial practice that he, personally, abhorred, he was going to be denied the woman he loved.

Oh, what in life was fair?

That he had denounced the Morning Star ritual long ago, and that he had been ignored, did not count for anything?

If Sun Eagle were to reveal his feelings to Kiriki's father he would not even listen, for when her father saw Sun Eagle, he also saw generations of Skidis before him who had taken the lives of innocent women in hopes that their corn crop would be wealthier because of it.

The elders of Sun Eagle's tribe believed in this practice wholeheartedly. Sun Eagle's father had only recently begun to falter when the mention of the sacrifice again this year came into the elder's conversations.

"Tomorrow I will arrive at Kiriki's village with many warriors," Sun Eagle whispered, his jaw tightening. "That is the only way she will be mine. Let Lone Chief set his warriors against mine! Mine will be the victory, and I shall ride away with Kiriki!"

He bowed his head. "Kiriki," he whispered. "My sweet and lovely one, that is the only way it can be done. And you must go with me willingly, or the deaths of many Pawnee, perhaps even your father, will be in vain."

The sudden sound of thundering hoofbeats behind him made Sun Eagle draw his reins tautly around his fingers. He stopped his horse and spun around just in time to see many horsemen headed his way. A warning shot through him. Was it Kiriki's father?

Visually counting the warriors, Sun Eagle knew that he would not have any chance of surviving if he stood his ground and fought. He wheeled his horse back around and snapped his reins. Nudging his horse in the flanks with his heels, he rode away in a fast gallop.

But his flight was not fast enough. Soon arrows began whizzing past his head.

Sun Eagle had no choice but to stop. . . .

The smell of scorched flesh rose up into Kiriki's nostrils. Pain bore into her skin. Tears streamed from her eyes as she jerked her wrists away from the flames, the leather strips only smoking. The damage had been done to herself, not to the bonds at her wrists. She could not escape. She was still at Brown Bear's mercy.

Her wrists paining her too much from the burns to continue, Kiriki managed to get back to the wall of the cave where water trickled down in places. She held her wrists up to the water and enjoyed the cool wetness soothing her injured skin.

Then she turned with a start and placed her back up against the wall again when Brown Bear entered the cave, a large fish in his hands. Kiriki wiped her tears with the back of a hand and could not help but look at the fish with envy, the gnawing hunger pains at the pit of her stomach almost as bad as those burned into her wrists. She had gone a full day now without food.

And was it even today that she had last seen Sun Eagle? So much seemed so strangely distant.

"I promised food," Brown Bear said, settling on his haunches before the fire. "You will have food."

He prepared the fish for cooking, then cut a long forked stick, pierced the fish and began cooking it over the embers of the fire. He looked toward Kiriki, seeing her eyes filled with tears.

His gaze slowly lowered. He emitted a strange sort of

growl when he saw her burned wrists and the smoking strips of leather.

Slowly he looked up into her eyes. "You want to escape so badly that you damaged your beautiful skin to do it?" he asked thickly. "Is Brown Bear that much different than Sun Eagle that you would risk anything to be away from him?"

"Yes, anything," Kiriki hissed. She cringed when Brown Bear rose quickly to his feet, leaving the fish to cook slowly in the embers of the fire.

"I will make medicine for your burns," Brown Bear said, leaving the cave.

When he returned and brought several crushed leaves mixed with water to Kiriki, she did not deny him the opportunity to place them on her wounds. She scarcely breathed when he first untied the ropes, leaving her hands finally free. Guardedly, she watched him softly apply the herbs onto her flesh, feeling immediate relief.

Looking over at Brown Bear, she was puzzled by how complex he was. He could kill an innocent woman without even batting an eye, yet be so gentle and caring for another. Perhaps he felt more for her than just wanting her because he coveted his brother's woman. Perhaps he genuinely cared for her! If so, in time he might even release her if he saw that she most definitely could never care for him.

She would have to take things slowly, watch for every opportunity to make him want to care for her enough to never bring harm to her. . . .

"Why do you try and burn the ropes away?" Brown Bear asked, smoothing the last of the poultice onto Kiriki's arm. He looked at her, quirking an eyebrow. "Do you not know that even if you did manage to escape from me, you would have no knowledge of how to get back to your people? I have traveled far with you. I have brought you to a place known by no one but me and my brother, and I am sure that my brother forgot about it long ago. This was a place of childhood friendship between brothers. In adulthood, it has never even been mentioned."

He gestured with a hand toward the cave entrance. "Outside the cave you will find land that will not be kind to you if you travel alone by foot," he further explained. "Even the white pony soldiers rarely come this way. The terrain is too puzzling to them. If they look one way they see what looks the same the other! They would move in circles trying to find their way. So would you also, beautiful Pawnee maiden."

Kiriki swallowed hard, realizing the truth in his words. She had rarely traveled from her village with her parents, much less alone. She would never be able to find her way home.

Not unless Sun Eagle managed to be near and found her while she was escaping. . . .

Tomorrow Sun Eagle would surely know of her abduction and would come for her.

A thought struck her with paralyzing fear. Once she was discovered abducted and Durah was found murdered, her father would suspect no one but Sun Eagle! By tomorrow, Sun Eagle could be dead by the hand of her father, for a crime he did not even do!

Desperation rose inside her. She reached a hand to Brown Bear's cheek and touched him with a forced gentleness. "I will be your wife if you will do something for me," she said in a rush of words.

Brown Bear was taken aback by not only what she said, but by the mere fact that she was touching him. He looked down at her with wavering eyes. "What are you saying?" he asked, feeling cornered, for he did not want her to be his wife. And he could not tell her exactly what he *did* want from her. This abduction was not at all as easy as he had planned it.

"You must go to Sun Eagle and tell him to be prepared for my father's wrath," Kiriki begged, moving to her knees before Brown Bear. She took his hands and squeezed them desperately. "You do not have to tell him anything except that you have heard that my father is after him, to kill him! For, Brown Bear, my father *will*. He will think that Sun Eagle is responsible for everything that

happened today! My father will go and kill Sun Eagle if
Sun Eagle is not prepared for him.''

Brown Bear's eyes lit up. He had not thought of that
possibility. If Kiriki's father killed Sun Eagle, then
wouldn't Brown Bear have everything that Sun Eagle now
boasted of having? Brown Bear would even be next in
line to be chief! Oh, but his plans *were* working in ways
that were good for him after all!

He looked guardedly down at Kiriki. He could not let
her know that he wanted Sun Eagle dead. He had to play
along with her. He would leave and let her believe that he
was going to warn Sun Eagle, when all along he would
not. By tomorrow Sun Eagle would be dead, and Brown
Bear could play the innocent one, saying that he had done
all that he could to stop the killing—that Sun Eagle had
most surely gotten careless after being warned by his
brother.

''I will go and warn my brother,'' Brown Bear said,
nodding anxiously. He looked down at her freed wrists,
then up at her again. ''But I cannot leave you untied
during my absence. I must tie you again.''

''That is all right,'' Kiriki said, her eyes wide. ''All
that I am concerned about this moment is Sun Eagle. Go
to him! Save him! Then, as promised, I will be your wife.
I will even tell Sun Eagle that it is *you* I love, not he.''

Smiling smugly, Brown Bear nodded. He looked down
at her wrists, worrying about them becoming scarred,
making her imperfect for the Morning Star ritual if he did
not treat the wounds with care. He must protect them from
the narrow leather strips that he had used to tie her.

He eyed the abundance of soft buckskin material in her
skirt. ''Tear some of your skirt away,'' he ordered flatly.

Kiriki paled. ''What?'' she gasped. ''Why should I do
that?''

''It will be used to protect the flesh of your wrists from
further harm,'' he said. ''Tear it away. Then I will leave
and go speak with Sun Eagle.''

That Brown Bear cared at all about her comfort confused Kiriki now more than ever. Perhaps he did have a

streak of kindness running through his veins after all. She
must take full advantage of it.

Anxiously, she tore two wide strips of soft buckskin
away from the bottom of her skirt and handed these to
Brown Bear. Scarcely breathing, she watched him gently
wrap these around her wrists before applying the leather
strips that secured her wrists together, assuring that, along
with her tied ankles, she would not escape.

Patience!

She must now . . . practice . . . patience. . . .

Brown Bear rose away from her and eyed the fish that
was for the most part cooked, then plucked some pieces
of it and placed it on Kiriki's lap. "You eat while I am
gone," he said. "You can manage. Your arms and fingers
are free. Only your wrists are bound."

"You are going now to find and warn Sun Eagle?"

"Yes. I shall return by morning."

"I will eat, then sleep," Kiriki said, feigning a yawn.
"Tomorrow you can take me on to your village? We can
be wed?"

"No, not tomorrow," Brown Bear said, slipping several
bites of fish into his mouth. "I will still wait a few more
days. It is best that way."

Kiriki looked up at him, puzzled. Yet did it truly matter
when he did deliver her to his village? If Sun Eagle
believed Brown Bear when he told him that she was going
to marry him, would not Sun Eagle abandon her forever
to this madman?

Her eyes narrowed and hate surged within her when she
looked up at Brown Bear, who was taking his time leaving. Oh, how she hated him! In truth, she would not lie
to Sun Eagle. As soon as she got the opportunity, she
would tell Sun Eagle exactly what had happened today.
She would laugh when Sun Eagle then stood over his
brother's dead body! Brown Bear had been just as merciless when he had slain Durah.

Tears clouded Kiriki's eyes when she thought of Durah.
It did not seem real—that Durah was dead. Never in life
could anyone have had such a dear friend as Durah!

Never would Kiriki, again.

"I shall leave now," Brown Bear said, bringing a blanket to Kiriki. "When the sun rises in the morning, I shall be with you again."

Kiriki nodded, settling in to wait.

Sun Eagle found himself surrounded by many warriors, then he was not at all surprised when Lone Chief dismounted and walked stiffly toward him, several warriors alongside. Sun Eagle itched to raise his rifle, or at least his knife, for protection, but realized that the effort would cost him his life.

He instead waited to see what fate had in store for him tonight on this lonely prairie, where only the stars had been his companions before the warriors had interfered with the silence of the land.

"Step down from your horse," Lone Chief said, his voice bland.

"And if I do not?" Sun Eagle challenged, squaring his shoulders proudly.

"You will be shot from it," Lone Chief said, emotionless.

Sun Eagle inhaled a shaky breath, then slipped slowly from his saddle to the ground. He looked guardedly around him, then into Lone Chief's eyes. "Today, when you refused my bride price, you knew that you would come and kill me before I had a chance to bring you more horses, did you not?" he asked, his voice showing no fear.

"It was not then that my decision to kill you was reached," Lone Chief growled. He looked up at Sun Eagle's horse, past him, then at Sun Eagle again. "Where is she, Sun Eagle? She is not with you, so you must have hidden her." Lone Chief tried to control his temper by holding his knotted fists tightly to his sides. "My daughter, Sun Eagle?" he repeated, his teeth clenched. "Where have you taken her?"

Sun Eagle's eyebrows rose. A coldness swept through him, for if this chief was asking for his daughter, did that not mean that she was gone? "Lone Chief, I do not have your daughter," he said, daring to take a step closer to Kiriki's father. "What has happened? Is she gone? How? When?"

"You play the innocent one," Lone Chief snarled. "You try and make me believe you did not steal my daughter away. Do you even deny killing Durah?"

Sun Eagle gasped and a sick feeling invaded his insides. He teetered. He swept a hand across his face, shaking his head, for if Durah was dead, what . . . of . . . Kiriki?

Then he closed his eyes and gritted his teeth. His brother! Could his brother . . . ?

Before he had time for much more thought, Sun Eagle was brought back to his senses by Lone Chief's loud command.

"Seize him!" Lone Chief shouted. "He must be made to confess! My daughter's life lies in the balance!"

Sun Eagle held himself proudly tall while he was flanked by warriors whose fingers sank painfully into the flesh of his arms. He did not flinch or show his fear when he was witness to a deep pit being dug in the ground at his feet. He knew his doom. He had seen ways of forcing truths from a man used before.

But this time? There was nothing to tell!

While Sun Eagle was being tortured, Kiriki was somewhere, perhaps being tortured herself.

And he could do nothing to save her. Nothing! Lone Chief would never believe the truth, for it seemed that his hatred for Sun Eagle was blinding him of what truths there truly were.

Nine

SUN Eagle was ready to be thrust into the open pit feet-first at any moment, and his eyes were riveted as he watched stakes being driven into the ground close beside the hole.

He gave Lone Chief a questioning glance, then his whole body jerked as he was shoved past the deep, black and narrow pit, and forced to lie on the ground between the four stakes. Without uttering a sound, staring blankly into the star-sequined heaven, he let his arms and legs be outstretched and secured with ropes to the stakes.

"You do not question why I do not place you in the pit?" Lone Chief asked, standing over Sun Eagle, his fists on his hips.

"I only question your reasoning," Sun Eagle said, his voice tight. "Nothing else. You waste time with me while Kiriki is being taken away by someone else. Why can you not see this? My love for her is strong. I would have never stolen her and then hid her away as though something shameful. I would have fought valiantly for her!"

He looked away from Lone Chief, his jaw tight. "I will say no more," he said thickly. "If you continue to waste time here with me, it is your daughter and yourself who will suffer. Not I, Lone Chief."

He swallowed hard, knowing that he *would* be the one to suffer the most if anything happened to Kiriki. But he would not confess this to her stubborn father. If Sun Eagle possessed nothing else at this moment, while lying prone and at the mercy of other thoughtless Pawnee, at least he still had possession of his pride.

Never could anyone take that away from him. Never!

He placed a barrier, as though a sound stone wall, between himself and Kiriki's father. He would now let the chief's words bounce off him, conditioning himself for what was to come. He was to be tortured, a humiliation so keen to the Pawnee.

But for Kiriki, he was ready to endure suffering.

It was for her. *Everything* was for her.

Yet, where was she?

If Brown Bear was responsible for any of this, his life would be short-lived if Sun Eagle ever managed to escape. . . .

"You lie!" Lone Chief hissed. A slow smile crept onto his wide lips. "First you will be tortured and left to fight the chill of the night and then the baking sun of day. By then, if you do not confess to your crimes, you will be placed in the pit and buried up to the neck. Your death will come slow, Sun Eagle."

Lone Chief bent a knee over Sun Eagle and spoke into his face. "*Sickstah,* give me the answer, Sun Eagle," he said resonantly. "You will be released. No harm will come to you. All I want is my daughter's safe return! Not *nahosah,* tomorrow. Today!"

Sun Eagle stared blankly ahead, awaiting the first blow to his powerful chest, and then knife wounds that would be inflicted on various parts of his body. He would bear the pain in silence, just like he was bearing the pain of worrying about Kiriki. One pain would be no less than the other. It was as though his heart was being torn in shreds, the worry of Kiriki was so intense!

Seeing that Sun Eagle was not ready to cooperate, Lone Chief rose angrily to his full height. He glared down at him and gave the first order to one of his warriors to make slight slash marks with a knife on Sun Eagle's abdomen.

Lone Chief grimaced, when in the moonlight he could see minute bubbles of blood ooze to the surface of Sun Eagle's flesh.

Yet still the powerful warrior did not speak or cry out. Not even an eyelash did he blink. Nor did a muscle flinch when the sharp knife was placed on one of Sun Eagle's inner thighs, and again was drawn across his flesh, leaving behind a track of red.

"You are foolish!" Lone Chief said, his frustration showing. "Speak! Confess! And all of this will stop!"

Sun Eagle kept the mental barrier that he had built intact. He could hear Lone Chief's rage, but he did not listen to what he was saying. The chief was beyond comprehension of what was true or false. He thought that he was doing what was best for Kiriki, when in truth it was the worst of all the decisions that he may have made in his lifetime. In the end, Lone Chief would surely see that and fall upon his own knife in his grief. . . .

But that would not bring Kiriki back! Not even that. . . .

Again his thoughts went to Brown Bear. Could his brother hate him this much? Should he tell Lone Chief that perhaps the true abductor was his brother?

He closed his eyes, torn with what to do. If he sent Kiriki's father up against Brown Bear, and Brown Bear was innocent, Sun Eagle would forever be laden with guilt!

No. He could not go against his brother unless he was positively sure of his brother's guilt. But if Brown Bear *was* guilty and Kiriki was harmed, because of his silence Sun Eagle would be at fault almost the same as Brown Bear.

Oh, but he was so torn!

A fire was built close beside Sun Eagle. He could feel the heat radiating on his face. He did not watch, but knew what to expect next. Small, flaming twigs were going to be thrust beneath each of his fingernails. They would burn slowly to his flesh. If he cried out as the fire reached his skin, he would be ridiculed and called a woman!

If he bore the pain, he would be regarded as an even mightier warrior than the reputation already gained by him!

But the whole reason behind the test was not to test his cowardice, but to get him to tell the truth before he had to endure any of the fiery pain!

He had already told the truth, but his words had fallen on deaf ears.

Brown Bear rode into his village, welcomed by silence at this midnight hour, except for a few dogs barking in the distance. He looked at Sun Eagle's dwelling, smiling smugly. Soon his brother would know of Kiriki's abduction! It had been best for Brown Bear to return to his village, to make an appearance to draw attention to himself so that he would not be accused of having abducted Kiriki.

"Soon I shall bring Kiriki to the village with me," he whispered to himself, dismounting before his own private earthen lodge. "Should Sun Eagle be here, he will not dare speak up against her being the sacrifice. There is no denying that she is the most beautiful woman among the tribes of neighboring Indians. She, only she, will make the appropriate sacrifice!"

If Sun Eagle *did* speak up in her behalf, swearing that she was Pawnee, not Comanche, by then the whole village would be already awestruck by her beauty and realize that no one but her would please the Morning Star! They would turn deaf ears to anything that Sun Eagle had to say, for the pleasing of the Morning Star was far more important than anything else.

The moonlight was silvering the land, illuminating everything within sight. Brown Bear peered through the darkness and saw the absence of Sun Eagle's black gelding that was usually tethered close at the entrance of Sun Eagle's dwelling.

Brown Bear stared at Sun Eagle's earthen lodge, feeling strangely ill at ease about his brother. If he was not there, there were many possibilities of where he might be! He may have heard of Kiriki's abduction and was now searching for her.

Or perhaps Lone Chief had captured Sun Eagle, blaming him for Durah's death and Kiriki's abduction.

"I must see if he is truly gone," Brown Bear whispered, moving stealthily through the night. He stepped up to Sun Eagle's dwelling, stooped, and moved slowly inside. He grew tense when he discovered there were not even any charred embers in Sun Eagle's firepit.

Stepping lightly on into the lodge, Brown Bear went to the firepit and bent an elbow to the ashes. He drew back quickly, frowning. They were cold! There hadn't been a fire in the firepit for hours!

He turned and stared down at the thick pallet of furs unslept in this night. A rush of fear spread through him. What if Sun Eagle suspected his own brother of having abducted Kiriki? Would Sun Eagle recall the cave of his childhood? Could he have already found Kiriki and have taken her away? Would the morrow bring Sun Eagle in search of Brown Bear, so that he could capture him and take him to Lone Chief for punishment?

Pale and shaken from such sudden fears, Brown Bear left Sun Eagle's dwelling quickly. He stopped at his parents' earthen lodge, remembering that he had returned to the village to draw suspicion away from himself. He must still let his parents, at least, know that he was there, so that if on the morrow they were questioned about him, they would give him the defense that he needed—perhaps even to save his life.

Creeping into his parents' lodge, Brown Bear went to his mother and touched her gently on the face. When she opened her eyes and stared up at him, startled at first, he took her hand and placed its palm to his lips in a kiss.

"I am sorry if I frightened you," Brown Bear whispered, leaning closer to speak to her. "But I awakened from a bad dream about Sun Eagle and went to his dwelling, and he was not there. Mother, did you see him tonight before you retired?"

Kidibattsk rose up on an elbow. "He is not there?" she whispered, her face furrowed into a frown.

"No. He is not," Brown Bear said, trying to show concern in the way he spoke and looked.

"He was not there earlier, either," Kidibattsk murmured, then reached a hand to Brown Bear's cheek. "But neither were you. Where were you, my son? Where do you think Sun Eagle is? I thought that perhaps you had

decided to go on a hunt together. It has been a great while
since brother hunted with brother.''

"I have been asleep for some time, Mother," Brown
Bear lied. "I must have arrived home just after you looked
in on me." He smiled down at her. "How old do sons
have to be for mothers to quit worrying about them?"

"Ninety-nine winters, my son," Kidibattsk said, laughing softly. She patted Brown Bear's cheek. "You go back
to bed. Your brother will be home soon."

She lowered her eyes and smiled a secret smile, envisioning her eldest son in the arms of Kiriki, somewhere
out away from everyone. He would be returning her home
to announce that there would soon be a wedding
ceremony.

Ah, yes, that was surely where Sun Eagle was, but it
was best not to reveal her thoughts to her youngest son.
She knew of Brown Bear's jealousy toward Sun Eagle. It
was best not to arouse jealousies over a woman.

"Now that I am awake because of the troubling dream,
I do not think I want to go back asleep so soon," Brown
Bear said. "I am afraid I would have the same dream
again. It is not good to see a brother killed even in a
dream, Mother!"

Kidibattsk gasped and dropped her hand away from
Brown Bear. "You dreamed of death?" she said, her
voice drawn.

"Yes," Brown Bear lied. "Sun Eagle's."

Kidibattsk implored Brown Bear with her eyes. "My
son, perhaps it is best that you go and see if you can find
Sun Eagle tonight," she said, casting thoughts of amorous
embraces from her mind. Perhaps Sun Eagle had been
denied Kiriki! Perhaps his bride price had not been enough
and he had become enraged, angering the wrath of Lone
Chief! Lone Chief had a great following of warriors! They
could kill Sun Eagle and swear they had cause to.

"If that is what you desire of me, I shall do it," Brown
Bear said, his mother having fallen right into his plan.
"But do not be frightened if we do not return by morning.
We may decide to go on that hunt we have put off so

long.'' He leaned down and kissed his mother gently on
the cheek. ''Perhaps tomorrow we shall bring you much
food for your pot, Mother.'' If there was any food
brought, he would do it alone, and alone gain praises from
his mother.

''That is good,'' Kidibattsk nodded. She gave Brown
Bear a gentle shove on the chest. ''Go. Ride with care.
The night has a thousand eyes!''

''Yes, Mother, this I know,'' Brown Bear said, inching
away from her, then lunging outside and rushing to his
horse. Time with his mother had been necessary, but much
too long! If Sun Eagle had found Kiriki, oh, what then?

Mounting his horse in one leap, Brown Bear leaned low
over its mane and galloped hard from the village, stirring
dust behind him, many dogs yapping and following him.
He kicked them away as they leapt at his feet, laughing
when one spun away from him, rolling from head to toe
across the land, yelping with pain.

''That is the way it will be for my brother when Lone
Chief accuses him of Kiriki's abduction,'' he whispered
harshly. He frowned, filled with doubt. ''If only that could
be so!''

The sun was just beginning to pour its orange light
along the horizon, erasing the velveteen black of night.
Brown Bear kept a lookout for any undue movement
ahead. When he heard the thundering of horse's hooves,
he guided his steed into thick brush and watched, breathless, as Lone Chief rode on past, many warriors dutifully
following him.

''They are looking for Kiriki!'' Brown Bear gasped,
paling. ''If they had seen me, they would have suspected
me and followed!''

He looked in the direction from whence Lone Chief had
just traveled. He would change his course of travel and
go *that* way. At least then he would not have to worry
about running into Lone Chief.

Nudging his horse with his knees, Brown Bear resumed
his travels, his chin held high. At least for now he felt
safe. He was being given more time to make definite plans

for his arrival into his village with Kiriki. It must be at
just the right moment. Nothing could get in the way of
being given the full honors of delivering the perfect
maiden for the sacrifice. . . .

Something just up ahead drew Brown Bear's rapt attention. It was now light enough to make out the figure of a
man staked to the ground. He swallowed hard and leapt
from his horse, tethering it to a tree so that he could
approach closer by foot, to see who it was and to possibly
offer help. He had never actually witnessed such a punishment before, but he had heard that it was the most severe
of all, except for when a man was buried alive—all but
his head.

Brown Bear's heart skipped a beat when he got close
enough to recognize the victim. It was Sun Eagle!

He eased behind some bushes and moved closer, staying
hidden behind them. His gut twisted and bitterness rose
up into his throat when he saw the slashes on his brother's
flesh, the blood dried to them. He could see bruises forming on his brother's face, his eyes black and swollen.

Then he saw his brother's fingers. They had obviously
been burned. They were red and raw!

The brother in Brown Bear wanted to go and release
Sun Eagle, but he knew that if he did there would be too
much for himself to explain. Surely by now Sun Eagle
suspected that Brown Bear was responsible for Kiriki's
abduction. If Brown Bear set Sun Eagle free, it could be
Brown Bear that would soon be lying there in his place!

He corded his shoulder muscles as he fought back the
urge to cry. He did not truly hate his brother this much!
Brown Bear only wanted the recognition that Sun Eagle
always stole from him. Now was the chance for all of that
to change.

"I cannot release him!" Brown Bear said to himself,
turning his eyes away from Sun Eagle who seemed, at
least for the moment, to be escaping his miseries in the
mercy of sleep or unconsciousness.

His eyes narrowed in anger. "Now I know why Lone
Chief was traveling from this direction," he hissed. "It

was *he* who put my brother here and tortured him! It was as I thought it would be. Lone Chief suspected Sun Eagle.''

He turned slowly around to look at Sun Eagle again. He bit his lower lip in frustration. ''Will Lone Chief return and kill Sun Eagle?'' His gaze shifted to the pit dug in the ground close to his brother. ''Yes, he plans to return. My brother will die in the pit!''

A slow smile lifted his lips. At Sun Eagle's expense he could not help but see a much brighter future for himself. Without Sun Eagle, everything was possible for Brown Bear. Everything!

He would force sadness from his heart and reflect on all tomorrows.

Brown Bear's tomorrows.

He would not waste any more time here with a brother who soon would be dead. He had to go to Kiriki and stay with her, until all threat was past that Lone Chief would change his mind and search for the true culprit.

Then he smiled smugly. ''But with my brother out of the way and soon dead, I can arrive victoriously in my village with my offering to the Morning Star,'' he said, thrusting his chest out proudly. ''Lone Chief will never know. He will think all along that Sun Eagle did away with her in some way. By the time Kiriki is the actual sacrifice, it will be too late if he finds out where she truly is.''

Brown Bear leapt onto his horse and rode away, confident that even if Lone Chief ever did find out about his daughter being used as the sacrifice, the warriors of *Alligatus*, Chief Antelope Buck, were stronger than *Skur-ar-a-le-shar's*, Lone Chief's. If a battle ensued between these two factions of Pawnee, Brown Bear had to believe his tribe would be the victor! The Morning Star would shine its greatness upon his people, blessing them because of the sacrifice.

''Yes,'' Brown Bear said smugly, nodding. ''Everything that I do is right. Everything.''

*   *   *

Kiriki awakened when she heard a rustling sound close by in the cave. Blinking her eyes open, having gratefully slept the night through from sheer exhaustion, she looked guardedly around her.

She emitted a soft cry of alarm when she made out the distinct outline of a she-bear standing on its hind legs at the entrance of the cave, two cubs standing beside her. She could hear the bear sniffing the air. She could hear its low, daring growl, knowing that it had more than likely picked up her scent.

Kiriki was too afraid to move. She lay stiffly watching for the bear's next movements, then died a slow death inside when the cubs came to her and began bouncing all over her as they romped and played.

But still Kiriki did not move. Nor did she hardly breathe! The bear had fallen to its four legs and was coming toward her, its rear end slowly swaying.

And still the cubs bounced and played all over Kiriki. It was as though they did not even know that she was there. Surely it was because they had never been near a human before and did not know to fear them.

Then the outline of Brown Bear appeared at the entrance of the cave, his rifle poised, aimed at the mother bear. A shot rang out loud and clear. The cubs jumped at least two feet in the air from fright, then scampered away farther into the cave, while the mother's body lurched and lunged forward, dropping in a crimson pool of blood.

Kiriki closed her eyes and heaved a sigh of relief. Brown Bear came to her and cupped her chin within the palm of his hand. "You are all right?" he asked thickly.

"A moment longer and I would have been the bear's morning meal," Kiriki said, moving to a sitting position. Her eyes began darting around, remembering the cubs. "Also her cubs'. Where did they go? They were here only moments ago. They weren't frightened of me."

"They have been frightened away by the gunshot, at least for the moment," Brown Bear said, turning back to the bear. He knelt down over it and touched her sleek, thick fur, the body still warm. "Now the bear will be food for us. The pelt will be my gift to you, Kiriki."

For a moment Kiriki had forgotten the dilemma she was in, with Brown Bear as her captor. Though she owed him thanks for saving her life, she could not utter the words, for in truth she would have not been put in such danger had Brown Bear never abducted her.

"I do not wish to have any gifts from you, thank you," she murmured, again looking over her shoulder for the cubs. She was afraid that he would heartlessly kill them also.

"It will be given to you anyhow," Brown Bear grumbled. "Preparing the bear pelt will occupy my time while I am waiting for the proper moment to take you to my people, to introduce you to them."

"Your people?" Kiriki said guardedly, not liking the sound of that. Why would it be so important to his people that he was merely taking a wife? He was not to be their chief in the future. As far as she knew, he was just another Pawnee, with no special status at all.

"Yes, my people," Brown Bear said, taking out his knife to begin removing the bear's pelt. "Never will they have seen such a lovely woman who will soon be a bride enter our village. I will boast of being the one to have offered you to them."

Brown Bear's heart lurched, having forgotten for the moment how cautious he must be about letting Kiriki know the exact purpose for her abduction. If she ever guessed that it was for the sacrifice, he would not be able to get her to willingly enter the village with a smile on her face.

She must never suspect. Never!

Kiriki was growing cold inside. She was recalling the band of Pawnee into which Sun Eagle had been born. Would not his brother, also, be born into the Skidi? Was he truly wanting her as his bride, or—for the bride of the Morning Star?

She closed her eyes and lowered her head, not letting herself venture any further with that dreadful thought. Her captivity was unbearable enough without having such thoughts added to it.

A warm soft tongue on her arm jerked Kiriki's eyes quickly open. She looked down into the dark brown trusting eyes of one of the bear cubs. When he settled down beside her, watching his mother's carcass being dismembered, her heart poured out to him. She was like that cub, a future which was questionable ahead of her, if there was to be any future at all. . . .

The sun was high enough in the sky to start beating down on the wounds of Sun Eagle's body as he instantly awoke. He groaned and felt lightheaded as he turned his head one way and then another, looking for signs of anyone observing him there in his misery. Only a short while ago he had thought that he had heard a lone rider coming close, then stopping. Had that been his imagination? Or had someone seen him and heartlessly left him there to die?

Licking his parched lips, Sun Eagle squinted his eyes as he looked up at the pulsing sun. "How long can I last?" he whispered. "Perhaps another hour or so. . . ."

He tensed when his body recognized vibrations in the land which meant the approach of many horsemen. He glanced over at the pit that lay waiting for him. Surely the horsemen approaching were Lone Chief and his warriors coming to finish what they had started.

Sun Eagle tried to seek within himself for that small measure of remaining courage that had not yet been drawn upon, to sustain him through the next ordeal of his life. Then he closed his eyes, envisioning Kiriki standing before him, her arms outstretched for him.

If he concentrated hard, he could feel her embrace as he went to her.

He could smell her sweetness. He could taste the wonders of her lips. . . .

As the horses grew closer, these thoughts of Kiriki were his courage—his hopes.

But where were his dreams? Were they truly to be denied him?

Ten

FROM weakness caused by the loss of blood, the swelter-
ing sun robbing him of his strength, and from having
endured such intense pain, Sun Eagle began to drift in and
out of consciousness. The horse's hooves that were nearing sounded muffled as they made contact with the ground,
and Sun Eagle found it hard to grasp onto sounds as he
mentally drifted . . . drifted . . . drifted. . . .

Even when the horses stopped and men dismounted
close beside Sun Eagle, he heard voices as though they
were being spoken from inside a deep cavern.

Even when he slowly opened his eyes and tried to focus
on the men who stood over him, he could not see them,
feeling as though he was nearly blinded from the sun's
rays that had incessantly beat down into his eyes. He could
only see shadow and light. He could only hear words that
came to him a jumble.

Yet, he could hear enough to know that it was not
Pawnee words. They were words of the white man!

Major Roger O'Fallon, the Indian agent from Fort
Redington, knelt quickly down beside Sun Eagle, soldiers
already following his orders to untie him.

"Sun Eagle?" Major O'Fallon said, looking his friend
up and down, seeing his sources of mistreatment. "Who
did this to you, Sun Eagle? Who?"

Sun Eagle's mind swam. He slowly moved his head
from side to side, unable to grasp onto what Major O'Fallon was saying enough to reply.

But deeply within his heart Sun Eagle was rejoicing!
This man, this Major O'Fallon, was a friend from long

ago. As a tribe, the Pawnee were friendly to the Americans whom they served as scouts against other hostile Indian groups. Sun Eagle had served as Major O'Fallon's scout more than once. He was now going to repay Sun Eagle for his loyalty. Major O'Fallon was going to rescue Sun Eagle!

Sun Eagle would live. . . .

"Damn," Major O'Fallon growled beneath his breath. He glanced over at Lieutenant Harper. "I think we may have gotten here just in time. Had he been here much longer, he would have been a goner." His blue eyes were haunted as he lifted his coonskin hat from his head and raked his fingers through his brown hair. His fringed buckskin outfit rippled against his muscled body as he rose back to his full height. "We'll take him to my cabin. It's closer than the fort. My wife Carin can do wonders with burns." He swallowed hard, again looking at the slash marks on Sun Eagle's body. Blood was dried into them with flies buzzing around them. "Also with knife wounds."

Sun Eagle could feel himself being lifted by strong arms. He groaned as he was draped gently over the back of a horse and secured there with ropes. He continued to drift in and out of consciousness as the horse began to travel in a lope across the land.

Now that he had been rescued, his mind was just alert enough to think: *revenge!*

Once well, he would find Kiriki's abductor. He would first question his brother and hope that he would discover that he had been wrong to suspect Brown Bear of any wrongdoing.

Oh, but should Kiriki die before Sun Eagle could rescue her, would it not be simpler for him to accept death as the answer, himself?

Suddenly there was darkness. He was in a deep sleep, for the moment void of pain, of worry, of dreams of revenge.

Even of Kiriki. . . .

*　　*　　*

The aroma of bear meat cooking over the flames of the campfire wafted across the cave toward Kiriki, making her stomach growl with hunger. She watched the two bear cubs at play close beside her, having noticed that even they had stopped to sniff the air from time to time, revealing their own hunger. Little did they know that soon they would be eating portions of their own mother.

When one of the cubs bounced over to Kiriki and began playing with the loose ends of the leather bindings at her wrists, she watched with amusement, then her face changed into a mask of seriousness. The cub's teeth sometimes grazed her flesh, drawing her attention to them. Though small, the teeth were sharp. Could they possibly be sharp enough to gnaw on the strips of leather long enough to chew through them?

Kiriki looked at the fat dripping from the meat into the fire, sizzling as the flames were fueled by the grease. If Kiriki could manage to smear some of the bear fat onto the leather bindings, would not the cubs be attracted to it? Would they not chew on the leather to draw the flavor of the meat from it?

Smiling, Kiriki encouraged the cubs to continue playing with the dangling strips of leather, to keep their attention on them. It would not be all that noticeable if she did it later, for Brown Bear would be used to seeing her attention to the bears and never suspect her true reason for offering the leather bindings as toys to them later. . . .

Brown Bear dropped his bloody knife to the pebbled floor of the cave and jerked the slab of cooked meat from the spear on which it had been lodged while cooking. He went and settled on his haunches before Kiriki. He tore off a piece of the meat and held it out to her.

"It is time to eat," he said, his body reeking of perspiration and dried bear's blood. "You eat. I will go to the waterfall and fetch us some fresh water."

Kiriki took the meat anxiously, her mouth almost watering from hunger. She took a quick bite, eagerly watching Brown Bear as he rose and placed the meat back on the spear that was thrust into the ground, now moving the meat high enough on the spear above the fire so that it would discourage the cubs from getting it.

When a cub went and playfully batted at his ankle with a paw, emitting a pitiful sort of growl from the depths of his throat because it had been ignored when the food had been given to Kiriki, Brown Bear kicked the bear cub away.

"I should run them off," he said, kicking at the other cub. "But they seem to amuse you. That is the only reason I allow them to stay."

"I thank you for the cubs, not myself," Kiriki said, taking another bite of meat. Her eyes wavered as she looked at the cubs who were now sitting side by side, looking forlorn as they watched her eating. "I would thank you for them again if you would give them at least a little food." She sighed. "Even if they will be eating their own mother, at least they will be fed something."

"If you want them to eat, feed them your own food," Brown Bear said, turning to leave. "I do not cook food to feed animals."

Kiriki shook her head in disgust, then when Brown Bear was gone, she placed a big chunk of the meat in her mouth and raised her wrists to the meat, rubbing the ropes back and forth across its greasiness. She watched the cubs who were watching her with a curious sort of interest. One cocked his head as he watched; the other rose up on its hind legs and went to her, resting his front paws on her shoulder as he reached with his tongue for the meat, her upraised arms in the way.

Kiriki grabbed the meat from her mouth with her hand and lowered her arms. "You're hungry, aren't you?" she whispered. She hurriedly placed her chunk of meat beneath her, out of the cub's reach, then offered him the grease-soaked leather at her wrists. "Chew on them awhile and I promise that I will give you the rest of my meat. But first, little ones, help me get free."

The other cub came sniffing. For a moment they fought over who would do the biting and chewing first, but then seemed to settle in at taking turns. Kiriki winced when their teeth would occasionally slip and sink into her flesh instead of the leather. But a few nips had been expected; anything was worth getting free.

Yet Brown Bear's earlier warning kept troubling Kiriki. Once she got free, what then? She had no idea how to get home. The only solution, as she saw it, was to somehow manage to steal his horse and let it lead her to civilization.

Of course, Brown Bear's horse would not take Kiriki to her village, but to Brown Bear's, which, in turn, was— Sun Eagle's.

But would Sun Eagle be there? Could he even now be dead at the hands of her avenging father? Her father would have to believe that Sun Eagle had abducted her; there was no reason to suspect anyone else.

Kiriki's breathing became shallow with anticipation. Her scheme was working—the ropes were weakening at her wrists. As starved as the cubs were, they were taking full advantage of the grease they could chew from the leather. She watched for Brown Bear's reappearance and grew tense when she heard the crunching of rock at the entrance of the cave.

"Shoo! Scat!" Kiriki whispered, nudging the bears away. Slipping her bound hands beneath her, she grabbed the chunk of meat. She tossed it farther into the cave and sighed with relief as the bears scampered after it, leaving her alone with her loosened bonds and a few anxious hours of waiting ahead of her.

After Brown Bear went to sleep, she would make her escape!

The necklace that Sun Eagle had given her pressed into her flesh beneath the protective covering of her buckskin blouse. As long as it was with her, she seemed closer to Sun Eagle and felt a small measure of hope.

Lone Chief rode in a hard gallop across the land of flowing rivers, ignoring a herd of buffalo and flocks of big horn sheep perched on the vistas of buttes and pinnacles in the distance. His prime interest at this moment did not lay in the hunt for food. He was anxious to get to Sun Eagle to

see what the cold of night and the heat of day had done to
his ability to tell the truth! If his life was of any value to
him, he would be ready to tell Lone Chief everything.

"Kiriki has been gone a full night now," Lone Chief
whispered to himself. He shook his head woefully. "That
is too long. That is far too long!"

"Look ahead!" one of Lone Chief's warriors shouted.
"He is gone! The stakes are bare!"

Lone Chief's heart lurched as he peered ahead and saw
that what his warrior spoke was true. There was no sign
of Sun Eagle anywhere. He had somehow managed to
escape!

"It cannot be!" Lone Chief shouted in frustration.
"Search the land. See if he got far!"

He reined in his horse close beside the stakes and slid
from his saddle. The astute person that he was, he quickly
noted and determined the route of Sun Eagle's escape, and
the manner in which he had achieved it.

"Stop, my warriors, look no further!" he shouted, raising a fist into the air. "Do you not see the horse's hoof-
prints that do not belong to our people? Can you not see
they belong to the white pony soldiers? That is how Sun
Eagle escaped! The white pony soldiers happened along
and found him."

He lowered his fist to his side, his face twisted with
anguished pain. "The prints do not lead in the direction
of Sun Eagle's village," he said from between clenched
teeth. "They lead elsewhere, either to the white man's
fort or to our friend Major O'Fallon's cabin. His wife is
noted for her skills with medicine. They say her skills rival
our own shaman. Sun Eagle will be made well again."

One of Lone Wolf's warriors stood next to him. "Let
us go and take him back!" he grumbled, his dark eyes
filled with fire.

Lone Chief slipped an arm around his friend's shoulder.
"No," he said, his voice low. "We will not go against
our friend Major O'Fallon. It is because of him that we
have a measure of peace in our land. He does not send
the pony soldiers to attack us—he makes them treat us as

though friends. He is being a friend to Sun Eagle, just as he would to you or I should he find us in trouble." He nodded, his face lined with sorrow. "So be it. So be it."

"But your daughter?" the warrior persisted. "We shall never know where she is."

"She will be to us as dead," Lone Chief said, walking square-shouldered to his horse. "Do not speak to me of her again. It is finished!"

He swung himself up into the saddle and rode away, his heart breaking, yet his head held nobly high.

Sun Eagle awoke to a cool compress on his brow and soft green eyes staring down at him. He was aware of pain in various parts of his body and that he seemed to be on fire from head to toe.

"Where am I?" he said weakly, licking his parched lips.

"Roger found you and brought you home for me to see to," Carin O'Fallon said in a lilting voice, removing the damp cloth from Sun Eagle's brow. "Sun Eagle, you had been tortured. Who would do such a thing?"

It was all coming back to Sun Eagle in flashes. Lone Chief and his warriors capturing him and staking him to the ground. But the various methods of torture were like a blur to him. One painful slash to his flesh had blended into the next. . . .

He tried to get up but a keen dizziness swept through him, discouraging further attempts. A gentle hand on his arm made him look up at Carin again, seeing in her a gentleness that he wondered if all white women possessed. She was not a pretty woman, with a square face that was too fleshy. Her rust-colored hair was tied in a tight bun atop her head, and a gap in her front teeth made her whistle strangely when she spoke.

But she was ever so sweet and kind. That was surely what had attracted a man like Roger O'Fallon to her, for he was of the same breed as she.

Never had Sun Eagle met such a kinder white man. Roger O'Fallon was a man of all heart, and he always

listened to the Pawnee's complaints no matter how large
or small. Even now, Major O'Fallon was taking a chance
by bringing Sun Eagle to his dwelling. How did he know
but that it was the war-hungry Comanche who had left
Sun Eagle to die in the sun, and that they would soon be
on the warpath while searching for him again?

"Lone Chief is the one responsible for my being staked
to the ground," Sun Eagle said, wanting to set Carin's
mind at ease.

He turned his head slowly and looked toward the door
as Roger came lumbering into the cabin, all six-foot-four
of him, a small son, David, at his side. Roger was tall
and lanky, yet could boast of much muscle. His hair was
brown and his eyes were blue like Kiriki's, reminding Sun
Eagle anew of perhaps what he had lost if her assailant
had captured, then slain her after possibly raping her.

Yet he still could not get his brother's jealousy from
his mind. Rather it be his brother, than a stranger. . . .

Resting his rifle against the wall, his son racing across
the room to pet his dog, Roger looked over at Sun Eagle,
then at Carin. "I see our guest has regained consciousness," he said. He went and stood over Sun Eagle. "How
are you farin', friend?"

"I have to get out of here," Sun Eagle said, his voice
raspy, his head throbbing. Again he tried to get up but
fell back down onto the bed, gasping for breath. "I am
so weak!"

Carin began caressing his brow with the cool, damp
cloth again. She glanced up at her husband. "He still
has a temperature," she murmured. "But it has dropped
somewhat." She looked at Sun Eagle's wounds. She had
spread her own recipe of herbs and creams into them, and
they were already looking better. Even the burns at the
tips of his fingers. "Everything about him seems better."
She smiled sweetly at Sun Eagle as he looked over at her.
"But, Sun Eagle, you must practice patience. You can't
leave this bed until your fever is gone. Until it is, you
won't have the strength to even walk from this cabin."

Sun Eagle looked desperately up at Roger. He trembled

as he leaned up on an elbow. "My woman was abducted!" he cried. "I do not know by whom. I do not know where she is or what has happened to her. I was accused of the ugly deed! That is why you found me staked to the ground. Her father thought that I abducted her because he did not agree to my bride price and sent me away from his village without her."

He fell back down onto the bed and closed his eyes, breathless. "I must leave," he whispered, panting for breath. "I must . . . find . . . her. . . ."

Roger and Carin exchanged troubled glances and shook their heads slowly. Sun Eagle drifted off into another troubled sleep, his body betraying him at his time of need.

Eleven

THE fire had died down to glowing embers. Kiriki watched Brown Bear stretch out on a blanket; the bear pelt that he had just prepared from the dead carcass was folded at her feet, a gift from him. She shoved the fur away with her bound feet, then choked on a sob when the bear cubs cuddled up into the fur, obviously still smelling their mother on it. It wasn't long before they were sleeping soundly, yet Brown Bear seemed to be having trouble going to sleep. He tossed from one side, then to the next, grumbling and fussing to himself.

Then finally he seemed to have managed to fight the devil within him that was keeping him awake, for his breathing became even, his body no longer twitching. . . .

Her heart beating erratically, Kiriki looked down at the leather strips at her wrists. Slowly, she began twisting them back and forth. Her eyes lit up when one snapped in two, the other hanging just by a narrow thread.

Her hands now completely free, Kiriki looked intensely at Brown Bear before reaching to untie her ankles. Her shoulder muscles became somewhat relaxed, for he still seemed to be sleeping soundly enough. His breathing was coming in an easy rhythm, yet was it appearing to be *too* easy? Could he be feigning sleep, expecting her to try and flee?

Kiriki scoffed at the idea. As far as Brown Bear was concerned, she was still tightly bound. If he had noticed the bears' attention to the greased ropes at her wrists, he had not shown that he had, and would be none the wiser of what they had achieved with their sharp teeth.

No. He did not know of her plan—he was asleep. She could continue her escape plan, unfoiled. . . .

With trembling, anxious fingers, Kiriki worked at the leather strips at her ankles, the knots in them as tight as the Pawnee warriors place their shafts on the tips of their arrows! Sweat beaded up on her brow, her fingertips becoming sore with her efforts, then she smiled slyly when finally the knot opened and the leather hung slack—leaving Kiriki *free*.

Rubbing the flesh where the ropes had cut into her ankles, Kiriki once again looked at Brown Bear, her moment of escape near. Her gaze traveled over his bronze body, from his heavily beaded moccasins, up his bare legs, past his loincloth and across his flat abdomen, then slowly upward until she rested her eyes on his face. It was expressionless, his eyelashes lowered, black on his copper cheeks.

Doubts began assailing Kiriki, still feeling that perhaps Brown Bear appeared to be sleeping *too* soundly which could mean that he was not asleep at all. She inhaled a shaky breath, turning her eyes to the cave entrance, then back at Brown Bear. She was so close to escape; she would not let anything stop her. If he were truly awake, surely he would not harm her if he stopped her. Somehow she seemed too precious to him, yet she was puzzled by the fact that he had not approached her in any intimate way. If he did marry her, was he the sort who did not have those special feelings for women?

A feeling of disgust swam through her, wondering if he favored male companionship in bed, over women. Were his plans to keep her for himself just so that Sun Eagle could not have and love her in the way that was normal between men and women?

Determined not to let this happen, that escape was vital to separate herself from any sort of life that Brown Bear had planned for her, Kiriki rose quietly to her feet.

Again, she paused long enough to look down at Brown Bear. He had not moved an inch. Still his breathing came slowly . . . shallowly. . . .

I must do it now! Kiriki thought desperately to herself.

She turned and moved stealthily around the sleeping cubs, then broke into a quiet run, her bare feet scarcely sounding on the pebbled floor of the cave. She could already feel the soft spraying mist of the waterfall as the night breeze blew it inside the mouth of the cave. She could see the rays of the moonlight that were silvering the water below as she inched her way out of the cave onto the small ledge that led behind the waterfall.

The ledge was slippery from the constant moisture, along with dampened, spongy moss that grew from the rocky shelf. Kiriki placed her back against the wall of rock behind her, and inched her way along until finally her feet made contact with solid ground.

Her pulse racing, Kiriki began to move through knee-high grass toward Brown Bear's horse, which was tethered to a tree closeby. She was only a heartbeat away from true escape! If Brown Bear's horse did not whinny as she mounted it, surely Brown Bear would sleep undisturbed until morning.

Kiriki grinned widely, envisioning his reaction when he awakened and found her gone. . . .

After reaching Brown Bear's proud stallion, Kiriki gained its confidence by smoothing a gentle hand along its muscled body, whispering sweetly into its ear. Then, when she felt that her friendly overtures had worked, she reached for the reins—

Suddenly her breath was knocked from her as she was tackled from behind and thrown to the ground. Already aching from the fall, Kiriki blinked her eyes nervously as she rolled slowly to lie on her back. A moccasined foot stamped down hard onto her stomach, pinioning her in place and making her feel as though she might retch from the pressure being put on her delicate, inner parts.

"Please . . ." she whispered harshly, coughing. She looked up into two slits of maddening eyes. "Brown Bear, don't. You . . . are . . . hurting me terribly!"

"That is good!" Brown Bear hissed, his teeth grinding together with a strange rasping noise as he spoke in anger down at Kiriki. "You try to escape from Brown Bear? That is unwise!"

"How could you expect me *not* to try?" Kiriki sobbed. "I hate you, Brown Bear. You are repulsive to me in every way!"

Brown Bear was taken aback by her venomousness. Strange, how it stung his heart. Yet surely it was because he wanted her to admire him as much as she admired Sun Eagle. No matter what his planned fate was for her, he did not want to think that he was repulsive to her, while in her eyes Sun Eagle was the epitome of man.

"You are a woman with a forked tongue!" he defended. "Did you not tell me that you would willingly be my wife if I went and warned Sun Eagle of your father's wrath? You lied! Even then you were planning your escape!"

"I doubt if you told Sun Eagle anything!" Kiriki cried, wincing when his foot became heavier, seeming to push clean through her stomach to her back. "He is probably even dead now! If so, Brown Bear, you will carry the burden of his death in your heart forever!"

Brown Bear laughed awkwardly, feeling uneasy about what she was saying. Could it be true? If Sun Eagle was dead, could it be something that Brown Bear would find hard to live with? Though jealous of Sun Eagle, it was true that guilt over a brother that was dead could be a much heavier burden to bear than jealousy of a brother who was alive.

Lifting his foot, Brown Bear reached down and grabbed Kiriki by the wrist. He yanked her to her feet and held her closely to him—so close that he could feel her heaving breasts against his bare chest and could smell her utter sweetness. If he could forget everything at this moment, perhaps he could prove that he was as skillful a lover as his brother. Perhaps he would not want to offer her as a sacrifice at all, and instead keep her as his woman.

Yet, that would require a physical battle with his brother, if indeed his brother was still alive. Never had Brown Bear won those sorts of battles with Sun Eagle, for he was much more muscled than Brown Bear!

But still, Brown Bear could not pass up the temptation to kiss Kiriki. His heart was thundering like a thousand horses set loose as he forced her lips to his mouth. An unfamiliar heat raged through him as he kissed her passionately, a hand wandering between their bodies to cup the magnificence of one of her breasts.

The moment was short-lived. Kiriki jerked a knee up quickly and smacked it into his groin. She fell backward with a jerk when Brown Bear set her free to cup his wounded mass of flesh within his hands. He danced around, yowling and groaning, reminding Kiriki of a jackrabbit that had just been shot.

Kiriki glanced quickly over at his horse, surely having been given a second chance to escape because of her quick thinking and cunning ways.

Making a mad dash toward the horse, she managed to grab its reins and mount it this time. But that was not enough. Brown Bear leapt onto the horse behind her, grabbed her by the hair and yanked her face around so that their eyes met.

From that point on, everything seemed to happen so quickly that Kiriki did not have the time to think or react. She was thrown to the ground. Her skirt was hiked up. She felt herself being violated and unable to stop it.

When Brown Bear's body lurched and spasmed into hers, she turned her eyes away, silvered with tears. . . .

Her whole body wracked with sobs, Kiriki was too weak to fight back when Brown Bear lifted her and carried her back inside the cave. Ashamed and filled with revulsion, she would not look at him as he secured her wrists and ankles again. She could feel his eyes branding her as he stood over her, then she winced when he touched her face gently.

"That was not part of the plan," he said, his voice breaking. "Never had I planned to defile your body. I must leave now. I have need to speak with Tirawa, the Supreme Power, about what I have done."

Kiriki looked slowly up at him. Tears continuing to flood her eyes, she spat at him. "One day you will pay for everything you have done to me," she hissed. "You will die for this, Brown Bear. You . . . will . . . die!"

Brown Bear felt that time was running out for him. He was not leaving Kiriki to go commune with Tirawa, but rather to go and see if Sun Eagle lay dead beneath the sky, or if he had been rescued and taken to their village. He had to see if the time was ripe for his arrival at the village with Kiriki.

Brown Bear did feel that he had overstepped the boundaries of what was right since he had chosen her for the Morning Star sacrifice, yet now, as each moment passed after having achieved the bliss of being with her in such an intimate way, he was glad that he had done it. Left alone now, she would have time to compare the brothers. Although she behaved as though his act had been vile, she had to have felt something while within his arms. All women who had shared lovemaking with him had always wanted to be with him again. Why would Kiriki be any different?

Shrugging, Brown Bear left the cave. When he mounted his horse, only then did his worries return to Sun Eagle. Sun Eagle was the only man who could stop his advance into the village with Kiriki.

"*If* Sun Eagle is alive," he whispered harshly, wheeling his horse around, riding away. "If he is, I won't allow his interference. This is my time of glory! Only mine!"

His mind filled with dark, resolute thoughts, he left the cave and his captor behind. He glanced up at the sky, searching for the morning star. . . .

Kiriki curled herself up into a fetal ball on her side, feeling degraded and empty. Lovemaking with Sun Eagle had been so wonderfully sweet! With Brown Bear, it was like being with the lowest of reptiles, the snake. If things ever worked out for her and Sun Eagle, so that they could be together again, could she ever forget the moments within Brown Bear's arms?

Could making love ever be sweet again?

Feeling a cold nose nudging her neck, Kiriki found one

of the cubs settling in beside her. She rolled over and snuggled against the cub, sobs engulfing her again.

Brown Bear had discovered that someone had freed Sun Eagle from his bondage at the stakes. Brown Bear was now being closely scrutinized as he entered his village on his mount, the village already stirring with early morning chores. Was he being watched because Sun Eagle had been brought to the village, weak and near death?

Or was it because no one knew of Sun Eagle's fate yet, and everyone was curious about Brown Bear's recent comings and goings?

Or had Kidibattsk confided in them, telling them that Brown Bear had been valiantly searching for his brother, and now that they saw Brown Bear entering the village alone they could not help but think the worst—that perhaps Sun Eagle was dead?

Soon all of his people would know *all* truths that would please them! They would be given cause to forget Sun Eagle when they discovered that Kiriki would be theirs! That she would be Tirawa's!

Dismounting outside his parents' earthen lodge, Brown Bear followed the scent of rabbit stew simmering over his mother's fire. The aroma of the wild onions that had been added to the stew was enticing, yet he had not come to share a meal with his parents. He had come to check on Sun Eagle—to see if he was in the village.

Guardedly, Brown Bear entered his parents' lodge and was met by his mother's sudden glance as she looked up and saw him standing there, broodingly watching her adding more vegetables to the stew.

Dropping the uncut carrots back inside the wicker basket that had been used to collect them from the garden, Kidibattsk rose quickly to her feet and rushed to Brown Bear. "My son," she murmured, embracing him. Then she stepped away from him, imploring him with her dark, wide eyes. "Sun Eagle? You have found him and brought him home? He is now in his dwelling?"

Relief flooded Brown Bear's senses, glad that Sun Eagle

was not there, yet his worry of where he was and with whom filled him with expectant wonder. The dark side of Brown Bear wanted his brother to be dead.

"No, I do not return to our village with Sun Eagle," Brown Bear said, clasping his hands to his mother's heavy shoulders. "Are you saying that he has not returned on his own?"

"Sun Eagle is not here," Kidibattsk said, her voice breaking. "And Sun Eagle is not with you?" She jerked free of her son's grip and put her back to him, holding her face with her hands. "Where can he be?"

"Mother, I have searched high and low for him, and I did not find him," Brown Bear lied, stepping around so that she would be forced to look at him. "Now what would you have me do?"

Kidibattsk wiped tears from her eyes and looked slowly up at Brown Bear. "Brown Bear, until now I was not all that concerned over Sun Eagle's welfare," she said hoarsely.

Brown Bear raised an eyebrow inquisitively. "Why now, if not earlier?" he asked.

"Because I thought Sun Eagle was with a woman," Kidibattsk said, choking on a sob that she tried to stifle in the depths of her throat. "I thought he was with the woman that was soon to be his wife."

Alarm distorted Brown Bear's face. "A wife . . . ?" he asked with a low gasp.

"He shared the secret with me, his mother," Kidibattsk said, turning from Brown Bear to go and sit down beside the fire. To busy her hands, she began cutting carrots into the stew again. "He had gone to this woman's village to offer a bride price." She looked up at Brown Bear. "It was a great bride price of many horses. I do not think the bride price would have been refused."

"This woman," Brown Bear asked guardedly, kneeling down on a knee beside his mother, "did he tell you her name? Do you know her by appearance, Mother?"

"Her name?" Kidibattsk repeated. "Her name is Kiriki." Kidibattsk picked up another carrot and began to dice it into the stew. "I would not know her if I saw her," she continued, her voice bland. "But I have heard many say that she is very beautiful."

She got a forlorn look in her eyes as she looked over at Brown Bear. "Of course any woman that Sun Eagle would choose would have to be beautiful as well as sensitive and sweet," she said softly. "For he is the kind of man who would deserve all of these qualities in a wife."

Jealousy stung Brown Bear's insides. He doubled a hand into a tight fist behind him, out of his mother's eyesight. "And this son who is with you now?" he said thickly. "Does this son deserve such a woman, also, for a wife?"

Kidibattsk reached a hand to Brown Bear's cheek and caressed it. "Yes, my son, even you, though many times you fill me with worry over the jealousy that eats away at your heart over your brother," she murmured. "But that will fade in time. You will one day be as genuinely sincere in all that you do as your older brother always is. Then I would like to see you bring a woman into our village for celebration. But for now, you still have some growing up to do."

Rage scorched Brown Bear's insides. Soon he would show his mother how wrong she was about him. It was *he* the Morning Star had spoken to in a vision. Not Sun Eagle! It was *he* who had chosen the most perfect sacrifice!

He smiled smugly to himself. His mother would not know Kiriki when he saw her enter the village. She knew her name, but that was all. Brown Bear would have to make sure that she knew nothing more of Kiriki until she was already dead!

Sun Eagle's absence, no matter the cause, was in Brown Bear's favor. He would seize this time to go and get Kiriki and bring her to his village, so that finally all could see her and share in the promise of the upcoming sacrifice. Soon he would be the greatest of all warriors in his people's eyes.

He looked tight-jawed at his mother. Even she would

finally have to accept that he was the greatest of her two sons.

Brown Bear bent and kissed his mother on the cheek. "I must leave," he said thickly. "I have my own personal life to tend to. Much has been neglected while searching for Sun Eagle."

Kidibattsk reached an eager hand toward Brown Bear. She grabbed his arm, delaying his escape. "If your duties take you away from the village, be gone not long, my son," she said, tears silvering her eyes. "With Sun Eagle gone, your nearness comforts me." She sniffed back her tears. "Your father says that he will give Sun Eagle another full day and night to arrive home safely before he goes and searches for him. It would humiliate Sun Eagle if he was searched for prematurely. It would show that neither your father nor his warriors had enough faith in Sun Eagle's ability to tend after his own welfare."

Brown Bear's lips curved into a slight grin, feeling confident now that everything was going his way. Everything! Even his mother was showing more affection for him. So much of what he did was to win her love—her admiration.

"I will be home soon, Mother," he said, easing her thick fingers from his arm, to draw her into his embrace. "You can depend on me. Always."

Kidibattsk smiled warmly at Brown Bear as she hugged him, then stepped away from him. "It is good to see your concern for your brother," she said, nodding. "It warms my heart, my son."

His eyes wavering, Brown Bear backed away from her then turned and fled from the dwelling. Sighing heavily, he took wide strides that took him to the Morning Star Priest's earthen lodge. His head bowed humbly, he entered. A voice deep and gravelly met his approach.

"*Lau*," the Morning Star Priest said in greeting. "I have been expecting you." He took Brown Bear gently by the arm and led him to the fire and urged him to sit down. "Now tell me all about this woman you have found for the sacrifice. You do plan to bring her to your people soon, do you not?"

Brown Bear was in awe of the priest's ability to read his thoughts. He swallowed hard. "Yes, I will bring her this evening," he said, nodding. "While I am gone to get her you can begin preparing our people for the arrival of the woman."

Brown Bear's mind strayed to the wonders of Kiriki's body as he had taken her sexually, hating now that he would actually never be able to be with her in such a way again.

But she would not be wasted. From now on, she was going to serve many more functions other than pleasing a man's hungry lusts.

"Tell me about her, my son," the priest said, placing a heavy hand on Brown Bear's shoulder. "Is she as lovely as other maidens of our past sacrifices?"

Brown Bear's eyes became clouded as he looked away from the priest. "She is the loveliest of them all," he said, unable to stop his voice from breaking. "She will please the Morning Star more than all past sacrifices."

The priest sighed heavily. "Then we shall be blessed with continuing bountiful crops until the Morning Star comes in a vision to another warrior in the future," he said, patting Brown Bear fondly. "You have proven that the Morning Star chose wisely this year. Go now. Return with the maiden. I am anxious to see her loveliness."

When Brown Bear rose to his feet and began moving humbly toward the door, he could feel the priest's eyes following him .

"Brown Bear, when you speak of this maiden, there is a measure of sadness in your voice," the priest said, rising to his feet. "Why is that? Are you being swayed by your brother? Are you also beginning to doubt the benefits of the sacrifice?"

Brown Bear turned and faced the priest. "How can you ask that?" he said. "Do I not willingly bring you a maiden that I see as the most beautiful of all? It would be easy, would it not, to keep her as my own, to be my wife, if I did not believe wholeheartedly in the Morning Star ritual?"

"That is so," the priest said, nodding. He patted Brown Bear on the shoulder. "Go, in peace and love. I shall take care of everything here."

Brown Bear left the priest's dwelling, feeling uneasy. It was not good that the Morning Star Priest showed signs of doubting him. Now it was more important than ever to get Kiriki here quickly, to set the Morning Star Priest's mind at rest, and even more important, his *own*.

Swinging himself up into his saddle, he paused for a moment to look at Sun Eagle's lodge.

He quirked an eyebrow. Where *was* his brother? Where? Was Sun Eagle even alive? . . .

Twelve

▼ ▼ ▼

THE cabin was filled with the tantalizing aroma of eggs, bacon and coffee, drawing Sun Eagle awake. He leaned up on an elbow and looked across the room. Carin was stooped before the massive fireplace, preparing the early morning meal. Her face was flushed from the heat of the fire; her apron with its gathered ruffles was worn over a high-necked, floor-length cotton dress, and her hair was drawn back from her face in its usual tight bun. Beneath her breath, she was humming a merry tune; contentment always seeming to radiate from her. Her son David was playing with building blocks at her side, a pleasant child of six, with blond curly hair that reached to his shoulders, and deep blue eyes.

Sun Eagle looked at the bedroom that was separate from the rest of the living quarters. He could hear Major O'Fallon stirring, rustling into his clothes. Sun Eagle was reminded of both the major's age and his wife's, and was glad for them that they, after many years of trying, had been given a child.

Sun Eagle's heart ached at the thought of perhaps not bearing any children with Kiriki now that misfortune had interrupted their courtship.

Where was she now? Would he ever see her again?

A raw sort of pain gnawed at his insides when he thought of Kiriki and that he was, at the moment, unable to go search for her. It was almost inconceivable that it had been her father who had stood in his way. He, Sun Eagle, would stop at nothing until she was found!

"I cannot wait any longer," he growled, his voice only barely audible. "I *must* go and find her. Today!"

Trembling from not having yet regained his strength, the raging temperature having almost totally debilitated him, Sun Eagle moved himself into a sitting position. His heart thundered wildly inside him as he took a deep, shaky breath before attempting to rise from the bed.

Having gulped in several swallows of air, he reached for a blanket and circled it around his waist, his bloody loincloth having been removed after being brought to the major's cabin.

Taking another deep swallow of air, he swung his legs over the side of the bed and placed his bare feet on the floor.

"Mercy be!" Carin said, turning with a start when she saw Sun Eagle's movements from the corner of her eye. She wiped her hands on her apron and rushed to the bed just as Sun Eagle attempted to place his full weight on his feet. . . .

Sun Eagle's head began swimming. His knees were so weak they buckled beneath him. He crumpled back onto the bed, breathing hard.

"Sun Eagle, why on earth can't you listen to me?" Carin fussed, wringing her hands nervously. "You're too weak to leave. You'll need at least one more day of rest and nourishment. Your wounds and your burned fingertips are healing quickly enough, but your body as a whole is healing much more slowly. You must remember that you had a scorching fever when you arrived at my doorstep. The fever has sapped you of your usual energies. Please be patient, Sun Eagle. Tomorrow will come soon enough."

"And even *then* he may be too weak to attempt mounting a horse," Major O'Fallon said as he walked from his bedroom, buckskins clean and fresh on his tall, lanky body. He smoothed his fingers through his brown hair, straightening it back from his face as he went and towered over his wife at Sun Eagle's bedside. "Sun Eagle, take my advice. Lie back down and let your body further heal itself before you do anything crazy like take off on your own.''

Not to be dissuaded, and with a silent audience, Sun Eagle once again swung his legs over the side of the bed and made a struggling attempt to stand. He swayed suddenly, the weakness grabbing him so violently that it felt as though someone had knocked the breath from him.

Strong arms caught him this time. He leaned against Major O'Fallon and let himself be lowered to the bed. It was evident that he could not stand even long enough to get to his horse.

A desperation seized Sun Eagle. Eyes wild, he grabbed the major's arm. ''My *arrus,* horse!'' he said, his voice weakened by his attempts to rise from the bed. ''Did they take . . . my . . . horse . . . ?''

Major O'Fallon eased Sun Eagle's hand from his arm and placed it on the bed as Carin removed the blanket from the Indian's body and drew it up over him. ''Your horse?'' he said, chuckling. ''Seems you trained him well, Sun Eagle. I don't know if Lone Chief and his warriors took it with them, but I *do* know that it's outside my cabin now, awaiting your recovery.''

Sun Eagle smiled, at least this one good piece of news was in his favor. ''My horse and I are as brothers,'' he said, then his smile faded, his comment causing him to think of his *true* brother. Something deep within Sun Eagle kept warning him that his brother did have a part in Kiriki's abduction and Durah's death. But he still did not want to think that his brother, his own flesh and blood, could so easily murder one lovely maiden just to steal another one away to spite his brother.

Major O'Fallon saw the change in Sun Eagle's mood. He knelt down on a knee beside the bed. ''Sun Eagle, what can I do to alleviate this torture you are going through within your heart?'' he asked. ''Though I am the Indian agent in these parts, I have not been given the power to intervene in personal problems among tribes. I am only here to make sure you have enough food, and that shelter is made available.''

He cleared his throat nervously. "I have gone beyond my boundaries at times, so perhaps I should now," Major O'Fallon continued. "But I would have to do so alone. I could not order the men under my command to go against rules set down from Washington. Only I could do this for you, Sun Eagle, and it would be done because of our special friendship."

Sun Eagle's eyes misted with grateful tears, so taken by the major's thoughtful nature. "It is kind of you to make such a generous offer to me, a Pawnee, but I cannot be the cause of you being forced to leave your post," he said, his voice drawn. "Too many Indians of all surrounding tribes depend on you. It would be selfish of me to ask that you risk it all for me, one Pawnee."

"You are not just a mere Pawnee," Major O'Fallon fussed. "In you, Sun Eagle, I see hope for the future of the Skidi. I know your feelings for the sacrifice that is so wrong. You want such practices banished! I want to work with you, to see that it is done."

Major O'Fallon swallowed hard. "But we must take this one step at a time," he said softly. "I must first see that you are well enough to travel again. Everything will fall into place after that."

He placed a firm hand on Sun Eagle's shoulder. "But now is now, and you are pining away for your woman," he said. "I will go and search each separate village for Kiriki. I will find her for you."

As badly as Sun Eagle wanted the major to do this for him, he still had to forbid it. The major's career would not be the only thing at risk. His life would be endangered. "My friend, I must again say that I thank you for your generous offer," he said, his jaw tight. "But it is my private affair. Soon, I will take care of it."

"If that is what you wish," Major O'Fallon said, taking a deep, shaky breath.

Sun Eagle nodded. "That is the way it must be," he said flatly. Closing his eyes, he fought back the urge to cry out to the major to go and find Kiriki.

Yet, still Sun Eagle could not go himself. He could not! Whatever was to be, would be.

The lowering sun was casting rivulets of light into the entrance of the cave, shimmering as it lay across Kiriki's sleeping form. Brown Bear stepped lightly into the cave and knelt down to caress the fur of one of the cubs that had bounded toward him, then rested at his feet. Brown Bear noticed the other cub curled up next to Kiriki, causing a melancholia of sorts to move through him. Though he had been forced to kill the mother cub, and had even kicked one of the cubs to show that he was not a weak, soft-hearted man, he had much feelings for these special animals. The Pawnee looked to bears in reverence, as though gods themselves. They were only killed when it became necessary.

Was he not even of their namesake? Only moments after he had given birth, he had looked upon a brown bear. So then had he been given his name.

And there was Kiriki lying asleep so soundly, so beautifully. Never would he forget the moments of lovemaking with her, even though she had not participated. It was the memory of how she had felt in his arms that would sustain him through the night after she was sacrificed. Never would he find another woman who would feel as good— as natural—within his embrace.

But he could not keep her as his own. Either way, dead or alive, she would never be his. Either she would be Sun Eagle's or Tirawa's!

"Better it be Tirawa!" he whispered harshly to himself.

He gently shoved the cub away from him and rose to his full height, still watching Kiriki sleep. On his journey here from his village he had adopted a plan within his mind that could possibly work—a plan that would get Kiriki to his village without the use of force. If he was skillful enough at lying to her, he would be entering his village triumphantly.

And it had to be now. Sun Eagle was missing.

But who was to say for how long? Sun Eagle seemed

to be kin to the cat family. He always came through scrape after scrape as though he had nine lives!

Going to Kiriki, Brown Bear nudged the cub aside, eliciting a low, tiny growl from the depths of his throat. He began loosening the tied strips of leather at Kiriki's wrists, all the while watching her face as her eyelids began to flutter open.

Kiriki jerked with a start when she saw Brown Bear sitting so close, observing her. Then she looked down at what he was doing and became suddenly afraid. Pale, she silently implored him with her wide, fearful eyes.

"Why are you untying me?" she asked, her voice quavering, expecting to be raped again by him.

"I have just returned from my village and have spoken with my mother about you," Brown Bear said, telling a half-truth. "She revealed to me how much she wanted you to be a part of our family."

He feigned an awkwardness by looking down, away from her. "But it is Sun Eagle she wishes to be your husband," he said humbly.

Slowly he raised his eyes back to hers. "My father also voices this wish," he said, drawing one of the leather strips away from her wrists. "So be it, Kiriki. My parents' desires always come before my own."

Kiriki raised an eyebrow, finding it hard to believe that Brown Bear would put anyone's wishes ahead of his own, even his parents. He had not slain sweet Durah to get Kiriki to himself only to give her up so easily.

No. Something did not ring true here. But how could she prove it but to go along with whatever he said or did? With her hands free, she could at least hope to be given the chance to escape again.

"So what are your plans for me?" she asked guardedly, as he moved to her ankles and began untying the bonds there.

"My parents have asked that I bring you to their village where preparations are even now being readied for your marriage to Sun Eagle," Brown Bear said, the lie so easy on his lips.

"If that is so, why did not Sun Eagle come, himself, for me?" Kiriki asked, watching him cynically. "If I am to be his wife, how will you explain what has happened here? How it was that you abducted and raped me, and that you even killed my very best friend!"

"I was wrong to do all of those things, and I have vowed to make it all up to Sun Eagle and Durah's parents," Brown Bear said solemnly. "Sun Eagle is showing trust and giving me the chance to show that I will keep my word by letting me come for you, to bring you to our village for the ceremony, while he readies himself for the ceremony by spending time in silent meditation and sweat baths."

"So he does know everything?" Kiriki asked, slowly beginning to see how what he said could be true. "He is all right? He was not harmed by my father? Sun Eagle is waiting for me at your village? We will be married soon?"

"As soon as the village celebration is organized," Brown Bear said, nodding. "You see, you are going to be wed to a noble warrior! The celebration must be grand, to fit his greatness!"

He smiled down at her. "Soon you will see," he said. "Soon you will be readied by the women of my village to be made beautiful for Sun Eagle, so that you will be pleasing in his eyes when you meet with him before my people to pledge your love forever with marriage vows."

"If only it could have been achieved without the loss of my friend's life," Kiriki murmured, casting her eyes downward, trying not to envision in her mind's eye the last moments of Durah's life. Could she ever forget the blood? The utter stillness of her friend when she had fallen to the ground, dead? It was a death she would never be able to forget, or accept. "And if only you had not violated my body. . . ."

"Both acts were unfortunate," Brown Bear said, nodding. "And I will make it up to you by being a most pleasant brother-in-law. Whatever you wish in life, I will see to it that you have. I will forever be in your debt, Kiriki, if you forgive me of my hideous acts of murder,

rape, and abduction. Had I known my parents' strong wish
that you become my brother's wife, I would have never
interfered!''

He looked deeply into her eyes. "You see, you do not
know how beautiful you are, and the effect that you have
on a man," he said, swallowing hard as he ached to have
her again, to taste of the forbidden fruit at least one more
time before giving her away forever. "Most men would
kill to have you. I am performing a great act of sacrifice
by giving you up to my brother."

Kiriki watched as her bonds were loosened. She eyed
the knife sheathed at Brown Bear's waist. If she only
knew if he were lying! In only a matter of moments she
could grab his knife and sink it into his black heart!

But she could not recognize a lie on his lips any more
than she could the truth, and could not take the chance
that he was not being sincere. Sun Eagle *could* be awaiting
her arrival. She *could* become his wife soon.

She had to take the chance with Brown Bear—that he
was telling the truth.

As Brown Bear continued loosening her bonds, his hand
grazed against the flesh of her ankle, causing a slow fire
to begin in his loins. He truly understood Sun Eagle's
infatuation with Kiriki. Brown Bear, himself, wanted her
so much that he could barely resist.

His jaw tightened and he pursed his lips together in a
straight, hard line. The art of restraint must be practiced
now more than ever before in his life. How easy it would
be to take Kiriki as his woman at least one more time
before giving her up for the Morning Star sacrifice.

Yes, easy! But wrong.

Thus far his scheme was working. Kiriki was being
drawn into his plan. Just a few more lies and he would
have won something more valuable than Sun Eagle ever
had, or ever would have.

That is, if Sun Eagle was even still alive. While staked
to the ground, he had looked dead.

Yes, Sun Eagle could be dead, and Brown Bear would
then have it *all!* The blessing of the Morning Star, the

admiration of the Skidi as a whole, the wonderment that he would see in his parents' eyes, finally realizing his worth!

He had waited so long for the latter. . . .

"There is one thing," Brown Bear said, drawing the last of the leather strips away from her. "When we arrive at our village it is a ritual of my people before a wedding ceremony that there is no conversation between the bride and the wedding party who will be preparing you for the wedding. It is all done in silent reverence. And you will not see Sun Eagle before the wedding. It is said that it causes an unhappy marriage if husband and wife see each other just prior to the ceremony. Do you understand all of this, Kiriki? It is important that you do."

Kiriki screwed her face up into a frown, finding these practices much different from those in her village, yet she knew that there were many differences between their two factions of Pawnee.

She would never forget how Durah had described the Morning Star ritual. . . .

Her eyes widened and her mouth went suddenly dry with the thought that she had fought against time and time again, fearing to lose her sanity if she let herself think it could be true. Could Brown Bear actually be readying her for a marriage to the Morning Star instead of to Sun Eagle?

Yet, surely his mother would not allow it! Sun Eagle had told his mother of Kiriki and of his love for her. His mother had even given Sun Eagle the special gift necklace to give to Kiriki, a gift she would not give unless from the heart.

No! Kiriki would not be foolish enough to fear something that surely would never be. She would make herself believe that she would soon be seeing Sun Eagle again. She would even be his wife!

Moving shakily to her feet, Kiriki looked up at Brown Bear with a proudly lifted chin. "Take me to Sun Eagle," she said. "I am ready to become his wife."

"And how do you feel about me, Kiriki?" Brown Bear

dared to ask. "Can you find it in your heart to forgive me for all the wrongs that I have recently done?"

"If Sun Eagle forgives you, then so shall I," Kiriki said, rubbing her raw wrists. "Perhaps one day I shall, Brown Bear, but not now. The death of Durah lies too fresh on my mind. The vile rape still stings my heart!" Her eyes began to flash as she looked up into Brown Bear's face. "Did you admit the rape to your brother?"

Brown Bear's eyes wavered, then he squared his shoulders. "I could not tell him that," he said, his voice breaking. "Had I, he never would have let me come near you again, and it was important for me to come and release you of your bondages, for in doing so it will prove much to my brother. I implore you not to tell my brother, Kiriki. It is done. It is behind us. Soon you will forget it."

His eyes lowered. "But never shall I!" he said, torment evident in his voice. "Even now I want you, Kiriki! Even now!"

An uneasiness grabbed Kiriki's insides, remembering how hungry he had been for her when he had raped her. It seemed that his hunger was no less now, even though he had made promises to his parents in order to win favor in their eyes. "You say that Sun Eagle is preparing for the marriage rites. Then let us leave now, Brown Bear, to go to him," Kiriki encouraged, inching toward the cave entrance. "I promise that I won't tell Sun Eagle that you raped me. It will be our secret, Brown Bear—yours and mine alone. I want you and Sun Eagle to be friends, not the bitterest of enemies, which you would be should he know that you defiled my body."

"That is what I want also," Brown Bear said eagerly. He glanced down at the cubs as they scampered after Kiriki. He looked up at her, seeing how pleased she was over their attentiveness to her. The cubs could be a way to appease Kiriki while they traveled to the village. The cubs would give her entertainment enough to keep her mind off any doubts that might suddenly seize her. It was imperative that she continue believing in him! Even up to that

moment when she would be placed in bonds as the sacrifice, she must believe in him totally!

"The cubs have found a second mother," Brown Bear
said, forcing his voice into a teasing fashion. "They can
go with you, Kiriki. Once at the village they will be placed
inside a pen until after the ceremony. Then you can do
with them what you wish."

"For awhile I will look after them, then Sun Eagle and
I will return them to the forest after they are old enough
to fend for themselves," Kiriki said, bending to pet one,
and then the other cub. She nuzzled her nose into the
depths of the cubs' fur. "It shall be hard to part with
them, ever, but when I do it will be for their own good."

"And yours, also," Brown Bear said, chuckling.
"Soon the cubs will be the size of their mother. I would
not think it best to sleep cuddled up next to a bear that is
twice your size."

For the first time since her abduction, Kiriki felt light-
hearted enough to laugh. "No, I don't think that would
be too wise," she giggled. "Once they are grown, the
cubs will surely see me in a different light."

"Perhaps as their dinner?" Brown Bear further teased.
He reached for Kiriki's hand and held it gently. "Let us
go. Much excitement—more than sharing laughter over
cubs—awaits you, beautiful Kiriki. There will be much
dancing and celebration. You will be adored. Adored!"

A sweet sort of peace soared through Kiriki at the
thought of finally being with Sun Eagle again. If only
Durah were alive to realize that her best friend's dreams
had been fulfilled. That would make everything, oh, just
too perfect!

Laughing as the cubs romped along after her, even man-
aging to maneuver themselves along the slippery rock that
stretched narrowly out behind the thundering splash of the
waterfall, Kiriki was for the moment able to forget the
recent unhappy ordeals of her life. All that lay ahead of
her now was a promise of all tomorrows—tomorrows
spent with the man she loved!

She let Brown Bear help her onto his horse, even wel-

comed his arm around her waist as he mounted behind
her. The wind lifted her hair from her shoulders as the
stallion began to ride through the forest at an easy canter,
the bears tumbling sometimes head over heels in their
clumsiness after it.

Kiriki could not help but hope that perhaps the best of
times was only a few heartbeats away.

Thirteen

ANXIOUSNESS to see Sun Eagle turned quickly to apprehension when Kiriki entered Sun Eagle's village on the horse with Brown Bear. Oddly enough, it seemed that the whole village had turned out to meet her—men, women, and children alike. There was a look of profound reverence on everyone's faces as they peered in wonder at her, as though she were a goddess!

Intimidated by this unexpected behavior toward her, Kiriki's eyes raked over the crowd, looking for one face in particular.

Sun Eagle's.

Though Brown Bear had warned her that she would not see Sun Eagle until they were ready to exchange their vows, she could not fathom him staying hidden somewhere while she was entering his village.

It was *their* moment, not his people's. Surely he wanted to take at least a glimpse of her. Soon they would be man and wife and could map out a future of togetherness.

Though it had been hard at first, Kiriki had been able to place all dreams of living in the white world behind her. Sun Eagle was now her dream. Only he!

The crowd parted as Brown Bear rode further into the village. His arm tightened around Kiriki's waist, showing a possession that puzzled her. She was not entering the village to become *his* wife. Why was he acting as though he were a hero, bringing home a trophy of war? The people were even looking at him as though he were something special!

But why? In truth, he was a murderer. An abductor. A

rapist! How could anyone ever look to Brown Bear with anything but contempt?

Yet little did they know all truths about Brown Bear, and Kiriki doubted if they ever would. For now, he was bringing his brother's woman to him so that a wedding could take place. Surely her treatment was because she was marrying the man who would one day be their chief.

Yes, that must be the answer to how everyone was reacting to her arrival today. Had not Brown Bear warned her that there would be a great celebration? She had to relax and enjoy these moments that would lead to finally seeing Sun Eagle again and being held within his powerful arms while he whispered words of love to her. . . .

Kiriki looked questioningly over her shoulder at Brown Bear as he drew rein before a great earthen lodge—a lodge highly decorated with symbols on the outside—a lodge that lay in the center of the village, close to the chief's own large earthen dwelling.

"Do not question anything that is to happen," Brown Bear said, dismounting, lifting his arms to her to help her from his steed. "Just remember that everything required of you is another step that will lead you closer to the moment of your marriage."

Stepping lightly to the ground, Kiriki straightened her buckskin skirt around her slender figure. She stared up at Brown Bear. "You puzzle me so!" she whispered. "First you show hate for your brother, even condemn him with every breath that you take, and now you act as though you would even die for him. How can I believe this, Brown Bear? How?"

Brown Bear touched her face gently. She was the captured maid for the Morning Star ritual and must be treated with utmost courtesy and kindness. Not a whisper of the approaching ordeal must she hear from anyone. It was the sole aim of Brown Bear, and everyone else that came in contact with her now, to keep her in ignorance of the ritual and to lull any fears or suspicions she might have.

"My mother shamed me into realizing that I could not keep you for my own when my brother had already planned to marry you," he said quietly. "He is the eldest. He will one day be chief. I must learn to respect that. From this day forth, I will not waver in my dedication to my brother. If I do not show total loyalty to my brother, the next chief-in-line, I may one day be banished from my people! I cannot let that happen." He paused, then smiled slowly. "Not even for you can I let that happen. I will take another woman as my wife—one that will be rightly mine, not my brother's."

Kiriki sighed resolutely. "I so want to believe you," she said softly. "And I guess I have no choice but to." Her eyes darted around again, in search of Sun Eagle. "But I would feel much better about things if Sun Eagle would make himself known to me."

"I have explained—" Brown Bear began, but was interrupted by Kiriki.

"Yes, I know," she said, sighing again. "Sun Eagle is readying himself for the marriage by sweat baths and communing with Tirawa, the Supreme Power."

"You will not see him until the moments just prior to the marriage," Brown Bear said, taking her by the arm and walking her toward the entrance of the highly decorated lodge. "Let us now proceed." He glanced down at her. "Remember, Kiriki, do not question anything that happens. It is required. All of it."

Kiriki still could not shake her doubts, for every so often she would remember Durah's tale of the Morning Star ritual. Brown Bear would become great in his people's eyes if he offered such a sacrifice.

But surely he would not offer his own brother's woman. How could he, except that his hate for Sun Eagle could be this intense?

A chill coursed through her, not wanting to think such morbid thoughts.

No brother could hate a brother that much. Never!

"We will now go and meet with the priest who will perform the marriage ceremony," Brown Bear said, again walking Kiriki toward the door. "It is I who will present you to him. It is I who will win favors for this."

Kiriki gave him another quick, wondering glance, then tried to keep calm under the circumstances of the Skidi, letting Brown Bear take her into the priest's dwelling.

Once inside, she found herself alone with a small man whose gray beard almost grazed the floor. He was dressed in a loose robe, and rose from beside an altar to come to her, his face solemn.

"This is Kiriki," Brown Bear said, nodding toward her. "She has come to wed our people's hero. She is prepared to participate willingly in the various rituals. I have told her that her groom awaits the ceremony with an anxious heart."

The Morning Star Priest looked up at Brown Bear, and within his eyes was a strange sort of torment that Kiriki could not help but be aware of.

But be as that may, she knew to not question a man of religion. A priest could be trusted implicitly.

"That is good," the Morning Star Priest said, taking Kiriki's hand. "Come. We will begin. What must be done here will take only a moment, then you will join many of our village's maidens who will be at your beck and call. Though instructed not to converse with you, you may tell them what you wish, and if at all possible, it will be yours."

Kiriki felt somewhat better after hearing his generosity. She smiled warmly at him. "I am sure I will have need to ask for nothing," she murmured.

She wanted to add, *except for Sun Eagle*. Oh, how badly she wanted to ask to see him. Yet she knew that was forbidden, and would have to learn the art of patience quite well in these next several hours.

The sleeve of the priest's thick, heavy robe slipped up past his wrist as he placed a hand to Kiriki's arm and led her away from Brown Bear. "You will stand here beside the fire," he said, his voice now filled with more command than kindness. "I am going to make smoke from buffalo fat mixed with sweetgrass. The smoke will pass over you, purifying you for the ceremony that awaits you. In a sense, this is the beginning of the ceremony. Be

happy, my child, for you have been chosen from among
hundreds of lovely women to wed the Skidi's favored
hero."

Again an uneasiness swam through Kiriki. She did not
like the way both Brown Bear and the priest kept referring
to Sun Eagle as their "hero." It was true that he was a
special Pawnee who would one day be their chief, but had
he achieved a heroic deed of which she was not aware?
He was the epitome of man, in that he was a man of great
strength and ability. Surely *that* was the reason they made
reference to him as a "hero."

Yet were not all villages filled with warriors who were
also strong and courageous? Why was Sun Eagle singled
out to be celebrated in such a way?

Except that he was one day to be their chief. Yes, that
had to be the answer!

Forcing all of her troubled thoughts aside, Kiriki held
her chin proudly high and watched the priest stir buffalo
fat into a vat of sweetgrass. Soon smoke billowed up into
the air. The priest began fanning the smoke with his hand
in the direction of Kiriki, causing it to pass over her. Then
the priest went to Kiriki and held his hands in the smoke
again and passed his hands over her.

"It is done," the priest said. He walked away from
Kiriki and knelt down onto the floor and searched with
his hands through a large bundle. Taking from it a dress,
he handed it toward Kiriki. "After you are taken to the
dwelling in which you will stay until the ceremony,
change into this dress. It is a special dress, for a special
woman."

Kiriki let him lay the dress across her outstretched arms.
"Thank you," she murmured.

She gazed down at the garment. It was made of a calf-
skin hide, white-colored from having been sprinkled with
white clay on the skin while it had been stretched. It would
come to just below her knees. The waist would be folded
up, and a buffalo-hair rope would be wound tightly around
her waist to hold her skirt in. It was decorated beautifully
with many colored beads.

She looked up quickly when the priest placed a little soft down feather on top of her head in the folds of her hair, then stepped away from her, his head bowed.

"Now you will go," he said solemnly. "The maidens assigned to you will be waiting outside. Go with them. Rejoice in what is happening here. Everyone rejoices with you."

"Thank you," Kiriki said, humbly taking steps backward toward the door. She glanced up at Brown Bear when she passed by him, then was relieved when she stepped outside the dwelling. Several giggling young women surrounded her. One took her hand and led her through the throng of people who still gawked silently at her. When they finally reached a smaller earthen lodge, she walked inside and was greeted with vase after vase of wild flowers positioned around the small cubicle of a room, and bowls heaped with all sorts of food.

She was taken aback by this, never having expected to be treated this grandly. She went from vase to vase, touching the flowers, then the same girl that had led her from the priest's lodge took the dress from her arms. Another began undressing her, soon tossing her normal clothing aside and then replacing it with the wedding garment. The pink necklace drew much interest. Kiriki covered it with her hand, never wanting to part with it. To her at this moment, it *was* Sun Eagle. It was as though he were there, touching her where the necklace lay so close to her heart.

"No," she said, shaking her head at the girls. "You can't remove the necklace."

One of the women gave her a stern look, her eyes flashing haughtily, then very determinedly removed the necklace and placed it on the floor with the rest of Kiriki's discarded garments.

Kiriki stomped very determinedly to where the necklace lay and started to reach for it, but was stopped when another one of the women stood in her way, shaking her head, while her hands were placed stubbornly on her hips.

"I don't see why I can't wear the necklace," Kiriki

fussed. "It was a gift from Sun Eagle to me. His mother gave it to him for my special gift." She looked angrily from woman to woman. "Where is his mother? She will tell you that I should be able to continue wearing it."

Kiriki's breath was stolen away when she saw the women looking guardedly from one to the other, then they all smiled at her again and she was taken by the hand and led to a pallet of furs on the floor beside the fire.

"All right, if I can't wear it now, I will later, after the ceremony," Kiriki fussed, her lips pursed angrily, wondering why the priest had told her that whatever she asked for, she could have, when it was obvious that these women were not ready to totally please her.

With her eyes, she questioned the women who sat down around here, but knew that it would be futile to question them. She could tell that all of them were following the command of silence.

But, oh, it was going to be so hard for Kiriki not to continue speaking or be able to stand not to be spoken to! She was filled with so much anticipation bubbling over inside her. Surely these women knew where Sun Eagle was keeping himself! If only Kiriki could sneak out and find him and draw comfort from his arms. He could wash all doubts from her mind with only one kiss!

Comfortably positioning herself on the pallet, Kiriki accepted a tray of fruit. She popped a grape into her mouth, again looking from woman to woman.

"Surely one of you will tell me where Sun Eagle is," Kiriki said, moving to her knees, looking one woman in the eye, and then another. "If I can see him for only just a *moment!* It isn't fair that we are forced to stay apart. Please? Will one of you break your silence just this one time and tell me where he is? Will one of you take me to him? Please?"

Exchanged looks of confusion made an iciness steal through Kiriki. Why was the mention of Sun Eagle, even his mother, causing such a reaction? It was as though they did not comprehend what she was saying!

Dread began to fill Kiriki. She inched away from the silent women and pushed the tray of fruit away from her. Suddenly she was not hungry. She was afraid.

The Morning Star Priest embraced Brown Bear. "She is all that you said she would be," he said. "The Morning Star will be pleased."

The priest stepped away from Brown Bear, his dark eyes weary. "No one but you and I know of her relationship with Sun Eagle," he said, his voice drawn. "Your mother knows of Sun Eagle's love for Kiriki, but only knows her by the mention of her name. She has never seen her? Is that not right?"

"That is so," Brown Bear said, nodding.

"Much care has been taken that your mother does not know that the sacrifice's name is Kiriki," the priest said, settling down onto a pallet of fur before the fire. "Your mother will not be allowed to visit her, either. But that is not a difficult thing to explain. Most women, except those assigned, do not meet with the captured maiden."

"My mother, the wife of my father, Chief Antelope Buck, will not disobey the rules handed down by our ancestors," Brown Bear said. "But she is most anxious to have a daughter. When she discovers that one has been stolen from her, as well as her elder son's woman, she will be devastated! She may never claim me as her son again!"

"You must choose now which you want out of life, Brown Bear," the priest said, looking up at Brown Bear with guarded eyes. "Recognition and acclaim for being the Morning Star's chosen one, or the need to have a mother's pamperings as though you were still a whimpering child!" He paused and leaned forward, resting his hands on his knees. "Which is it to be?"

"I have already made my choice," Brown Bear said, his jaw tight.

"Then, dreamer of the Morning Star, continue with your assigned duties," the priest flatly ordered. "Send for

a man descended from the Wolf bundle keeper. A heredi-
tary office, it is his duty to guard the captive.''

"That I will do," Brown Bear said, nodding.

"Then you must go and kill a buffalo for the ceremony,
choose the location of the place of sacrifice, and build the
scaffolding," the priest added. "Then it will be time for
the ceremony."

Brown Bear's eyes wavered. "This must all be done in
haste," he said. "I do not know where Sun Eagle is, or
when he might return. We must not take the usual time
that is taken for the ceremony. We must make the sacrifice
tonight!"

"It will be up to you, Brown Bear," the priest said,
frowning up at him. "Kill a buffalo and bring it to me,
build the scaffolding with chosen friends to aid you, then
I will tell our people that it is time for the sacrifice!"

"It will all be done by tonight," Brown Bear con-
firmed, squaring his shoulders. He was recalling a herd of
buffalo that he had seen on his approach to the village.
They had been grazing on rich grass only a short distance
away.

He had already chosen a place of sacrifice. It would be
located on a high, level spot among a number of rough
ravines. The altar could be seen there for many miles
around, and the various stages of the death of the maiden
would be plain to the many watching eyes of the assembled Skidi Pawnee.

A thrill swept through him at being so near the time of
total recognition from his people!

"Before you go to hunt for the buffalo you must first
anoint yourself with red ointment," the priest said, rising
to go to a bundle that lay near his altar. He removed a
small buckskin pouch and handed it to Brown Bear. He
watched Brown Bear sink his fingers into the red ointment,
coloring his whole body except for where his loincloth
covered his private parts.

"It is done," Brown Bear said, then accepted some
special eagle feathers from the priest in order to decorate
the mane and tail of his horse.

Turning, he left the priest's lodge and eagerly decorated his horse, then mounted him. He looked proudly around himself—at the feast and celebration that was filling his village with much laughter and dancing. Many drums, nearly two feet in diameter and made of tanned hide stretched over bent saplings, were beating to the rhythm of feet pounding the earth in a frenzy of dancing.

For music other than drums and rattles, the Pawnee were clapping their hands and shouting *"Ki-ya! Ki-ya!"*

There were songs of rejoicing and thanksgiving. Before riding away, Brown Bear joined in to sing one of the rejoicing songs. His voice was deep and gravelly as he sang:

> *"Nawa Atuis*
>   Now, O Father
> *Iri ta-titska*
>   Our thanks be unto thee,
> *Iri-asuta-hawa*
>   Our thanks! Renew our plenty!
> *Iri-rurahe!*
>   Our thanks!
>   Renew these tiny gifts to us!"*

Filled with much enthusiasm, Brown Bear took a final look at the people, adults and children alike, dancing around in rhythmic movements. Then he rode away, hearing the chants and music following along after him. It was now that he *knew* that what he was doing was right. His people were happy! They saw the promise of all tomorrows because of the sacrifice that would be offered to the Morning Star!

"And all of this is because of Brown Bear!" he shouted, his voice echoing back to him.

He rode across the fertile land, into the river valley, then drew his steed to a quivering halt when the herd of buffalo came into view. There was one straggler that had separated itself from the rest. It was quite a fat cow, the best for the offering to the Morning Star.

He took his arrow and notched it onto his bow. Just before he shot it, he shouted to the heavens, "It is consecrated to the big star!"

Sun Eagle awakened from a fearful dream, perspiration soaking his flesh. He rose quickly to a sitting position and looked across the room. Neither Carin, David, nor Roger were there. They were surely outside tending to their cattle, or working in their garden.

Sun Eagle lowered his face within his hands, cradling it, unable to get the fretful dream out of his mind. It had been about his beloved Kiriki. In it, he was seeing her lithe body filled with many arrows!

"That means only one thing!" Sun Eagle groaned, gritting his teeth. "I was sent a dream of what is to be if I do not stop it. Now I know why Kiriki was abducted! She is to be the Skidi sacrifice to the Morning Star. Tirawa, who is in and of everything, does not approve and has warned me in my dream!"

His head spinning as he rose from the bed, Sun Eagle fought his weakness. He dropped the blanket away from himself and reached for his loincloth. Hardly able to stand, he finally managed to get the loincloth in place.

Then, forcing himself to take one step after another, no matter how his head was beginning to swim again, he finally reached the door. Stepping out into the sunshine, he shielded his eyes with the back of a hand, then smiled when he discovered his dutiful gelding tethered only a short distance away.

His feet shuffling, his body seemingly heavy, Sun Eagle finally managed to mount his steed. Taking the reins, leaning down to hug his arms around his horse's strong neck for support, he ignored Carin and Roger's shouts of complaint as he swung his gelding around and began to ride away.

"This I must do!" he shouted back. "It has to be now or never!"

Clinging with all of his might to his black gelding, Sun Eagle directed his attention straight ahead. He had to move steadily onward, for it would not be long before the morning star would appear in the heavens.

And at that moment in time, Kiriki could be taking her last breath.

The buffalo was shot and skinned. Brown Bear spread the hide on the back of his stallion, then put the meat on the horse, placing the forelegs with the feet upward in front, at the shoulders of the horse, then arranging the buffalo hindquarters with the feet upward, at the horse's rump. He was then ready to lead his horse into his village. The people would know that the meat was to be prepared for the human sacrificial ceremony. . . .

Left alone except for two women, Kiriki glanced over at her discarded clothes. This was perhaps her only chance to confiscate her necklace. She was determined to wear it to her wedding ceremony. Sun Eagle would want her to.

Scooting toward the clothes, Kiriki was glad that the women were too occupied looking out the door at the excitement to notice what she was doing. When she reached her clothes, she lifted them up and grew cold inside. Her necklace was gone! One of the women had taken it not only from her, but also away from the lodge. And she knew that demanding its return was useless.

Anger flashing in her eyes, she decided that now was not the time to argue for the return of her necklace. But after the wedding to Sun Eagle, if indeed there was to be a wedding, he would find the one who had taken her precious gift. It would be returned to her and the one responsible for the theft punished.

She scooted back close to the fire, suddenly chilled, for the excitement outside seemed more than what was normal for a marriage ceremony.

Everyone seemed crazed!

Yet there was no way for her to escape to see the true cause of the celebration. Her thoughts went out to Sun Eagle's mother. Oh, where was she? Perhaps she could explain all of this to Kiriki, her soon to be daughter. . . .

Fourteen

▼ ▼ ▼

TORN with conflicting emotions, everything too peculiar for her liking, Kiriki was tense as she was being prepared for the wedding ceremony. She had never observed a ceremony such as this before—a ceremony celebrating the wedding of the next chief-in-line. In her village there had never been cause for such a celebration. Since she had been born, her father had been the chief of his people, and since he did not have a son, there would never be such a ceremony in her village.

Soon cousins would be looked over carefully, a favored one to be designated as the reigning chief once Kiriki's father had parted to the hereafter. A mere cousin would never have the attention of a true next chief-in-line!

Standing nude, Kiriki tried to separate herself from what was happening to her, embarrassed that others were seeing her undressed. She was letting her body be painted freely, for at least she *did* know that women of her village were painted thusly before their wedding. It was a custom of the Pawnee to paint their women freely as an ornamentation, especially on the face and breasts.

She sucked in her breath when the cold wet bristles of a small brush were used to stroke soft colors of yellow in a circle around one breast and then the other. She blushed when the coldness caused her nipples to tighten and stand out more erect, as though a man's tongue were there, pleasuring her.

The women's giggles embarrassed her anew and she was glad when they finally slipped the lovely white dress over her head, giving her the privacy that she desired.

The drumbeats outside increased into a maddening tempo. Singing and shouting penetrated the walls of the earthen lodge, echoing and vibrating all around Kiriki. Her heart began to pound in the same frenzied rhythm, fear building within her.

To soften her fear, she kept concentrating on Sun Eagle and his sweetness.

He *had* to be the cause of this celebration. He *had* to. . . .

Her hair was now being weaved into two long braids, the part in her hair being daubed with fresh red paint, and Kiriki had the strong urge to flee.

But she knew that she could not. She had seen a massive Pawnee warrior guarding the dwelling just outside the door.

This, alone, gave Kiriki cause to believe that she had been lied to. If she was being readied for a marriage to Sun Eagle—he whom she loved with all of her heart— why would they have the need to guard her like a prisoner?

Anger filled her eyes and heart. Brown Bear! He was the one responsible for however this day turned out.

Kiriki became suddenly aware that there were more shadows in the lodge. She looked up at the smoke hole and emitted a quiet gasp when she saw that the sky was lightening in color. Soon it would be morning! Soon the morning star would appear bright and beautiful in the sky!

Kiriki looked quickly away, closing her eyes. This morning could be the last time that she would ever see the morning star. If her fears were founded, in the eyes of the Skidi, she would be wed to it!

There was suddenly a commotion at the door. Kiriki opened her eyes and swung around just in time to see one of the bear cubs rush inside. Her eyes lit up as the cub went to her and plopped down at her feet, seemingly contented.

When a Pawnee brave followed closely behind, Kiriki knelt low and wrapped her arms protectively around the cub.

"Leave it alone," she said, her voice quavering. "At

least give me this to enjoy before . . . before the
ceremony.''

"He broke free from the cage we placed him in," the
brave said, looking humbly down at Kiriki, as though she
were someone revered. "I must take him back. Soon it
will be time for the ceremony."

Kiriki kept her arms locked around the cub, warming
inside when his tongue leapt out and began licking her
hand. "Leave him be!" she cried.

Then she blanched, wondering about the welfare of the
other cub. "Where is the other cub?" she dared to ask.
"Surely it broke free, also."

The brave looked down and locked his gaze onto his
moccasined feet. "One of the young boys who were
readying their arrows for the celebration shot the cub,"
he said thickly. "It died instantly."

A sickness swept over Kiriki. She swallowed hard, tears
hot in her eyes. "The cub was so sweet," she said, her
voice breaking.

Again she defied the brave with her eyes. "I cannot ask
that this cub be left with me now, for once I leave the
dwelling, there would be no one to care for it," she said
firmly.

She squared her shoulders angrily. "It would be shot
by a child also, no doubt!" she hissed.

Releasing her hold, she pushed the cub toward the
brave. "Take him but see to it that he is protected," she
said, her voice mellowing. "If anything happens to me,
see to it that he is taken to my village. Explain that the
cub was mine. My parents will care for it!"

Everyone looked on, dismay in their eyes. They now
understood that Kiriki suspected exactly why she was
there, and that she was taking her fate like a true Pawnee
princess.

Never had they seen such a courageous, proud woman.
She would make the best bride of all past women for the
Morning Star!

The brave swept the cub into his arms. "The cub will
be seen to properly," he said, then rushed from the lodge.

Kiriki had seen that the man had not questioned the meaning behind her words—that perhaps something would happen to her.

Now she knew.

She held her chin proudly high. If she were to die this morning, she would do so bravely!

Wherever Sun Eagle was, he would be proud of her.

Sun Eagle clung to his horse, weakness causing sweat to sheen his bronzed body. He breathed hard, fighting the lightheadedness that threatened to prevail over him, looking up into the heavens and realizing that soon the morning star would appear there in all of its bright glory. If Sun Eagle was right, this morning there would be much blood spilled! If Brown Bear *had* abducted Kiriki for the sacrifice, the usual preliminaries of taking days upon days for the sacrifice to be offered would not be practiced. She would be killed in haste. For if not, Brown Bear would chance losing her to Sun Eagle again.

"I must get to her," he whispered, his voice filled with anguished pain. "If I am wrong, if Brown Bear has not abducted her and taken her to my village for all of the wrong reasons, there will still be cause for a celebration. Mine!"

Yet, though he would know that Kiriki was not being used for a sacrifice, he still would not know where she was, or with whom.

Unable to hold onto his horse any longer, weakness overcoming him, Sun Eagle fell to the ground. He lay there, panting. Slowly he curled his fingers into the dirt, then groaned as he pushed himself up again. He leaned against his horse, bowing his face into his hands, as he again felt the swimming inside his head.

In a matter of moments the fuzziness had passed and he struggled until he was once again on his horse's back. He looked up at the sky, seeing streaks of dawn along the horizon. Peering across the land, seeing much that was familiar to him, Sun Eagle knew that he was not all that far from his village.

''Just a little farther,'' he whispered, nudging his horse with his knees. ''I must make it. I . . . must!''

Brown Bear was proud to be the one to have been chosen to choose the place of sacrifice and now to be the one officiating the building of the scaffolding on which the sacrifice would be placed and offered to the Morning Star. As several warriors worked eagerly alongside Brown Bear, he glanced eagerly at the sky. There were light streaks along the horizon. The Morning Star was already awaiting its turn in the sky! Surely at this very moment it was thrilling over what was soon to be offered.

A wife!

A bride of all brides!

Perhaps no sacrifice would even be needed for the next growing season. So intriguingly lovely, Kiriki could perhaps sustain the Morning Star's appetite, even *forever*.

Having need to concentrate hard on the completion of the sacrificial scaffolding, knowing that the priest would lead his people and Kiriki there within a matter of moments, Brown Bear's fingers worked eagerly at building it. He knew that the scaffold must be erected according to the ancient ritual. One upright was of elm, and the other of cottonwood. The four lower cross bars were of elm, box elder, cottonwood, and willow. Kiriki would be forced to climb up the lower three cross bars and would stand upon the fourth, her hands tied to the fifth.

She would stand between the two willows, for they were water trees. At the top would be tied otterskins, because the otter was a water animal. At the lower willows on which she would be standing, would be wolf skins, then mountain lion, bear, and wildcat, in that order.

In this position she would be standing when the chief executioner launched his sacrificial arrow. Soon a small opening would be cut over her heart. Meat from Brown Bear's slain buffalo would be held under the scaffold to catch some of the drops of blood from her body.

If the blood did not drip on the meat, bad luck for all would follow, for it was a bad omen. . . .

After the blood had soaked into the buffalo meat, a man would approach Kiriki with a warclub. He would make four feints at each of the four points of her body, and then would touch her upon the heart. As he would do so, he would give a war whoop and run away—the idea was that by this blow, the spirit of the sacrifice would leave Kiriki to go up into the heavens to become one of the stars, where she would watch over the people for whom she had died.

In the meantime, the priests would have kindled a fire nearby, to the southeast. When the blood had ceased to drip upon the meat offering, its bearer would wheel around and go to the fire, circle the fireplace four times, and standing west of it, would raise the meat toward the heavens, lowering it gradually, dropping it into the fire where it would burn—the idea being that the smoke would go up and join the Morning Star in the heavens.

Brown Bear winced when he thought of the most prominent, meaningful actions of the ritual. Though he knew that it was required, he would find it hard to join the others—when the men and boys would come up and begin to shoot Kiriki in the back. As they would shoot her, they would sing war songs. Even the children would be told to shoot.

At last there would be so many arrows in Kiriki's back there would be room for no more. Even the mothers of little children would shoot small arrows for them.

A procession of all the people would then be formed, and led by the priest, they would circle the scaffold and the fire where the meat offering was burning. The priests would sing: "Let the sacrifice alone."

While the smoke of the blood and the buffalo meat and the soul of Kiriki ascended to the sky, all the people would be praying to Tirawa to take pity on them, and to give them health, success in war, and plenteous crops.

The priest would then send the people home.

It would be daylight. The Morning Star would have seen the whole performance. Assistants to the priest would go forward, untie the body, take it down, and carry it about a quarter of a mile from the scaffold onto the prairie, where they would lay it face downward with her head to the east. The men would sing a song, saying that the sacrifice would turn into or become a part of the earth through this great ceremony. The idea was that all the animals mentioned in the song would now become a part of Kiriki because some of them would come out from her and others would eat of her.

There would then be a general rejoicing and celebration through the village. The women would get out their husband's war bonnets and spears and mimic war parties around the village. Men and women would dance. The soul of Kiriki had gone straight to Tirawa, who sent it to the Morning Star. The Morning Star would clothe the sacrifice with flint from his fireplace and would place it among the stars in the heavens. Her body was thought to be not like ordinary bodies. Even after her death it would possess life. Things would be born from it and the earth would be fertilized by it.

Brown Bear turned around when he heard the sound of many feet rustling along the ground behind him. His people were arriving, Kiriki flanked by two of the Skidi's most able warriors. Brown Bear's eyes wavered as he looked at how proudly Kiriki walked toward him. Dusk still caused the scaffolding to be hidden in shadows—surely she had not yet seen it. Did she still believe that she was being brought to Sun Eagle? Did she expect to share vows with him soon?

Or was that look on her face one of defiance, proving that she knew everything without even having been told.

Feeling numb, death surely only moments away, Kiriki challenged Brown Bear with a set stare. She did not bother to look around for Sun Eagle. She now knew that he was not there. More than likely he was dead. The one beautiful thing of what was happening here on this early morning—where the tall grasses and fields of flowers were still dew-laden—was knowing that soon she might be joined, hand-in-hand, with Sun Eagle in the hereafter. Brown Bear could not do anything about their happiness then! They would run across the fields laughing and rejoicing in their newly found peace and happiness. Sun Eagle would pluck roses and place them in her hair. They would embrace and forever whisper love to one another without anyone's interferences. Brown Bear would not have won anything at all from Sun Eagle or Kiriki. In truth, they would have become the victorious ones—victorious over life and death!

The shadows now slowly fading, the sky lightening, caused Kiriki to emit a quick gasp of terror. She was looking past Brown Bear where something grotesque was reaching up into the sky.

It was a scaffold!

It did not take much thought to understand why the scaffold had been built. For her!

Had not Durah warned her? Was Durah's spirit looking down from the hereafter at this very moment, mourning what was to become of her best friend?

Kiriki wanted to turn and flee, but she would not get far. The whole Skidi village was following her, chanting. They had already celebrated her death. They would not let her disappoint them or the Morning Star.

It was now sunrise. The Morning Star Priest approached Kiriki and while she stood helplessly watching, he undressed her. Trembling, she further watched as he painted the right half of her body red, and the left half black. The two warriors who had accompanied her to the scaffold came forward and placed thongs around her wrists. She was encouraged to approach the scaffold.

Kiriki paused, tears streaming from her eyes, then she held her chin proudly high and began to ascend the steps that had been built on the scaffold. . . .

Sun Eagle's mother stood beside her husband Chief Antelope Buck, observing without approval. Kidibattsk's lips were pursed tightly together as she watched the lovely woman being forced to climb the scaffolding. She was not sure if she could bear watching another woman's body become filled with arrows. It was a practice that should be banned!

Yet Kidibattsk could not voice her opinion aloud. She was the wife of the chief. She knew that deep within her husband's heart he was weary of such practices, also. It was the elders that he was continuing to please.

Not wanting to watch the young lady being tied to the scaffolding, Kidibattsk turned her eyes away and looked at a maiden standing beside her whose hands were covering something at her neck.

Then Kidibattsk's eyes widened in surprise as the maiden's hand lowered and unconsciously revealed the shell necklace that she had taken from Kiriki.

Kidibattsk turned to the maiden and clasped her hands onto her shoulders. "The necklace!" she demanded, her voice a forced whisper. "Where did you get it? I know that necklace! I made it with my own hands!"

The maiden paled and gasped, covering the necklace with her hand again. "I took it from the woman who is the sacrifice," she defended. "Why should I not? She will soon be dead."

Kidibattsk's eyes wavered as she turned and looked up at Kiriki, confused.

Then she looked over at Brown Bear, seeing the gleam in his eyes as he waited patiently for the ritual to be completed. He had known all along who he had abducted for the ritual—he had taken his brother's intended!

Rage filled Kidibattsk's veins. She reached for the necklace, yanked it from the young woman's neck, and started to rush toward the scaffold, but was stopped by strong hands.

"Do not interfere," Chief Antelope Buck said, his voice drawn. "It is too late."

Kidibattsk looked up into her husband's eyes, stunned. Then she humbly went to his side and joined the others in watching, the broken necklace still clutched within her hand. Tears rushed from her eyes when she looked up at Kiriki's innocence. Sun Eagle had been right when he had described the loveliness of his woman, and also her courage.

After Kiriki reached the top of the scaffolding and was being tied to it, the men chosen for the last rites had assembled in the ravine to the east of it, where they were concealed from her view. A small fire was kindled there and they prepared their paraphernalia.

Just at the moment of the morning star's appearance in the sky, the two men came forward bearing firebrands. They were dressed as priests and had owl skins hanging from their necks, showing that they represented the messenger of the Morning Star. They took their places on either side of Kiriki, and with their brands, touched her lightly in the groin and armpit, smiling smugly when she did not cry out, proving to everyone that she was worthy of the sacrifice!

They then turned to the ravine and a third man ran out, carrying the bow and arrow made for the sacrifice. As he came running, he gave his war cry, and the people called to him and encouraged him as though he were attacking an enemy. . . .

As Sun Eagle rode across the land he became aware of a fire up ahead, and then his insides froze when he saw the definite outline of a scaffolding against the dawn sky.

His eyes searched wildly around and saw the throngs of Skidi also outlined against the horizon.

He looked at the scaffold again and as he rode closer he saw the lovely nude maiden tied to it.

Fear soared through him when he heard the war whoop and saw the warrior running from the ravine, toward the scaffold. In a matter of minutes, it would all be over!

Somehow able to gather up the strength that had been denied him since his fever, Sun Eagle straightened himself up on his horse, dug his heels into his gelding's flanks, and encouraged it to gallop across the dew-laden grass.

What seemed a blur to him in his mind, he managed to be suddenly riding alongside the running warrior. He reined his horse so suddenly that it reared, its hind legs knocking the warrior to the ground.

Then Sun Eagle dismounted. Grabbing his knife from its sheath he ran toward the scaffold. In a few quick movements he was up the steps, cut Kiriki's bonds, and was carrying her back down the steps to his waiting horse.

Sun Eagle was aware of utter silence around him as he was being observed defying all of his people, and especially the Morning Star.

But he ignored everything but the weeping woman in his arms—even the morning star as it now shone brightly overhead, as though singling him out with its silver light.

"Sun Eagle," Kiriki cried, clinging to him around his neck as he mounted his horse, still holding her. She looked up at him, devouring him with her eyes, loving him so intensely that it hurt. "Oh, Sun Eagle, I thought you were dead. In a matter of moments I would have been!"

Holding her on his lap, Sun Eagle wheeled his horse around and thundered away from his people. "What I have done may never be forgiven!" he shouted. "But for you, Kiriki, I would defy anyone!"

"Will they search for you and kill you?" Kiriki asked, her hair coming loose from its braids, flying in the breeze, her naked body chilled to the bone. "Oh, Sun Eagle, where can we go so that you will be safe?"

"I will take you with me to the hills," Sun Eagle said, then teetered as a surge of weakness reminded him that he had been given enough strength only to rescue Kiriki.

Sun Eagle glanced down at Kiriki and the way her body had been defiled with the hideous paint. He saw the burns at her groin and armpits. Rage tore through him. "Who is responsible for you being in my village, to be offered as a sacrifice?" he growled. "Or need I ask? It was my brother. It was Brown Bear!"

Kiriki swallowed hard, regretting having to reveal a brother who could hate so much. Yet she must. Sun Eagle would eventually want to seek ways of revenge!

"Yes, it was your brother," she said, lowering her eyes. "He planned it well, Sun Eagle."

Then she looked quickly up at him, and as daybreak diffused the land in streamers of glorious light she noticed the slash wounds on his chest. Even his powerful hands showed signs of torture! His fingertips were now healing from burns.

"Sun Eagle, who made you suffer so?" she cried.

Sun Eagle inhaled a shaky breath. "Your father blamed me for your abduction," he said, his voice neutral. "He sought to get truths from me that I was incapable of giving, because I knew not where you were."

"Yet you are alive?" Kiriki marveled.

"Only because Major O'Fallon discovered me and took me to his dwelling," Sun Eagle said. "His woman doctored me well."

Kiriki lowered her eyes again. "My friend, Durah, is dead," she said, finding the truth so hard to speak aloud. "Brown Bear murdered her! She was all sweetness and kindness in this world, and now she is dead."

"Yes, this I know," Sun Eagle said, leading his horse up a butte and into a thick forest that would then again lead to higher country. "That, too, I was being punished for."

Kiriki placed her cheek to his bare chest. "It is all too unfair," she sobbed. "Oh, Sun Eagle, everything is so unfair!"

"But we will endure, Kiriki," Sun Eagle said, drawing her closer, reveling in the touch of her flesh against his.

"Thank you, my handsome warrior, for saving my life," Kiriki murmured, looking adoringly up at him. "How can I ever repay you?"

"You are repaying me even at this moment," Sun Eagle said, smiling down at her. "Just knowing that you love me is payment enough, and I know that you do, for, my woman, your eyes are revealing all truths to me!"

Kiriki returned his smile, then lifted her mouth to his lips and kissed him sweetly.

Fifteen

▼ ▼ ▼

CHIEF Antelope Buck moved slowly to the scaffold and climbed it halfway to the top. He spread his arms, as though embracing his people, his eyes roving over them, but not with apology. The throng was quiet, stunned by Sun Eagle's daring escapade and also from no longer having a sacrifice for the Morning Star.

"My people!" Chief Antelope Buck cried. "In your eyes my son, Sun Eagle, has done the unmentionable! You see him as one who has defied Tirawa the creator of the universe. You see him as having denied the sacrifice to the Morning Star. You see him as having defied you, his people. Perhaps this is so, yet in my eyes, my son is a man of great courage! He has voiced aloud many times his distaste for the Morning Star sacrifice, and today he has acted upon his convictions. He saved a woman from the sacrifice! My people, you must see him as I see him and be in awe of his courage and admire his daring and ability to act upon his convictions. Did he not prove today that he is to one day be a great leader? As I prepare myself to cross over into the hereafter, I will hand over my title of chief to him with enthusiasm."

Chief Antelope Buck lowered his arms and doubled a hand into a tight fist and placed it over his heart. "Hear me well, my people!" he said, his voice soft and with deep emotion. "My son deserves praise, not condemnation."

Utter silence followed the chief's pleadings, everyone's eyes on him. Kidibattsk wiped a tear from her eyes, moved deeply by her husband's words, for she feared that

perhaps he did not have the courage of his son required
to voice his feelings aloud to his people. The elders of the
village swayed him more oft than not about things. This
time he spoke on his own, from his heart. Surely the
people would be moved by his pleadings for a son that
would one day rule as their chief.

Shifting her gaze, Kidibattsk looked sourly over at
Brown Bear. Oh, what a disappointment he was to her,
always. She could not understand how two sons could be
formed in the same womb and be so different. One was
a man of courage. The other a man of jealousy and
hatred—in truth, cowardly. It ate at her heart that they
could not have been the same in bravery, so that she could
love one the same as the other.

Oh, but she could not! Brown Bear did not deserve
praise of any sort. He had stolen his brother's woman,
and had passed her off as someone different. Had Kiriki
actually been slain before Sun Eagle had arrived to rescue
her, Brown Bear would have been condemned in his mother's eyes forever.

As it was, she now only pitied him.

Her fingers still clutching the broken necklace, Kidibattsk looked down at it. For Kiriki and Sun Eagle, she
would repair it. Hopefully, Kiriki would have the opportunity to wear it on her wedding day.

Slowly she began looking around her, assessing the attitude of the silent Pawnee. If they did not agree with their
chief, Sun Eagle would be hunted down and killed. Kiriki
would be brought back to the village and the sacrificial
ceremony would be continued. . . .

"My people!" Chief Antelope Buck shouted, lifting his
fist into the air. "Let me hear your words! Do we celebrate
a son who has proven his courage beyond any Pawnee
you have ever been witness to before? Or do we hunt him
down and kill him like a dog?"

There was a sudden stirring among the people. Brown
Bear became restless, looking from his father back to the
people, wondering if his father's words had stirred them
in the wrong way. If they saw Sun Eagle as a hero, then

all was lost to Brown Bear again. All the gain that he had achieved by having brought the most lovely of sacrifices to his village would be gone.

Instead, he might even be scorned. Once they all learned who the sacrifice truly was, that it was Kiriki—the woman Sun Eagle had chosen to sit at his side when he eventually reigned as their chief—Brown Bear would be scorned, perhaps even banned from the tribe.

He shifted his feet nervously, his heart pounding as murmurs began to ripple through the crowd, their eyes fixed admirably on their chief.

"Sun Eagle is a hero!" one Pawnee shouted, waving a hand in the air. "Surely the Morning Star—surely even Tirawa—recognizes his courage! It was not meant for this particular woman to be wed to the Morning Star, or it would have been so! She would be dead now! Surely Tirawa did not look favorably on this woman, and gave his blessing to Sun Eagle to take her away!"

Eyes turned to Brown Bear. "Your son, Brown Bear, brought us the wrong sacrifice!" another Pawnee shouted scornfully. "Send him out to find another!"

"Send him away!" another shouted. "Because of him we have no sacrifice!"

"We want Sun Eagle!" another shouted. "Bring him to us so that we can celebrate his prowess!"

Voices rang in unison. "Send Brown Bear away!" they shouted. "He does not deserve to be among our people!"

Seeing the mood change to anger, and not wanting either of his sons to suffer because of this ill-fated day, Chief Antelope Buck motioned for Brown Bear to come to him, to stand by his side. Once there, he placed a firm arm around his son's shoulder.

"My son, Brown Bear, will not leave our village except on a mission of the heart," he shouted, glancing over at Brown Bear, trying to understand a son who would steal his brother's woman.

But even if Brown Bear was someone he did not know or understand, he could not see him condemned in the eyes of his people. He deserved another chance to prove himself. He was the son of Chief Antelope Buck! Somewhere, deeply within him, there had to be a trace of courage and pride running through his veins.

Chief Antelope Buck faced the crowd again. "Brown Bear will go and find Sun Eagle and Kiriki, and bring them back to the village!" he said firmly. "If need be, he will voice a public apology to Sun Eagle and his woman!"

A gasp rippled through the crowd. Chief Antelope Buck had forgotten that only he, his wife, and Brown Bear knew that Sun Eagle had not only rescued this woman today because of his beliefs against the Morning Star ritual, but also because the woman on the scaffold had been the one he had earlier chosen to be his wife.

Tightening his hold on Brown Bear's shoulder, not only for Brown Bear to understand that he was being protected by a father but also to try and convince himself that he was doing what was right, Chief Antelope Buck spoke more softly to his people, explaining about Sun Eagle's relationship with Kiriki. That was hard, for he did not know the full details. He had only become aware of who Kiriki was when Kidibattsk had grabbed the necklace from the squaw. . . .

Brown Bear listened intently at what his father was saying to his people, in his own mind already planning what he was going to do. He would agree to go after Sun Eagle and Kiriki, but taking only his own warriors, the ones most loyal to him.

In truth, Brown Bear would kill Sun Eagle and Kiriki. They had shamed him!

"Brown Bear will ride now and return with Sun Eagle and his woman," Chief Antelope Buck said in conclusion. "We will celebrate Sun Eagle's courage! My people, we shall shower him and his woman with gifts."

Shouts and chants rose from the crowd, approving the chief's decision. Chief Antelope Buck turned to Brown Bear and looked deeply into his eyes, causing Brown Bear to grow numb inside for what he, himself, had silently planned. He then challenged his father with a set stare, for what Brown Bear did, he did for his own survival.

"My son, ride with the wind," Chief Antelope Buck said. "Bring your brother and his woman back to me. Then you will be pardoned for the wrong that you have done here today."

Brown Bear knew deep within himself that he would never be pardoned for anything. He had lost not only his pride, but any chance of ever getting the recognition that he needed from his people to be their great leader.

"I shall do as you ask," Brown Bear said, forcing humility into his voice. "I, too, see my brother as courageous!"

He lowered his eyes humbly, yet his jaw was tight with hate. "I am sorry for having disappointed you, Father," he said between gritted teeth. "I will await anxiously for you to embrace me with pride again."

"Then go," Chief Antelope Buck said, his voice drawn. "Return soon."

"Soon," Brown Bear said, backing away from his father, his head still bowed. Then he spun around and raced from the crowd, his private set of warriors already mounting their horses.

When he reached his horse and swung himself up into the saddle, he looked from one warrior to the other. "Without saying the words, you already know what must be done!" he said, his eyes narrowing angrily. "If none of you approve of my plan to see my brother dead, do not join me on this mission. You must know that if my goal is achieved, we shall never be free to return to this village again. We will have to go far away."

"You are our leader," one of the warriors said, the others agreeing with silent nods. "Wherever you go, we will follow. Whatever you choose to do, we will go with you. In our eyes, you are the greatest warrior of them all. Not Sun Eagle!"

His chest swelling with pride, Brown Bear smiled smugly. "Then, my warrior friends, let us ride!" he shouted, wheeling his horse around, kicking up sprays of grass as he rode away from his father's village. A choked sort of feeling was embedded in his throat, so wanting to

turn and take a last look at his village. Perhaps this would
be the last time he would see it. Perhaps he should have
embraced his mother, for even that would be denied him
forever, should he be victorious in what he was now
driven to do!

High up in the hills, the breeze so soft they could not
feel it, Kiriki and Sun Eagle sat beside a quiet stream, a
great rock outcropping at their backs. "I fear that we are
not far enough away from the wrath of your people,"
Kiriki worried, looking down across a flat stretch of land
that lay beneath her in the distance. "They surely will not
give up hunting until they find us. Even you will be killed
now, Sun Eagle."

She looked at him, her lashes heavy over her sad eyes.
"Though I am ever so grateful for having been rescued,
I do not like to feel that it is because of me that you will
be forever scorned in the eyes of your people, perhaps
even until they kill you for what you have done."

Sun Eagle put his finishing touches on the loose buckskin dress that he had fashioned out of one of his blankets
for Kiriki. Slipping another blanket away from her shoulders that he had placed there to ward off the evening chill,
he started to draw the dress over her head, then stopped
to take another look at her skin where the torches had
been touched to her groin and armpits. The herbal mixture
that he had prepared for her only moments ago was already
working. The red marks were fading.

"Do you hurt?" he asked, his voice thin. He lay the
dress aside and sank his lips to the skin close beside the
burns.

Kiriki's breath was stolen. She gasped with pleasure as
Sun Eagle's hands swept over her stomach, then past the
burns at her groin, cupping her at the juncture of her
thighs where she was just beginning to throb.

"Darling, do I hurt?" she asked in a whisper. "Yes, I
am being tormented terribly!"

Sun Eagle drew quickly away, his eyes wide.

Kiriki reached a hand to his face and touched him gently. "My darling, my torment is not the painful sort," she reassured. "It is the torment of the heart caused by your kisses."

She snuggled into his arms, pressing her breasts into his bare chest. "Darling, I want you so much," she whispered, clinging. "So very, very much."

Sun Eagle twined his fingers through her hair and drew her lips up to his. "We have time before traveling onward," he said, his gaze burning down into her eyes. "But I would not want to hurt your wounds."

"Nor I yours," Kiriki said, reaching to touch his scarred fingertips. "Oh, my darling, how could my father have done this to you?"

Sun Eagle brushed a soft kiss across her lips. "How could my brother have done so much to *both* of us?" he growled. "Seems both my brother and your father are misguided."

Kiriki looked past Sun Eagle's shoulder, down into the valley again. "Are we truly safe enough here?" she worried.

"For awhile," he said, placing his hands to her shoulders to stretch her gently onto the ground. "We will ride onward. Soon. I know a place to make camp. My brother and I found it in our youth while exploring."

Kiriki tensed. "And you will go there?" she gasped. "He will surely follow!"

Sun Eagle smoothed Kiriki's hair back from her brow and softly kissed her eyes closed. "My brother has surely forgotten about this special place," he tried to reassure her. "We were there only once. It has never been mentioned again, not even briefly. But I have been there many times. I go there to meditate—to commune with the Spirit Father."

Kiriki leaned away from Sun Eagle. She looked up at him, her jaw tight. "Sun Eagle, your brother took me to the cave of your boyhood explorings that you told me about earlier. Please don't go there!" she said, her heart pounding when she recalled the vile moments shared with

him there. "He would surely find us if he is sent by your
father to search for you."

Oh, she did not have the heart to tell Sun Eagle that
his very own brother had raped her! He would not ask her,
surely never believing his brother could be *that* deranged.

"The cave is not where I am taking you," Sun Eagle
said, his heart growing cold at the thought of Kiriki having
been abducted and taken there. He did not have the courage to ask if she had been raped by his brother. Surely
Brown Bear would have never defiled her in that way!

"The cave was only one of many of our boyhood
places," he said somberly, looking away from her, his
mood becoming haunted by memories that tore at his
heart. "That was a time when brothers were friends!"

Kiriki reached her arms around Sun Eagle's neck and
drew him back down above her. She kissed his face with
butterfly kisses. "I am so sorry that he continues to do
nothing but hurt you," she murmured. "That sort of hurt
is unfamiliar to me, for I have never been blessed with a
brother or sister. Durah is the closest to a sister that I ever
had."

She looked away from Sun Eagle, filled with remorse
again at the thought of Durah no longer being there, to
confide in, to laugh with, to *love*.

Sun Eagle sensed her withdrawal and swept his arms
around her, drawing her against him. He ground his body
into hers, reveling in the touch of her breasts against his
flesh. "There is much to forget," he whispered, flicking
a tongue across her pouting lips. "We shall be together
forever to help one another forget. You are my life, Kiriki.
Tell me that I am yours."

Kiriki raised her hips to his, feeling his hardened shaft
exploring between her thighs. She opened herself to him
and let him enter her, sucking in a deep breath as pleasure
soared through her.

"You are all that I ever want," she whispered, smoothing her hands down his back, locking her fingers on his
buttocks. She pressed him harder against her as his thrusts

began within her. "Love me now, Sun Eagle. Love me forever!"

"All tomorrows are ours," he said, whispering against the slender column of her throat. "No one will take them away from us. Especially not my brother!"

Slipping her legs around Sun Eagle's waist, Kiriki locked her ankles together. "Let us not speak of your brother while we are making love," she whispered.

"That is so," Sun Eagle whispered back, then crushed her mouth with a fierce, savage kiss. His hands traveled over her body, taking in the gentle curves, the sudden peaks, and the utter softness of her skin. Lost in the silken sheath of her, he loved her with an exquisite tenderness. The ultimate of sensations was just beyond reach, yet he slowed his pace. He wanted her to follow along with him, to feel the explosion of ecstasy at the same moment as he.

Kiriki was drowning in the almost unbearable sweetness building up inside her. It was a relief, for she had feared that Brown Bear's invasion to her body would make all lovemaking ugly to her.

But now, while with Sun Eagle, she was finding nothing but ecstasy again. Total ecstasy!

She moved with him as he stroked gently within her, her entire being throbbing with a quickening passion. His tongue parted her lips and sought the depths of her mouth, causing her to respond with a fierce, fevered kiss. Her pulse raced when his hand crept between their bodies and cupped one of her breasts, tweaking a nipple to a hardened peak between his forefinger and thumb. Her skin quivered, and a sob of bliss leapt from her throat when his hand moved slowly downward and his fingers began skillfully caressing her swollen nub that lay only a fraction from his hardened shaft moving in a steady rhythm within her.

Then suddenly their bodies jolted and quivered. They cried out against one another's lips as the peak of passion was reached. Their bodies strained together, taking from one another all that each was offering, then they lay quiet, nestled close. . . .

"Had Brown Bear succeeded at what he tried, never would we have shared in such joy again, my love," Kiriki cried, her cheek resting against Sun Eagle's chest. "Oh, Sun Eagle, that we have made love again so wonderfully free is beyond belief! But shall we again? What if we are sought and found? Oh, Sun Eagle, it could all be over so quickly for us."

"Never will you be taken from me again," Sun Eagle growled, holding Kiriki away from him, looking down at her with fire in his eyes. "Whoever tries will die!"

"You may have to kill your brother," Kiriki said somberly.

"It will be no different than were he a Comanche!" Sun Eagle said, his voice a deep growl.

He reached for the makeshift dress that he had made Kiriki and began drawing it over her head, strips of buckskin at the sides serving as ties to hold the garment together. "Now let us be on our way," he said further. "There is no sense in tempting fate. Though my brother deserves to die because of what he has done, it is not my wish that he dies at *my* hand."

Kiriki smoothed the dress down past her hips and tied the pieces of buckskin at both sides, hiding the truth within her heart that would make Sun Eagle change his mind about not wanting to be the one to kill his brother.

Oh, but if he only knew!

She would not be the one to tell him. She would not go to sleep at night for the rest of her life knowing that she gave Sun Eagle the cause to take his own brother's life.

Sun Eagle would *never* know. Never!

She followed him to his gelding, desire melting her as he placed his hands at her waist to lift her onto his horse. His mere touch fired her love for him!

She smiled to herself as he mounted behind her and swept an arm around her waist possessively. She leaned into his embrace, her back against his chest as he spurred his horse away from the stream, riding higher into the hills.

* * *

Brown Bear rode stiffly on his horse, his gaze straight ahead. In the distance he was seeing the hills of his boyhood past. Sun Eagle would not expect him to remember! They had explored those hills only once, but Brown Bear knew that Sun Eagle had returned often, to meditate. Brown Bear had followed him one day, curious about his brother's private place for communing with the Great Spirit. What better place to take the woman he loved?

Brown Bear then looked down at the crushed grass. Surely this was the path of his brother's escape! When the morning came, Sun Eagle would be in for a great surprise. The attack would be quick. The deaths of Sun Eagle and Kiriki would be swift!

Smiling smugly, thrusting his chest out and his shoulders back, Brown Bear urged his horse into a softer lope. There was time. Let his brother and woman make love at least one more time before they said goodbye forever!

His smile faltering, Brown Bear was thrust back into time, when he had felt the wonders of Kiriki's body against his own. There was no denying that his feelings for her had gone further than what he had planned. He loved her. When he killed her, a part of him would die.

But wasn't he dead inside already? So much in life was going to be forever denied him now. So much that he was not sure if he could bear it.

Hate swelled within his heart for Sun Eagle.

It was all *his* fault.

Sixteen

MORNING was upon the land, the silhouettes of the buttes rising into the sky purplish hazes; the horses' hooves on the gravel-pocked land a sound that seemed like thunder inside Kiriki's head. Bone-weary and sleepy, she pleaded silently up into Sun Eagle's eyes. They had ridden all night without stopping. Kiriki had no idea how many miles still stretched out before her, for it seemed that Sun Eagle was taking her to the ends of the earth for protection.

Feeling Kiriki's eyes on him, Sun Eagle eased his hold around her waist and leaned her partially away from him. "It has been a long night," he said, seeing that weariness was causing small lines in her soft features. "For that I am sorry."

"Are we just about there?" Kiriki asked, her voice lilting.

"As you look around you, you will see the place of my childhood adventure," Sun Eagle said, smiling reassuringly down at her. "I am now choosing a safe place for us to make camp."

"You think I am weak because I complain?" Kiriki asked, her gaze lowering. "For this I am sorry."

"You complain only once and that you are ashamed of? Kiriki, you are a woman of great strength and courage," he defended stoutly. "Never doubt what you are!"

"You say these things only because you love me, Sun Eagle," Kiriki murmured, looking slowly up at him. "Of late, I have felt anything but strong—anything but courageous. So much has rendered me weak within, especially inside my heart."

"And that is going to all be made up to you," Sun Eagle growled, reining in his horse behind a great outcropping of rocks that were formed like a wall. He lifted Kiriki from the horse and held her close. "Somehow I shall make it up to you."

"I know," Kiriki whispered, clinging to his neck, his arms so powerful as they held her within their grasp.

"Soon I will be certain of whether or not my father hates me for defying Tirawa," Sun Eagle said, lowering Kiriki to the ground on a thick pallet of grass. "We will stay here a few days, and then I shall go alone to see if any of my father's warriors are searching for us. If there are none, then perhaps I shall attempt going to see my father. I shall talk with him and explain to him about the wrongs of Brown Bear. The wrongs of the sacrifice! If he will listen to reason, and will welcome you back into the village as my wife, then I shall return for you and take you home with me."

Kiriki lifted a hand to his copper cheek. She reveled in the soft, smooth touch of his flesh. "And, Sun Eagle, should he not welcome you or me?" she asked, her voice shallow. "What then? Perhaps he won't even allow you to return to me. I shall be left alone in these hills, to die."

Sun Eagle clasped his hands to her shoulders. He glared down at her, determination tightening his jaw. "That will never happen," he growled. "I have friends. I shall seek them out before I enter my village. I shall explain exactly where you are and what is to become of you should I be detained by my father or his warriors."

Kiriki paled at the thought. "And what would your instructions be?" she asked, her voice breaking.

"That you are to be returned to your people," he said, searching her face, moved again by her innocent loveliness. He took her into his arms and hugged her fiercely. "At all cost you are to be protected. You have already been put through an ordeal that may cause you to have hideous dreams throughout the rest of your life."

"As long as I am with you, my dreams are only filled with sweetness," Kiriki said, tears wetting his cheek as they began to flow from her eyes. "Oh, Sun Eagle, hold me. Never let me go. Though my dreams are filled with sweetness, it is now, while I am awake, that I am troubled. I am suddenly so afraid!''

Sun Eagle held her tightly. He rested his cheek against the soft satin of her hair. ''My woman, have I not promised that no harm will come to you?'' he asked thickly. ''Do you not trust my ability to protect you?''

Kiriki pushed away and looked quickly up at him, not having realized how doubtful she had sounded. ''Sun Eagle,'' she gasped. ''I did not mean to show any doubts of you! I am sorry. It is just that . . . that so much has happened. The ordeal that I was forced to endure because of your brother! It is only that, Sun Eagle, that causes me to say things that are wrong.''

She lunged into his arms and hugged him again. ''Please forgive me?'' she murmured. ''I never want to cause you pain.''

''Nor I you,'' Sun Eagle said, then swung her away from him, smiling. He held her hands. ''Let us speak no more of doubts or fears. It is time to find nourishment for our bodies. I know this place well. There are many wild grapes to be plucked, and many wild vegetables to be dug.''

When Kiriki's stomach growled at the mention of food, she giggled. She blushed. ''I am hungry,'' she murmured.

''Words were not needed. I have heard the protest of your stomach,'' Sun Eagle said, grabbing his rifle. With his free hand, he took Kiriki's hand and began leading her toward the forest, enjoying this moment of lightheartedness. He feared that it would not last long. Though he had spoken of going to his village to speak with his father, he truly doubted if he would have the opportunity. Surely he was banned from the tribe, forever.

His heart was heavy with such a thought. It was almost unbearable to think that perhaps he would have to wander with Kiriki forever, with no true destination or people to reach out to.

Even their children would be cast out as renegades!

It was not fair, yet he had no choice but to have to wait

and see what fate handed him, Kiriki, and the children that would be born to them.

Life had its many pitfalls. The worst, it seemed, was having a brother who was filled with tormented jealousies, for if not for Brown Bear, even now Sun Eagle and Kiriki would be married.

Sun Eagle swept an arm around her waist and led her beneath the shadows of the great oak trees. Birds chattered overhead. Squirrels scampered along the ground, their bushy tails twitching nervously. There were distant sounds of water cascading across rocks, and the smell of damp earth and rotting leaves.

Huge, purple clusters of wild grapes up just ahead caught Kiriki's full attention. She slipped from Sun Eagle's grip and ran to the vines. Without hesitation she plucked some of the grapes and thrust the plump, sweet morsels into her mouth. They not only began quenching her hunger, but also her thirst. She smiled up at Sun Eagle as he began to pick his fill, also.

Kiriki's smile faded when she saw a sudden look of alarm on Sun Eagle's face as he turned with a jerk and looked back in the direction from whence they had just come. Then she dropped the remaining grapes that she had had in her hands, understanding Sun Eagle's alarm. She now heard the thunder of horses, also. She rushed to Sun Eagle's side and clutched his arm, looking up at him wildly.

"They are here!" she cried. "They followed us, Sun Eagle. They will kill both of us!"

Sun Eagle's anger was rising inside him, knowing that only one Pawnee would have found him this quickly. Did his brother's wrath go even this deeply? Would he not stop until he killed both Sun Eagle and Kiriki?

Well, he would not do so without a fight!

Sun Eagle framed Kiriki's face between his hands. "You must stay here," he commanded. "I will go and fight my brother and his warriors, then slip away and come to you. Be ready to ride, Kiriki. I will return for you. Soon!"

Fear burned into Kiriki's heart, afraid of being left alone. But she knew by the sounds of the horses that she was safe. The riders were way below the butte. It would take them at least one hour to climb their horses up the slippery rocks to get to the top. It was not even required for Sun Eagle to fire upon the assailants once—escape could be had now!

Grabbing Sun Eagle's hand, Kiriki pleaded up at him with her eyes. "Get the horse and let us leave before firing upon those who are coming for us!" she cried. "Let us leave quickly, Sun Eagle! Quickly!"

"It would be dishonorable for me to flee without showing the warriors that I fight first," Sun Eagle said firmly. "My shots will find targets. Let those who do not feel the piercing pain of my bullets know that to follow me means possible death. If bloodshed is what my brother and his warriors are after, then so be it! But it will not be my blood or yours that will be spilled. Never!"

He took a quick step away from her. "Now I must go," he said, his voice void of emotion. "I shall return in the blink of an eye. My woman, be ready to ride for another full day. My brother will follow us until he waits for us to drop from exhaustion." He smiled smugly. "It will be he who will fall first!"

Kiriki watched Sun Eagle break into a run, soon out of her sight. She crumpled down on the ground, feeling defeated. Wrapping her arms around her legs, she began rocking herself back and forth . . . back and forth . . . staring into the distance.

She dreaded the sound of the first shot.

Sun Eagle moved stealthily from the forest, then positioned himself behind tall boulders of rock, close to his tethered horse and where he could get a straight aim at the approaching horsemen. Squinting his eyes, shielding them from the rising sun in the distance, he began looking from warrior to warrior, recognizing them all.

But most prominent of all was his brother who rode before them all, the leader.

"Brother seeking brother to take back for chastisement, possibly death? How could it be?" Sun Eagle said through gritted teeth. "How has it gotten to this? Where are the days we lay side by side studying the stars in the heavens, whispering secrets that only brothers have? Brown Bear, it cuts deeply into my heart, this hate that you have for me!"

He watched as Brown Bear wheeled his horse to a stop and dismounted. He could hear the orders being shouted, his brother's voice threatening—thick with *hate*. Some of his assailants stayed on horses. Others fled to hide behind trees and rocks.

Soon bullets were pinging all around Sun Eagle, glancing off rocks overhead and at his sides. His gelding whinnied and dug at the rock beneath his front right hoof, shaking his mane nervously.

Taking perfect aim, Sun Eagle got off his first shot. He winced and felt a strange sort of pain pierce his gut when one of the Pawnee warriors fell from his horse, blood gushing from his chest. Never could he be proud of shooting any of his own people. In doing so, the future generations of Pawnee were being cheated of sons—of daughters!

Bullets again whizzed and bounced all around him. Again he took aim, and another Pawnee warrior hit the ground.

Then everything was quiet. Sun Eagle searched with his eyes very carefully, then caught sight of Brown Bear as he was creeping from tree to tree. Sun Eagle's heart began to race as he slowly lifted his rifle in place again, taking careful aim. The gun moved slowly along with Brown Bear's movements. One shot and he would be dead.

But Sun Eagle could not pull the trigger. He could not find it in himself to kill his own brother.

He . . . just . . . couldn't. . . .

Breathing hard, sweat pouring from his brow, Sun Eagle lowered the gun to his side. He had to get out of there. If not now, and Brown Bear persisted to shoot at him, Sun Eagle would have no choice but to fire back and kill him!

"I cannot do that!" Sun Eagle whispered harshly to himself. "He is my brother! The same blood runs through our veins! I will do anything to prevent being forced to kill him."

Moving stealthily to his gelding, he swung himself onto his blanket saddle. Gripping his rifle and leaning low, he led his horse away, into the outer fringes of the forest. Kiriki was there. Sun Eagle offered her a hand, and in one sweep he had her up on the horse in front of him.

"Is it over?" Kiriki asked, looking over her shoulder at him, so relieved that he was safe. She had heard the volley of gunfire. Each had torn away a little corner of her heart, not knowing if Sun Eagle had been hit by any of them.

"For now it is over," Sun Eagle said, leading his horse farther into the dark shadows of the forest. "But my brother is clever. He will follow."

"Your father sent your own brother to kill you?" Kiriki said, shaking her head in disbelief. "That is heartless, Sun Eagle. How could your father do that?"

Sun Eagle did not respond. His mind was busy trying to sort through all that was troubling him. There was no doubt now that he was considered a renegade. But he was finding it hard to believe that his father would hate him *this* much.

And to assign Brown Bear to pursue and kill him?

No. It did not seem at all like Chief Antelope Buck—fine warrior that he was!

Something seemed amiss here. Quite amiss. . . .

Brown Bear looked up at the butte that shadowed him in grays. "He is no longer there!" he growled, casting a fierce look at Flying Deer, his favored warrior companion. "He managed to flee." His gaze went to his fallen comrades. "He killed two of my best warriors. Do you now see the sort of Pawnee my brother is, Flying Deer?"

Flying Deer looked from the dead warriors back up at the butte, then at Brown Bear. "Your brother was only defending himself against those who were firing upon him," he said guardedly. "Brown Bear, you would have done the same had you been cornered."

"Cornered?" Brown Bear exclaimed. He waved a hand wildly in the air. "Do you call him cornered? Why, he is no longer even there—he has escaped! It will now take us another full day, perhaps longer, to find him!"

"Then perhaps you will find it best not to pursue him any longer," Flying Deer dared to say, knowing Brown Bear's temper. "You can return to your father and tell him that either they are dead, or that they have fled further into the hills. You have made it look to Sun Eagle as though he is being pursued because of your father's anger toward him, instead of how it truly is—he is supposed to be returned home, a *hero*. Sun Eagle will forever believe that he is a renegade, Brown Bear. He will never return home to cause you trouble again. Leave it be, Brown Bear. Leave it be!"

Brown Bear grabbed Flying Deer by the shoulder, digging his fingers deeply into his flesh. "Hear me well, warrior," he growled. "My mission is to see to it that my brother is *dead*. Only *then* shall I be assured that he will never interfere in my life again. You ride with me, or you turn around and leave in disgrace, a *coward*."

Flying Deer jerked himself free of Brown Bear's grip. His eyes filled with fire, he challenged Brown Bear's steady stare. "I choose to ride away, but not in disgrace," he fumed. "Never shall I be labeled a coward. I ride from you who is filled with too much jealousy and hate. You are to be pitied, Brown Bear."

Turning on a heel, Flying Deer began to walk away from Brown Bear, his head held high. His shoulder muscles tensed when he heard the swish of an arrow and then felt the piercing pain in his back. He looked down, shock registering on his face, as he saw the arrowhead projecting through his abdomen. A lightheadedness swept over him. He clutched at the arrow shaft as he sank slowly to the ground, and was lost to everything in a dark void of unconsciousness.

There was a strange silence as the warriors looked down

at Flying Deer, then up at Brown Bear, questioning him with their dark searching eyes.

Brown Bear challenged them with a set stare. "Never forget who I am!" he shouted. "I am the chief's son! I will be the next chief! Sun Eagle will never have that opportunity!" He motioned with a hand toward Flying Deer who lay in a pool of blood. "Any of you who question my authority will join Flying Deer in the hereafter." He doubled a hand into a tight fist and held it in the air. "Now let us ride! Sun Eagle is already too far ahead of us!"

Flying Deer was coming in and out of consciousness, yet he lay perfectly still. He did not want Brown Bear to know that the arrow had not killed him. The pain was almost unbearable, yet Flying Deer could think logically during his bouts of consciousness. His thoughts were filled with Sun Eagle. He needed to be warned! . . .

Sun Eagle suddenly drew his horse to a halt. He looked over his shoulder, one eyebrow quirked. Then he looked down at Kiriki who was questioning him with her eyes.

"If we continue to travel in this direction, we will be playing exactly into my brother's hands," he said, swinging his horse around in a wide circle. "I shall backtrack to confuse Brown Bear, then take a side route that will take me back exactly to where Brown Bear and his warriors were firing upon us." He laughed throatily. "While Brown Bear is traveling one direction, we shall be traveling another. I will not take you farther into the hills. There are too many other places that I know can just as easily fit perfectly into our plans until we decide where we will go to begin our lives anew."

"You are certain now that you can never return home again?" Kiriki asked softly.

"No, never shall I be certain of that," Sun Eagle said, nudging his horse into a steady lope with his knees. "In time, I shall test my father's love for me. But for now, you are the most important, Kiriki. We will bide our time.

I cannot believe that fate will only hand us the life of the renegade. Never shall I accept that!''

Sun Eagle was careful to backtrack for several miles, then spun away into the forest where the dried spongy leaves made it impossible for him to be tracked. At this point Brown Bear would be confused as to which direction to go. If he chose the right course, then Sun Eagle would have to do the inevitable. He would have to kill his brother and any warrior that fought alongside him.

If Sun Eagle and Kiriki didn't get killed first. . . .

Seventeen

THE moon topped the trees with its silver light. A lazy campfire burned within the shadows of a butte, a speared fish cooking low over the coals. Kiriki and Sun Eagle lay beside one another on a spread blanket, having fallen into a deep exhausted sleep after arriving at Sun Eagle's planned destination.

Kiriki stirred in her sleep, a dream troubling her. She began tossing from side to side, reliving Brown Bear's rape in her dream. She gasped and fought in her sleep, then awakened with a start as tears became cold on her cheeks.

Her breath was momentarily stolen from her when she found Sun Eagle's dark eyes looking down at her, concern in their depths.

"Kiriki, you were dreaming," Sun Eagle said, smoothing a comforting hand across her sweat-beaded brow. "Was it all that bad? Do you want to tell me about it?"

Ashamed, feeling the violation to her body anew—as though Brown Bear were there, forcing himself upon her—Kiriki turned her face away from Sun Eagle. "No," she whispered, wiping the tears from her cheeks. "I do not wish to talk about it. It—it—was the sort of dream that one wishes to forget quickly."

"It is because of my brother that you dream, is it not?" Sun Eagle asked venomously.

Kiriki looked quickly up at him, stunned. Had he read her thoughts? Did he somehow, in his great wisdom, know that she had been raped?

She had not wanted him to know. Ever!

It was too shameful. It was something a woman never forgot, nor would the man that loved her, should he find out. . . .

"It is because my brother abducted you," Sun Eagle continued, then drew her within his arms and held her tightly. "The dreams will end one day, Kiriki. You will be able to forget them forever."

Kiriki sighed deeply, grateful that she had been wrong about what Sun Eagle had been thinking when he had spoken of his brother. He knew not of the rape at all. Only the abduction . . .

"Yes, I will soon forget," she murmured. "But will you? Your brother wronged you greatly. How can you ever forget that?"

"One day he will pay," Sun Eagle said, looking into the darkness, smiling when he thought of his brother being confused about the direction of Sun Eagle's travels. "But for now, you are all that concerns me. We must soon make plans for our future. It will be a future of total togetherness."

"Oh, how wonderful that sounds," Kiriki said, snuggling closer. "I love you so much, Sun Eagle. Oh, so very, very much."

She looked past his shoulder, at the outline of the butte in the distance. It was the exact butte upon which she and Sun Eagle had been camping when Brown Bear and his warriors had begun firing upon them. A full circle had been traveled.

But where would they go now? Brown Bear searching for Sun Eagle was absolute proof that he was being looked upon as a renegade. Never could he return home again. He would be captured and more than likely put to death.

She peered up at the sky, at the blinking stars. Soon the morning star would appear in the heavens again. Would she now cringe every time she looked at the star that she almost died for?

She had been only moments away from death. . . .

A stirring not all that far from where Kiriki and Sun Eagle still lay caused them both to tighten within one another's arms. Kiriki's breath became shallow as she looked guardedly up at Sun Eagle.

"You heard it also?" she whispered.

Sun Eagle gently eased her away from him, his eyes searching around them. "Yes, I heard it also," he whispered, reaching for his knife that he had placed close beside him before he had fallen asleep. Circling his fingers around the handle he rose stealthily to his feet, Kiriki following his lead.

Sun Eagle glared down at her. "You stay!" he commanded in a harsh whisper. "It could be one of Brown Bear's scouts. If so, I will be forced to kill him. There is no need for you to see Pawnee blood spilled!"

Trembling, Kiriki nodded. She hugged herself, her pulse racing when she heard the rustling sound again, this time closer. She focused her eyes on a thick grove of cottonwood trees nestled beside a meandering stream, knowing that was where the intruder was positioned.

Then she moved her gaze slowly to Sun Eagle. He had also heard and was almost there. The intruder could jump out at any moment and kill Sun Eagle with one plunge of a knife. An arrow could move silently through the night and become embedded in Sun Eagle's powerful chest. A bullet could very easily find its home in her loved one's body. . . .

Lunging forward, Sun Eagle became lost to Kiriki's sight among the trees. She covered her mouth with a hand and stifled a gasp of fear behind it. Any moment now she could lose the man she loved!

Her gaze shifted to the rifle that lay on the ground within her reach. Her heart raced. Should she get the gun and follow Sun Eagle?

But she had never fired a weapon before! Her father had warned her of the dangers of firearms introduced to the Indian by the white man.

"I am part white," she whispered. "*I* should be able to use the firearm of the white man."

"Kiriki!" Sun Eagle shouted, kneeling down beside a

Pawnee warrior that he had found dying beneath the cottonwoods. "Come quickly!"

Flying Deer looked up at Sun Eagle through pain-hazed eyes. He reached for Sun Eagle's hand and grasped onto it. "I . . . saw . . . the campfire," he said hoarsely. "I did not expect it to be you, Sun Eagle. It is so good that it *is* you."

Sun Eagle placed his free hand beneath Flying Deer's head and lifted it from the hard ground, fearing that it was he who had shot him. He had been forced to return the fire when Brown Bear had begun the shooting. Never would Sun Eagle have wanted to shoot and kill Flying Deer. He was one of the most compassionate of all Pawnee.

"Flying Deer, I am saddened to see you suffering so from a wound," he said, his voice drawn. "It was not my wish to shoot you or any of our Pawnee comrades!"

Then one of Sun Eagle's eyebrows quirked when he searched Flying Deer's body for a wound, flinching when recognizing that which would be made by an arrow, not a bullet. Sun Eagle had fought with a rifle—not bow and arrow!

Flying Deer coughed, his whole body twitching from the pain. He held more tightly to Sun Eagle's hand. "You did not shoot me," he whispered harshly. He looked past Sun Eagle as Kiriki stepped into view, water cupped within her hands. When she fell to her knees beside him and offered him the water, he drank thirstily, then began coughing again, the water almost choking him.

Sun Eagle stroked Flying Deer's fevered brow, his heart anxious for answers. "My friend, it is good to know that it is not I who is responsible for your pain," he said thickly. "But I do not understand. If not myself, then who? What Indian shot you with an arrow? Was it the Comanche?"

Flying Deer inhaled a shaky breath, then tried to lean up on an elbow, to get closer to Sun Eagle's face, but weakness caused him to collapse back to the ground. Breathing hard, he stared up at Sun Eagle. "No. Not the

Comanche. One of our own Pawnee is responsible," he said weakly. "It has been hard to force myself not to give in to death. But I could not leave this earth until I managed to tell someone of the wrong that Brown Bear is doing you, his brother. When I saw the campfire, I began scooting toward it. I had to tell whoever it was that Brown Bear is not following his father's commands. He is going against his father! He is going against *you*, Sun Eagle! Above all else, he wants you dead. He will stop at nothing until you are."

Sun Eagle's mind was spinning, trying to grasp onto the truths of Flying Deer's words. What did it all mean? Was Brown Bear doing exactly the opposite of what his chieftain father had ordered? Had his father possibly forgiven him this bold act of saving Kiriki from the Morning Star sacrifice?

"My wound is from your brother's arrow," Flying Deer continued. "The wound is mortal. I have not long to live." He squeezed Sun Eagle's hand more fiercely. "But it is long enough to tell you that you are being celebrated as a hero in your village! Your courage to rescue Kiriki made everyone look upon you as a hero. You are not the renegade your brother wants you to believe that you are! It is because I could no longer allow your brother to search and kill you that he decided to take *my* life. When I walked away from him, he shot me in the back. He saw me as a threat."

Flying Deer managed a weak smile. "He was right," he said, then he looked wildly up at Sun Eagle as his body convulsed. "Go home, Sun Eagle . . ." he said, his voice strangled. Then he stared unseeingly ahead as his body relaxed and his breathing ceased.

Kiriki turned her eyes away, a keen sadness filling her over this man whose allegiance to Sun Eagle had caused him his life. Yet a part of her was exceedingly happy, for Sun Eagle was able to return home, and not only as another Pawnee, as a great *hero!*

Then her eyes wavered. What was *her* status in Chief Antelope Buck's village now? Would she also be as welcomed? She *was* to be Sun Eagle's wife! Surely no one would look to her as anything less. Oh, surely they would not continue looking to her as the woman who had cheated them of the sacrifice.

She wanted to be loved—to be accepted as one of them. . . .

Strong hands on her shoulders caused Kiriki to turn slowly around. She looked up into Sun Eagle's eyes, scarcely breathing, for surely he was having his own moments of doubts.

"It is time to return home," he said, looking sternly down at her. "We will return Flying Deer to his family for burial. We will let the people of my village see you ride with me on my horse, knowing that you are mine, *forever*. We then shall go to my father and tell him what Flying Deer has told me about the ugliness of Brown Bear's intentions toward me—that he came to kill, not spread good tidings from our chieftain father."

"What will your father do about Brown Bear?" Kiriki dared to ask.

"It is for my father alone to decide," Sun Eagle said, a sudden pain entering the depths of his voice. "I am sure that Brown Bear will not be free to return home again. *He* will live the life of a renegade, not *I*."

Tears of happiness streamed down Kiriki's cheeks as she eased into Sun Eagle's arms. "Is it really true?" she murmured. "Are we truly free to enter your village? Will we soon be wed, Sun Eagle?"

"All of these things are true," Sun Eagle said, stroking his fingers through her hair.

Kiriki looked quickly up at him. "My parents!" she gasped. "I must go to them soon! They must be told that I am alive and that I am well!"

Sun Eagle smiled down at her. "After we make things right in my village I will go with you to yours," he said. "I must take many horses as an apology to them for the inconvenience that Brown Bear caused by abducting you."

He cast his eyes downward, then looked slowly up at Kiriki again. "Even Durah's parents will be given many horses in hopes that their loss of a daughter will not be as great in their hearts and eyes any longer," he said solemnly.

Kiriki was at a loss for words for a moment. "You would do that?" she finally said. "You would be that generous? That kindhearted?"

"It is a small thing to do when considering why I am doing it," Sun Eagle said, swinging away from her to bend down over Flying Deer. "Now we must prepare a travois for my fallen comrade. He must be returned home with dignity." His jaw tightened. "Perhaps my brother will not only be banned from his people, he may be hunted and killed for what he did to Flying Deer. Shooting a man in the back is the ultimate act of cowardice." He lowered his face into a hand. "How could he do this? How? And all because of me? How could he hate *this* much?"

Kiriki knelt down beside Sun Eagle and slipped a comforting arm around his shoulder. She was silent, her own concerns heavy on her heart. Though Sun Eagle had all of the good intentions in the world of returning her home and offering many horses to two different families for restitution, would these families accept the gifts? They could still look upon Sun Eagle as an enemy. He even bore the scars of their wrath!

It was up to her to set things right. Oh, but what if she couldn't! What if Sun Eagle was taken prisoner? What if he was shot quickly for Brown Bear's crimes?

She looked over at Sun Eagle, seeing his total innocence. Nothing could be allowed to happen to him. Nothing!

There would never ever be another Sun Eagle.

The moonlight streaming down through the trees overhead in spirals of silver light spreading across the ground at his feet, Brown Bear knelt to a knee and kneaded his chin in contemplation. "My brother is more shrewd than I have given him credit for!" he said, his teeth clenched angrily. He looked up at the warriors circled around him. "Do not just stand there. Search the land for other signs of Sun Eagle's gelding! It cannot go in two directions at the same time.''

"Brown Bear, your brother is leading us in circles," a warrior dared to say, knowing Brown Bear's temper. "It is no use. He is long gone."

Brown Bear rustled quickly to his feet and stood face to face with the warrior. "What are you saying?" he growled. "That we give up the chase?"

"No," the warrior said, standing firm beneath Brown Bear's threatening stance. "I say let us ride back to our village and see if Sun Eagle chanced returning to speak to your father. He is not the sort to give up easily. He would not give up a future that would include the title of chief!"

Brown Bear spun around on a heel, placing his back to the challenging warrior. He began to pace back and forth, his head bowed, his fists clenched. Would Sun Eagle dare return to his village after having defiled the Morning Star's wishes? Could he truly believe that he had been pardoned of such a vile act? Or had he found out somehow that he had been forgiven and was being looked upon as some sort of hero? If he returned and discovered exactly what news Brown Bear was supposed to have brought him, Brown Bear was doomed for eternity!

The thought frightened him, sending icy currents of dread through him, and Brown Bear ran to his horse and quickly mounted. "We must ride toward home!" he shouted. "We must overtake Sun Eagle if he is on his way there. He must not be allowed to arrive alive. Nor should Kiriki! Both can tell much that would harm Brown Bear."

Wheeling his horse around, Brown Bear sank his heels into its flanks. The night air cold on his face, his insides as cold from fear, he rode hard through the darkness. He held his chin high, as was expected of a noble warrior, but he could not help but already feel the label of coward being attached to his name! If Sun Eagle or Kiriki told the actual truth of what had happened today, Brown Bear's future would be worth nothing at all. He would have to steal to live, for he would be a wandering renegade, the most hated of all Indians.

Eighteen

▼ ▼ ▼

IT was growing dusk again, the return to Sun Eagle's village having taken the remainder of the night and the whole day. Though so tired that she felt like she might fall from Sun Eagle's gelding, Sun Eagle's strong arm thankfully holding her in place, Kiriki sat with a lifted chin and straight back as eyes began to follow her entry into the village. Fires burned brightly outside the earthen lodges, lighting their entrances where more Pawnee stepped into view, silently watching Sun Eagle's return, triumphant over his brother who continued to wrong him. Kiriki was closely scrutinized, embarrassing her as she realized that in most minds she was being remembered as nude and painted for the sacrifice.

Yet these people were all probably also remembering how she had been tied to the scaffold—courageous and ready to accept her fate. If she looked closely enough, she could see not only happiness at seeing Sun Eagle, but a sense of relief in also seeing her. She hoped the reason for this relief had nothing to do with the Morning Star sacrifice. She wanted to place all thoughts of it behind her. This was the beginning of her new life. She was soon to be wed to the man she loved. Never again would she dream of being married to a white man. Sun Eagle was all that she would ever want in life. Even if she developed a curved back while pleasing him from day to day by doing her daily chores that would be required of her, even that would be accepted. Did not her mother accept her dues as a wife? So would Kiriki, and be happy for it.

Kiriki became aware of something else. Everyone's

gaze was settling on the body that was being drawn behind
Sun Eagle's horse on the travois. Covered with a blanket,
no one could tell who was being returned, dead.

Sun Eagle reined his horse in before his father's large
earthen lodge. Before dismounting, he met his father's
steady stare with one of his own, his heart thundering
wildly inside him. Had Brown Bear succeeded at killing
Sun Eagle, this son and father would have never been
reunited again until they both passed into the hereafter.
This way was better. They had so much more to experience in life before embracing in the hereafter. Though it
was a place of no more fears or worries, it was only meant
for loved ones to join there once everything of *this* life
had been achieved. Sun Eagle and Chief Antelope Buck
were being given this second chance.

It made Sun Eagle's heart sing. . . .

Dismounting, Sun Eagle lifted Kiriki from the horse and
stood her beside him as they faced Chief Antelope Buck
and Kidibattsk as she joined her husband outside the
earthen lodge. Sun Eagle saw immense joy in his mother's
eyes, and knew that it was taking all the restraint taught
to her as a child not to rush to him and embrace him. It
was the same for him. But both knew the dignity that
must be maintained, for Sun Eagle was no longer a mere
child. He was a great warrior—the man who would one
day be a great Pawnee chief.

He must be treated thusly. He must *act* thusly.

Chief Antelope Buck stepped forward. His eyes wavered
as he looked Sun Eagle up and down, seeing the scars of
his torture. Then he stepped to him and solidly embraced
him.

"My son," he said, his voice drawn. "My son, Brown
Bear searched and found you. You have come home."

Chief Antelope Buck stepped away from Sun Eagle
when Sun Eagle did not reply. He quirked an eyebrow as
he silently looked into Sun Eagle's eyes, then slowly
moved his gaze to the body that lay covered on the travois.

Something grabbed at his heart. Brown Bear? Could
that be Brown Bear?

He looked past the travois and became puzzled when he saw no warriors returning behind Sun Eagle. If Brown Bear had found Sun Eagle and had told him to return to his village for the recognition that he deserved, would not Brown Bear and his warriors return with Sun Eagle? Everyone would want to participate in the celebration!

Chief Antelope Buck once again peered questioningly down at the covered body, aware of his people walking toward him. He became rigid when Sun Eagle came to his side and placed an arm around his shoulder.

"My father, I have much to tell you," he said. He flinched when his father drew away from him and knelt to a knee beside the travois. He watched his father raise a trembling hand to the blanket. "Father, I have much to tell Flying Deer's . . ."

His voice trailed off as his father peeled a corner of the blanket away, revealing the death mask of Flying Deer. Others also saw. A keen wailing began in the midst of the crowd of Pawnee making Sun Eagle's heart ache, for he recognized Flying Deer's mother's voice. She now understood that she had lost a son—an *only* son. . . .

"Flying Deer?" Chief Antelope Buck gasped, glancing quickly up at Sun Eagle.

Sun Eagle placed a hand on his father's shoulder. "You thought that it might be Brown Bear?" he asked quietly.

"That is so," Chief Antelope Buck said, nodding.

"Father, Brown Bear killed Flying Deer," Sun Eagle said solemnly, feeling his father's flesh flinch beneath his grasp. "My brother, your son, shot Flying Deer in the back because he refused to accompany Brown Bear on a chase that meant eventual death for me."

Chief Antelope Buck rose abruptly to his feet. His face became lined with deep grooves as he frowned at Sun Eagle. "What do you mean?" he said, his voice drawn.

Sun Eagle looked slowly around him, at the questioning eyes. He inhaled a shaky breath when Flying Deer's mother and father came and took him from the travois and carried him away, wails erupting all around them, to show everyone's remorse for the fallen son.

"Let us go into your lodge so that we can speak of Brown Bear in private," Sun Eagle said, once again placing a hand on his father's shoulder. He glanced down at Kiriki. "Let us speak of Kiriki, also, and of our plans to be man and wife."

Kidibattsk moved to Kiriki's side. She placed a heavy arm around her waist and looked adoringly up at her. "It is good that you are alive and well," she murmured. She then frowned. "Had I known in time that it was you who was being readied for the sacrifice I would have personally whisked you away!"

Kiriki smiled down at Sun Eagle's mother. "Thank you," she said, warming all over inside. It was wonderful to know that she was welcome not only in Sun Eagle's village, but also inside his people's hearts. She was being treated as though she were already wed to Sun Eagle. Just perhaps things in life were finally going to be good!

Kiriki and Kidibattsk followed Sun Eagle and Chief Antelope Buck into the large earthen lodge. Kiriki was almost knocked from her feet when she felt something lunge at her ankles. She gasped with delight when she looked down and saw the one surviving bear cub there, playfully trying to tackle her, its whole body shaking in its playful state and delight in recognition.

"Oh, how wonderful to find that you are all right," Kiriki said, falling to her knees to hug the cub. "My sweet little cub. You are all right!"

Kidibattsk laughed softly as she patted Kiriki fondly on the head. "It was I who kept the cub for your return," she said. She glanced over at Chief Antelope Buck as he was settling down before the fire, Sun Eagle sitting opposite him. She giggled. "In my husband's eyes, it was not the most favored thing to do."

"I think you are very thoughtful," Kiriki said, looking up at Kidibattsk. "I now see why Sun Eagle is so compassionate. It is because of you, his mother."

"Let us go and sit beside the fire and listen to what Sun Eagle has to say," Kidibattsk murmured. "I fear the news of my other son is not good. Oh, how Brown Bear disappoints me!''

Kiriki rose to her full height and went with Kidibattsk and sat down with her with a view of Sun Eagle across the fire. The bear cub curled up in Kiriki's lap as she began listening earnestly to Sun Eagle explaining about Brown Bear's disloyalty to his father, of how Brown Bear had not only abducted Kiriki, but also had killed Durah. He explained his long hours of torture in the sun at the hand of Kiriki's father who had accused him unjustly.

Everything became quiet in the lodge after Sun Eagle stopped talking. Kiriki looked from his mother to his father, seeing pain in the depths of their eyes, and understanding why. Brown Bear was not a son to be proud of. He was also a son who was now the same as dead to his parents. He had been disobedient to them both.

''It is with a heavy heart that I had to bring you the news of Brown Bear,'' Sun Eagle said, his voice breaking. ''Let us now speak of more favorable things.''

He beckoned with a hand for Kiriki to come to him. Breathlessly, Kiriki set the cub aside and went to Sun Eagle and obediently sat down beside him. She thrilled inside when he took her hand and held it on his lap.

''Kiriki was never meant to be wed to the Morning Star,'' Sun Eagle growled. ''It is for *me* that she was brought into this world. Soon we are to be wed. Mother and Father, it is my wish that I have both your blessings.''

With tears in her eyes, Kidibattsk went to her cedar box and opened it. Her pudgy fingers brought out the pink shell necklace all repaired and beautiful again. She took it to Kiriki and placed it around her neck. ''It is with a happy heart that I return this gift to you,'' she said hoarsely. ''It is with a happy heart that I accept you into our lives. You will be a special daughter-in-law.''

Touching the necklace tenderly, Kiriki looked down at it, then with misty eyes looked back up at Kidibattsk. ''I thank you with all of my heart for everything,'' she murmured. ''I look forward to having you as my mother-in-law. It will be a most perfect arrangement.''

His chest swelling with pride, Sun Eagle looked from Kiriki to his mother, then over at his father, who still had yet to say anything about the upcoming marriage. "Father?" he asked. "And what do you have to say? Is Kiriki welcomed by you, also?"

Chief Antelope Buck rose to his feet and went to Kiriki. He gestured with his hands for her to rise before him. Her knees weak, feeling dwarfed by this mighty Indian chief, she did as she was bid and melted inside when he clasped his hands gently to her shoulders.

"From this day forth I shall address you as 'daughter,' " he said, his voice deep and resonant. "You make my son proud. So shall I be as proud."

Kiriki flicked tears from her thick lashes with a finger, then smiled warmly up at Chief Antelope Buck. "I shall never disappoint any of you," she said, swallowing hard. "From this day forth, Sun Eagle shall be my life." She laughed softly and corrected herself. "From the moment I *met* your son, he has been my life, I should say."

Sun Eagle chuckled and went to place an arm about her waist. "And with that I must return Kiriki home so that her parents can rejoice in knowing that she is all right," he said, smiling down at her.

Chief Antelope Buck's shoulder muscles knotted as he tensed with uneasiness. "And if you are not welcome in her village, my son?" he asked, now knowing the entire story of how Sun Eagle had been accused of Kiriki's abduction.

"That I will be bringing Kiriki back to her people alive and well should be all that they need to realize that they accused me wrongly," Sun Eagle said, his eyes darkening with an unspoken fear of that which he did not want to reveal. He still felt the soreness of his wounds inflicted by Kiriki's father's warriors. He would be scarred for life because of him.

"I will also be taking a great bride price to her father," he said quickly. "And enough horses to pay Durah's family to help lessen their hearts' pain over their loss."

"That is very thoughtful, and I am sure that you will

be welcome by all as soon as they see what your intentions are toward Kiriki,'' Chief Antelope Buck said, placing an arm around Sun Eagle's shoulder. ''Who could not be proud to have my son as part of their family?''

Sun Eagle smiled crookedly, recalling exactly how Kiriki's father had rejected his first offered bride price. In her village, Sun Eagle was nothing special. Perhaps once they realized that he had saved her life they would feel differently.

They left the lodge, Kiriki leaving her cub in the care of Sun Eagle's mother just this one more time. She was given a strawberry roan mare on which to make her journey back to her village. She waited for Sun Eagle to round up the many horses, feeling guilty that he felt that he must offer so much in order to have her as his wife. In truth, she would go with him anyway. Even if she did not have her family's blessing, she would marry Sun Eagle.

But she admired him for being gallant enough to want to make a good, lasting impression on his soon to be in-laws, for she did love her parents so very much.

As they rode from town, they looked remorsely up at the funeral scaffold being built in a tree at the edge of town. Flying Deer would rest there soon.

Brown Bear raised a hand and stopped his warriors when he looked ahead at his village and saw a body being placed on a scaffold at the edge of town. His insides recoiled, wondering which of his people had died while he was away.

''Go and inquire as to who it is before I make my entrance into the village!'' he ordered one of his warriors.

He watched, fidgeting with his reins, as the warrior rode dutifully up to the small band of Pawnee who were surrounding the tree upon which the body was being placed. Squinting his eyes, he leaned low over the mane of his horse when some of the people looked suddenly his way.

Then he straightened his back when the warrior wheeled his horse around and started riding back, so quickly it was as though a bolt of lightning had struck him. Knowing that the news was not good, Brown Bear edged his horse back into the cover of some low hanging branches of a willow tree, then paled when the warrior reined in beside him, breathless.

"Flying Deer is the one who is being mourned in our village!" the warrior said, his eyes wild.

"How can it be?" Brown Bear gasped. "You know where he died. That is a day's ride from here!"

"That is so," the warrior said, nodding. He panted for breath. "He was brought to the village for burial."

"By whom?" Brown Bear asked, impatience thick in his words.

"You will not be happy with my answer," the warrior said, his voice fading.

"Tell me!" Brown Bear said, leaning over to grab his arm.

"It was Sun Eagle," the warrior said, wincing when Brown Bear's grip strengthened painfully. "It is rumored that he found Flying Deer before he had died. Flying Deer told him everything, Brown Bear—everything about you."

Brown Bear dropped his hand away from the warrior. He hung his head, having just been told the worst of anything that could be told him. He knew that at this moment he had lost his family. Instead of just a brother, an entire family! And it ate away at his heart to realize that he was the cause.

"What are we to do, Brown Bear?" the warrior dared to ask. "It is also rumored that should you return, you shall be punished severely by your father and then banished from the tribe. So will all of the warriors who joined you in this vengeance against your brother. We are all guilty in our people's eyes. I am lucky I was not grabbed from my horse and slain only moments ago. We are as one in our guilt for the death of Flying Deer!"

Brown Bear slowly lifted his eyes and looked past the warrior. His insides grew numb when he saw several of his father's most valued warriors ride from the village in his direction. "We must flee!" he shouted, spinning his horse around, digging his heels into its flanks. "We must ride into the hills and find a safe hideaway! I do not wish to fire upon anymore of our people. Not even in defense of myself."

The horses thundered away in a cloud of dust, soon lost in the thick cover of the forest. Brown Bear was cursing himself beneath his breath, his eyes lit with points of fire. Still, he would somehow find a way to get even with his brother.

Kiriki's smile broadened as she spied the protective wall of her village just up ahead. She looked over the fields now awash with pale colors of predusk, the ground evenly furrowed, sprouts of corn and cabbages anew all across the land. A rabbit stopped to sniff the cabbage leaves, then bolted away with alarm when the sound of the approaching horses frightened it.

"I am home," Kiriki whispered, then shouted her father's name as she saw him appear at the gate on his horse. She waved frantically as he rode toward her, flanked on each side by two massive warriors that she readily recognized.

"Father!" she shouted. "Sun Eagle rescued me! He has brought me home! Oh, Father, if not for Sun Eagle I would be dead!"

Her father drew his horse to a shuddering halt before Kiriki and Sun Eagle. There was a blissful sort of joy in his eyes as he looked Kiriki up and down, and then there was a strange, doubtful coldness in his eyes when he looked over at Sun Eagle.

"As I promised, I have brought many more horses for you as bride price for your daughter," Sun Eagle said, gesturing toward the horses with a sweep of the hand. "I have even brought many horses that I will offer to Durah's family in compensation for their daughter's death. You see, it was my brother who is responsible for Kiriki's abduction and Durah's death. He is responsible for the misunderstanding between us as well."

Lone Chief's mouth opened. "Your brother?" he said thickly. "He is responsible? Not you?"

"Did I not tell you while you were torturing me that I could never do anything to hurt your daughter?" Sun Eagle responded, his voice bland. "Let us go and talk beside your fire. Let us share in a smoke. I will explain everything to you and then I wish to take Kiriki back with me to my village. You are invited to come and share in the wedding ceremony."

"And what if I still do not approve of you being my daughter's husband?" Lone Chief asked, leaning closer to Sun Eagle, his eyes dancing.

Kiriki moved her horse closer to her father. "Then, Father, I will be forced to go against your wishes for the first time in my life," she interjected. She reached for Sun Eagle's hand. "He *will* be my husband. No matter what anyone says." She swallowed hard. "Even you, Father."

She looked past him. "Before I leave, I must visit Durah's grave," she said, tears near. "I have much to say to my dear friend."

Lone Chief wheeled his horse around. He looked over his shoulder. "Sun Eagle, you are welcome to my dwelling," he said, then lifted his lips into a slow smile. "Any time. Once you become my son-in-law, I hope to see you often."

Kiriki beamed from ear to ear. She was so happy she wanted to shout. But she held herself at bay and rode proudly into her village with Sun Eagle at her side.

It was like a wonderful dream that she was afraid she might awaken from at any moment.

Nineteen
▼ ▼ ▼

ATTIRED in a white doeskin dress, the necklace of pink shells worn proudly around her neck, Kiriki sat beside Sun Eagle at the celebration in his village marking the return of a hero.

Inching closer to Sun Eagle, Kiriki slipped one of her hands into his and sneaked him a sweet smile as he glanced down at her. When he smiled at her, it was as though the beautiful sky they were sitting beneath had embraced and kissed her. Her insides thrilled at the thought of being free to be with him, their wedding the cause for the next celebration.

Snuggling close to him, Kiriki's eyes were drawn to the dancers who pranced and leaped around the great outdoor fire in time with the great booming of many drums. The dancers were young boys attired only in breechclouts, their whole heads shaved except for a narrow roach which ran from the forehead to the back of the head. This roach, less than an inch long, had been stiffened at the sides with grease and paint to make it stand up well. From the roach, the boys' scalplock fell back in its natural position.

Young girls stood around in clusters, giggling, watching the loose flapping of the breechclouts as the boys' legs lifted feverishly as they danced. The girls' faces were painted freely and their hair was worn in braids, their attire a loose buckskin garment called a smock.

Kiriki's eyes were drawn across the fire, pride burning inside her as she looked from her father and mother to Sun Eagle's father and mother who sat side by side, enjoying the celebration. They had smoked the pipe of peace

and were united in feelings about the upcoming marriage
between their son and daughter, whereas only a few days
ago Kiriki's father had tortured and humiliated Sun Eagle.

She thanked Tirawa for making everything possible.
Because of Sun Eagle's courageous rescue, everything had
changed.

A cold nose burrowing into the back of Kiriki's arm
made her turn with a start, then she smiled pleasantly
when she discovered the bear cub poking and sniffing at
her, obviously feeling neglected.

Turning, Kiriki reached for the cub and lifted it, placing
it on her lap. She stroked its thick fur as it settled down
in a round ball, closing its eyes with contentment. Kiriki
continued stroking the cub as she observed the celebration,
enjoying the chants and music, now watching the rhythmic
movements of the elders who performed in full tribal
dress, then watching the celebration change from dancing
to games, all the while Sun Eagle beside her, his chin
held proudly high.

First there were the shooting matches. During this exer-
cise of keen competition, the young braves wore a stiff
piece of leather around their left wrists to protect them
from the bow string, and every time the bow string hit
this leather, it cracked.

Kiriki noticed that the braves held their bows at an
angle, or very nearly perpendicular, and then with a quick
release sent the arrow whizzing through the air. They used
the hide of a coyote hung up to resemble the shape of a
man as their target. They were able to hit the target shooting their arrows at an angle that flew over three hundred
yards, if not more.

Bows used by the younger braves were smaller than
those used by the men. The arrows were blunt, without
either barb or feathers. The adult bows were made of a
very tough wood and were about four and one half feet
in length. They were almost two inches wide and tapered
at either end. On one end they had a buttonlike affair over
which the tendons were put, thus making the tendon as
tight as a fiddle bow. When not in use, they would release

the tendon by simply slipping the tendon off the buttonlike affair.

The braves, both young and old alike, made their own arrows. They were for the most part two feet long, fastenening their arrow heads with tendons to the arrow shaft. Their arrow heads were mostly of steel although they had some that were flint.

On the opposite end of the arrow they had feathers that had been taken from a hawk or an eagle, and were split lengthwise and fastened to the arrow with the same substances that they used on the arrow heads.

Kiriki watched the braves place their arrows aside. It was now lance-throwing time. The braves were to throw their lances through hoops while the hoops were rolling on the ground. The same boy that threw the hoop often threw the lance, and this called for very quick action.

This continued for some time, and then a great abundance of food was served. While eating fruit and all assortments of roasted meat, Kiriki and Sun Eagle were joined by their parents.

"It is with a warm heart that I tell you news that may help the future of our people," Chief Antelope Buck said, his eyes dancing as he looked over at Sun Eagle. He wiped grease from his wide lips with the back of his hand, smiling.

Sun Eagle sorted through the tray of fruit and chose an apple. "What news, Father?" he asked. "I am anxious to hear."

"Major O'Fallon would like for you to accompany him, along with many other representatives of our Plains Indians, to Washington to meet with the great white chief," Chief Antelope Buck said, leaning closer to Sun Eagle. "My son, you have been chosen, personally, to represent your people. Major O'Fallon even said that you could be singled out for a special honor for your courageous rescue of Kiriki. It is with pride that I accepted for you. I told Major O'Fallon that you would willingly go to represent our band of Pawnee."

Kiriki's eyes lit up, her heart pounding wildly as she

looked over at Sun Eagle. Never had she heard such exciting news. Sun Eagle was actually being given the opportunity to go to the great city of Washington where the streets were filled with white men dressed in ruffled shirts and expensive suits, traveling in fancy carriages, and women were dressed in silks, satins, and wore flashing diamonds about their necks. Could it be?

Oh, but if only she was being given this opportunity!

It would be a dream! A dream!

Sun Eagle lay the apple aside, his eyes troubled. His shoulder muscles and his jaw tightened as he looked at his father. "It has never been my desire to mingle with the white man," he said in nearly a growl. "It is not my desire now to do so!"

"But you *have* mingled with the white man right here in our village!" Chief Antelope Buck argued. "You speak with Major O'Fallon as though he is a brother."

Sun Eagle stole his gaze away from his father and looked studiously into the fire. "That is different," he said flatly. "Major O'Fallon is different. He has a heart that does not react in ugly ways to the Indian." He glanced quickly over at his father. "He is one of a kind, Father. I would not find such camaraderie among the white men in Washington."

Chief Antelope Buck placed a hand on Sun Eagle's arm. "But, son, you must try," he said thickly. "Our future could be better because of it!"

"I am only one Indian, Father," Sun Eagle said. "Do not put so much faith in me, alone, to make things better for our people. The burden would be too great. I am not sure that I want to walk around with such a burden on my shoulders."

"You can move mountains if you put your mind to it," Chief Antelope Buck growled. "Did you not prove that you can do this when you chose to rescue Kiriki from the scaffold? Who else would have chanced performing such a daring feat? Who else would manage to come out of the performance unscathed, instead, being celebrated as a hero? Only you, my son. Only you."

"You say that many others are going to Washington for the same purpose?" Sun Eagle asked reflectively.

"That is so," Chief Antelope Buck said, nodding.

"That journey would take weeks, Father. I am not sure I wish to take that much time for efforts that will in the end be futile," Sun Eagle argued. He gave Kiriki a slow look, taking her hand, squeezing it affectionately. "I do not want to take the time away from Kiriki. I do not want to postpone our wedding."

Kiriki smiled up at Sun Eagle, yet it was not as sincere a smile as she wanted it to be. She was feeling torn about his decision not to want to go to Washington, thinking that he *should* go, for perhaps he would never get this opportunity again.

Yet she did not want to postpone the wedding, either! Perhaps if they did, something would happen to cause it never to happen! She realized just how quickly these bad things occurred in life. So much had happened to her and Sun Eagle these past several days.

Chief Antelope Buck looked from Sun Eagle, to Kiriki. "Take Kiriki with you, my son," he suggested whole-heartedly. "Then, once you finish the mission that is most important to your people, we will have a wedding upon your return. You will begin your marriage with much gladness in your heart if you first carry out this mission that I see is so important to our people."

Kiriki's knees grew weak and her eyes widened into great pools of blue at the prospect of being included in Sun Eagle's special journey. Could it actually be happening? All of her life she had wanted to have a part in the white man's culture, because a part of her was white, and now she might be given the opportunity to at least observe how the white men lived and acted in a big city of whites.

She pleaded with Sun Eagle with her eyes, so afraid that he was determined to say no, not realizing what going to Washington would mean to her.

But the wedding . . .

How could she be willing to accept the decision to postpone the wedding so easily? Was it the part of her that was white talking to her heart now? Did the part of her that was white still want to think of a future with the white people?

Oh, but she felt as though she was betraying Sun Eagle with such thoughts and doubts! Yet still, if all truths were known, she knew that she would give her left arm to get to go to Washington.

Sun Eagle smiled warmly down at Kiriki. "It is in your eyes what you want my answer to be," he said. "My woman, do you not realize that I know your mixed feelings about your heritage that is part white? I will take you to the city of the great white father with me."

An intense feeling of joy overtook Kiriki. She could not refrain from lunging into Sun Eagle's arms, hugging him fitfully. "Thank you," she whispered, tears wetting his bare chest. "Oh, thank you. I will cherish each moment while there!"

Sun Eagle framed her face between his hands and held her away from him, their eyes locking. "But will you want to return to live the life of a Pawnee wife once you see the riches of the white women?" he asked, his voice thick. "Will I be taking you there, only to lose you? We will not yet be man and wife, Kiriki. You will be free to go wherever you choose, and with whom."

Kiriki swallowed hard, recalling the many times that she had vowed never to become the wife of a Pawnee brave. She had not wanted to become old before her time! She had not wanted her shoulders to become curved and her back bent!

Oh, but what if she *did* become swallowed up in the wonders of the white women and how they lived? What if she *did* find it hard to return to Nebraska with Sun Eagle?

The thought frightened her, yet deep down inside, she knew that she could never turn her eyes, nor her heart, away from Sun Eagle. No one could love as fiercely as she loved him! It was a love that would endure all the pain and hardships of being a Pawnee wife who labored from day to night.

"My love, how could you doubt my love for you so easily?" she murmured, then moved into his arms again, embracing him.

Sun Eagle held her tightly, inhaling the sweet fragrance of her hair as he placed his cheek on her brow. He so badly wanted to believe her! Yet he could not help but worry about this journey that was to benefit his people, whereas in the end, he, alone, could lose so much.

His victory, his success, depended on Kiriki. Only Kiriki . . .

Sun Eagle was delivering Kiriki home after the celebration, his grip around her waist strong as his gelding rode in a gentle lope across the land. The sky seemed dressed in sequined velvet this night, so beautiful and peaceful that Kiriki was not even once reminded of the ordeal of the Morning Star sacrifice. It was behind her now, as were her harried moments with Brown Bear. It was the future that mattered, and at this moment Kiriki saw it as wonderful.

"You are in no hurry to be home in your parents' dwelling, are you?" Sun Eagle asked, directing his horse away from the wooded bluffs he was traveling along, across a fertile plain of goldenrod and bluestem grass, toward a river valley. "Will your parents worry?"

"Not as long as they know that I am with you," Kiriki said, turning to smile up at him. "Did you not see the admiration in both their eyes during the celebration? They see how you are honored as one who is important. They will no longer question your worth as a husband, either."

Sun Eagle frowned as he emitted a low grumble, his thoughts momentarily straying to the hours he had been forced to endure the heat of the sun as he lay spread-eagled across the land, his ankles and wrists secured to stakes in the ground. The same man who had hated him then, admired him now.

But Sun Eagle could not forget that quickly how Kiriki's father had been so unreasonable, not listening to reason, while all along, she had been with Brown Bear. Had

Brown Bear raped Kiriki, not only Brown Bear would be accountable, but also Kiriki's father.

"Do not blame me for questioning your father's worth as an in-law," Sun Eagle said, regretting his haste in speaking condemning words of Kiriki's father when he heard her gasp of shock. "Kiriki, do not blame me for speaking in haste. It has not been that long ago since your father treated me as though I were less than a dog. The moments of torture are too fresh on my mind."

Kiriki lowered her eyes, not wanting to envision her father being that cruel to the man she loved. She did not want to envision Sun Eagle being forced to endure such pain. It was all because of her!

"Oh, Sun Eagle, I am so sorry," she murmured, turning to slip into his embrace. She kissed his bare chest, then flicked a tongue about one of his tight nipples. "Let me make it up to you, darling. Let me help you forget."

When her hand slipped low, seeking entrance at the waist of his buckskin breeches, Sun Eagle inhaled a shaky breath of anticipated pleasure. He guided his horse beneath the rustling leaves of a cottonwood and dismounted. He lifted his arms to Kiriki and took her from the horse, then swept her up fully into his arms and carried her toward the shine of the river.

Kiriki thrilled when he kissed her passionately. She clung to him as he lowered her to the ground beside the river and spread himself out over her, his hands already smoothing her doeskin dress down from her shoulders, soon revealing her peaks of breast to his feasting eyes.

His mouth left her lips and his tongue made a warm, wet path down the column of her neck, across the hollow of her throat, and then engulfed the nipple of a breast, suckling hungrily from it as he swept her dress on away from her and tossed it aside.

Kiriki's breath was being stolen away by Sun Eagle's lips and tongue. She moaned softly as he left her breast behind and kissed his way across her abdomen, flicking his tongue quickly in and out of her navel, then lower, where she throbbed with wondrous need of him.

Placing his hands beneath Kiriki's hips, locking his fingers into her soft flesh, Sun Eagle lifted her mound toward his waiting mouth. He flicked a tongue across her throbbing center, causing her to flinch with anticipation, then devoured her there with his full mouth.

Kiriki tightened her hands into tight fists at her sides as she tossed her head, the pleasure so intense she could hardly bear it. And still Sun Eagle tormented her with his tongue and lips. When he nipped her with his teeth, she sucked in a wild breath and had to fight back the climax that waited to spill forth from within her.

"Sun Eagle," Kiriki whispered, placing a gentle hand to his cheek. "Please. Do not love me in that way any longer. I want you, darling. I want you to feel the same pleasure as I."

Sun Eagle drew away from her and stood above her, removing his breeches. Then he leaned down over her, anchoring himself on each side of Kiriki with both his hands. He smiled down at her, his eyelids passion-heavy. "Never think that what I was just doing gives no pleasure to me," he said, softly probing between her thighs with his hard, throbbing shaft. "To give pleasure is also to receive it. Never forget that."

"Then, my darling, let me give you pleasure now," Kiriki said, lifting her hips so that it made it easier for him to enter her. She gyrated her body as he began his strokes within her, causing him to go deeper with each added thrust. She splayed her hands on his muscled thighs, encouraging him to move faster. Kiriki closed her eyes and absorbed the muscled feel of him inside her, filling her magnificently—filling her fully. Yet in small flashes she recalled when being with a man in such a way was painful and intolerable.

While with Brown Bear! Oh, could she ever forget?

Kiriki tried to force Brown Bear from her mind. The euphoria caused by Sun Eagle was helping her forget. She abandoned herself to the torrents of pleasure that were sweeping over her. She trembled with readiness as Sun Eagle's body hardened against hers. She absorbed the bold thrusts and cried out her fulfilled pleasure as an explosion of ecstasy claimed her, spreading a delicious tingling heat throughout her.

Sun Eagle's mouth bore down hard upon Kiriki's lips, kissing her hungrily as he became drenched in great surges of warmth traveling through his arteries and the sinews of his thighs, across his back and up to his brain, giving him a message of intense pleasure that outdid anything ever experienced before by him. His body shook and quaked, his seed spilling deeply within her velvet canal.

And then all was quiet, and Kiriki and Sun Eagle lay, clinging, Sun Eagle still atop her.

"Sun Eagle, you are a masterful lover," Kiriki whispered, caressing his muscled buttocks. "Do you promise me such ecstasy forever?"

"And if I were to say no?" Sun Eagle teased, tweaking one of her nipples between a thumb and forefinger. "Would you love me still? Or leave me?"

Kiriki looked up at him, puzzled, then laughed, knowing that he was teasing her. No one who loved as wonderfully as Sun Eagle could ever forget the art of doing so. In fact, she expected that he would become even more skilled as the years went along.

"Oh, I guess I would just have to go and find me another brave and turn you out to wander alone without me," she teased back.

Sun Eagle swung away from her and picked her suddenly up into his arms and began running with her toward the water. "We shall see about that!" he said, laughing. "Let me show you what I will do to you if you ever leave me! I shall find you and do *this!*"

He ran with her into the water and dove beneath the surface, taking her with him. Kiriki clung to him, holding her breath, then ecstasy claimed her again when she felt herself being caressed beneath the water. As they both popped back to the surface, Sun Eagle did not abandon his assault on her swollen mound. His fingers worked their magic, eliciting a faint sigh from Kiriki as she held her head back and closed her eyes with pleasure.

Standing on the bottom of the lake, Sun Eagle positioned Kiriki at his waist, locking her legs around him. He slipped his hardness within her and began stroking eagerly. His hands claimed both her breasts, then his lips sent butterfly kisses across them.

Together they soared and flew again, as though on wing. . . .

Twenty

Washington, D.C.

KIRIKI peered down from the Pennsylvania House Hotel window, where she and Sun Eagle had been given a room on the fourth floor. She clutched at the windowsill, dizzy as she looked down at the street that she had been told was called Pennsylvania Avenue. She had been on many buttes in her life in Nebraska, and had not let dizziness spoil the moment of looking out upon the beautiful creations of Tirawa. This building was not even as high as some buttes she had stood upon, yet its height troubled her senses.

Spinning around, to place her back to the window, sweat beading her brow, Kiriki now clutched her hands at her sides, wondering still about this weakness that was engulfing her. This was the wrong time to reveal to herself that she was not a strong person who could endure all challenges of life. Why, this moment in her life was even greater than what she had dreamed when she had let herself get caught up in hopes of one day being a part of the white man's culture—at least being able to observe it much more closely than she had been able to in Nebraska. She was in the city of the great white father. She was being thrust in the middle of the excitement that surrounded his great white mansion. The streets and sidewalks were busy with the hustle and bustle of people.

Slowly turning around, looking out the window again, Kiriki sighed with relief when she discovered that the dizziness had passed on over her. It had been only for a moment. Surely it was just the excitement of being in Washington with Sun Eagle. . . .

"Sun Eagle," she whispered, missing him. He had been whisked away by Major O'Fallon and his entourage almost the minute they had been settled into a room. Kiriki had been left alone, after being cautioned not to leave the room, since everything of the white man's world was unfamiliar to her.

Major O'Fallon had promised that she would be included in the evening's activities. She would be taken on a grand carriage ride through Washington. She would be shown all the points of interest, and then a meal would be shared by all in one of Washington's finest restaurants.

A shudder of excitement flowed through her at the thought of being able to actually view so much from a grand carriage. But an iciness of fear grabbed at her heart at the thought of eating among the white men and women in what they called restaurants. She did not even know the skills of eating with tableware! She would most surely embarrass herself.

And what of Sun Eagle?

Would he not be mocked by those watching if he did not know such skills, also? He was to one day be chief. He should never be mocked, by anyone!

"Though I am glad to be here to be able to observe so much, I fear that it could, in the end, prove to be an unwise journey!" Kiriki said to herself, closely watching the men and women scurrying along the sidewalk down below her. "Could we not be made fools of? That could benefit no one but the white man!"

Thoughts of gentle Major O'Fallon came to her mind. Surely he would not allow anyone to ridicule the Indians who had come to Washington with only the best of intentions on their minds, their hearts filled with hope. He would not allow them to leave filled with despair.

Restless, the minutes having grown to hours, Kiriki began pacing the room, then her reflection in a gilt-edged mirror hanging on the wall above a fancily carved oak table made her stop and stare at herself. It seemed strange to see the full length of herself in a mirror. As she slowly turned from side to side, she marveled at how the reflection was so real—as though she were two people! Until today, she had only seen her reflection in the mirroring of the lakes and rivers.

Stopping, Kiriki slowly smoothed her hand down the softness of her deerskin blouse. Having sewn it herself, she was familiar with how the rectangular piece of deerskin had been cut in half, a neck and hole and two arm holes then cut into it. The blouse had been sewn down both sides with an awl and sinew.

Her hands continued their journey downward, now touching the tanned deerhide fabric that had been sewn into a wrap-around skirt that extended from the waist to below the knees, fastened at the waist by a woven yarn belt. Leggings were fastened at her knees. Moccasins graced her tiny feet.

Though her attire was simple compared to the white woman's fancy, lacy clothes, it looked beautiful to her today as she was able to admire her handiwork as it shaped itself on her, revealing the soft curves of her breasts and hips, now seeing what Sun Eagle observed when he looked so admirably at her.

"I *am* pleasant to look at," Kiriki whispered, giggling, then blushing at the thought of her admiring herself in such a way.

The blaze of the sunset suddenly reflected through the window behind her and into the mirror, all bronze and brilliant, blinding Kiriki. She turned and stared at the window, her heart racing. The first day in Washington was almost gone, and she had seen nothing except what was visible from the window of her hotel room. Though it was an honor to be in such a grand room, where she and Sun Eagle would even be sleeping on a bed, it seemed not enough for her adventurous heart. She felt as though she was wasting time while waiting for Sun Eagle and Major O'Fallon's return. She wanted to experience, firsthand, those things that had been a part of her dreams and fantasies.

How could she be expected to wait and wait and wait?

"It surely won't matter if I leave for a little while to walk along the fancy avenue," Kiriki contemplated aloud, again looking down at the activity below. "Though my clothes are Indian, surely the people will recognize the part of me that is white! Surely I will be accepted as part of them as I wander down the avenue."

Again she turned and gazed into the mirror. Her hands went to her hair. She had not painted the part in her hair red, as most normally done while in her Pawnee Indian village. Nor had she painted her face, sensing that these customs would make her look peculiar in the eyes of the white women whose faces were peachy white. Only on occasion, while watching through the window, had she seen women with painted faces, and they seemed peculiarly different from the other women. Their attire had been skimpy and of bright fabrics, whereas most of the women were dressed in full-length dresses and pretty bonnets.

To Kiriki, the ones who were more subdued in their attire were the most attractive.

Grabbing a buckskin jacket from the bed, Kiriki slipped it on. Her fingers trembled as she opened the door and stepped lightly out into a corridor lighted by candles burning in sconces along the long walls where closed doors were on each side of the corridor as far as the eye could see. There were hardly any sounds, each room of the hotel seeming to lock away secrets for those who were momentarily in them.

To Kiriki, everything about Washington was like being in another world—in a fantasy land. She wanted to experience as much as she could before she returned to the *real* world. . . .

Tossing aside all warnings not to stray from her room, Kiriki moved on down the corridor. When she came to the staircase that would lead her down to the hotel lobby and then to the intrigue of the Washington streets, she stared down at the steepness, and a dizziness once again swept over her. She clutched at the railing until her bal-

ance returned, then, feeling foolish, moved stealthily on
down the stairs, her moccasins making no sound on the
plush red carpet beneath them.

One floor and staircase conquered, then a second and
third, Kiriki swept from the staircase into a fancy lobby
where fancily dressed people stood in throngs, talking.
The aroma of sweet perfume scented the air, causing Kiriki's nose to flare in enjoyment. She had heard of such
wonderful smells that women could anoint themselves with
from bottles. It was surely true, for never had she smelled
anything as wonderful, except for roses she had plucked
wild along the creek beds.

Oh, but to have such a bottle of perfume to take back
with her to the Pawnee! Would the women not marvel at
being able to smell sweetly all day while laboring in the
gardens?

She inched along the outskirts of the room, staring at
the beautiful plumes that hung from fancy hats worn by
the women, the sleek lines of their velveteen, silk, and
satin dresses, and where at their lowswept bodices so
many displayed sparkling diamond necklaces lying against
their pale, white skins.

And then she became aware of attentions turning to her.
She smiled at those who had turned to stare openly at her,
making her feel as though she were a fish out of water.

When only a few returned a smile, the others remaining
cold and aloof, Kiriki rushed on from the building, her
heart pounding. She now knew, beyond a shadow of a
doubt, that no one recognized in her that part that was
white. Even the color of her eyes did not matter to them.
She was Indian in dress and skin coloring—they saw her
no less than a total Indian.

Once outside, on the thoroughfare, Kiriki wiped tears
from her eyes and began walking with her chin held
proudly high among the people who seemed in too much
of a hurry to be on the street to enjoy it as she hoped to
do. But of course these people must do this every day.
This was the first time for Kiriki.

Hearing the tinkling of a piano surfacing from somewhere close by, Kiriki followed the sound. Was it not a beautiful way to make music? Up till now, she had only heard the magic of the Pawnee drums and rattles. But this instrument being played with vigor made all sorts of different sounds, even prettier than the evening breeze whispering softly through the leaves of the cottonwood trees.

"I must see how this is done," Kiriki whispered, her pulse racing as she stopped and gazed through a window, seeing a man sitting at a piano, his fingers moving wildly across the white and black keys.

Intrigued, Kiriki stepped closer to the glass pane of the window, her nose touching, and watched, hypnotized not only by the sound, but by the man's ability to move his fingers so quickly across the keyboard.

"Like what cha see, ma'am?" a voice rang out beside Kiriki.

Kiriki jumped with alarm. She turned and found herself face to face with a short and squatty man, his face almost completely hidden behind a thick, rust-colored beard. He wore a raccoon hat and fringed buckskins, stinking with dried perspiration.

"Let me take you inside so's you can get a better look," the man said, circling an arm around Kiriki's waist. His eyes gleamed down into hers. "I can tell this is the first time for you to visit the white man's world." He chuckled low. "Myself? I ain't never been this close to such a beautiful savage." He leaned into her face and quirked an eyebrow. "A savage with blue eyes?" He chuckled. "Seems your mama came in contact with the white man way before you did."

A sudden rage engulfed Kiriki. She jerked away from the man, seething. "You insult *me* when you insult my mother," she hissed, aching to slap him, yet fearing what he might do. He looked far less than a man who could be trusted. "And if I wish to enter this establishment, I do not need such an escort as you."

The man's dark eyes danced with amusement. "My Lord, she speaks in English better than most white folk I know," he teased. He grabbed her wrist and held onto her tightly. "How'd you learn the English tongue? Was your father white?" He looked over his shoulder, then back down into Kiriki's daring eyes. "Is he here now? Or did you come with that passle of Injuns I seen comin' into town earlier this mornin'?" He guffawed as he leaned closer to her. "I ain't never seen such a sight as Injuns tryin' to act as though they are civil like normal folk. Don't you savages all know that you cain't make a pussy-cat outta mountain lion?"

"Let me go," Kiriki said, fear entering her heart. This man's grip was like iron! If he wished, he could drag her away into the fast falling dusk! And if she screamed, who would pay heed to an Indian woman in danger? To most she was worthless, when in truth this man who was confronting her was the one who was less than human.

"And what if I don't?" the man said, leering down at her.

"If anything should happen to me, Sun Eagle would hunt you down and kill you," Kiriki dared to say. "Even in this city filled with white men and women he would find you! He would kill you slowly."

"You scare me to death with talk of a savage named Sun Eagle," the man said, laughing throatily. He nodded toward the saloon. "Come on. Let me buy you some firewater. I've heard how Injuns react after drinking whiskey. Damn, I could have some fun with you if you took a few swallows of what I plan to buy you."

"I will not drink anything you give me and I will not go inside the establishment with you," Kiriki said, stiffening her back and lifting her chin defiantly. "I wish to return to my room. I . . . I made a mistake leaving."

She was startled when he suddenly freed her wrist and gestured with an arm for her to walk on past him. She had not expected to be let go this easily. What had she said that had made him change his mind?

Rubbing her sore wrist, Kiriki edged around the man, watching him for a moment, then she broke into a run and ran breathlessly through the crowd. When she reached the hotel, she did not stop until she had raced up the four

flights of stairs and was inside her room. Crying, she
threw herself on her bed. She had proven unable to fend
for herself in the eye of danger! It was not meant for her
to be in this city. She was misplaced!

The sound of the door opening behind her made her
heart thrill. Sun Eagle had returned. Oh, just at the most
perfect time, he had returned to the room! She needed his
muscled arms around her to comfort her. She felt only
half a person at this moment. He would make her feel
whole again.

Scooting to a sitting position, Kiriki wiped her eyes and
looked toward the door. But her insides froze when she
saw who was standing there, larger than life, a symbol of
hatred and bigotry to her. It was the whiskered man! He
had tricked her! He had let her return to her room only to
give him a chance to follow her.

She felt her stomach do a strange sort of flip-flop as the
stranger closed the door and began walking toward her.
When he placed his hands to his belt and began loosening
it, Kiriki could not move, fear having stolen her ability
to.

"You dumb savage," the man said, laughing. "You
don't even know what a key is or what it's used for, do
you? If'n you'd have locked the door with a key, it
would've protected you from the likes of me."

Kiriki still could not speak or move. Her only hope was
that Sun Eagle would arrive at any minute. He was her
only hope.

"You are a strange one, ain't you?" the man said, his
voice husky with lust. He yanked his belt away from his
breeches, then pulled his buckskin garment away, revealing his nudity, rust-colored hairs thick on his torso and
thighs. "You have blue eyes, yet the skin of an Injun.
What else about you is intriguing?" He leaned over her.
"Here. Let's have a look."

Kiriki gasped and felt faint when the man ripped her
blouse down the front, causing her copper breasts to spill
out. When the man touched a breast, then squeezed her

nipple brutally, Kiriki found the strength that was required
to raise a knee and thrust it hard into his groin.

When he grabbed at himself, tumbling backward off the
bed, Kiriki jumped from the bed and searched around
the room for something to protect herself with. She spied
the water pitcher and grabbed it, but the man was too
quick for her. He lunged for her ankles and wrestled her
to the floor.

His face red with rage, he moved over her and jerked
at her skirt until it was down below her knees, then on
the floor beside her.

A bitter taste swam inside Kiriki's mouth as the man
nudged her thighs apart with his knees and she felt the
probing of his manhood. In her mind's eye she was recalling Brown Bear raping her!

Oh, could it be happening again?

Could she bear it?

The man's lips seared Kiriki's lips as he bore down
upon her with a painful kiss. She tried to bite him, but
all was in vain. The man was getting the best of her. She
had no more strength to fight him.

No more strength. . . .

Suddenly there was a great flurry of activity in the
room. Kiriki's eyes opened widely as she saw Sun Eagle
approaching the man from behind, his face twisted angrily.
Before the man's hardness entered Kiriki, Sun Eagle
jerked him from above her and wrestled him across the
floor. The shine of a knife suddenly in Sun Eagle's hands
filled her with horror. If he killed the white man, Sun
Eagle would be hanged by a noose. No white man's court
would ever find him anything but guilty of murder, even
if he *was* defending Kiriki's virtue. She was an Indian.
Most Indian women were looked at as objects to be used.
That was exactly what the white man was going to do,
had he succeeded. Use her! And he would have not been
condemned for having done so.

"Sun Eagle, stop!" Kiriki shouted, jumping to her feet.
She started to go to them, to try and intervene, but she
was too late. While the white man was trying to strangle

the last breath out of Sun Eagle, Sun Eagle had no choice but to plunge the knife down, into the evil man's hairy back. . . .

Taking a shaky step back, covering her mouth with a hand to stifle a choked scream behind it, Kiriki watched the man's body convulse as blood spurted from the wound.

And then he was still.

Sun Eagle removed the knife from the man and wiped the blood on the man's breeches that lay on the floor beside the bed.

"You killed him," Kiriki finally managed to say, but in a strained whisper.

Sun Eagle replaced his knife in its sheath at his waist. He drew Kiriki into his arms and held her tightly. "Had I not, he would have killed me, then raped and killed you," he said, his voice thick with apology. "Somehow he got the advantage. He was only moments away from succeeding at choking the life from me."

"What can we do, Sun Eagle?" Kiriki cried, closing her eyes so that she would not see the blood or the body. "Perhaps we can go to Major O'Fallon. We could explain what happened. Perhaps even President Monroe will understand. We must at least try, Sun Eagle."

"No. We cannot do that," Sun Eagle said, pushing her away from him and looking into her eyes. "Listen to me. Not even they can help us now. They cannot defend an Indian who has killed a white man in the white man's city. We have no choice but to flee and hide, Kiriki! Hide!"

Kiriki blanched. Her eyes wavered. "But, Sun Eagle, this is not Nebraska!" she cried. "There are no hills or caves that you are familiar with. We are in a distant land unfamiliar to both of us. Where *can* we hide? Where can we go?" She lunged into his arms, sobbing. "Oh, Sun Eagle, I am so afraid! This is not the way it was supposed to be. I had hoped—had wanted for so much more. How could I have fooled myself into believing that I could leave the land of our people and be happy? I want to go home, Sun Eagle. Please, take me home."

Sun Eagle stroked her hair gently. "We will go home," he said. "In time. But for now, we must separate ourselves from this place. When the body is found we must be far away."

"Oh, but where?" Kiriki cried.

"I have seen a body of water that runs through the city," Sun Eagle said. "We will follow it. It will take us to land that is forest. We shall hide there for a few days. In the meantime, we will try and steal two horses. We shall return to our homeland."

"And what if we become the hunted?" Kiriki asked, looking slowly up at Sun Eagle. "You know that we *will,* Sun Eagle. How can we elude the white man who will come ready to hang not only you but I?"

"I am not promising that we can," Sun Eagle said, holding her away from him. He eyed the ripped blouse, anger rising more fiercely inside him. "But we will give it everything we can, Kiriki. That is all that we can do."

He looked at the other clothes that she had brought with her. She had hung them carefully on the back of a chair. He waved his hand toward them. "Get into something that will be comfortable for several days," he ordered flatly. "Then let us leave this place. I believe there is a back stairway. We shall sneak out that way. We would have the opportunity to steal a horse from in front of the establishments along the street, but we would draw undue attention to ourselves. We will find horses later."

Sniffing, her knees weak with fear, Kiriki did as she was told. After getting fully clothed, she glanced over at the dead man, his eyes staring lifelessly ahead, causing goosebumps to rise on her flesh.

"Let us go," Sun Eagle said, offering Kiriki a hand.

She took his hand and left the room with him. They moved in the shadows of the corridor and down the back staircase until they stepped out into a dark alley. Kiriki clung to Sun Eagle as she looked one way and then another.

Sun Eagle nodded to his right side. "This way," he whispered. "We must avoid the busy street. Remember, we are searching for the river that runs through the city. Once there, we will not be far from safety."

Kiriki nodded. She stayed close beside him as they ran stealthily behind the buildings. The sound of the city seemed to be mocking her as she tried to close her ears to it. The tinkling of a piano. The sound of laughter. The clip-clop of the horses on the cobblestone streets.

All of those things were of an environment—a culture—that were apart from her.

No matter that she was part white.

No one seemed to truly care, but her. . . .

Twenty-one
▼ ▼ ▼

THE long train ride and the lamplights and noise of the city behind them, Kiriki and Sun Eagle continued running alongside the Potomac River. Kiriki placed a hand at her side and moaned to herself, not wanting Sun Eagle to know that she needed to rest—that her side was paining her so much that she could hardly bear it. She was responsible for this dilemma in which they had found themselves. If she had listened to the warnings of both Major O'Fallon and Sun Eagle, she would have never left the hotel room. There would have been no evil man following her to the room, and Sun Eagle would have been given no cause to kill the man.

She had spoiled everything for Sun Eagle! He had come to Washington to be honored, and now that could never be. How could she ever repay him for the disgrace that he would take home to his people?

Could he even *go* home? Would not the white man follow and arrest him, even there?

Sun Eagle swung around and stopped in Kiriki's path, taking her hands as she came to a teetering halt before him. "My woman, it is safe enough now for us to walk, not run," he said. "We have traveled far."

He looked over his shoulders at the forest that stretched out behind them in all directions. He looked back down at Kiriki. "We will find safety among the trees," he assured. "Tomorrow, when the sun rises early in the sky, we will travel onward. We will search for a white man's dwelling so that we can take horses and flee this troublesome land and go back to Nebraska."

"Sun Eagle, Nebraska is so far," Kiriki complained, her side, and now even her abdomen paining her so strangely. "How can you know in which direction to go?"

Sun Eagle looked up at the sky. "I shall follow the stars," he said, looking back down into Kiriki's troubled eyes. He drew her into his strong embrace. "The morning star always shines brightest over our villages of Pawnee, does it not?"

The mention of the morning star caused Kiriki to shudder, recalling the scaffold and her near death. She was reminded of Sun Eagle rescuing her, defying the Morning Star, refusing it its sacrifice this year.

"The morning star may not be shining as brightly," she whispered, afraid to say much about the defied star aloud, especially now that it was needed to guide them back home. "It is surely very angry at both of us, Sun Eagle."

"Look to the heavens, my love," Sun Eagle said, leaning away from Kiriki. He gestured with a hand toward the lightening sky as dawn began to be evident along the horizon. "Do you not see the morning star in all of its glory? Does it shine any less than before I rescued you? Do you not know that it saw the wrong in what Brown Bear had done? It is Brown Bear that should be wary of the wrath of the Morning Star! Not you or I!"

Kiriki looked slowly up at the sky. Her insides grew warm and the pain in her body subsided when she saw the morning star shining more brightly than any other star in the sky. It was twinkling as though it was dancing.

"It is not angry at us," she murmured, sighing. "Sun Eagle, it *can* lead us home!"

"And so it shall," Sun Eagle said, taking her hand, again leading her alongside the Potomac, but this time in an easy, relaxed gait.

Kiriki inhaled the aroma of wild flowers and pine as she and Sun Eagle moved into the shadows of the trees. The moon was spinning its white threads only occasionally through the branches, yet it was mirrored brightly in the river. There was a sudden frenzied flutter of wings overhead, and Kiriki looked up and saw the outline of several

birds take flight, having been frightened from their night's
nesting. This saddened her, for the birds would become
as she and Sun Eagle—lost.

Holding more firmly onto Sun Eagle's hand for reassur-
ance, Kiriki walked alongside him farther and farther into
the woods, then suddenly up ahead there was a flicker of
lamplight through a break in the trees.

Sun Eagle's eyes squinted narrowly as he saw the light.
He stopped Kiriki and studied the area, assessing the danger of having come across a white man's dwelling nestled
within the forest.

Kiriki sensed Sun Eagle's wariness. "What shall we
do?" she whispered, snuggling closer to him. "We can
pass on by in the dark and surely not get noticed."

The sudden barking of a dog made Kiriki grow tense.
The dog would alert the people in the house that intruders
were near.

"Sun Eagle, the dog—" Kiriki whispered harshly, then
jumped with alarm when the dog, a beautiful collie, came
bounding toward them through the brush.

But it was no longer barking. It was wagging its tail,
its eyes bright and friendly as it stopped and looked up at
Kiriki, then jumped up on her, whining.

"It senses that we are friends," Kiriki said, smoothing
a hand over the dog's thick coat of fur. "Perhaps its own-
ers are just as friendly. I have been told that a dog's
personality often matches its owner."

"Perhaps," Sun Eagle said, looking at the dog, then
the lamplight again. "But it could be something else, Kiriki. Do you not know your unusual ability to charm animals? I saw it in the way the bear cub took to you so
quickly. It could be the same with this dog. He senses
your kindness, your gentleness. An animal is never wrong
in his choice of friends."

Kiriki laughed softly. "Let us go and take a look at the
house, Sun Eagle," she said. She hoped that somehow
they could be taken in and be fed and given a place to
sleep. She was bone-weary and the strange ache in her
side and abdomen was troubling her again. She did not

want to be forced to complain to Sun Eagle about her weaknesses. He had always looked to her as strong. If he doubted this, would he even want to marry her? The strength of a Pawnee wife was important.

Sun Eagle's eyes wavered, sensing there was more in Kiriki's desire to see the white man's house than she was saying aloud. He could see the weary lines beneath her eyes, and her color was not good. All of this trauma was proving to be too much for his woman. How could he expect otherwise? Everything was too different from that which she was accustomed. He had to get her back to Nebraska and forget there ever was a journey to the city of the great white father.

"Yes, we will take a look at the house," he said, circling an arm around her waist. "Perhaps near it we can find the horses that we need for our journey home."

Leaning into his embrace, walking alongside him, Kiriki inhaled a trembling breath. She must prepare herself for the long journey that lay ahead of them.

The dog bounding at her side, its tail wagging, helped lighten Kiriki's mood. She reached toward the dog, giggling as his long wet tongue took a lap at her hand.

"I wish we could keep the dog, also," Kiriki murmured, knowing that stealing a horse would cause punishment enough if they were caught. "He is so lovely, Sun Eagle. And so very, very gentle."

"Perhaps one day when we are settled, after we are married, I will get you a dog for entertainment in the evenings while we are resting before the fire," Sun Eagle said, glancing down at the dog, also admiring it. "After our children are born to us, the dog will then be their playmate."

"Children?" Kiriki said, her eyes lighting up. "Oh, Sun Eagle, to have children with you would be so wonderful!"

Then she stopped in mid-step and turned to him. She took his hands. "You must think I am terrible!" she said, gazing lovingly, yet apologetically, up at him. "I did not ask how your day was before I turned it into chaos. How did you find President Monroe? Did you and the other Plains Indians find comfort in his words? Did he promise assistance to the Indians? Did you meet his wife? Was she pretty? Were you, personally, honored, my darling?''

"President Monroe is a kind man with a deep crease in his chin which I was told is called a 'cleft,' " Sun Eagle said. "His presidency is being hailed as the 'Era of Good Feeling.' He seems to care what happens to the Plains Indians, but much is being said among our delegates about President Monroe's part in the Seminole War."

"The Seminole?" Kiriki said, raising an eyebrow questioningly. "I do not know about them."

"They are the Indians who are from the land that is called Florida," Sun Eagle explained. "The war that President Monroe is responsible for began over attempts by the United States authorities to recapture runaway black slaves living among the Seminole bands. Under a General Andrew Jackson, the United States forces invaded the area, scattering the villagers and burning their towns. Soon after, the Seminoles were forced to go live on a reservation. If the Plains Indians are forced to live on reservations, I, nor any of our people, will have anymore kind words for President Monroe or his successors!"

"Do you think that is the true reason behind the President inviting the Indian delegates to Washington?" Kiriki asked in a hushed whisper. "To prepare us for what is to come?"

"Nothing has been said about reservations," Sun Eagle said flatly. "Thus far only words of kindness and promise of aid to our people has been said."

Kiriki reached a hand to his coppery cheek. "And what was said about you and your bravery, my darling?" she asked, her voice lilting. "Were you looked to as the special man that you are?"

Sun Eagle looked momentarily away from her, casting his eyes downward. Then he looked at her, his shoulders proudly squared. "Tomorrow there was to be a medal placed around my neck to honor what I did in the line of danger," he said hoarsely. "I am being called courageous.

I was to be honored for my bravery in a special ceremony.''

Kiriki inhaled a quick gasp of breath, then broke away from him and began running. Her sobs filled the air, filling Sun Eagle with despair and wonder. He ran after her and grabbed her around the waist, spinning her around to face him.

"Why do you run from me?" he asked, their eyes locked. "Are you not also proud of me?"

"Oh, Sun Eagle," Kiriki said, sniffling as tears streamed down her face. "No one could ever be as proud as I am of you! I cry because I have taken so much away from you because of my foolishness today. Because of me you will not have the medal placed around your neck. Because of me you are now a renegade. You must hate me! I wouldn't blame you if you did."

Sun Eagle studied her for a moment, then held her tightly. "My woman, I could never hate you," he said, his voice breaking. "My love for you is as strong as those of the stars for the sky. It is as everlasting."

"But I have stolen so much from you because of my careless behavior today." Kiriki sobbed. "How can you ever forgive me? How?"

Sun Eagle held her away from him. "Do you think a mere medal is important to me when there is *you?*" he said huskily. "Kiriki, *you* are the most valuable of all to me." Again he held her close. "And you cannot blame yourself for anything. If you had not let your adventurous nature lead you from that room to explore, you would not be the woman I knew you to be. It is the man who is to blame. Only the man! He took advantage of your innocence. It is good that he is dead."

Again he held her away from him. He framed her delicate, tear-streaked face between his hands. "My woman, had I not returned when I did, you would have been raped by the man," he said thickly. "Had he defiled your body, I—"

Kiriki laid a finger on his lips and sealed his further words, in her heart feeling guilty for having kept the one true rape from Sun Eagle. But she could never tell him it was his very own brother who had done the vile deed!

"Let us speak no more of what could have, or might have been," she encouraged softly. "It is the future that we must face now. Because of me, we may never see one that is full of happiness and promise. I should have never—"

Sun Eagle stopped her in mid-sentence by brushing his mouth across her lips. "Let us hear no more self-blame," he whispered. He took her hand and began trotting ahead. "Let us go and see if there are any horses. I am a master at capturing horses!"

"But these are not Comanche horses," Kiriki said, finding it hard to keep up with him, her side aching again.

"It matters not who owns the horses," Sun Eagle said, casting her a troubled glance when he heard her cry out softly with pain and grab at her side. He stopped and placed his hands on her shoulders. "You are not well. Tell me. What is hurting you?"

Cold sweat was beading Kiriki's brow. She rubbed her sore side, the pain now excruciating.

But she would not show her weakness. Sun Eagle already had too much on his mind—he did not need to bother himself with more worries of her.

"It is nothing," she said breathlessly. "Only that I am tired. Let us walk, Sun Eagle. Not run."

"You are in pain," Sun Eagle said more adamantly. "I can see it in your eyes. I can hear it in your voice. Tell me where you hurt!"

"Please, Sun Eagle," Kiriki begged, then winced when a fiery pain stabbed at her side again, causing her to double over.

Sun Eagle jumped with alarm, then swept her fully into his arms and held her close. He could hear the raspiness of her breath. He could see the pallor of her cheeks. "You *are* ill," he said, his voice drawn.

He began running, carrying her snuggled closely to his chest. When he came to the clearing where he could see the house in full view, he was tempted to go to the door and demand attention for Kiriki, yet a great surge of fear urged him not to. His fear was not for himself, but for Kiriki. Should she be ill and taken to a white man's prison in such a condition, she would be neglected and could possibly die.

No! He had to take her somewhere safe, where he, himself, could look after her. Surely whatever was ailing her would pass. Perhaps she had eaten something of the white man's food that had poisoned her.

His gaze shifted to a barn at the far edge of the farm grounds. Surely within its confines some refuge and safety could be found. At least for awhile. . . .

Again running, clutching Kiriki close to him, the collie bounding along behind them, Sun Eagle reached the barn and slipped inside. He scarcely breathed as he looked around, assessing the area for danger.

His gaze stopped at a ladder that led upward to the loft, where he could see thick layers of straw spread out. It would be a comfortable place for Kiriki while she was resting. It would be a place where Sun Eagle could minister to her until she was faring better.

The whinny of a horse drew Sun Eagle's eyes elsewhere. Along the far wall several horses were in separate stalls. His heart thumped wildly—their means of escape was there, so close!

"Sun Eagle, I feel so . . . so suddenly hot," Kiriki said, everything spinning as she opened her eyes. "I . . . I am so *ill*."

Sun Eagle gazed longingly down at her then went to the ladder and managed to get her up to the loft, leaving the now barking dog below. When in the loft, Sun Eagle lay Kiriki down on the straw and leaned over her, his hand on her brow. He flinched. She was burning up with fever. What was ailing her was not from bad food. Something else was going wrong in her body, and he knew not what.

Kiriki grabbed for her right side and drew her legs up to her abdomen as another sharp pain pierced her side. She cried out, and then felt a bitterness rise up into her

throat. She flashed Sun Eagle a desperate look. "Sun
Eagle, I believe I am going to—"

Kiriki did not get the words out. She held her head
away from Sun Eagle. Her body convulsed as she retched,
her throat and nose burning from the vile liquid that was
erupting from inside her.

Sun Eagle rose quickly to his feet, a desperation seizing
him. He *had* to go for help! Kiriki was ill in ways that
he knew not how to help her. If he did not find someone
quickly who knew the art of medicine, Kiriki might even
die.

He looked down the ladder, searching for the dog, only
now realizing that it had stopped barking. He plopped
down to his belly beside Kiriki when he saw a wavering
light outside approaching the barn. He watched cautiously
over the edge of the loft when the dog bounded into view,
panting, then looked up at the loft and again began its
incessant barking.

Grabbing his knife from its sheath, Sun Eagle waited
to see who the dog had brought with him. If it was a man
with a gun, then Sun Eagle would have to be quick and
accurate with the knife. He did not wish to kill again, but
when cornered, he would do what must be done to save
Kiriki.

"Laddie, hush that barking," a woman's soft voice
said. "Every night now you bring me out here to find
that raccoon. I know it disturbs the horses when it comes
noseying around in the barn, but, Laddie, it isn't here for
long. You know that. Always by the time I get out here,
it's gone. Laddie, you are the true nuisance here."

Kiriki moaned to herself, the pain continuing its assault
on her body. Again she felt the urge to retch, but knew
that there was great danger in making any sort of noise.

Someone was approaching the barn.

Kiriki's eyes opened, and she felt some relief when she
recognized that it was a woman who came into the barn.
Sun Eagle's hand loosened on the knife, and he watched
with caution as the woman moved around inside the barn

below him, her lantern being held in all sorts of positions as she began searching for the raccoon.

Then his breath caught in his throat when she stopped and looked at the collie whose intent eyes were on the loft overhead.

"Laddie, don't tell me that darn raccoon scooted up the ladder to the loft," the lady said, sighing resolutely. "I'm not about to go up there." She lifted the tail of her dress with her hand and spun around, heading back toward the door. "I've had enough for tonight, Laddie. I'm going back inside the house. Drat that William. If he wasn't so absorbed in his senatorial duties, he'd be here nights to help find that crazy raccoon, and then you'd leave me to my knitting and cozy fire."

Kiriki could not hold back the bile bitterness that was invading her throat any longer. The muscles of her throat spasmed as she retched again, making a horrible noise in the process.

Sun Eagle grew rigid as he saw the woman spin around and look up at the loft, her face having gone white with fear.

Twenty-two
▼ ▼ ▼

REALIZING that speed was of the essence in order not to use violence to silence the white woman, Sun Eagle rose quickly to his feet and rushed down the ladder. Petrified with fear, the woman had not moved. She looked up at Sun Eagle disbelievingly.

"Do not be afraid," Sun Eagle tried to reassure. "I am not here to harm you. I have come to your dwelling because my woman needs help."

"Your woman?" the woman asked, her voice drawn.

Kiriki knew the position that Sun Eagle had put himself in by having been forced to reveal himself to the white woman. She listened intently to their conversation, and when she heard herself mentioned, she knew that she must reveal herself to show the white woman that Sun Eagle spoke the truth. There was no telling what the next moments would bring for her and Sun Eagle. The white woman could pretend to befriend them and then turn them over to the authorities at her first opportunity, or she could have a warm heart and understand their dilemma once they revealed the events of the evening to them.

Her abdomen causing her such distress, Kiriki found it hard to move. But she must. For Sun Eagle, she must. . . .

Dragging herself across the straw-covered floor of the loft, sweat beaded Kiriki's brow. She winced with pain, then managed to grab hold of the top rung of the ladder to pull herself to the edge of the loft so that she could look down at the drama being acted out below. Her face was flooded with lamplight as the woman held up her lantern to take a better look.

"My word, there *is* a woman in the loft," the white woman gasped. She held the lantern higher, taking a closer look at Kiriki's pain-stricken face. "And she does appear to be in pain."

"My woman is very ill," Sun Eagle said, finding it hard not to go back to Kiriki, to hold her protectively within the muscled strength of his arms. "It is an illness I am not familiar with."

"I could take a look at her," she said, looking cautiously up at Sun Eagle. "My name is Madeline Jones. My father is a doctor. I have assisted him many times."

She paused, then lowered the lantern as she took a step backward. "I first must know who you are," she murmured. "I know of no Indians in these parts, so close to Washington."

"My woman and I have come in peace from Nebraska along with other Plains Indians," Sun Eagle confessed. "We traveled here with Major O'Fallon."

"You are among those my husband met today?" Madeline gasped. "Why, then, are you this far from Washington? My husband said that all of the Indian delegates were to stay in the Pennsylvania House Hotel. My Lord, you are far from the comforts of a hotel."

"It is something I do not wish to take time to tell at present," Sun Eagle said, looking nervously up at Kiriki. "My woman is too ill. She must be attended to."

Madeline cleared her throat nervously, then squared her shoulders. "Get your woman and follow me," she said flatly. "Let us get her inside my house on a comfortable bed and see just what the trouble is."

She started to walk away then stopped. She turned and eyed Sun Eagle again. "Your name?" she asked.

Sun Eagle stiffened. If he told her his name and she knew of the murder, she would be afraid all over again. Yet he was not one to ever speak with a forked tongue. He told truths, always.

"Sun Eagle," he blurted.

Madeline's face lit up with recognition. She smiled widely. "You are Sun Eagle?" she asked, admiration thick in her words. She looked up at the loft again. Her eyes wavered as her smile faded. "Then that must be Kiriki? The young woman you saved from the Morning Star sacrifice?"

"That is so," Sun Eagle said, squaring his shoulders proudly.

"I know of you both," Madeline said. "My husband is a senator from Washington and has been in the city all day attending the meetings. Perhaps you know him? Senator Jones?"

She lifted the hem of her skirt in her free hand. "But of course that is not important now. Let us waste no more time talking, young man," she said, turning to walk away from him. "Bring Kiriki. We must not let anything happen to her now, after having been rescued so valiantly before!" She looked over her shoulder at the collie. "Come along, Laddie. Stay out of the young man's way." The dog bounded dutifully along behind her.

Sun Eagle rushed up the ladder. He stepped up on the loft and lifted Kiriki gently into his arms. He kissed her hot brow. "Everything is going to be all right," he reassured. "We have found a friend in the white woman."

"But will she be a friend when she hears the truth of tonight's events?" Kiriki asked, locking an arm around Sun Eagle's neck as he began his slow descent down the ladder. "She talked of a husband. He has been in Washington all day. It appears that he has not arrived home yet. When he does, he could carry with him the news of the murdered man and that he was found in our room. He will know that either you or I are responsible."

"This is not the time to worry about it," Sun Eagle said, running with her from the barn. "We must concern ourselves with seeing that you are taken care of. You heard the woman say that her father is a doctor. Perhaps she has enough knowledge, herself, to care for whatever is ailing you."

"Her father is not a shaman," Kiriki fussed, wincing

when a sharp pain in her abdomen, shifting around to her side, troubled her again. "Do you put trust in anyone if they do not have the knowledge of a Pawnee shaman?"

"I have learned much from Major O'Fallon," Sun Eagle said flatly. "I know that white man doctors know much about illnesses that our shamans do not know. We must put our trust and faith in whatever this woman knows tonight, Kiriki. There is no shaman here to perform his special magic."

Kiriki laid her head against Sun Eagle's chest. "I am so afraid," she murmured. "Sun Eagle, we are in a strange land among strange people and I am rendered helpless with sickness. I feel that perhaps we will never see Nebraska again. Oh, Sun Eagle, I so badly want to go home."

"We will. Soon," Sun Eagle said, faltering a moment when he reached the steps that led up to the white woman's house. She was on the porch gesturing with a hand for him to come ahead, but still he could not help but hesitate. Once inside those walls, would he not feel as though imprisoned? Had he not already experienced such feelings while in such establishments in the city of Washington?

"We must hurry," Madeline said, opening the door, motioning with the swing of her lantern for Sun Eagle to follow her. "Take Kiriki into the house. Follow me to my bedroom. I shall see to her quickly."

"Do not be afraid, Sun Eagle," Kiriki whispered. "The white woman seems sincere enough. And I am so ill. So ill."

Hearing the tormented pain in Kiriki's voice, Sun Eagle hesitated no longer. He took the steps in wide strides and walked past Madeline inside the house. He looked guardedly around him, seeing a home filled with many white people's fancy treasures, then stopped his gaze on a gun rack that displayed all styles and makes of rifles. If this woman wanted to, she had many defenses against two Pawnee intruders!

But he had to cast doubts aside. For Kiriki, he had to have faith. . . .

Madeline blew her lantern out and set it on a table. She eyed Kiriki for a moment, then swung around and walked in haste toward a room at the far end of the corridor. "In here," she said, motioning with a hand. "This is my bedroom. We shall make Kiriki comfortable and then I shall examine her."

Sun Eagle followed Madeline into the bedroom. Without any further hesitation he walked to the bed and gently placed Kiriki on it. Then he stood back out of the way as Madeline moved to the bed and stood over Kiriki, touching her brow with a delicate hand. She flinched when she felt the fire of Kiriki's flesh. She spun around and rushed across the room, toward the door. "I must first get cold compresses and try and get her temperature lowered," she said over her shoulder. "I shall return quickly."

Sun Eagle went to Kiriki. He knelt beside the bed and took her hand, clasping it hard. "Kiriki?" he whispered, noticing how she breathed so heavily, her eyes closed as though in a deep sleep.

Kiriki just barely heard Sun Eagle, as though he was speaking from deeply within a dark tunnel. She licked her parched lips and tried to reply, but she no longer had the strength to speak, nor the ability to open her eyes. But she could manage to gently curl her fingers around his hand.

Madeline rushed into the room. Seeing the intimate scene between Kiriki and Sun Eagle, she chose to go to the other side of the bed and let Sun Eagle continue holding Kiriki's hand on the other. Quickly she placed the wet, cold cloths to Kiriki's brow. Then she eyed Sun Eagle warily, wondering if she should undress Kiriki for the examination while in his presence.

She chose to ignore that he was there, understanding his devotion to Kiriki. There would be no embarrassment when Kiriki's clothes were shed. Sun Eagle's prime concern was that his woman was taken care of in the proper way.

Madeline hoped that she could remember all that her father had taught her through the years while assisting him—enough so that she could help the lovely Indian maiden.

If not, she feared Sun Eagle's reaction. It was apparent that he possibly loved Kiriki more than life itself. . . .

Madeline deftly removed Kiriki's clothes. She began gently poking around her abdomen, seeing how Kiriki winced with pain even though she was now in a semicoma. A keen sadness entered Madeline's eyes, for she was almost sure of what was wrong with Kiriki without even examining her internally. At first she had thought that it might be the young woman's appendix. But it was something even more severe than that. Kiriki had been pregnant but no longer was. The dead fetus was spreading infection throughout Kiriki's body.

The fetus had to be removed immediately, or Kiriki would die.

"What is it?" Sun Eagle asked anxiously. "What do you find wrong with my woman?"

Madeline looked guardedly over at Sun Eagle, then went to him and urged him to his feet. She led him out of the room then stopped, looking up. "It is not good," she murmured. "I must operate on Kiriki immediately. And *I* must do it, because we do not have time to go into Washington for my father." She placed a hand on Sun Eagle's arm. "You must place all faith in me, Sun Eagle. It is up to me, alone, to see Kiriki through this traumatic moment in her life."

Sun Eagle's pulse was racing. His eyes were wild. He clasped his fingers to Madeline's shoulder. "What is wrong with Kiriki?" he said, his voice shallow. "Why do you say that a knife must be used on her? Why?"

Madeline stiffened beneath his hands, fear entering her heart. Though she did feel that she was capable of doing the surgery that was required, she feared what might happen to her if Kiriki did not survive. As she saw it, she had no choice but to risk her own life in order to save another.

"Did you know that Kiriki was with child?" Madeline asked softly.

Sun Eagle was taken aback by the news that Kiriki was carrying his child. She had not told him! Yet had she known herself? She would never withhold such wonderful news from him. Never!

"No, I did not know," Sun Eagle said thickly. "Nor did Kiriki. She would have shared the news with Sun Eagle."

Madeline swallowed hard. She lowered her eyes, then slowly looked back up at Sun Eagle again. "I am more than positive that she was pregnant, but isn't any longer," she said, her voice breaking. "I am going to ask you to stay out of the room long enough for me to examine her. And then, if I am accurate in my assumptions, you will have to assist me while I do surgery."

"Why is the knife required?" Sun Eagle asked, shuddering at the thought of his lovely Kiriki's skin being defiled in such a way.

"To remove the dead fetus from within your woman's body," Madeline said, wincing when she saw Sun Eagle's reaction as he jerked away from her and became tight-jawed, with his hands clenched into tight fists at his sides.

"The child is dead?" Sun Eagle asked, his voice breaking.

"I am almost certain of it," Madeline said, then moved determinedly around him. "I am going to examine her now. I shall be certain in a matter of moments."

Sun Eagle watched her go into the room, feeling empty inside. He kneaded his brow feverishly, then began pacing back and forth, awaiting the white woman's word. That Kiriki may have lost his child made him want to cry out and curse mankind. If she lost one child, would she be able to carry another? Would there never be an heir born to him, to carry on the chieftain title? Could he bear not to have a son in his image?

Madeline soon came from the room, wiping her hands on the skirt of her dress. She looked glumly up at Sun Eagle and nodded her head. Sun Eagle did not have to hear the words spoken. He knew. A child, perhaps no larger than a walnut, lay within Kiriki's womb, and it was dead. Dead!

"I must prepare a lot of hot water and gather up some cloths," Madeline said, rolling the sleeves of her dress up to her elbows. "Sun Eagle, I shall pray while I operate. Surely God will assist the movements of my hands. I promise you that I will do the best that I can."

Suddenly an overpowering fear seized Sun Eagle. He could not let a white woman cut into his beloved's body with a knife! She was a mere woman. Women did not know the skills of a man. He could not leave Kiriki lying there on the woman's bed to be carved up like she was an animal! It did not seem right. None of it!

His heart thundering like a drum beating out of control, Sun Eagle bodily set Madeline aside and rushed into the bedroom and swept Kiriki up into his arms. He grabbed a blanket and wrapped it around her, then raced from the room, past Madeline, and outside. He began running through the darkness, tears streaming down his face, while Kiriki lay limply within his arms, unaware of anything amiss, for she was still in a stupor.

Madeline was stunned for a moment, then she ran outside and down the steps. She began flailing her arms in the air. "Sun Eagle!" she shouted. "Do not be foolish! Bring Kiriki back! If you don't, she will die!"

Sun Eagle closed his ears to the woman's pleadings. He stumbled on through the darkness, past the barn, then stopped in mid-step when a man on horseback was suddenly there, staring blankly down at him.

"Sun Eagle?" William Jones said, struck dumb from seeing Sun Eagle there, and with a woman in his arms. "What is this, Sun Eagle? Why are you here? Who is the woman?"

Sun Eagle's back became rigid. He recognized the senator from having been congratulated personally by him earlier in the afternoon. He was one of the more personable white men of the many with which Sun Eagle had become acquainted.

But now he meant nothing to Sun Eagle but a *threat*.

Breathless, Madeline ran up to William as he dismounted. She grabbed him by the arm. "Darling, I am so glad you are home," she said, casting Sun Eagle a worried glance. "You must help me convince Sun Eagle that his wife must be operated on soon, or she will die! I, William, must be the one who operates. We have no time to go for Father!"

William slipped his top hat from his head and ran his fingers nervously through his silver threads of hair. "Will someone please tell me what this is all about?" he said, looking from Sun Eagle, to his wife, then back at Sun Eagle. "Sun Eagle, what in tarnation are you doing this far from the city? Who is that in your arms? And what on earth is this about an operation?"

Madeline shook her head in despair. "Darling, I have no idea why Sun Eagle is this far from the city, but I do know that his wife needs attention immediately," she blurted. "Darling, a dead fetus is poisoning her insides. If it is not removed immediately, Kiriki may die of peritonitis." She clutched feverishly to her husband's arm. "Please convince Sun Eagle that it must be done. Please!"

William's brow furrowed into a frown. "Sun Eagle, I don't know what took you away from Washington," he said slowly. "Perhaps someone said something insulting to you after the reception. I don't know. We can talk about it later. But for now I urge you to listen to my wife. She is very knowledgeable about all manners of medicines and illnesses. If she says that Kiriki needs an operation, she needs an operation. I urge you to return to the house and let her proceed with it."

Sun Eagle challenged William with a set stare, torn inside with what to do. This man did seem to speak with a straight tongue. He did move one's heart with words. He was not devious. He would not encourage anyone to do anything that may end in disaster.

"I hand over my woman to your wife because you say that it is best to do so," Sun Eagle said flatly. "Should the knife betray us all—"

Kiriki stirred in Sun Eagle's arms. She groaned and spoke his name softly beneath her breath. Then she was silent again.

"We must not waste any more time," Madeline said, going to Sun Eagle to place a comforting hand on his arm. "The knife will not betray us. It will make Kiriki well again."

His shoulders squared, Kiriki strangely light in his arms as she lay so limply, Sun Eagle carried her back to the house and eased her down on the bed. William came into the house and nodded to Sun Eagle as Madeline began carrying hot water into the room, then spotlessly clean cloths.

"It is best to let her work alone," William said. "Let us go to the parlor and wait."

"The wait will be too long if I am not with my Kiriki," Sun Eagle said, refusing to go. "I stay by her side. I watch. If she calls for me, I will be there for her."

William nodded and left the room. Sun Eagle folded his arms across his chest and watched tight-jawed as Madeline took the first clean swipe with a sharp knife across Kiriki's abdomen. He fought wild tears as he watched her remove what had not yet taken the shape of a child from inside Kiriki. Nevertheless, he knew that it would have been a being that would have breathed and loved. . . .

Fighting emotions battling within him, Sun Eagle watched Madeline as she skillfully sewed Kiriki back up and medicated her wound with some sort of brown liquid, then covered it delicately with clean, white dressings.

Madeline wiped beads of perspiration from her brow and drew a soft blanket up over Kiriki, then turned to Sun Eagle and smiled slowly up at him. "It went well, Sun Eagle," she whispered. "Now Kiriki will be all right. It should not be long before you will see that what I have done was right." She swallowed hard. "I am not sure it will make any difference to you at this time, but they say that when a woman miscarries, it is always for a good reason. Should she have gone full term, the child may have been deformed. God saw to it that you did not have to see such a sad childbirth.''

Sun Eagle nodded silently, then went and knelt beside the bed. He took Kiriki's limp hand and kissed it, then took a damp cloth and began caressing her fevered brow with it.

A knock on the front door drew his attention momentarily away from Kiriki. He bent his ear in that direction when he heard what the man was telling William Jones.

"Have you heard about the murder in town, William?'' the man said anxiously.

"No, I can't say that I have,'' William said. "Who was murdered? By whom?''

"Thomas McKittrick was killed. That's who,'' the man said. "He was knifed and you'll never guess by *who*.''

"Who did it?'' William prodded.

"Well, there's no actual proof that the Injun did it, but Thomas was knifed in Sun Eagle and his squaw's room,'' the man said, laughing beneath his breath. "It seems the savage is a savage after all, huh?''

Sun Eagle leapt to his feet, feeling trapped and wanting to flee. He looked down at Kiriki. He saw how vulnerable she was as she lay so still, so pale.

Slowly he knelt back down beside the bed. He would not leave her. He *would not* leave her. His spine stiffened when he heard footsteps behind him. Slowly he turned around and challenged William with a set stare.

"Sun Eagle, I sent the man away,'' William said softly. "He does not know that you and Kiriki are here.'' He took a step forward into the room. "Now would you like to explain to me why you are so far from Washington?''

Sun Eagle pushed himself up from the floor and folded his arms across his chest, his eyes not wavering as William waited for his answer.

Twenty-three

▼ ▼ ▼

"WELL, Sun Eagle? What do you have to say for yourself?" William said, meeting Sun Eagle's stare. "It doesn't make sense—you being so far from the city, especially with Kiriki being so ill."

"Kiriki was not ill when we fled the city," Sun Eagle said defensively. "She became ill suddenly. Had I known that the trauma of everything that happened tonight would cause her to . . . to lose our child, I would have done things differently."

"The trauma of things happening tonight?" William prodded. "What things, Sun Eagle?" He took a step closer to Sun Eagle and placed a gentle hand to his shoulder. "It would be best if you confide in me before others discover that you are here. Tell me everything, Sun Eagle. Everything."

Sun Eagle placed a hand to William's and eased it away from his shoulder. He then turned and eyed the door that led into the room where Kiriki lay, perhaps somewhere between life and death, then turned and faced William Jones again.

"It is because of the whiskered man that my woman was traumatized tonight," Sun Eagle said, trying to keep his anger at bay. "If I had not returned to the hotel room when I did, she would have been raped. The man had already wrestled Kiriki to the floor and had ripped off her clothes so that he could touch her with his filthy hands. He was fully prepared to rape her."

"And that is why you killed him?"

"I was angry enough to kill him for that reason alone,

but I know the feelings of the white man toward the red man, and would have refrained from going as far as actually murdering the vile man except that he was strangling me," Sun Eagle said, his voice drawn. "Had I not plunged the knife into his flesh, I would have been killed and my Kiriki would have been raped." His voice faded, then he added, "Then she would have been killed so that she could not reveal to anyone who was responsible."

William went to the fireplace, knelt, and began feeding wood into the flames. "Sun Eagle, I understand that you felt that you would not have been believed had you stayed," he said, glancing over his shoulder at him. He smiled slowly. "But being who it was who was killed, *no one* would have condemned you except for Jonas who came and told me about what had happened. He's the sort who always likes to see the red man condemned. Had he told me all of the facts of the situation, like how glad the authorities are that that bastard Thomas McKittrick finally got what was coming to him, I'd thought more of him for it."

Sun Eagle was taken aback by what William was saying about the murdered man. "You are saying that you and the authorities are glad that this Thomas McKittrick is dead?" he gasped, hope spiraling inside him.

William rose to his full height and patted Sun Eagle fondly on the back. "Young man, you did the city of Washington a great service by killing him," he said, laughing lightly. "You see, he's wanted by the law for several rapes and murders in the area. He just kept giving everyone the slip. His beard and unkempt appearance is a disguise. He is normally clean-shaven and wears the best of clothes, sporting diamonds on his fingers. That's how he managed to charm the women to his hotel suite those times he raped then stabbed them to death."

"Then Kiriki and I do not have to fear being placed in the white man's prison for what I did?" Sun Eagle asked disbelievingly. "It was right? It will be acceptable?"

William went to the fireplace mantel and picked up his pipe. He filled it with tobacco and lit it, then turned back to face Sun Eagle. "No, you won't be condemned," he said. "I will explain everything to the authorities. They will understand. They may even give you a commendation for your deed."

"But I am Indian," Sun Eagle said, gesturing toward himself with his hand. "Can an Indian kill a white man and his reason for having done so be understood?"

"Most of the time, no," William said, coughing nervously. "But this time? Yes. Many times yes."

Sun Eagle exhaled a trembling, relieved breath. His shoulders relaxed. "Sun Eagle is glad," he said, turning to look at the bedroom door again. "Kiriki will be glad."

Madeline appeared at the door. She went to Sun Eagle, wiping her hands on a blood-soiled apron, then she slipped the apron off and laid it aside. "Sun Eagle," she said, placing a gentle hand on his arm. "Kiriki is awakening. She will need you. She will be in much pain, for all I have for the pain is Valerium. While she has been awakening, I have managed to get her to take a few spoonfuls. But that won't be enough to make her comfortable. I am sorry for that, Sun Eagle."

Sun Eagle swallowed hard, nodded, then walked on past Madeline into the bedroom. The room was dark with shadows, a lone candle flickering low on a table beside the bed. Kiriki looked so small on the bed, her face pale and drawn, a sheet drawn up to her chin to hide her nudity and bandaged body beneath it.

Sun Eagle choked back a sob of remorse, then knelt beside the bed. He reached beneath the sheet and found Kiriki's hand, and clasped his fingers around it. His throat tightened when her eyelashes began to flutter and her mouth opened in a slight, quavering moan.

"Kiriki?" Sun Eagle said, his free hand softly caressing her brow. "Darling Kiriki, it is I, Sun Eagle. I am here. Can you hear me?"

Kiriki was consumed with fiery flames of pain. She gasped for breath as she slowly opened her eyes and found Sun Eagle looking devotedly at her. She licked her parched lips. "Sun Eagle, what has happened to me?" she whispered. She looked past him and slowly around the room. "Where am I?" She winced and cried out as a sharp pain grabbed at her abdomen. "Oh, Sun Eagle, why do I hurt so?"

Sun Eagle leaned closer to her. He kissed her brow. "I am so sorry that you are hurting," he said hoarsely.

"Why do I?" Kiriki prodded, vaguely recalling the pain that she had experienced earlier while fleeing the city of Washington. This pain she was having now was far more severe. She could hardly bear it!

"Kiriki, how do I tell you?" Sun Eagle said, her pain transferring to him, his heart aching.

"Tell . . . me . . . what . . . ?" Kiriki asked, chewing on her lower lip to stifle another cry of pain.

"You were with child, Kiriki," Sun Eagle said, now holding both of her hands. "But you are no longer. The white woman had to use a knife to remove the dead fetus. That is why you hurt so badly, Kiriki. Your abdomen was opened. You will now have to have time to heal before we travel back to our people."

Kiriki's mind was spinning. A child? She had been pregnant and she had not known it? And she had lost it? It tore at her senses to realize the truth of what had happened.

"A child?" she finally said, tears wetting her cheeks.

"Yes, but do not be so remorseful," Sun Eagle said, his face etched with worry. "The white woman. Madeline? She said that often when one miscarries it is for a *good* reason. The child was not meant to be born."

A strangling sort of feeling invaded Kiriki's throat and her heart skipped a beat. The child! Whose had it been? Brown Bear's or Sun Eagle's? Both had been with her in that way.

She turned her eyes away, sobbing softly. She had to believe that the child had been Brown Bear's or she would not have lost it. Any child conceived of Sun Eagle would have been too strong.

Yes, she had to believe that Tirawa had blessed her by taking the child from her. Though she, herself, had been born of a rape, she did not wish to ever carry such a burden around inside her, as her mother had been forced to do. Nor would she ever place such a burden on the child.

"Kiriki, please do not be so saddened," Sun Eagle said, placing a finger to her chin, directing her eyes back around to look at him. "We will have many more children. We will have a son to be next chief in line, and then a daughter in your likeness so that I can marvel over her as I do you. Our future is bright, Kiriki. Even the white men do not condemn us for the murder that was forced upon us this night. The man was evil. He was hunted by the white authorities. It is said that we did the white man a favor by ridding the city of him."

Kiriki's eyes widened. "Then I did not ruin everything for you?" she whispered, her throat dry. "You will still be awarded your special medal?"

"As soon as you are well enough to be witness to the white man awarding it to me," Sun Eagle said, squaring his shoulders proudly.

Kiriki clutched her fingers desperately around Sun Eagle's hand. "I am not going to be there to see you get the award," she said, her voice anxious. She gasped for breath as pain again assailed her in great, fiery sweeps. She closed her eyes, trying to fight the pain, then slowly opened them again and pleaded with them up at Sun Eagle. "Sun Eagle, I am going to die. Oh, Sun Eagle, do you hear me? I am going to die! I shall never see our people again. I shall never see the beauties of Nebraska again. Oh, please hold me, Sun Eagle. Please hold me!"

Sun Eagle was stunned by Kiriki actually believing that she was dying. He would not accept that as true, himself. He knew her strength. He knew her courage. She would not let herself be taken from him before they had shared everything in life together.

Leaning down over her, Sun Eagle gently embraced her. He placed his cheek to hers, his heart pounding. "What you say is foolish!" he whispered, aware of the heat of her flesh against his. She was still awash with a fever. Perhaps she *was* going to die. The thought cut away at his insides. He would not allow her to say it anymore. He would not allow himself to think it.

"No, it is not foolish," Kiriki whispered, lifting a shaky hand to his unbraided hair. She wove her fingers through its thickness, reveling in its softness. "We must prepare ourselves for my death, Sun Eagle. I want to marry you. Please, let us be married. *Now*."

Sun Eagle could not fight the tears that burned the corners of his eyes. They rolled onto Kiriki's cheek. "You wish to be married?" he asked, his voice breaking.

"Yes, my love," Kiriki said, choking on a sob. "Do you not see? It is necessary so that one day in the future when your soul also leaves your body we can be together forever in the hereafter. Oh, Sun Eagle, am I selfish for wanting to claim you at death's door? Am I? I do not want to be, but I love you so."

"You are not going to die!" Sun Eagle said between clenched teeth. "Do not speak of dying!"

"Are you saying by *not* saying it that you will not marry me now?" Kiriki asked, placing her hands at his cheeks, easing his face away from her own. She implored him with her eyes. "If you do not wish to, I will try and understand. You wish to save your hereafter love for the woman you will marry and who will bear your children. I will try and understand, Sun Eagle. Truly, I will."

Sun Eagle took her hands and kissed both palms, then held them to his chest. "I am not saying that at all," he said hoarsely. "It is only that to be married now under such circumstances will be the same as admitting that I, also, do not think that you will live, and I believe with all of my heart and all of my faith in you that you *will* live."

"Then if you are right, and I do live, we will have no marriage ceremony to prepare for when we return to our people," Kiriki said. "We will return with the news that we are already man and wife."

"How could it be possible?" Sun Eagle said, his defenses crumbling. "There is no one of our village here to perform the wedding."

"That is not necessary," Kiriki said, wincing when pain

shot through her again. She gasped for breath, then continued speaking. "Am I not part white, Sun Eagle? Was not my father a white man?"

Sun Eagle nodded. "Yes, that is so," he said, quirking an eyebrow. "But why do you now mention a father that you never knew? You only knew a father who was Pawnee."

"I mention my white father because it is the time to do so," Kiriki said, clasping onto his hands again. "I am part white and part Pawnee. I can choose from two sorts of marriage ceremonies, can I not, because of my two heritages? We are among the white people now, not the Pawnee. The ceremony must be performed by a white priest, not Pawnee."

Sun Eagle tried to refrain from showing his alarm at her suggestion, knowing that it was important to please her at this time. She could not be allowed to become displeased or unhappy. Her life depended on so much at this moment. Being content was of the utmost importance.

"Kiriki, is this what you truly wish?" he finally said, his voice drawn.

"I fear that we may never have another chance to join hands and hearts for eternity," Kiriki said, tears streaming down her face again. "My love, do this for me? Let me become at peace with myself before I take my last breath of life."

Sun Eagle gritted his teeth at her mention of death again. There seemed to be no stopping her thoughts. Perhaps agreeing to the marriage just might fill her mind with hope instead of despair.

"It will be done," Sun Eagle said, rising to his feet. "I shall ask that a priest be sent for. Also perhaps something to help lessen your pain."

He looked toward the window, seeing the darkness of night. "When morning comes I shall go to the forest and gather some herbs for your fever," he said. He looked determinedly down at her. "You are not going to die, Kiriki. I will not allow it!"

Kiriki smiled weakly up at him, then closed her eyes

and drifted off into sleep, the only escape from her miserable pain. While she slept she dreamed. She was in a field of wild flowers, laughing and singing, a child clasped to each of her hands. Sun Eagle was there, carrying a third child. Never had she seen him so happy! Nor had she ever felt such intense contentment. . . .

Sun Eagle looked down at her and his heart sang when he saw a soft smile flutter across her lips. By agreeing to the marriage, he had made her feel a measure of happiness.

Oh, but if only he could feel as happy! If he could only see a future of togetherness! If he could only see into the future and be shown that she would be alive to share a future with him!

At this moment in time, he could not have faith in anything. Not even himself.

Twenty-four

▼ ▼ ▼

THE bedroom no longer smelled of sickness, instead its aroma was that of a Nebraska plains in the spring when wild flowers bloomed in abundance, filling the air with heady, wonderful fragrances. She smiled as she looked around the room, touched by Madeline's generous nature as to have taken the time to bring in so many beautiful flowers from her garden to share with Kiriki and Sun Eagle on their wedding day.

"It is our wedding day," Kiriki murmured as Sun Eagle entered the room alongside Major O'Fallon. She reached a hand to both of the men as they flanked her bed. She looked from one to the other. "I do apologize for having distracted you from your journey to Washington. I do hope not too much has changed."

Sun Eagle knelt beside the bed and touched his hand to Kiriki's brow, his eyes lighting up when he discovered that she was not as hot as before. Could it be the herbs that he had administered to her early in the morning? Or could it be the medications that William Jones had obtained from Madeline's father late last evening?

"Do not worry yourself over such trivial matters on your wedding day," Major O'Fallon said, patting Kiriki's hand. His blue eyes wavered as he looked down at her. "I am so sorry about what has happened to you. I feel somewhat responsible. Had I not encouraged you and Sun Eagle to come to Washington, perhaps you wouldn't have miscarried."

Kiriki looked away from him, ashamed when she let herself recall that deeply within her she was happy that

256

the child was no longer living. She had no doubt that it had been Brown Bear's child—a child conceived in violence.

She now understood what her mother had surely gone through while carrying her child securely within her womb. She had probably seen the leering eyes of her assailant every day. Kiriki was blessed that she would not have this burden—a burden that she would forever have to keep secret from everyone.

"Kiriki? Have I said something to wound you?" Major O'Fallon asked, kneeling beside the bed. He grasped her hand and leaned closer to her, speaking in almost a whisper. "If so, I am sorry. I . . . I never want to cause you harm. Never have I meant for harm to come to you. Only recently have I realized that I am the cause of so much heartache on your part. Oh, God, how can I ever make it up to you?"

Kiriki blinked back a tear and slowly turned her eyes to the major. "What do you mean?" she asked, her voice weak. "How could you be responsible for how I feel about anything? You are our Pawnee Indian agent. You are our friend. You could never hurt any of my people. You have always looked out for our welfare. We love you as though you were a part of us—as though you are our brother."

Major O'Fallon looked over at Sun Eagle and questioned him with his eyes, having spoken to Sun Eagle in confidence only moments ago. Sun Eagle had encouraged him to tell Kiriki the truths that had been revealed. He felt that she should have been told long ago. She would have been more at peace with herself. Even with her mother. . . .

Sun Eagle nodded. He kissed Kiriki's hand, then left the room, knowing that she was following him with questioning eyes. But truths between a daughter and father must be spoken without an audience.

"Kiriki, how do I tell you?" Major O'Fallon said, clearing his throat.

"Tell me what?" Kiriki asked, blinking her eyes nervously. "Why did Sun Eagle leave? Why do you see a need for you and I to be alone?"

Major O'Fallon rubbed a hand gently over her forehead, stopping to smooth his fingers over her brown eyebrows. "You have been questioned often about the color of your eyes, haven't you?" he asked, smiling down at her. "I am sure you have noticed that they are the exact color of mine." His hand went to her hair. His fingers wove through the silken texture. "Even your hair. It is the exact color of mine." He caressed her cheek. "But, my dear, the color of your skin and mine differs so. It is the color of your mother's."

Kiriki was feeling stronger, not only physically, but mentally, as well, yet was finding it hard to grasp onto what the major was leading to. It made no sense whatsoever to compare her eyes and hair with his. She knew where she had gotten them—from her father.

And her father was . . .

Sucking in a great gasp of air, Kiriki leaned up on an elbow, suddenly seized with an idea that was too far-fetched. This man that she had idolized since she was a child? This Major O'Fallon? Surely he was not the man who had raped her mother! This man had a heart of gold and could never do any wrong, to anyone.

Yet it was the way he was addressing her—the way he was comparing her to him that made her heart begin to pound crazily and tears pool her eyes. If she discovered that all along she had been lied to—that this gentle man was capable of rape, she would lose trust in mankind. Totally!

"All of my life I have wished that my true father could have been like you," she said, her voice quivering. "Upright, honest, caring. Have I been wrong to think so highly of you? Have I?"

"Why would you ask such a thing?" Major O'Fallon asked, his gaze becoming unsteady under her close scrutiny.

"It is because of your comparisons," Kiriki said, then lowered herself back to the bed, exhaustion overcoming her. "Why would you compare my eyes and hair to yours? Why?"

"Why?" Major O'Fallon repeated, wringing a cloth out in a basin of water, applying it to her perspiring brow. "Because I see you lying there so helpless. So ill. I feel that it is time to reveal secrets to you that I have been withholding since even before the day of your birth. Not only because of seeing you lying there so innocently, so wracked with pain, but also because I believe that my daughter needs secrets revealed to her on her wedding day."

Kiriki looked up at him, shock registering across her pale face. She stared at him for a moment, then turned her eyes away, groaning. "No," she cried, doubling her hands into tight fists beneath the blanket. "It cannot be! You *can't* be my true father. He was a demon! A man who thought so little of women that he raped them!" Slowly her eyes moved back to him. She blinked tears from them as she glared up at him. "My true father is dead! He was killed for his ugly deed! How can you explain that? How?"

Outside the room, Sun Eagle had heard Kiriki's distress, and even though he had agreed that Kiriki should be told the truth—that the time had come for *all* truths, a truth that he had only moments ago been told, himself—he now regretted his decision. It was obvious that it was a strain on her. Worse even, that she was not believing the gentle major as he tried to explain to her that he was her father.

He rushed into the room and knelt down beside Kiriki's bed. He reached beneath the blanket, took her hands, and squeezed them affectionately. "I am here if you need me," he said, eyeing Major O'Fallon wearily. He looked down at Kiriki. "My sweet Kiriki, what Major O'Fallon is trying to tell you is that he *is* your father, and that there was no rape at all those eighteen years ago. Your mother and Major O'Fallon were in love, but it was a forbidden love. When your mother discovered her pregnancy shortly after her marriage to Lone Chief, the story of the rape was contrived to save face."

"But there was a man slain for the rape," Kiriki said, looking up at Major O'Fallon, trying to grasp onto the truth. A part of her was glad, but a part of her was wary.

"Kiriki, that is the most unfortunate thing about what happened those eighteen years ago," Major O'Fallon said, lowering his eyes as he recalled the innocent man's murder. "The Pawnee needed someone to blame when your mother lied and said that she had been raped by a white man." He raised his eyes and implored her with a set stare. "She refused to point an accusing finger, so the Pawnee came to their own conclusions as to who it was. There was this soldier. He taunted the Pawnee all of the time. He called them names. He was forever going to the village and openly teasing the women. One of the women even confessed that he had raped her. Well, it gave the Pawnee much pleasure to accuse this man of your mother's rape and get their vengeance. He was sought and killed. His scalp still hangs among those in Lone Chief's lodge."

Kiriki eyed Major O'Fallon speculatively. "All of this because you and my mother—?" Kiriki said, then turned her eyes away, not able to continue. All of this was too much to comprehend. She did not know whether to hate or love Major O'Fallon. At this moment he was someone that she had never truly known at all. Nor had she known her mother—a woman capable of lying to a daughter. . . .

"Kiriki, let me continue explaining about your mother and me," Major O'Fallon said, removing the cool cloth from her brow. He dropped it back in the basin of water, then smoothed some damp locks of her hair back from her eyes. "Kiriki, I was at that time, as now, the Indian agent, admired by all. I had succeeded in matters where no other agent had before me. I had managed to get help from the government that gave your people better living conditions. Then something unforetold happened. Your mother was young and beautiful. I was young and free. We fell madly in love. But we had to meet in secret, for you see, it was a forbidden love. We could never get married. My work was important for your people. Your people could have suffered had I married your mother, for both your mother and I would have been ridiculed by the white man, and my powers at bargaining in Washington would have been lost. Your mother and I sacrificed our love to do what was best for your people.''

He hung his head in his hands. "I thought her pregnancy was the result of the rape," he said, his voice drawn. "Only when the child was born and I looked into the child's eyes, and saw the color of her hair, did I know whose child, in truth, that it was. I confronted your mother in private. She told me the truth. That this child—that you—were mine. But she made me promise never to tell anyone. Not even you. She had already lived through the horrors of the condemnation of her women friends for having been raped by a white man, and giving birth to his child. She did not want to chance living through that again, and as before, she did not want to chance ruining my career since my word still carried so much weight for the Pawnee in Washington.'' He gulped hard. "I have regretted not telling you for years but I did not know how to. My promise to your mother was that. A promise. I did not want to give her cause to hate me. Though I am married, I still love your mother with all of my heart.''

Kiriki's pulse was racing. She looked up at Major O'Fallon with tear-soaked lashes. The story was beautiful! She had been conceived of a pure love instead of a cruel rape. Her true father sacrificed his love for a woman for the Indian people. He had sacrificed his own happiness for the Indian people. His heart was good! His intentions were pure just as that moment when she had been conceived by two people who loved each other so innocently.

Major O'Fallon looked slowly over at Kiriki. His eyes filled with tears when he saw that she was looking adoringly up at him. It was in her eyes and expression that she bore no ill feelings for him. She had understood.

"If only I had known," Kiriki whispered, sobbing. "We could have shared so much together. My life has been filled with so many questions. So many guilts. Had I known you were my father, I could have come to you

and you could have given me answers. You could have
helped lift my burden of guilt for how I was conceived.''

Major O'Fallon nodded. ''Yes, my dear, I could have
done those things,'' he said thickly. ''But too many things
would have been jeopardized. Please try and understand.''

''Why did you tell me now?'' Kiriki asked, wiping tears
from her cheeks. ''Is it because I am dying?''

Major O'Fallon paled. He looked over at Sun Eagle
with alarm, then down at Kiriki. ''As I said before,'' he
murmured, taking her free hand and patting it. ''It is my
daughter's wedding day. I could not bear standing by
watching and not be recognized as your father.'' He
smiled softly. ''Don't you know that it is the custom of
the white man that the father give the bride away to the
groom? My dear, I want that honor today if you will allow
it.''

''And, Kiriki, you are not dying,'' Sun Eagle said
forcefully. ''You are much stronger today. Your color is
better. And your body temperature is only slightly above
what is normal. Soon you will be well enough to return
to Nebraska with your husband at your side.''

Kiriki was suddenly awash with a euphoric happiness.
''My father?'' she whispered, staring momentarily at
Major O'Fallon. She turned her gaze to Sun Eagle. ''My
husband?'' She swallowed back a sob lodged in her throat.
''I am very lucky. This is the happiest day of my life.''

Then her eyes widened and a strange, lopsided smile
appeared on her face as she stared up at Major O'Fallon.
''You have a son called David, do you not?'' she asked,
her pulse racing at the thought of what it could mean.

''Yes, I have a son,'' Major O'Fallon said, smiling.

''David?'' Kiriki said, blinking back tears. ''If he is
your son, can I not also call him my brother?''

Major O'Fallon nodded. ''Yes, Kiriki,'' he said, wiping
a tear from his cheek. ''You can call him your brother,
because, in part, he is.''

Kiriki choked back a deep emotion that was filling her.
For so long, she had wished for a brother and sister, and
through a twist of fate she now had one.

She had many reasons to live now. Many!

Through the long confessions, several carriages had arrived, filled with the wedding party which consisted of important dignitaries from Washington and their wives. Kiriki was now only aware of the buzzing of voices right outside her door. She looked at the closed door, panic seizing her.

"It is my wedding day and I cannot leave this dreadful bed!" she fussed. Her fingers went shakily to her hair. "And my hair! Surely it is a fright!"

Sun Eagle and Major O'Fallon exchanged quick glances, then broke into merry laughter. "My daughter is going to be all right," Major O'Fallon said, rising from his chair to go to the door. "She is worried about her appearance as only a healthy woman worries." He opened the door only slightly and beckoned for Madeline. "Kiriki would like to have her hair brushed for the ceremony. Could you please?"

Madeline came into the room and gazed in wonder at Kiriki, then smiled broadly. Kiriki had improved even during the past hour! She was actually beaming. Thank the Lord, she was going to be all right!

"I'd be happy to make her beautiful," she said, sighing. She got a brush and went to the bed. Sun Eagle helped hold Kiriki's head up while her hair was given several gentle strokes.

And then the guests were invited into the room, a priest in his black robe and stiff white collar in the lead, with the President of the United States and his wife, Elizabeth, at his side.

"I now pronounce you man and wife," the priest said, closing his Bible. He smiled at Sun Eagle. "You may kiss the bride."

Sun Eagle quirked an eyebrow and looked slowly around the room at the group of people watching and waiting for him to kiss Kiriki. Kissing her in public seemed out of place, yet had not the whole wedding ceremony seemed odd? It differed strangely from the Pawnee's wedding celebrations. This wedding was too subdued, with no drums, no dancing, no rattles. . . .

Major O'Fallon edged close to Sun Eagle. "Kiss her," he whispered, nudging Sun Eagle in the side. "Then the ceremony will be finalized."

Sun Eagle gazed down at Kiriki who lay in bed, beautifully dressed in one of Madeline's gowns that had a high neckline and eyelet trim. There was a look of radiance in her eyes, and he knew now without a doubt that she was recovering from her ordeal. And they were man and wife. Nothing could take that from them. Nothing or no one. Especially not Brown Bear.

Bending over Kiriki, Sun Eagle framed her face gently between his hands. He wanted to shout to the heavens of his gladness when their lips met, and he discovered that they were no longer hot to the touch. The fever had left her.

He kissed her softly, their tongues meeting in a quick flick, then he rose away from her and stood proudly by as a procession of senators, congressmen, and their wives began passing beside the bed, congratulating Sun Eagle and Kiriki.

Madeline Jones took her turn. She bent over Kiriki and brought something out from behind her that she had purposely not let Kiriki see until now. "Here is my wedding gift for you, Kiriki," she said softly. "Had I had time to go into town to shop for something special, I would have given you something else. As it is, I hope this will please you enough."

Kiriki's eyes widened with disbelief as Madeline placed a bottle of perfume within Kiriki's hand. Even with the lid securely sealed she could smell the sweetness of the gold liquid splashing around inside. She looked at the perfume, then up at Madeline. "I have longed so often for perfume," she murmured. "How can I ever thank you? I love it, Madeline."

"Shall I open it for you and put a dab or two on your wrists?" Madeline asked, smiling from ear to ear.

"Oh, yes, please do," Kiriki said, anxious to smell sweet and wonderful.

Madeline unscrewed the lid from the bottle and let several drops splash into the palm of her hand, then she transferred this to Kiriki's wrists. Kiriki sniffed her skin, then giggled as she glanced over at Sun Eagle. "I smell like roses!" she whispered. "Please smell me!"

Sun Eagle raised her wrist to his nose. He inhaled and smiled down at her. "It is a wonderful gift," he said thickly.

Another senator's wife presented Kiriki with a pair of solid gold earrings, that which stole her breath away. She thanked the woman and held onto them lightly as the President and his wife Elizabeth stepped away from their quiet conversation with William Jones and Major O'Fallon, and moved to the bed. Elizabeth handed Kiriki a package tied with a pink satin bow.

"If you are not up to opening it, I would be glad to do it for you," Elizabeth said, smiling down at Kiriki.

"Thank you, but I believe I can do it," Kiriki said, placing her perfume and earrings aside, touched by the fact that the President's wife was so generous and sweet. "It is so kind of you to bring me and Sun Eagle a gift."

Elizabeth laughed and glanced over at Sun Eagle. "The gift I give you is for you, alone, Kiriki," she said, then turned to her husband and locked an arm through his. "James has the gift for Sun Eagle." She batted her thick lashes nervously. "Please open your gift first, Kiriki."

Kiriki's fingers fumbled with the bow, having never seen one before. Finally she got it off, and with weak fingers tore the fine tissue paper away. Her eyes widened and she gasped when she discovered a shawl made of silk edged with delicate white lace. Never had she seen anything as fine or as beautiful.

"Oh, thank you," she said, clasping the shawl to her breast. "I shall treasure it. Always!"

"It seemed the perfect gift for such a sweet and charming young lady," Elizabeth said, pleased with Kiriki's reaction to the gift. She turned to President Monroe. "Darling, I believe you have something for Sun Eagle?"

President Monroe chuckled under his breath. He kneaded his cleft chin with one hand while his other hand fished for something deeply within his gray coat pocket. "Hmm, where is that thing?" he said, giving Sun Eagle a look of amusement. He nodded. "Ah, I think I've found it. Yes, here it is."

Sun Eagle and Kiriki exchanged quick glances, then Kiriki's heart warmed when the President stepped up to Sun Eagle and slowly placed a medal hanging from a fancy band over his head and around his neck.

"With this medal I honor you, Sun Eagle, for bravery in saving Kiriki from death during the Morning Star ritual," President Monroe said, arranging the medal so that the silver face picked up the glow of the sun shining through the window, revealing the engraved picture of a scaffold and Indian, representing the sacrificial spot, and an Indian fleeing with an Indian girl, beneath them engraved, "To The Bravest Of The Brave."

On the reverse side was revealed the depictions of two hands clasped, the sign of friendship, and laurel leaves around the edges.

"The medal also honors you for all of your efforts to help bring together much understanding between your people and ours," the President said. "Wear it proudly, Sun Eagle. Each and every one of us present is genuinely proud to know you."

A sudden burst of clapping made Sun Eagle's eyes mist with thanks, yet it was at this moment that his thoughts were more on Kiriki than himself. He bent to a knee and showed her the medal, then rose back to his feet and accepted each and every handshake, pride swelling within him.

Kiriki saw in her husband the wonders of a man who would one day rule his band of Skidi. He would be a leader of leaders. And he was hers.

Tired, yet pleasantly so, Kiriki closed her eyes and could not fight the sleep that crept over her. She sighed heavily in her sleep, causing Sun Eagle to look quickly over at her with alarm.

"She is only sleeping," Madeline reassured, touching his arm gently. "Though she has enjoyed today, it has worn her out." She looked around the room and addressed the crowd.

"We must leave Kiriki to rest," she said in a voice of authority. She glanced up at Sun Eagle. "We shall all be out in the parlor. Come and join us after you spend a few more moments with your wife."

Sun Eagle nodded. Everyone left but Major O'Fallon. He lingered, and went and placed a hand on Sun Eagle's shoulder. "Well, Sun Eagle, not only are you one of the best damn scouts in Nebraska, but I am sure you will make one damn good son-in-law," he boasted confidently.

They embraced, locking their arms tightly around each other.

Twenty-five

Nebraska

KIRIKI lay awake in Sun Eagle's arms, the morning light spiraling softly through the smoke hole in the ceiling of the earthen lodge. Home. She was home in Sun Eagle's dwelling as his wife. The journey from Washington had been long and arduous, but even so, while traveling in the stagecoach, she had healed more and more every day. Last night she and Sun Eagle had performed as man and wife for the first time since the marriage ceremony, and she was relieved that her traumatic experience had not lessened her ability to share in the lovemaking. It was still as sweet. It was still as wonderful.

Sun Eagle stirred beside her. She turned on her side and looked at him adoringly, gently smoothing some of his raven-black hair back from his eyes as he slept with a relaxed, contented look on his handsome face. She loved him even more than before because he had not once condemned her for having lost the child. Many Pawnee women whose babies died in their wombs were ridiculed and cast aside by their husbands because they were seen as weak and useless.

But Sun Eagle had not condemned or ridiculed her. He was a man of understanding—a man of deep love. Little did he know her true feelings about this child that she was convinced had been Brown Bear's.

Snuggling close to Sun Eagle as he turned on his side, resting her breasts against his back and letting a hand dangle over his broad chest, Kiriki thought about the past several weeks and what she had gained or lost. She *had* lost a child in Washington, but she had gained a husband, a father, and a brother!

Oh, how she wanted to shout the news of having a father she regarded with reverent admiration to the world! Oh, how she wanted to go to David and claim out loud that he was her brother!

But she had sworn to secrecy, not wanting to bring harm or disillusionment to her mother or her step-father. Even her true father's wife, the good woman that she was, would be hurt by such truths. Kiriki would just have to learn to accept what time she could have with her father and brother on the pretense it was for other reasons than being with kin.

"I shall think up many reasons to see and talk with them," she whispered, giggling.

Her heart lurched when Sun Eagle suddenly grabbed her hand and guided it downward. She sucked in a wild breath of passion when he led her hand to his manhood and urged her to wrap her fingers around it. She laughed softly.

"How long have you been awake?" she asked, hearing his moan of pleasure as she skillfully moved her hand on his smooth shaft. "Did my contentment—my happiness—awaken you? Could you feel it transfer from my body into yours, my darling?"

"Perhaps so," Sun Eagle said, chuckling. "But I would be more truthful in saying that your breasts teased me awake as they lay against my back." He turned slowly to face her, so carefully that her hand did not move from his hardness. "It is good that we can make love again. Soon you will be swollen with child. You will forget the one that was denied you."

Kiriki's smile faded and her hand slowed its pace. She was not sure that she could ever become with child again. Her body had been forced to endure much during the miscarriage. It may have been damaged in the process.

In her heart, Kiriki damned Brown Bear over and over again. Because of Brown Bear much could still be denied to her and Sun Eagle. A child! A child!

Sun Eagle sensed Kiriki's hesitation. He took her hand away from his hardness and rose above her, holding himself away from her with extended arms and the palms of his hands. "Kiriki, you will forget all sadness caused by the loss of the child soon," he said, his voice filled with compassion. "We will busy ourselves making a wonderful life together. Hopefully, soon a child will join us. But do not worry yourself over it. What is important now is that you are healthy again. We are able to share everything, Kiriki. You are now my wife. I am your husband."

Kiriki stifled a sob behind a hand, wondering how she could have ever found a man like Sun Eagle. How foolish of her in the past to only think of a future with a white man. Sun Eagle surpassed everything that she had thought to find in a white man. All that was being denied her by marrying him was a fancy house with fancy belongings. What Sun Eagle offered her, compassion and total commitment, was far more precious and everlasting than any mere possessions.

"My husband," Kiriki murmured, placing her hands behind Sun Eagle's neck, drawing his mouth down to hers. "Oh, how beautiful that word sounds on my lips. And to know that when I say it, I am making reference to *you*. Can it be possible? Are you truly mine? Is our future together truly guaranteed? Can Brown Bear never do anything else to prevent it?"

"Do not worry about that brother of mine," Sun Eagle said, kissing the column of her throat, and then trailing kisses down to her breasts. "He has fled. He is labeled a renegade. He would not dare show his face around here. My father and your father have cause to punish him severely!"

Kiriki was silent again, knowing that she had cause to make Sun Eagle hate Brown Bear so much that he would hunt him down until he thrust a knife into his heart.

But never would she tell Sun Eagle. Never. And not because she feared for Brown Bear. It was for herself that she would not tell. She did not want Sun Eagle ever to know about the vicious, ugly rape. It could possibly cloud his vision of her when they were making love.

Wanting to change the subject so that she could place Brown Bear from her mind, at least for the moment, Kiriki looked up at Sun Eagle, her voice anxious. "Today I will go and see my mother and father," she said, shimmering with rapture as Sun Eagle continued his sweet assault on her body, his tongue now flicking across one breast and then the other.

"Not my true father, Sun Eagle," she quickly corrected. "But the father who has been kind enough to call me his daughter through the years."

She paused and inhaled a shaky breath as Sun Eagle's tongue and lips made a slow descent along her body, her stomach quivering with pleasure as his tongue now flicked in and around her navel. "Darling, I am almost going mindless," she giggled, weaving her fingers through his hair, guiding him lower. "But I must tell you what I plan to do today. I am going to take the lacy shawl that Elizabeth Monroe gave me and present it to my mother. Oh, how she will love it! She has never had anything fancy in her life. Can you not see her prancing around before her friends showing off what her daughter brought her from Washington?"

When his mouth buried itself in the soft tendrils of hair at the juncture of her thighs, Kiriki's voice faded, rapture stealing her of all thought and reason. "I shall even sprinkle the shawl with the perfume," she whispered. "She will not only look beautiful, she will smell wondrously!"

Sun Eagle looked up at her and smiled. "My woman, are you through rattling on and on?" he asked, momentarily drawing his mouth away from her. "Close your eyes. Enjoy the pleasure that I give you. We can talk later. Much later . . ."

"It is only because I am so happy," Kiriki said, sighing.

"Let me make you happier," Sun Eagle said, lowering his mouth to her throbbing center again.

He loved her in a leisurely fashion with his mouth and

tongue, drawing pleasurable moans from her. She abandoned herself to the melting sensation that was encompassing her. Her blood quickened, and she could not help but let herself go all of the way, enjoying the pleasure to the uttermost limits. Her body quivered, a blissful joy overtaking her, so much that she did not even realize when Sun Eagle rose above her and entered her with his ready hardness.

She responded to his thrusts, lifting her hips to meet and move with him. Great surges of ecstasy welled within her, filling her with a lazy warmth. She welcomed his lips as they came to her mouth, his kiss daring to make her go over the edge into total ecstasy again. . . .

Sun Eagle stroked her breasts, his fingers teasing circles around the nipples, causing them to strain with added anticipation. Then she felt his body stiffen, and knew from past moments of lovemaking that he was near to reaching the same peak as she. They clung. They tangled. They kissed. They tremored and shook.

Then they lay parted, both breathing hard and pearled with sweat. Sun Eagle reached a hand to Kiriki and caressed her between the thighs. "You are so much woman," he said huskily. "I could have never asked for more than what you have given me first as a lover, then as a wife. I am fortunate. I shall always remember just how much."

Kiriki turned to him and snuggled within his arms. "I am the fortunate one," she whispered, kissing his sleek, copper chest. She flicked a tongue across one of his hard nipples, eliciting a faint groan from deep within him. "Because of you I have finally found my destiny. Everything is clear to me now, Sun Eagle. My past. My present. My future. Thank you, my love. Thank you."

A voice filled with panic outside the earthen lodge, asking for Sun Eagle, caused Sun Eagle to rise quickly to his feet. He drew a loincloth on, slipped into moccasins, and stepped outside.

Kiriki grabbed a buckskin dress and drew it quickly over her head and slipped her moccasins on, then went

outside to stand beside her husband. She saw a fierceness
in his eyes never seen before as he listened intently to the
brave tell him of his missing horses.

"It was Brown Bear!" the Brave said breathlessly.
"Some young braves had sneaked from their dwellings in
the middle of the night to swim in the river. They saw
Brown Bear steal your horses, Sun Eagle. They did not
come forward and report it to you at that time because
they feared being punished by their parents for having left
their dwellings without permission. They came forward
only moments ago, guiltily for keeping such information
from you. Sun Eagle, Brown Bear stole *all* of your horses!
All of them!"

"Then my brother knows that I have returned to my
village," Sun Eagle said in a low growl. "His jealousies
and hatred for me are no less than before." He doubled
a hand into a tight fist. "This time he has gone too far. I
cannot stand by and tolerate a brother who first steals my
woman, and now my horses. It must end!"

The brave looked anxiously at Sun Eagle. "We will go
after him? We will take what is yours back from your
brother?" he said, a hand clutched determinedly around a
long lance. "This time you will kill him, Sun Eagle? You
must. Brown Bear will not be satisfied until you are dead.
First it was Kiriki, then it is your horses. Sun Eagle, next
it will be you."

Sun Eagle's eyes wavered. "That is true," he said
thickly. "I know this. That is why I will ready many
poison arrows and then will go after my brother. By the
time the stars sprinkle the dark heavens with their lovely
light he will be dead."

"I shall go and give commands to many warriors to
ready their weapons," the brave said, his eyes alight with
excitement for the hunt. "We ride with you. We wish to
see Brown Bear take his last breath. He has caused not
only hardships to you and your family, but to our people
as a whole."

Sun Eagle nodded. "That is true," he said, a part of
him unable to shed thoughts of himself as a child when

Brown Bear rode at his side on the hunt. They had learned many things together, most of it good. When and where Brown Bear learned bad traits was beyond Sun Eagle's comprehension. It just seemed to have happened, and now nothing or no one could help Brown Bear. He had sealed his own doom by his evil deeds.

Kiriki walked beside Sun Eagle back inside the lodge. "Your heart is heavy," she murmured. "I can feel it as though it were in my own body!"

"It is not good to make plans to kill one's own brother," Sun Eagle growled, going to a large cedar box stored at the far end of his dwelling. He fell to his knees before the box and raised its lid. He peered down at all ingredients needed for the most deadly of warfare. There were buckskin pouches filled with dried leaves of poison oak and various other poisonous weeds. Slowly he lifted a vial that contained the venom from a rattlesnake. All of these things he took to the firepit and placed them in a small cooking vessel over the fire, adding a small portion of water. He let this all simmer together into a pasty sort of mixture, removed it from the fire, and sat and watched it until it cooled, a sharp knife held tightly within his hand.

"I have never watched this process before," Kiriki said, eyeing the knife that he held so determinedly. "What will you use the knife for, Sun Eagle?"

Sun Eagle did not answer her. He, instead, suddenly made an incision with the sharp knife just below his knee and slightly to the side so that the blood would run down almost to his heels.

Kiriki gasped and paled. "Why do you do this?" she cried in a tremoring voice, understanding most customs of the Pawnee, but not this. Not this!

"It is to test the strength of the poison," Sun Eagle said, no emotion in his voice.

Kiriki's breath became quick and frightened as she watched Sun Eagle apply a very small quantity of the poison to the blood that was running down.

"If the blood thickens and the thickness moves upward,

the poison is strong enough," he explained, understanding Kiriki's fright. "If it does not, I must add more rattlesnake venom to the mixture and start the process all over again until it is exactly as it should be to make my arrows deadly."

"But the poison can kill you, Sun Eagle!" Kiriki choked, desperation rising inside her. "Oh, Sun Eagle, please, please!"

Sun Eagle watched the clotting process very closely and then scraped the blood away so that none of the poison would reach the wound. "It is as I desire," he said, smiling over at Kiriki. "I must now prepare the arrows. While they are drying, I must join my warriors to prepare ourselves for the battle ahead against my brother and his companions."

Kiriki understood this custom well enough. She knew what to expect. Before starting on any war party, much time was spent in practicing and fighting imaginary battles. When the party was completely organized, a war dance would be held, and a special sacrifice would be offered for the safety and success of the expedition.

Most normally, the return of a successful war party was an occasion for great joy, and a scalp dance was usually held that night.

But she did not expect that to be so tonight. The one who would be slain would be the son of this village's great chief. But there were no assurances of which son it would be. Kiriki knew that Brown Bear could be setting a trap for Sun Eagle. . . .

She watched Sun Eagle kneel down before the fire again. He took soot from the burned wood and began painting his face black. Fear for his safety was overwhelming her. Things had just begun to look beautiful and right for them and now, in an instant, it had all changed.

Damn Brown Bear! He would probably even torment them after he was dead!

"Sun Eagle, I want to go with you," Kiriki blurted, positioning herself on her knees beside him. "I cannot stay behind not knowing what is happening to you. We have only found a measure of happiness and now are being separated again? It is not fair!''

His face blackened, Sun Eagle turned to Kiriki. "I cannot allow you to go," he said flatly. "It is not right for women to accompany warriors on a warpath." He took her hands and urged her to her feet. "And, Kiriki, you are not yet *that* strong that you could go to battle beside your husband. You have recently been weakened by the loss of our child."

"I have gained back my strength," she argued. "I can do the work of two women. I can ride a horse as skillfully as a man. I want to go! Let me be known as the woman who rides with her warrior husband to seek revenge for her own self. Do you not remember Durah? Brown Bear killed her. I must go and avenge her death!''

"I understand how you feel but you must understand how *I* feel," he said, his voice becoming stiff with impatience. "You are my woman. My wife. I am giving you a command, Kiriki. You must obey it. I cannot allow you to ride with me into the face of danger." He stopped and implored her with his dark eyes. "Now or ever."

"My husband, you give me a command as though I am one of your warriors?" Kiriki questioned, her voice wavering. "Is that the way it is to be? Is that what it will mean to be your wife? You will love me as though I am so special, and then you will give me a command as though I am nothing? Sun Eagle, please tell me that I am wrong— that I am not to be a thing used and tossed about like a leaf that blows across the land, soon to dry up and wither away into a nothingness!''

Understanding her confusion, hurting inside because he was the one who had caused it, Sun Eagle drew her quickly into his embrace. He hugged her tightly. "Never will I treat you as anything but good," he said. "But this time I must tell you that you cannot go with me to search for Brown Bear. It could take days and nights. You would feel awkward in the presence of my men. They would look to me as weak if I allowed you to go. Now do you understand, Kiriki? Do you?''

Kiriki squeezed her eyes shut and forced back tears. "I so want to," she sobbed.

"Kiriki, I am a warrior who might have many battles ahead of me, and I do not want to always have to question you whether or not I can go," Sun Eagle said, leaning away from her, looking intensely into her eyes. "It is not manly. It is not what a great chief would do. My woman, there is much about me that has changed since I have declared my love for you, but never can I lose my manliness. For our people I must look strong. Always!"

Kiriki touched his face with her hand, seeing a face painted for war, and here she was, delaying him. Suddenly she felt ashamed. "Please go and be with your warriors," she murmured. "I am sorry for having caused you distress. I shall never do so again."

"I shall return to you unharmed, my Kiriki," Sun Eagle said, sweeping her into his arms. He kissed her long and savagely, then broke away and left her looking sadly after him.

Kiriki wiped tears from her eyes, knowing that her promise to him would be the hardest ever in her life to keep. How could she let him go without following him? How? Yet if she had gone, would it have not shamed him in front of his warriors' eyes?

A sudden thought occurred to her. She could go and he would not even be aware of it! She could follow along behind him far enough that he did not see her. She could not bear to part from him under these circumstances. She knew Brown Bear's evil side much more intimately than Sun Eagle did. She knew that Brown Bear was capable of anything. Anything!

But still, she could not go against her husband's wishes. He could hate her forever should she shame him in front of his warriors. . . .

A sudden pain at her wrist made Kiriki flinch. She looked down at the cub that had grown into a bear. He had a tooth lock on her wrist, looking up at her with mischievous eyes that were no longer those of a mere cub. The bear had grown in leaps and bounds since it had become Kiriki's special pet. When it played, it sometimes inflicted pain.

"Let go, sweetie," Kiriki said, small rivulets of blood smoothing across her flesh. Her free hand nudged at the bear, then she sighed with relief as the bear freed her wrist and plopped down beside her, looking innocently up at her.

Kiriki wiped the blood away and studied the teeth marks on her flesh. They were not all that bad, but they could have been.

She turned to the bear and lay down beside him, hugging him. "Though I love you dearly, the time has come to part," she murmured, she and Sun Eagle having come to that decision only last night. "Today, sweet bear, while Sun Eagle is away, I will busy myself with my own most dreaded chore. I must return you to your rightful place—to those of your own kind."

The bear snuggled against her and heaved a heavy sigh, as though it understood. Kiriki cried softly. She could lose so much more today than the bear. She could lose Sun Eagle. . . .

Twenty-six

▼ ▼ ▼

KIRIKI stood at the edge of Sun Eagle's village, a hand folded over her eyes as she looked into the distance. She could see a cloud of dust on the horizon, causing a sadness and sense of foreboding to enter her heart. Just how long would she have to wait to see which brother was victorious? If it was Brown Bear . . . ?

The weight of the bear pressing against Kiriki's leg as it sprawled on the ground next to her, leaning possessively against her, made her thoughts return to the chore that lay ahead of her. The bear no longer required the care of humans. Out in the forest now, it could learn to fend for itself. It had almost doubled in size these past weeks and she could not forget all that easily that its teeth were already as sharp as any arrowhead.

Bending to a knee, Kiriki petted the bear, tears near when it raised its dark, trusting eyes to her. "It is in your best interest that I do this," she said, smoothing her fingers through its thick fur. "Once you are back in the forest among others like yourself you will be happy to forsake your human friends."

Kiriki reached her free hand to her gold earrings hanging proudly from her ears. It had been easy to pierce her ears with a sharply pointed piece of metal that made holes through which the earrings hung. In a buckskin drawstring pouch hanging at her waist lay this metal pin. It had served her well once. So would it again!

"I shall give you something that is so precious to me to prove my love for you," she murmured, removing one of the earrings. "Little bear, once the earring is in place in your ear I shall always know you from the others in the forest. Perhaps you will still even know me.''

The bear growled and rocked its head back and forth, as though it knew and understood as she removed the metal pin from the bag.

"It will hurt for only a second," Kiriki said, hoping that the bear would not feel enough pain to feel threatened. It was important to Kiriki to leave him with sweet memories.

Settling down on the ground, the sun bright overhead, the breeze so light that it was hardly a breeze at all, Kiriki placed the bear between her legs and held it locked in place there with her knees. Steadying her hand, she took one of his ears and stretched it out against her palm, then with her other hand quickly jabbed the tip of the pin into the flesh of its ear, recoiling when the bear emitted a strange sort of bark, flinching, then stood trustingly still again.

"See?" Kiriki said, sighing with relief. "There was only a brief moment of pain. And now to make you beautiful.''

Smiling, Kiriki lifted the earring to his ear and clicked it into place. "We are now a matching pair," she said, laughing softly. She gently shoved the bear away from her and gazed at him. "My, but don't you look pretty? You will be the envy of all the female bears in the forest. And I bet you will attract a very beautiful female mate!''

Shaking its head, sitting down clumsily, the bear pawed at the earring for a moment, then looked resigned at having it to live with, and rose to all fours and waddled back to Kiriki.

"Now we must take that walk in the forest," Kiriki said, casting a quick glance over her shoulder at Sun Eagle's village and the activity of the people. Most were sullen, for everyone knew that one of the chief's sons would return for burial, a funeral ceremony the next sort of celebration for this Skidi band of Pawnee.

Goosepimples crawling along her flesh at the thought of which brother it could be—Sun Eagle—made Kiriki more determined to busy herself with things other than waiting and watching to see the end result of today's confrontation between brothers. It was good that she had the chore of taking the bear to the forest. Her sadness for having to do this could possibly overwhelm the fear for Sun Eagle that was clutching at her heart. Brown Bear was devious. Oh, what if he was drawing Sun Eagle into a trap!

"But Sun Eagle is the most cunning of the two brothers," Kiriki reconfirmed to herself. "He will not let his brother best him!"

Recalling the day by the river, when Brown Bear had appeared so suddenly and had killed Durah before she had been able to defend herself, Kiriki patted the knife that she had sheathed at her waist for today's outing. With Brown Bear running loose, always a threat, she had decided to make sure that she brought protection for herself. She could not shake the suspicion that Brown Bear would not just stop at stealing Sun Eagle's horses. He would continue to torment Sun Eagle forever, if given the chance.

"And after today?" Kiriki whispered to herself.

She hugged the bear fiercely as he came to her, nuzzling her lap with its nose. "I'm going to miss you, sweet thing," she whispered. She framed the bear's face between her hands. "I have let you remain nameless for a purpose. Had I named you, that would make leaving you in the forest so much harder. Nameless, you can blend much more quickly into your world. You still are just a bear— not a bear carrying a human name!"

Hardly able to stand having to part with the bear, lingering with him making it even harder, Kiriki jumped to her feet and began running away from him, toward the forest. Tears came to her eyes when the bear came bounding behind her, seeing all of these happenings today as a game to be shared with Kiriki. Would she, in fact, even be able to shake him once they were in the forest? Would he not just follow her from it again?

Hopefully, instinct would take over for the bear once it was among the trees and wild plants blooming beneath them. At present, many grapes were in abundance. Kiriki planned to lead the bear to some large tempting clusters, then sneak away from him while he feasted upon them. She would feel cruel not saying a final goodbye, abandoning him as something unloved, but this was the only way.

"Come, little one!" Kiriki said, laughing as the bear suddenly fell and rolled head over heels in the dust, then picked itself up and began following her again in leaps and bounds..

The shadows of the forest were soon reached. Kiriki slowed her pace, wary for herself and what might be hiding there, ready to pounce out at her. Brown Bear. She would never trust being alone as long as Brown Bear was alive.

Kiriki slipped the knife from its sheath, then forgot her fear momentarily when the bear began sniffing the ground and exploring in the nooks of trees and bushes. It seemed truly absorbed and content to be given this opportunity.

Kiriki was genuinely sad to know that in the next few moments she would be saying a final goodbye.

The sun's rays spiraled down through a break in the leaves of the trees overhead and caused the gold earring in the bear's ear to pick up the bright glint. Kiriki looked at the earring, hope rising within her. Would today's goodbye be truly all that final? Would she, perhaps sometime in the future, be able to see him again?

The earring. It would set him apart from all of the rest.

But if she *did* discover him wandering in the forest, would she dare approach him? Would he have replaced his love for her with fear and hate that most bears felt for humans? Oh, but if only a trace of remembrance could remain within his mind. . . .

A rustle in the foliage ahead made Kiriki's heart skip a beat. She grasped more tightly to the hilt of her knife and looked cautiously around her. Then she laughed lightly when she saw two squirrels scampering just a few feet ahead, their jowls filled with the meat of acorns.

But this scare had been enough for Kiriki to know that she must get her chore done and behind her. Safety

awaited in numbers back at the village. Alone, she was
far too vulnerable to the evil of man!

Searching with her eyes, walking stealthily onward, Kiriki watched for a vine of wild grapes with which to entice
the bear's interest and empty stomach. Kiriki had purposely failed to feed him both last evening and this morning. He would eat eagerly as soon as food was found and
offered him. . . .

His jaw tight, his dark eyes suspicious, Sun Eagle drew
his reins tight and wheeled his black gelding around to
face the warriors who had joined him on this mission to
find and kill Brown Bear, and to reclaim his stolen horses.

"My brother was not as careful as he most normally
is," Sun Eagle said in a snarl. He pointed down at the
tracks in the dust. "Yet, is it for a purpose that he leads
us so easily to him and the horses? There has been no
effort whatsoever to lead us away from them." His eyes
became two points of fire, and he tightened a fist and
motioned with it angrily over his head. "I fear that we
are riding toward a trap."

Sun Eagle turned and looked in the direction of an
approaching horseman. It was his trustworthy scout returning to give him news of what lay ahead. Soon he would
know just how clever his brother was.

The scout drew rein beside Sun Eagle. His breathing
was harsh. His chest heaved with exhaustion. "I found
the horses!" he said, looking wildly at Sun Eagle. "They
have been led to a canyon and left there. There is no one
there guarding them. We can ride in and take them. Sun
Eagle, the horses are yours again."

"So easily?" Sun Eagle said, quirking an eyebrow.
"My brother is careless, but not *that* careless!"

He looked over his shoulder in the direction of the village. Thoughts of Kiriki sprang forth, alarm shaking him
from his head to his toes. "My brother does not truly
want the horses at all," he said in a growl. "The horses
were only to lure me and the most skillful braves away

from the village so that Brown Bear can sneak in there and steal Kiriki away.''

Sun Eagle shook his head as a sick feeling impaled his insides. ''That is his intent!'' he said, his voice drawn. ''He wants my woman and will not stop until he has her.''

Without taking time to instruct his warriors, Sun Eagle spun his horse around and urged his steed into a hard gallop across the land back in the direction of the village. He was no longer concerned about horses—only his Kiriki. Only his wife!

His warriors followed dutifully.

''Ah, finally there is a good bunch of grapes,'' Kiriki said, running toward them. She looked over her shoulder at the bear as he followed her, his nose twitching from the sweet smells of the fruit wafting through the air toward him. ''Come, my little friend, you shall have a feast!''

When she reached the grapes, Kiriki stepped aside and watched the bear pounce on them. Tears streamed from her eyes as she watched the grapes being consumed in huge mouthfuls, and when she realized that the bear was not paying any attention to her, whatsoever, she began moving back away from him.

Then Kiriki broke into a mad run, hoping to put space between them before the bear got its fill. Twinges in her abdomen made Kiriki recall her recent surgery, yet she did not slow down. When the bear would look around for her, she must be gone. Even if he came sniffing the ground for her scent, she hoped that other more interesting things of the forest would lure him away from it. She had watched his fascination of everything as he had moved more deeply into the forest. He was becoming as one with nature—his true habitat.

Almost reaching the outskirts of the forest, Kiriki stopped quickly and looked with alarm at a warrior walking stealthily up just ahead, trailing his horse behind him, and then she recognized his stance, his profile. It was Brown Bear! He was not with the stolen horses at all. As she had surmised, he had plans other than that which only included horses. Surely *she* was his next target!

Hiding behind a tree, hoping that he had not caught her movement out of the corner of his eye, Kiriki scarcely breathed. Where were the rest of the warriors that usually accompanied Brown Bear's travels? Had he instructed them to wait? Or was there a plan for them to follow shortly?

She swallowed hard, fear building within her, waiting and wondering what she should do! When she caught sight of many warriors following on foot in the distance, her insides froze. Perhaps she was not the only reason Brown Bear was returning to his village. Perhaps he had lured Sun Eagle and their most dependable warriors from the village for a more lurid reason. What if an attack on Brown Bear's own village was imminent? Oh, how could he?

The knife still clutched within her hand, Kiriki studied it. She could at least stop Brown Bear with one plunge of the knife. Perhaps if he was stopped, the others would flee. Without their leader surely they would not follow through on such an undesirable attack. What would they gain but further shame? Most were from Sun Eagle's village, having been drawn into wickedness under the command of Brown Bear.

"I must!" Kiriki whispered, cold inside at the thought of what she was about to do. More than likely she would not survive her attack on Brown Bear. But she must chance it. She would be doing it for Sun Eagle. Did she not owe him so much? Had he not rescued her twice? Would she not even be avenging her friend's death? Durah would finally be able to rest in peace in the hereafter if Kiriki snuffed the breath from her murderer.

Her heart pounding, Kiriki slipped from behind the tree and ran cautiously to the next tree, then the next, and then the next, until she was so close to Brown Bear she could hear his steady breathing as he moved past the tree behind which she was lurking. Her knees weak with fear, her fingers trembling, Kiriki looked to the heavens. She silently prayed to Tirawa to give her strength to do this, and to guide her hand so that one stab wound would be all that was required to kill Brown Bear. Then she lunged from behind the tree and stopped Brown Bear dead in his tracks as he looked at her, his eyes startled wide.

"Die!" Kiriki hissed, bringing her knife down in the death plunge. As the knife entered his chest and he grabbed at it, crumbling to the ground, groaning, Kiriki stood over him, feeling victorious. "That is for the child that you placed inside my womb!" she cried. "It is also for Sun Eagle and for Durah, my dear friend whose breath you stopped with the plunge of your knife into her heart. For the world, I have done this, Brown Bear."

Brown Bear looked up at her, blood streaming down his abdomen, across his loincloth, then pooling on the ground beneath him. "Kiriki, you speak of a child . . . ?" he said in strained whisper. "Our child . . . ?"

"It is no longer," Kiriki said coldly. "The child did not wish to be born because you were its father! I now wait to proudly carry Sun Eagle's child, for you see, Brown Bear, your brother and I are man and wife."

Brown Bear coughed, strangling on blood that was rising into his throat. Then he convulsed and stared lifelessly ahead, dead.

Kiriki gazed down at Brown Bear, finding it hard to realize that he truly was dead, no longer able to wreak havoc on all whose who could have loved him had he allowed them to. Then she flinched and screamed as strong hands circled her waist and began dragging her away from the death scene. Her knees grew weak, expecting to have a knife still her heart at any moment, but it was the voice spoken to her that made her look up with dismay.

"Sun Eagle!" Kiriki gasped. "How? . . ."

"Be still, my woman," Sun Eagle said, positioning her behind a tree. "My warriors are circling. Soon much blood will be spilled."

Sun Eagle started to walk away from her, then returned. He touched her cheek gently. "What you have done is brave," he said thickly, looking devotedly down into her eyes. "But, Kiriki, it was also foolish. Had Brown Bear's warriors seen you, you would now be dead."

"I understood the dangers," Kiriki whispered. "But I had to do it, Sun Eagle. He was on his way to our village. Had I not come in this direction to set our bear free in the forest I would not have seen him. What then? What if he would have entered the village and killed and maimed before you had arrived back? I *had* to kill him, no matter the risk."

"It is with a humble heart that I must leave you to go into battle," Sun Eagle said, drawing her into his arms, hugging her fiercely. Then he released her and moved stealthily away from her.

Kiriki held her breath when she heard sudden war whoops and screams of pain as the attack began on those who were unaware. She eased from around the tree and watched, aghast. There was little twanging of bow strings and not much thrusting of lances. For the most part the fighting was at quarters too close for this, and the combatants pounded at each other's heads with hatchets and war clubs. When she witnessed the first scalp being lifted from one's head, she turned away, ill with now understanding how it was done, remembering the many scalps hanging from her step-father's scalp pole in his earthen lodge.

The fighting continued for some time, and then everything was quiet. Kiriki dared to take another look. Something drew her attention to Brown Bear's body. His scalp was gone. . . .

Sun Eagle came walking proudly toward her, several scalps within the grip of his fingers. Kiriki gulped hard, but did not ask him to identify the scalps. She took it for granted that one was Brown Bear's.

Then the unforeseen happened. Sun Eagle separated one of the scalps from the others. He held it toward Kiriki. "This is yours," he said thickly. "It will be proof to my people of your courage! It will hang forever in our dwelling, my woman."

Kiriki placed her hands to her throat, paling. "I can't,"

she murmured. "How could you ask me to? That has to be Brown Bear's scalp!"

"Never speak of him again to me," Sun Eagle said somberly. "He is rightfully dead. You are the one to be honored for having taken his life."

"But he was your brother," Kiriki said, her voice shaking. "How could we hang his scalp in our dwelling?"

"Kiriki, when you look at that scalp you will not be seeing my brother in your mind's eye, but a man who I now know was guilty of raping you," Sun Eagle said venomously.

Kiriki took a step back. "How did you know?" she gasped.

"Only moments ago I witnessed you telling Brown Bear," Sun Eagle hissed. His eyes wavered as he looked down at her. "This was a secret that you were going to let haunt you for the rest of your life? My woman, never fear telling me *anything*. Never carry burdens that I could help lighten."

"The truth sometimes hurts too much to share with anyone," Kiriki said, lowering her eyes. "Even the man one loves. It sometimes destroys feelings, Sun Eagle."

"Never!" Sun Eagle said, taking a step forward. He reached for her hand and forced the scalp into it. "It is yours! Carry it into the village and show it off proudly!"

A shudder encompassed Kiriki as she looked down at the raven-black hair in her hand. Then suddenly her mood changed. She was victorious! She had beaten the man who had taken so much from her. She had made it possible that no one else would ever be hurt by him again.

Slowly she turned her eyes up to Sun Eagle. They exchanged winning smiles.

Twenty-seven
▼ ▼ ▼

Two Years Later

HEAVY with child, Kiriki sat with the women back from
the large communal fire where the men had collected. It
was the time for the great buffalo hunt. For several days
the priests and the doctors had been preparing for this
solemn religious ceremonial. They had fasted long; earnest
prayers had been offered. Now the twelve buffalo skulls
had been arranged on the ground in a half-circle, and near
them stood Chief Sun Eagle, his father having recently
left the earth to join his ancestors in the hereafter.

Sun Eagle and the other warriors of the Skidi were
reverently holding in their hands the buffalo staves, sacred
bows and arrows, and other implements of the chase. For
a little while they stood silent with bowed heads, but pres-
ently one and then another began to murmur their petitions
to Atius Tirawa, the Spirit Father.

At first their voices were low and mumbling, but gradually they became more earnest and lifted their eyes toward
heaven. It was impossible for Kiriki to distinguish what
each one said, but now and then disjointed sentences
reached her.

"Father, you are the Ruler."

"We are poor."

"Take pity on us."

"Send us plenty of buffalo, plenty of fat cows."

"Father, we are your children. Help the people."

"Send us plenty of meat, so that we may be strong,
and our bodies may increase and our flesh grow hard."

"Father, you see us."

"Listen."

As they prayed they moved their hands backward and forward over the implements which they held, and at length reverently deposited them on the ground within the line of buffalo skulls, and then stepped back, still continuing their prayers.

It was a touching sight for Kiriki to witness these men calling upon their God for help. They threw their souls into their prayers, and as a son might entreat his earthly father for some great gift, so did they plead with Tirawa. Their bodies quivered with emotion, and great drops of sweat stood upon their brows.

After the last of the articles had been placed upon the ground, their voices grew lower and at length died away.

A moment later a drum sounded, and a dozen or so young warriors sprang into the circle and began the buffalo dance. This was kept up without intermission for several hours, and then it was time to assemble at the horses to leave for the hunt.

Sun Eagle broke away from the throng of warriors and met Kiriki halfway as she hurried to him. She thrust her arms around him, her large ball of stomach impeding their complete embrace.

"Sun Eagle, the days and nights will be long without you," she cried. "It is time for our child to come into the world. If you are gone you will not have the chance to hear its first cries! Or see its first smiles!"

Sun Eagle stroked her back. "That is not what you truly fear most about my absence," he said softly. "You fear the birthing itself. You are afraid that perhaps things will go wrong since you did not carry your first child full term."

Kiriki held herself back and looked him in the eyes, hers wavering. "That is so," she said, choking back a sob. "Perhaps I will need your strength at birthing, Sun Eagle. I fear that I cannot do this all on my own. Must you go? Must you?"

"Kiriki, I am now the chief of my people and they

depend on me to see that enough food is brought back to sustain them through the harsh winter that lies ahead,'' Sun Eagle said, not sounding convincing enough to himself, for he truly did not want to go. He feared leaving Kiriki to this chore of birthing alone. If something caused her to fail this time, there may never be another chance. And Sun Eagle was depending on her to give him a son.

Perhaps many!

"Nothing you say will make my hardship of your absence any more tolerable,'' Kiriki pouted, placing her hand to the small of her back as it ached fiercely. Then her mood lightened, and she forced a smile for Sun Eagle's benefit. "I am being selfish, aren't I?''

Sun Eagle nodded and smoothed some locks of hair back from her sky-blue eyes. "Yes, you are, but you have reason to be,'' he said. He glanced down at her buckskin blouse that was drawn tautly across her swollen abdomen. He placed a hand reverently on her stomach. "You are the only woman in the village who is ready to give their chief the gift of child.''

Serious lines crinkled at the corners of his eyes as he frowned down at Kiriki. "While I am gone do no chores,'' he said sternly. "You sit by the fire and do what amuses you and let the rest of the village worry about carrying firewood and water. Do you hear me, my woman?''

"I believe I can manage that,'' Kiriki said, giggling. "Our child will appreciate it. Sun Eagle, it is so restless today. It moves around inside me constantly. First a knee pokes me, and then an elbow! It must be a son who is trying to wrestle free from its tight confines, Sun Eagle. Will that not make you anxious to return from the hunt? A son who will be waiting to be held?''

"You do believe you will have the child while I am gone?'' Sun Eagle asked, his jaw tight.

"It just cannot go on and on, Sun Eagle,'' Kiriki said, groaning as she once again placed a firm hand at the small of her back. "My back will not bear much more of the burden.''

Sun Eagle drew her near. He kissed her softly on the

lips. "Kiriki, make prayers often to Tirawa who is in and of everything," he said. "You must trust always in Tirawa. He made us, and through him we live. So shall he make us a perfect son."

Kiriki hugged Sun Eagle. "Yes, and so shall he make us a perfect son," she murmured.

Sun Eagle broke away from her. "It is time to leave," he said, casting nervous glances at his waiting warriors already mounted on their horses, their eyes anxious. He took Kiriki's hand and squeezed it, then walked square-shouldered to his black gelding and swung himself into the saddle.

Kiriki waved at Sun Eagle. He placed his fist to his heart as he looked proudly down at her, then wheeled his horse around and rode away.

Kiriki watched Sun Eagle until she could no longer make him out along the horizon. She listened to the sound of the horses' hooves on the earth, sounding as though distant thunder, then turned and sauntered back inside her house.

Glum, so bone-weary, the weight of the child and her milk-swollen breasts pulling her shoulders down, she stared blankly into the fire for a moment, then decided that she could not pass time away quickly enough by just sitting and staring into space.

First she busied herself making fresh bread. It was made from corn meal and flour and mixed with water, with a lot of small pieces of buffalo suet mixed into it. She buried this mixture in the hot ashes and left it there for only a short time. When it was baked, the bread would have a crust on it about an inch thick.

Still restless, overly so, for having recently not had any energy to do the necessary everyday chores, Kiriki decided to work on her pottery. With all of the necessary utensils and ingredients at her side, she sat down on the floor beside the fire and began shaping the clay that she had mixed with sand and water, molding it into shape with her hands and a paddle.

The pottery was treated with a grooved paddle to produce a ridged effect. The paddle was then wrapped with twisted cords to produce a cord-marked vessel. The rim was decorated in patterns by incised lines.

The pot was then placed in the oven and would be hard when it was removed.

A sudden pain tore at Kiriki's insides. She tried to move to her feet but no amount of effort she took would get her up.

She began to scream. . . .

A heavy mist hung over the prairie. Sun Eagle feared that if it lasted for much longer it would be impossible for the scouts that he had sent on ahead to see far enough to discover the buffalo. The first few hours of the march had been uneventful. Once or twice the huge bodies of a small band of buffalo loomed up through the white mist about them, their size and shape greatly exaggerated and distorted by the fog's deceptive effect.

As the sun climbed toward the zenith the air grew brighter and by mid-day the fog had risen from the ground, and though still clinging in white cottony wreaths about the tops of the higher bluffs near Sun Eagle and his hunting party, they now could see for quite a long distance over the prairie.

A little later the sun burst forth and the sky became clear. Soon after noon, a scout was seen coming at full gallop down the bluffs. He bent from his horse and spoke a few words very earnestly, gesticulating and pointing back over the prairie in the direction whence he had come as he came alongside Sun Eagle.

"Te-co di tub-tu-ta-rik-ti-ra-hah," he shouted. "I saw many buffalo!"

"Tu-ra-heh!" Sun Eagle shouted back. "That is good!"

Sun Eagle commanded his men to go at once and find them. At a moderate gallop, the riders all set off. Suddenly, without the slightest warning, the huge dark bodies of half a dozen buffalo sprang into view, rising out of a ravine on their left not a hundred yards distant. When the buffalo spied the multitude before them, they stopped and stared.

A thrill going through him at the sight of the animals, Sun Eagle lifted the reins from his horse's back and bent forward, the horse springing into a sharp gallop toward the game. As he did so, Sun Eagle saw his warriors falling into line, following him. The buffalo wheeled, and in an instant were out of sight, but when Sun Eagle reached the edge of the bank down which they had just plunged, he could see through the cloud of dust their forms dashing down the ravine.

Sun Eagle's horse, as eager for the chase as his rider, hurled himself down the steep pitch and sped along the narrow broken bed of the gully. Sun Eagle could feel that sometimes his steed would lengthen his stride to leap wide ditches where the water from side ravines had cut away the ground. Sun Eagle's eyes were fixed on the fleeing herd, his ears intent on the pursuing warriors behind him. He could hear the quick pounding of many hoofs and could feel that one of the horses was nearer than the rest, steadily drawing up to him.

But Sun Eagle was gaining on the buffalo. Already the confused rumble of their hoofbeats almost drowned those of the horses behind him, and the air was full of the dust and small pebbles being thrown up by their hurrying feet. They were still ahead of Sun Eagle but the gulch was so narrow that he could not shoot.

The leading horseman behind Sun Eagle drew nearer and nearer, and was now almost at Sun Eagle's side. Under his right arm, Sun Eagle could see the lean head and long, slim neck of the rider's horse, and could hear the rider speak to his horse and urge him forward in the race.

Sun Eagle's horse did his best, but the other was a young pony, filled with spirit and had the most speed. He shot by Sun Eagle's gelding, and a moment later was alongside the last buffalo.

As the young Pawnee passed Sun Eagle the lad made a laughing gesture of triumph, slipped an arrow on his bow-

string, and drew it to its head. But just as he was about
to let it fly, his pony, which was but a colt, took fright
at the huge animal that it had overtaken and shied violently
to the right, almost unseating its rider.

At the same moment the buffalo swerved a little to the
left, and thus lost a few feet. As Sun Eagle passed the
young warrior he could not restrain a little whoop of satis-
faction, and then swinging his rifle out of its gunboot, and
around, he fired.

The buffalo fell in its stride, tossing up a mighty cloud
of the soft yellow earth. Sun Eagle's gelding ran by him
fifty yards before he could be checked.

Then as he turned and rode back to look at the game,
the other Pawnee passed him like a whirlwind, and, close
at the heels of the herd, swept around a point of bluff and
out of sight.

Only Sun Eagle's rival remained and he was excitedly
arguing with his horse. The application of a whip-handle,
applied with vigor about the creature's ears, convinced it
that it must approach the dead buffalo.

The young brave then dismounted and passed his lariat
about the buffalo's horns, drew the pony's head to within
a few feet of the terrifying mass, and fastened the rope.

When he had accomplished this he grinned up at Sun
Eagle and Sun Eagle responded in kind, transferring to the
young, ambitious Pawnee all his right and title of the dead
buffalo. The young Pawnee was the future of his people!
He had showed much cunning that would be required of
him in the face of challenges ahead. Sun Eagle was proud
of him, as though he were his very own son, his flesh and
blood. . . .

At this, the lad smiled even more cheerfully and prepared to begin butchering.

Sun Eagle admired the buffalo. It was a superb speci-
men, just entering his prime, and was fat, round and sleek.
His horns were symmetrically curved and beautifully pol-
ished. Not a scratch marred their shining surfaces, nor a
splinter was frayed from their sharp points. The sweeping
black beard was long and full, and the thick curls upon

his hump and massive shoulders were soft and deep, while
the short hair of his sides and hips was smooth as the coat
of a horse. His size was enormous. It seemed that he
would weigh at least two thousand pounds.

Satisfied that the youth knew how to properly butcher
the handsome horned animal, Sun Eagle swung away from
him and rode on along the course taken by the remaining
buffalo, for he was anxious to see what had become of
them.

On rounding the point of the bluff, where he had last
seen them, his curiosity was satisfied. The valley widened
out until it was sixty yards across and on either side rose
vertical bluffs of yellow chalk to a height of forty feet.
Scattered about over the little valley lay half a dozen buffalo, over each of which bent one or two Pawnee warriors
busily plying the knife. Sun Eagle had not been involved
in the kill, but it was strangely more satisfying to see his
warriors' eager ambition as they prepared the carcasses for
the return home than perhaps to have participated in the
major part of the kill. Sun Eagle was pleased more today
with their skills with the rifle and bow and arrows, for the
hunt was not going to be strung out for days and days.
Soon he would return home to be with Kiriki. Perhaps he
would get to witness the birthing, after all!

Soon the broad disc of the setting sun rested on the tops
of the western bluffs, tipping their crests with fire. Sun
Eagle rode ahead of his warriors whose horses and travois
were piled high with dark, dripping meat, and with soft
shaggy skins. Before midnight there would be feasting and
merriment about the flickering fires of his village. Marrow
bones would be tossed among the red embers, calves'
heads would be baked in the hot earth. Fat ribs would be
roasted, ka'wis boiled, and boudins eaten raw. With
laughter and singing and storytelling and dance, the night
would wear away.

Nudging the flanks of his horse with his heels, Sun
Eagle rode in a brisker gallop, something nagging at his
heart. It seemed that something was beckoning for him.

Kiriki!

Could it be Kiriki?

Was the child making its way down the birthing canal even at this moment?

Over the plain where the buffalo had fallen, gray wolves were prowling. The coyote, the fox and the badger tore at the bones of the slain buffalo. When day would come, the golden eagle and the buzzard would perch upon the naked red skeletons, taking their toll.

Far away, a few frightened buffalo were cropping the short grass of the prairie, arrows sticking in their sore sides. . . .

Water was heating, several maidens were standing around Kiriki, fussing over her as she lay nude on a bear pelt away from the heat of the fire. Sweat pearled her brow as she breathed shallowly, the pain as she remembered it the one other time.

Tears flooded her eyes. Though she had carried this child full term, there appeared to be some doubt that she would have a healthy baby. Each time she bore down, it did not seem to mean a thing. There seemed little or no progress in the birthing canal. Was she destined to be motherless? Was Sun Eagle destined to have no sons?

Or would he be forced to seek another woman to share his bed, so that *she* would bear him a son?

"Oh, please . . ." Kiriki whispered, looking up at the heavens through the smoke hole above her. "This baby must be all right. My child must be healthy. It must be a son!"

Another pain seemed to tear her in half. She stifled a scream behind a hand and tried to relax, as many hands began caressing and kneading her stomach. When one of these hands reached up inside her, stretching her open more widely for the exiting of the child, she bit her lower lip. The pain was so excruciating, and a dizziness overcame her, threatening to cause her to faint.

She closed her eyes when the hand left her body and the pain was over for at least a moment. She began to drift, unable to fight for her child any longer. . . .

Twenty-eight

▼ ▼ ▼

THE hunters' return was met with muted enthusiasm, alarming Sun Eagle. From the sorrowful looks his people cast him he knew that something was quite amiss in his village.

He looked quickly toward his earthen lodge, seeing women moving frantically to and from the entrance.

He gazed down into the eyes of his mother who came to start unloading the pelts from his gelding, evading his eyes.

Sun Eagle dismounted quickly. He clasped his hands to his mother's shoulders, stopping her. With her arms filled with pelts she looked waveringly up at him. "It is Kiriki, is it not?" he asked, dreading to hear the answer.

Kidibattsk lowered her eyes and shook her head, the words not wanting to form on her lips. To tell her son that his wife may not be able to go through the birthing process normally to give him a son would be the same as telling him that the stars had each dropped from the heavens while he had been away on the buffalo hunt! He loved Kiriki so much, yet it was in his destiny to have many sons. If his wife could not give them to him, then he would have to seek others out.

Kiriki would be devastated. And so would Sun Eagle.

"Kiriki? She is not doing well?" Sun Eagle asked. Then, when he received no answers except for those that his mother purposely denied him, jerked away from her and began running toward his dwelling. Once there, he stepped into a room of fire and light. His heart wrenched and his back stiffened when he looked across the fire and

298

saw Kiriki stretched out nude on a pallet of furs on the floor, several women ministering over her. He noted her shallow breathing and that her eyes were closed. His gaze fell upon the round ball of her stomach, so copper and smooth—so quiet.

Rushing past the gaping women as they discovered him standing there, Sun Eagle fell to his knees beside Kiriki. He swept his arms around her shoulders and drew her face up to his. He kissed her closed eyelids and then her mouth.

"My Kiriki," he whispered, tears sparkling at the corners of his eyes. "Can this truly be happening? Have you given up?"

Determined not to allow her to give up on birthing this child that was so important to them both, Sun Eagle lay her gently back down on the pallet, then leaned down into her face. "Kiriki!" he said firmly.

He sat back from her and stared down at her when there was no response, then slapped her face slightly. "You must wake up, Kiriki!" he shouted. "You must put much strength behind your pains and help push the baby from your womb!"

There was no response. Again he slapped her. First one cheek, and then the other. "Wake up!" he cried, desperation thick in his voice.

His hands went to her abdomen. He began kneading it frantically, working his fingers downward across it. "This baby is going to be born tonight and it is going to be alive and healthy!" he said, his voice breaking. "Kiriki, help me! Awaken! Push!"

The women slowly clustered around him, watching him, having never witnessed a man so determined to see a child born into the world before.

But this man was the chief. To him, a son would be the world. His son would be the next chief-in-line.

Kiriki's eyelashes fluttered as she heard a voice entering her mind. She leaned into the direction of the voice, wanting to grasp onto it, it seeming to be a lifeline that she had been groping for while floating around in a dark void of nightmares of bloody clawing fingers reaching out for

her and her child. Until this voice had broken through her
unconscious state she had been afraid to awaken. Afraid
that whoever those claws belonged to would claim not
only her child, but also herself, for eternity.

Seeing the life in her eyes and her small, pointed tongue
brushing across her parched lips, gave Sun Eagle all of
the hope that he needed to continue with his proddings.
He kissed Kiriki softly on the lips, a tear from his eyes
dropping on her cheek. His fingers kneaded and kneaded
her abdomen. He kneaded even more feverishly when he
felt a small knot pushing up on her abdomen—a knee or
elbow of their child that he and Kiriki had discovered so
often these past months.

"Do you not feel it?" Sun Eagle asked anxiously. "Kiriki, our child is very much alive within you. It is eager
to join us and become a part of our world! Only you can
make it happen, Kiriki. Only you."

His thoughts went back to Madeline Jones in Washington and how she had opened Kiriki's abdomen to remove
the dead fetus. He grew cold inside as he stared down at
Kiriki, who still seemed unable to awaken and help give
the final pushes that were needed to free the child from
her womb. Was the knife needed again? What were the
chances of Kiriki surviving? Would he save the child, only
to lose Kiriki?

He rose to his feet and began to pace back and forth.
He lifted his eyes and called aloud to Tirawa. "Atius
Tirawa, my father in all places. It is in you that I am
living. You are the ruler. Nothing is impossible to you.
If you see it, make my woman well! Deliver our child to
us!"

Then Sun Eagle gained the strength and faith that was
required to do what he now knew had to be done. He
even recalled how the flesh had been sewn back together.

Ordering that sewing utensils be brought, along with
many containers of boiling water and clean buckskin
cloths, Sun Eagle prepared himself for the surgery.

Soon after, he steadied his hands as he knelt down
beside Kiriki, everything that was needed to perform this

risky task on all sides of him. Several women, including his mother, stood behind him and around Kiriki. There was no celebration outside to welcome the return of the hunters. Everything was stone silent as the village waited beside the large outdoor communal fire. Life stood still in this village of Pawnee until there was word of whether or not there would be a new life born inside Sun Eagle's dwelling.

Kiriki struggled to leave the dark pit that she seemed to have fallen into. She gritted her teeth when once again the bloody claws began reaching for her, only able to get so close to her, then stopped and hung there, suspended in air—the claws now seeming to be waiting for something. The voice was no longer there urging her onward. Just as she had begun to recognize who it was, it had faded away. Now all that she heard was someone breathing heavily over her body and something unidentifiable seeming to be drawing a line down the middle of her stomach. . . .

Sweat beaded on Sun Eagle's brow as he guided the sharp knife very delicately down her abdomen, careful not to insert it too deeply into the flesh.

The child. He could not harm the child!

Kidibattsk was busy patting Kiriki's body clean with wet, spongy buckskins. She watched anxiously as Sun Eagle dared to slice open the woman he loved. Not once did Kiriki's body flinch, as though somewhere deeply in her unconscious state she understood that her husband was doing this deed out of love. Never had Kidibattsk seen her son's hand move so quickly and lightly in motion. He was making a perfectly straight line with the knife. Now he was laying the knife aside and parting the flesh. . . .

His heart thundering wildly, Sun Eagle reached his hands inside Kiriki's abdomen and claimed his child. The women became quickly involved as he handed the child to them. He wanted to take pause and see if the infant was a son or a daughter, and to see if it was going to take its first breath of air.

But moments were passing that were important to Kiriki. She was his prime reason for living. Only she!

He grabbed the awl and sinew and began sewing up Kiriki's flesh. His heart melted and a warmth swept through him that was too wonderful to describe when he heard his child's first intake of breath as it began to cry. The women laughed merrily.

"My son, you are the father of a healthy son!" Kidibattsk said, holding the child over close enough for Sun Eagle to see as he took his last stitch in Kiriki's abdomen.

Sun Eagle lay the awl aside and wiped his perspiration-laced brow with the back of a hand as he looked admiringly down at his son. "Sky Hawk," he said, thrusting his chest out proudly. "We will name him Sky Hawk!"

Tears of happiness streamed from Kiriki's closed eyes. Her nightmares with the bloody claws were gone. The demons that had raged within her were gone. The cries of the child had reached inside her and had frightened everything evil away. She could awaken now. There was no cause to stay hidden behind that protective wall of darkness any longer. Though feeling a new sort of pain on her abdomen, it was a pain that was welcomed, for she had heard her child cry. Her child was alive! Her child was going to be able to laugh and sing and experience all that was sweet in life. . . .

Seeing a look of peace settle over Kiriki's face, knowing that somehow she was able to comprehend what had just happened, Sun Eagle bent to her lips and kissed her lovingly. "We have a son, Kiriki," he whispered against her lips. "He is all you could ever ask for in a son. I have named him Sky Hawk! We shall call him *Kutawikutz*, Hawk for short."

Choking back a sob, Kiriki fluttered her eyes open. She slowly lifted a hand and touched Sun Eagle on his face. "Sun Eagle . . ." she whispered shakily. "My darling Sun Eagle . . ."

She then drifted into a wonderfully peaceful sleep. She was tired. Oh, so sorely tired. . . .

Alarm shot through Sun Eagle. He wanted to try and

awaken Kiriki again, afraid that if she drifted off too far, it may be the last time. She may not awaken! Her body had gone through a major trauma. Could it endure much more? Was even this time too much?

Kidibattsk lay a heavy hand on her son's shoulder. "Put your faith in Tirawa," she murmured. "Tirawa is all things good. Tirawa will not let Kiriki die. She is part of Tirawa's goodness!"

She drew away from him momentarily and picked up her grandson, then spoke again. "Sun Eagle, also your son is part of this goodness of which we speak," she said, holding the child closer to Sun Eagle so that he could see him. "Share your son with your people. Take him outside. Hold him up for all to see. He will one day be a great leader of the Skidi Pawnee."

His gaze sweeping over his child, seeing its wonderful copper coloring, its dark shock of hair, and its fat arms and legs, he was so proud he felt as though he might burst. He opened his arms and let his mother lay the child within them, laughing lightly as Sky Hawk's lips began to smack, as though nursing.

And then the child opened his eyes. Sun Eagle's knees almost melted beneath him when he saw their color. It was as though looking into a mirror of Kiriki's eyes. It was as though looking into the sky on a clear morning of spring—a blue sky unspoiled by clouds!

"Yes, I saw them also," Kidibattsk giggled, leaning closer so that she could get a better look at her grandson's unusual eyes. "Though the eyes of the white man, they are beautiful, because they are also the eyes of Kiriki!"

Sun Eagle nodded. "That is so," he boasted. "That is so."

The women in the dwelling stepped aside, making way for Sun Eagle to wind his way past them. As he went outside, the reflection from the large communal fire cast its golden glow on him and his child. Everyone looked. Everyone marveled. Sun Eagle held the child high over his head so that all could see.

"My people, take your first look at your chief's son!"

he shouted. "He is called Sky Hawk! He will be most powerful! He will be a great leader!"

Great cheers and whoops filled the air. Drums began to beat and rattles began to shake. Sun Eagle lowered Hawk and nestled him close, content to see that his people were so proud. He chuckled when several smaller youths came bounding to him and began performing a skillful dance, the boys' loincloths skipping up from their thighs, the girls' newly blossomed breasts bouncing beneath their buckskin smocks. These were his people's future. His son was his people's future. At the moment, all seemed well!

A cry split the air, spoiling the moment of reverie and pleasure. "Sun Eagle!" Kidibattsk screeched. "Come quickly! It is Kiriki!"

His heart pounding so hard, feeling as though it might swallow him whole in his fright, Sun Eagle hurried back inside the dwelling. He expected to be told that Kiriki was fading away, moving toward the road to the hereafter.

Instead, he found her eyes open wide and her arms outstretched, beckoning for her husband and son to come to her.

"Is not my son hungry?" Kiriki asked, pushing thoughts of the ragged pain in her abdomen aside. As soon as she had her son suckling on her breast, everything in the world would be right.

"You are awake?" Sun Eagle marveled, dropping to his knees beside Kiriki. "You are alert? You are going to be well?"

"Yes, to all of those questions," Kiriki said softly, her eyes having not left the golden child held safely within Sun Eagle's arms. She reached out a hand and wove it through Hawk's thick, black hair. "Just like his father," she murmured.

Sun Eagle chuckled. "Not entirely," he said, gently laying the child at Kiriki's side, a shiver of pleasure coursing across his flesh as he watched his wife place a nipple within his son's mouth. "You have not seen his eyes, Kiriki. They are yours. They are as blue as the sky. Perhaps even bluer."

Kiriki reached her free hand to Sun Eagle. She twined her fingers through his, her face flushed pink as she watched and felt her child take nourishment from her body. "Sun Eagle, I am so happy," she said, sniffling back the urge to cry.

"Are you in much pain?" he asked, squeezing her hand affectionately.

"I was until my son placed his lips to my breast," Kiriki said, smiling down at Hawk. "But now all that I feel is an overpowering contentment." She looked slowly up at Sun Eagle. "I truly did not think that I would ever be able to give you this son. We are blessed, Sun Eagle. Blessed."

His gaze went to the puckering stitches at her abdomen. She had not questioned about them. Surely it was because she did not want to face the truth that this would be her last child. Sun Eagle would not allow her to go through this same sort of trauma a third time.

"Yes, blessed," he said, leaning to kiss first her cheek, and then his son's.

Five Years Later

Hawk was set securely on Sun Eagle's shoulders, his legs dangling around his father's neck. Kiriki warmed inwardly as she compared the two, their son almost an exact replica of his father, except for the eyes. Though only five, Hawk was showing signs of being a leader. The children of the village followed him around all of the time, him teaching them how to shoot a bow and arrow because he was the most skilled of them all.

"And how many squirrels have you slain today?" Sun Eagle teased his son, glancing up at him.

"Father, the arrowhead of my arrows are too blunt," Hawk fussed. "How can I ever boast of killing anything? You force me to practice with a weapon that is powerless!"

"That will do until you are older," Sun Eagle said flatly.

"I have heard tales of the Morning Star sacrifice when it was being practiced before you became chief, and that even the sons who were my age were allowed to shoot their arrows into the body of the sacrifice," Hawk still argued. "If there was a Morning Star sacrifice now, would you allow me to participate as the others would surely do? I *am* the son of the chief. I would be shamed in the eyes of the others if you would not allow me to take aim at the woman sacrifice with my bow and arrow."

Kiriki paled. Her eyelashes fluttered nervously as she looked up at her son whose determination and persistence were making her cold inside. "How did you hear of the sacrifice?" she asked, her voice quivering.

"Some of the older boys told me," Hawk said, looking down at his mother, shrugging. "I even know about father saving you from the sacrifice and that since then no sacrifice has been practiced among the Skidi Pawnee. Father, it is because of you there is never to be another Morning Star ritual, is not that true?"

"That is true," Sun Eagle said, casting Kiriki a nervous glance. "And, son, let us speak no more of it. It is best left in the past and unspoken. It is a custom that shall never be practiced in our village as long as I am chief."

Hawk's eyes lit up. "When *I* am chief I will have the say, won't I, Father?" he said, his voice proud.

Kiriki and Sun Eagle's eyes met and held. "Yes, when you are chief, you will have the say," Sun Eagle said thinly. "But of course you will do what is best for your people. You will do what is decent for mankind."

Sun Eagle slipped Hawk down from his shoulders. "Go on and play, my son," he said, swatting him playfully on his tiny bottom. "You are too young to be talking of sacrifices and weapons. It is a time of innocence. Let your father and mother enjoy this time without worries of a son whose mind goes beyond his years!"

Kiriki slipped an arm through Sun Eagle's as she watched Hawk scamper away, stopping occasionally to stoop and examine a rock or a flower. "Sun Eagle, I do worry," she murmured. "He is our only child! What if he continues to always be this restless? He will not live a long life. I don't think I could bear it should he die before me."

Sun Eagle swung Kiriki around to face him. "Do not fret so over a son whose questions and curiosities brand him as one who is intelligent," he said softly. "And let us never talk of death when in the same breath speaking of our son. Do you not recall how he battled so hard to be born? Kiriki, such a son would not die now all that easily. He will live a long life. He will one day rule our people."

"But his mention of the Morning Star ritual . . ." Kiriki said, shuddering at the thought of what she had endured because of Brown Bear.

"He is only a little boy who sees magic in such talk," Sun Eagle said dryly. "As he grows older, he will see the wrong in the sacrifice just as I did. He is my son. How could he accept something that I condemn so venomously?"

"Sometimes sons are not like fathers." Kiriki argued softly.

"When the father is a proud chief, the son knows it is best to behave as he is taught!" Sun Eagle said scornfully.

"But Brown Bear did not. You did not, Sun Eagle," Kiriki dared to say. "Your father believed in the Morning Star sacrifice. You never did!"

Sun Eagle felt as though his heart had been stung, her words bit so fiercely into him. He looked slowly over at Hawk, now not feeling so confident about his future. . . .

A rustling in the bushes up just ahead of Hawk made Sun Eagle grab his knife from its sheath at his waist. "Stand behind me," he whispered when a low growl reverberated through the air from behind the bushes. He looked at his son in terror as Hawk stopped and waited to see what was approaching him, curiosity a stronger drive in him than fear.

Kiriki could not stand the suspense. Her son's life was

at stake. She brushed past Sun Eagle and started to lift Hawk into her arms, then stopped, frozen to the spot, when a huge bear came looming into sight, walking erect on its hind legs.

"A knife will not be enough!" Sun Eagle cried, now recalling having left his rifle perched against the wall of his dwelling. "Kiriki, move slowly back toward me. Slowly . . ."

Kiriki managed to get Hawk in her arms and took one step back, then stopped and gawked at one of the bear's ears. The sun's rays were spiraling downward through a break in the trees overhead, shining onto a golden earring. There was only one bear that wore such an earring!

"It is you!" Kiriki squealed, placing Hawk back to the ground. She knew the dangers, that the cub who was now grown into a full grown bear may not remember her, yet she was too compelled to go to him to see than to take heed to the dangers that were truly at hand.

"It is I, Kiriki!" she said, holding her hand toward the bear as the animal fell to its four paws and stood there, watching her approach with a tilted head. "Oh, I was wrong not to name you! I could call you by a name now! You would probably recognize the name more than you do me!"

The bear emitted a low growl, then its huge body began to sway back and forth the closer Kiriki got. "I am so glad to see that you are all right," Kiriki said, now close enough to test the bear, to see if he was going to allow her to pet him. Slowly she moved her hand to his head, then jumped with alarm when the bear flopped suddenly onto the ground, on his side, and began licking at her ankles.

Kiriki looked over her shoulder at Sun Eagle, beaming. "He does!" she shouted. "He knows me! We are all safe, Sun Eagle. He would never harm us."

Kiriki fell to her knees beside the bear and threw her arms around his neck and began hugging him. "My friend, my friend," she whispered.

There was suddenly more rustling sounds in the bushes.

Kiriki moved slowly away from the bear and watched as two cubs came bounding out into the open, jumping all over their father playfully.

Sun Eagle moved to Kiriki's side. He reached a hand to her. "It's best that we leave while we can," he said. "Where there are cubs, there is also a mother. And, Kiriki, the mother has never known you. She will not understand, either, the love her companion has for you. We'd best leave. Now."

Tears came to Kiriki's eyes. She gave the bear another fierce hug, patted the two cubs, then went to Hawk and lifted him into her arms. As she fled alongside Sun Eagle toward the village, she gave the bear another wistful stare. It was sad leaving him again, yet it was wonderful to know that he had survived and had a family of his own.

She gave Sun Eagle a pleasant smile, sniffling back her tears. She, as well, had a family. Though blessed with only one son in her lifetime, it was no less a blessing than should she have had a dozen. Things were as one with Tirawa who is in and of everything. Tirawa had made life good—Tirawa had made all things possible for her and Sun Eagle, and hopefully would also for their son.